Harper
Monogram

DANNY
BOY

Leigh Riker

HarperPaperbacks
A Division of HarperCollinsPublishers

This is a work of fiction. The characters, incidents, and dialogues are products of the author's imagination and are not to be construed as real. Any resemblance to actual events or persons, living or dead, is entirely coincidental.

HarperPaperbacks   *A Division of* HarperCollins*Publishers*
10 East 53rd Street, New York, N.Y. 10022

Cover illustration by Jeff Cornell

First printing: July 1995

Printed in the United States of America

HarperPaperbacks, HarperMonogram, and colophon are trademarks of HarperCollins*Publishers*

❖ 10 9 8 7 6 5 4 3 2 1

ROMANTIC TIMES SINGS
LEIGH RIKER'S PRAISE

MORNING RAIN
"The emotionally charged story of one woman's coming of age as she gains the strength of purpose to finally change her own path."

UNFORGETTABLE
"Intense relationships in a small farming community whose past and present are closely linked together."

TEARS OF JADE
"Author Leigh Riker again demonstrates her ever-increasing talent as a Women's Fiction novelist."

JUST ONE OF THOSE THINGS
"A vivid portrayal of a woman in crisis; the decisions she makes will forever change the lives of both her and her daughter."

To Mona Perry Bartley
From the heart and all about home,
this one's for you, Mom.

ACKNOWLEDGMENTS

My thanks to the Beaverhead Chamber of Commerce for supplying the added visual information about my fictional characters' magnificent home state of Montana; to Hal for the great cowboy stuff; to the staff at the Professional Rodeo Cowboys Association for so promptly and cheerfully double-checking my facts about the exciting sport of bull riding; and to Bev Haynes for providing, as only another writer can, a firsthand look at Cheyenne. To friend and equestrienne Mary Kay Morel and her faithful sidekick Noël, thanks for all the rides. Trust me. The horse never dies.

THE COWBOY PRAYER

Heavenly Father, we pause, mindful of the many blessings You have bestowed upon us. We ask that You be with us at this rodeo and we pray that You will guide us in the arena of life. We don't ask for special favors; we don't ask not to draw a chute-fighting horse or never to break a barrier. Nor do we ask for all daylight runs or not to draw a steer that won't lay. Help us, Lord, to live our lives in such a manner that when we make that last inevitable ride to the country up there, where the grass grows lush, green and stirrup-high, and the water runs cool, clear and deep, that You as our last Judge, will tell us that our entry fees are paid. Amen.

1

There were only three songs that could make Erin Brodey Sinclair cry: "Auld Lang Syne," because she had spent most New Year's Eves alone; "My Funny Valentine," because she'd had only one memorable romance in her thirty-three years; and the song her mother-in-law was playing now.

But come ye back when summer's in the meadow. . . .

The soft piano strains echoed, bittersweet, from the living room along the hall to the kitchen. Meg kept playing. Her Saturday afternoon teaching finished, the last budding local pianist gone home, she was letting her fingers drift over the keys in the same skillful fashion, with the same result for Erin as always.

Without half trying, "Danny Boy" could make her weep buckets. For the song, and for the boy himself.

The man, she corrected. Though it became harder and harder, even with the passing years, to think of Danny as a grown-up. Maybe when his mother played her favorite piece, she too remembered the boy he'd once been, and that was what made Erin want to sob.

Slicing onions for supper, she wiped the back of her free hand across her cheek. It was the onions that made her cry, nothing—and no one—else.

Sending the paring knife through another fat chunk of onion, she stared down at the butcher-block table Danny had made for Meg in high school woodworking class for Mother's Day. It was a good table, its oak grain strong and straight, like Danny's body, its legs sturdy. When he put his mind and hands to a project, including the calling he had chosen over Erin, he approached perfection.

And when Danny laid gentle hands on her . . .

"Hey, Mom!" a shout sailed through the open window.

A warm June breeze wafted in, and Erin glanced up at the screen through which she could glimpse her seven-year-old son flying across the ranch yard on his new red bicycle.

She'd bought the bike to squelch his new demand for a horse of his own. She claimed they had no time for extra animals, and no money to spare. The rest of the truth was, she hadn't the heart to expose him to danger.

The craggy mountains behind him in the distance shadowing Paradise Valley, the rosy sun sinking below the sharp peaks to the west caught her attention, as they'd done for most of her life. Like nothing else except this ancestral land, this house, they soothed Erin's spirit. Then she jolted to awareness. Timmy sped by, one hand thrust overhead in a classic position.

"Watch me! I'm a bull rider!"

Erin peered out the window. "Both hands on the handlebars, or no elderberry pie for dessert!"

The fruit-filled treat was cooling on the nearby oak sideboard on top of a blue gingham runner that matched the kitchen curtains. Meg had set the dinner table before she went in to play the piano, and her well-worn but much-loved stoneware plates, white trimmed in cobalt blue, shone like mirrors at each of the four places. The smell of browning meat teased Erin's nostrils. Next to the simmering skillet a pot of new potatoes bubbled on another burner.

But neither the tantalizing aromas nor the homey scene could short-circuit her memories or her fears. Suddenly she could see a hundred dusty arenas, hear the roar of a crowd, and some announcer's hearty voice.

Here comes one of rodeo's finest. In Erin's mind the chute banged open and two thousand pounds of ill-tempered rodeo bull burst out. Her pulse went mad. *Danny Sinclair, folks, on Sassy Sam! Danny's from Sweetwater, Montana.*

"Mom! I'm ready!" Timmy slid the bike to a stop in the dusty yard underneath an old maple tree where the grass never grew. Solemnly, he looked in Erin's direction then nodded once. "Time me!"

Before she could respond, Danny's son shot forward, repeating the pose Erin had yelled at him about. One arm waving, the other gripping a length of dirty rope wrapped around the bike frame, his narrow butt flattened against the seat, both feet up and heels kicking high.

"Count 'em!"

The paring knife still in hand, Erin froze. She could hardly blame Timmy for wanting his eight-second ride. It was her own fault for falling in love with a bull rider, then marrying him.

"One . . . two . . . "

The bike careered toward the opposite side of the yard, perilously close to Erin's vegetable garden.

"Three."

Just her luck, to have had a son by that bull rider and to be raising that son alone.

"Four."

Except for the past few weeks. She leaned against the sink. She'd been alone most of June. She'd fought Danny hard but not hard enough this time, this summer. She'd finally given in and sent Timmy to his father for nearly a month on the circuit. His first. Two days ago he'd come home mouthing rodeo talk like church dogma and Erin was still paying the price, just as she'd paid for half of Timmy's plane ticket.

"Five—"

The number stuck in her throat. Time seemed to freeze too, as if everything happened in slow motion. Horrified, Erin watched the shiny red bike hit an exposed tree root. The wheel made an abrupt right turn, just like a Brahma trying to toss its rider in the ring. Timmy sailed over the handlebars, somersaulted in the air, then landed in the dirt with an audible thump.

"Timmy!"

The bicycle landed on top of him, but Erin hardly noticed it. "Meg!" she yelled, running for the back door.

From the living room "Danny Boy" stopped in mid phrase. Erin could hear Meg pounding through the kitchen behind her, but she was already down the back steps herself and pelting through the yard, the abandoned barn looming like the dark shadow of another tragic day.

She didn't hear a sound. Timmy lay on his side, one arm covering his face, the other pinned beneath him, his legs sprawled and looking limp. Erin felt dizzy. She'd seen that pose before too.

Years ago it had sent her running back to Sweetwater, and ended her marriage. And years before that . . .

"Timmy," she said. "Honey, are you okay?"

Shaking, Erin pulled the bike away then gingerly pried his arm from his face, which looked white and slack. The spray of freckles across his nose appeared darker, and his eyes were closed. The unruly hank of dark hair—Danny's hair—that never stayed in place had slipped over his forehead to graze his scraped cheekbone.

"Dear God." Wiping her hands on her jeans, Meg dropped down beside Erin in the dirt. Neither of them could look at each other. More memories. "Is he all right?"

Timmy's lips twitched.

"Gram, o'course I am." He opened one eye, in the same way his father might. "You think I'm a sissy?"

Erin noticed that his pupil looked larger, filling the beautiful green iris. His lips looked faintly blue.

"Lie still," she ordered but spoke too late. He rolled over, then flopped back with a groan.

"Ohhh, Mom. Ouuchh!"

"Let me see."

"Don't touch it!"

His arm dangled at a strange angle and Erin's stomach turned.

"It's broken," she said to Meg, who hovered at Timmy's other side, her brown gaze stricken. Meg nodded in mute agreement. "We'll have to get him to the doctor's."

"In Sweetwater? He may be gone for the day by now, Erin. He only works until noon on Saturday." Meg wrung her slender hands.

"Then we'll drive into Dillon to the emergency room." She slipped an arm under Timmy's small frame. "Go get my car keys and start the Jeep."

Meg stood but didn't move toward the house. "Can you manage him yourself?"

"I've been managing since the day he was born."

She knew the words sounded harsh but couldn't help herself. Terror quarreled with anger inside her. Struggling to her feet, she started toward the driveway with her child in her arms. Her child, she thought, trying not to jostle him. She'd learned just how alone she was a long time ago, and how unreliable Danny could be.

"I could kill him," she said under her breath. "I could just kill him for this."

Timmy's voice sounded weak but he knew who she meant.

"It's not Daddy's fault."

"He must have spent the whole month teaching you how to hurt yourself."

Timmy leaned his head against her shoulder. His skin felt clammy. "It's just part of rodeoing."

With the bad memories at her heels, Erin hurried to the waiting car. She hadn't meant to give orders to Meg, who'd taken enough during a nearly forty-year marriage to Danny's father. Meg had memories of her own, but Erin, despite her lifelong aversion to making quick decisions, had become used to taking charge in a crisis. She had no choice there. It almost came naturally by now. And the Jeep's engine purred, a blanket thoughtfully provided by Meg lay waiting on the seat. Maybe the hard words had helped them both to cope.

Erin gently laid Timmy down.

"You'll be fine," she said.

"Us bull riders get throwed lots of times. We're tough." He tried a smile that quavered. "Don't look sad, Mom. You always say I'm the man of the house here." His voice faded but its edge remained. "Get me a brace and some surg'cal tape, I'll be ready to ride tomorrow."

His eyes closed and Erin counted to ten not to say anything. She rolled her eyes at Meg, who climbed gray-faced into the back seat to cradle Timmy on her lap. Erin sped around to the driver's side, never thinking that she'd left ground sirloin browning on the stove and the pot of potatoes about to boil over. She'd heard Danny spout the same macho nonsense too many times.

"The gospel," she muttered, "according to Danny Sinclair."

Danny dreamed he died and went to heaven. Flat on his back, he opened his eyes, one at a time, and looked up into the face of an angel. A fuzzy angel with a radiant face, greenish eyes, and a halo of soft, reddish hair. The angel looked like Erin.

"Hello again," she said with a smile.

He gazed around the medical tent and groaned. She

wasn't Erin. She wasn't even an angel. Outside he could hear a horse's whinny, the muted blare of the announcer's voice calling someone else's score. A hot breeze ruffled the tent flap and he smelled the bulls in the nearby stock pens.

"How long have I been out?"

"About twenty minutes. This time. You passed out in the arena, on the stretcher, again as soon as you hit that cot."

He groaned again. Another time, it might have been a theatrical gesture. Danny, like most men he knew on the circuit, considered injury a normal part of the business, a mild inconvenience—and a way to meet nurses.

He looked at his bared chest. It was striped with white adhesive bandage.

"What's the damage?"

She only smiled. A small penlight flicked on, and she examined his pupils while Danny catalogued his aches and pains. It hurt to breathe. His elbow stung like hell and his face burned. His head throbbed. Par for the course.

"You'll have a great shiner by tomorrow. Two bruised ribs, some scrapes. Those horns missed you by an inch." The phony angel pulled back with another reassuring smile. "The usual. Next time try not to land on your face. It's too nice to mess up."

He barely heard the compliment. He had no memory of the fall. Or could he call it a fall? He'd been catapulted from that black bull's back like a man shot from a cannon in a circus, and when he landed, all the breath had been knocked from him, as well as his consciousness. He felt woozy.

"What's your name?" the paramedic asked.

He told her.

"You know what day it is?"

He'd heard the routine often in his eighteen years of professional riding. She wanted to know if he'd scrambled his brains. He thought a moment.

"June 25. Saturday." He paused. "The president's some

Democrat from Arkansas." He grinned weakly. "I rode in a go-round there once near Fort Smith . . . took second place."

"Do you know where you are now?"

"Sure." He gazed up at her. "Utah," he said, "Lehi. Town of about six thousand people. And one pretty bad bull."

"You'll do."

She straightened, giving his shoulder a light pat.

Then Danny remembered. He'd come to the first time in the dirt looking into a pair of panicked brown eyes.

"Where's my buddy? Is he all right?"

"What are rodeo clowns for, except to save people like you? He's fine," she said. "He's waiting for you outside."

Neither of them mentioned a hospital. He didn't feel bad enough to go and she'd obviously dealt with his kind before. Pick him up, dust him off, start him all over again. That was his motto and that of any other rodeo rider worth his pro standing.

"Thanks, Doc." Still, he sat up slowly, fighting the urge to hold his head on with one hand.

"Take it easy for a few days."

"I appreciate the advice but I've got a date with another bull in Colorado." He buttoned his shirt with shaking fingers. Damn, he felt weak. If she spotted that, she would slap him into bed somewhere and hide his boots.

"I wouldn't ride for a week or so," she added.

"If I don't ride, I don't eat." He slid off the cot, surprised to find his boots were still on. "Even when I do ride, sometimes I don't eat."

"Ever think about hanging up that bull rope?"

He jammed his hat on his head, and his elbow pulsed in time with the one he'd hurt. Quit? He still hadn't won his world championship.

The look on her face reminded him of Erin.

"Not yet," he said. "You can take the boy out of the rodeo, but you can't take the rodeo out of the boy."

"Except on a stretcher."

Unlike Erin she didn't try to change his mind. He guessed she'd treated others just like him and decided not to waste her time, or her breath. If only Erin had learned to hold her tongue . . . if she wasn't so stubborn. If only she believed in him.

Danny let the paramedic hold the tent flap back because he wasn't sure he could lift his arm, then made his way, one shuffling step at a time, outside. The paramedic handed him the brown leather chaps he'd worn in the ring, then his bull rope.

"Take care of yourself. Any vomiting, bleeding from your ears, excessive drowsiness, you come back."

Like hell. In the next ten minutes he'd be on his way to Durango, his next bull ride, and some prize money. Utah hadn't been kind to him. He owed the payment on his pickup camper, in fact two payments, and he hadn't sent Erin any money for Tim since the boy went home to her.

Something inside Danny turned. Home, he thought. The word made his chest hurt worse.

He found Luke Hastings sprawled not far from the tent on a hay bale in the dirt, his weathered hands laced across his stomach, his usual wad in his cheek, his eyes shut. Danny didn't bat an eye. The floppy straw hat he wore, a caricature of a cowboy's Resistol, his white clown face with its black-and-red paint, didn't faze him. He was used to seeing Luke in his red-striped shirt and suspenders, bright blue tights, polka-dotted knee pads and shin pads.

"You gonna get me out of here or wait until that lady doc decides I ought to stay a while?"

Luke's eyes remained closed. The star burst dark lines around them had started to run into the stark white on his cheeks and into the thick black outline around his mouth.

"Stay, and make her happy?" He grinned, showing strong white teeth. "I saw her looking at you. Even out cold you looked good to her."

Danny didn't answer. Luke knew better than to goad him about women. Somewhere along the way, he'd lost his taste for sexual adventure. No, he knew exactly where he'd lost it, and when. The day he first kissed Erin.

There'd been a few women in the eight years since she left him. Mind-saving sex, he called it. A buckle bunny here or there. Rodeo groupies.

They made Danny sadder afterward than he felt before. He couldn't remember the last time he'd wanted even that. And in recent years he'd become damn careful. He risked his life every time he climbed on a bull, never mind some strange woman.

"Sorry." Luke rose to his feet and peered at Danny. "You want to stick around anyway? I mean, we have plenty of time to get to Durango." He shifted the chaw inside his cheek. "We could get a room here in Lehi tonight."

Danny shook his head. He had no money to spare. In the dirt he'd not only bruised his ribs and his pride; he'd lost his rodeo entry fee, and his investment in gas and food for the trip. He was already in the red.

"I can cover the motel," Luke offered. He didn't work freelance but on contract for a big rodeo stock contractor so he still had his salary.

Danny hesitated. He had some money set aside for emergencies and Tim's college fund, but he never touched that.

"We could sleep in the camper," Luke added, making Danny wonder how bad he really looked. He drew himself up and set his teeth.

"No, let's put on some miles between me and that particular bull. I can rest in Durango for a few days."

"You sure?" Luke asked.

"I'm sure."

Luke took off his hat and flicked his surprisingly shiny, dark blond hair from his eyes. He knew better too than to press a cowboy about his wounded masculine pride. "Let's go then." His battered sneakers slapped the pavement with every step. Then abruptly, he stopped. "You want to eat or is your stomach—"

"My stomach's fine. I'm hungry, in fact."

"A quick stop at Burger King then and we're on our way."

"Burger King? Didn't we eat there last night?"

"I like their chicken sandwiches."

"Tell me something I don't know. Hell, it's my turn to pick. Taco Bell," Danny said, following him at a slower pace into the parking lot. His head thumped and his elbow felt like fire but he couldn't examine it. His arm was wrapped in surgical tape from forearm to biceps. "I love their Mexican pizzas."

"How many'd you eat last time? Five, six?"

"Seven." Danny waited while Luke unlocked the pickup camper's door. "I had a good ride that day, remember? Perfect landing. Got clean away too after I came off that mean Brahma—didn't even need you."

Inside the camper Luke creamed off his greasepaint to reveal a youthful-looking face for a man in midlife. It always startled Danny. Then Luke exchanged his costume for a pair of jeans as worn as Danny's. Danny exchanged his boots for a pair of high-topped sneakers that matched Luke's. Then they pulled out of the parking lot without looking back. At the last minute Luke turned his head.

"She was cute, wasn't she? That female paramedic?"

"Looked just like an angel," Danny repeated his earlier observation, when he hadn't been that sure he wasn't right. "Too good for you."

Propping one sneaker against the dashboard, Danny let Luke drive without any of his usual backseat comments. They headed southeast, that much farther away from Sweetwater and the ranch at Paradise Valley, and after a while Danny let his head fall back.

He'd swallowed three aspirins without water and he still hurt. Sometimes he thought he always would.

Night fell and stars strewed the big sky overhead. Through the open windows a sweet breeze seemed to kiss his cheek. On the radio Vince Gill sang about still loving a woman.

"You okay?" Luke finally asked.

"I'm okay."

"You don't sound it."

Danny sighed. "I was thinking, that's all."

"That stuff can kill you."

"Sure can."

But he couldn't stop thinking. Not when he felt bad, though he wouldn't admit it, and alone, even with Luke beside him. He welcomed the closeness they'd developed over the years, a closeness he hadn't felt with any other man except his brother, until he'd fallen out with Ken long ago. But tonight he just wanted to be quiet with his thoughts.

Ken didn't speak to him anymore. Erin spoke to him only when necessary, about Tim. Danny gazed out at the dark sky and the stars. His son, his only son . . .

Another ten miles down the road, Luke said, "You miss the little guy?"

Danny had had a nagging sense of loss ever since he put Tim on the plane to Montana. "Sure, but I'll see him again."

"Not if Erin has anything to say about it."

"I'm his father." He smiled a little, which made his face ache. "Ol' Tim sure did take to the circuit, didn't he? I could just feel rodeo goin' through him like it did me when I was his age. His first buzz."

"Wonder what Erin said when he got home and badgered her for a horse?"

"No," Danny said. "She always says no. If she figured the connection between Tim being here then asking her for a horse, she'd say no real quick."

Luke said nothing more. He'd been divorced for fifteen

years and mistrusted all women. Danny still wore his wedding band, but Luke knew the topic of Erin was off limits.

They'd had some good times, though. Danny hadn't felt that good again until Tim came to visit. Father and son, at last. Maybe Erin was weakening. Some night when he didn't feel quite so runover, he'd give her a call.

They'd patch things up. He'd stay on the circuit long enough to win the world—his championship buckle. Then at last he would go back to Paradise Valley, and she'd take him in. Erin, his brother, his mom . . . He could go home again, and they'd all forgive him.

"Hey, Luke?"

The truck engine whined up a long grade, and the mountains loomed out of the darkness, and the stars sprinkled the sky like silver candies on an ice cream cone.

"Thanks for jumping between me and that bull today."

"That's what I do best."

True enough, Danny thought. Luke was the finest rodeo clown he'd ever worked with. Danny knew what he did best too, even at thirty-six. They said bull riding was for younger men, and for those who stayed single. He wondered, as the pickup rolled toward Durango and the prize money he badly needed, whether he hadn't knocked his head once too often. Because he was neither that young, nor in his own mind that single.

No matter what Erin believed.

Half out of her mind, Erin paced the Barrett Memorial Hospital emergency waiting room. She didn't know what else to do except glance at the empty doorway every few seconds.

She'd tried to reach Danny's brother, Ken, at his construction office in Dillon, but he hadn't answered and his secretary didn't work on Saturday. She supposed he was home by now. The line was busy anyway—business, probably. He would have turned off the stove, but he didn't know where they were. He'd be frantic about Timmy.

She'd try calling again in a few minutes.

"Erin, sit down." Meg gazed at her from a plastic sofa in the corner. "I can feel gray hairs popping out from just watching you." She wrung her hands. "At times like this I feel ancient . . . helpless."

Stopping, Erin contemplated the older woman. Meg's soft, light brown hair had little gray, her brown eyes normally held humor and warmth. She had a slim, slight figure that still curved in all the right places, and her silky shirt and trim jeans still drew glances on the street. Not anyone's image of a grandmother, Erin thought.

"I feel helpless too. You're not old, Meg."

Her mother-in-law had married young, at sixteen. Maybe all that early living made a woman feel old before her time. She'd certainly suffered enough. She'd lost one son, and two years ago at fifty-four she'd watched her husband die. Erin shouldn't have insisted that Meg come along today. A broken arm couldn't be life-threatening. Could it?

She sank onto a hard-sprung chair. "I can't stand it myself. What's taking so long?" She jumped up. "I'll try Ken once more. I know he's home."

"Erin, I think you should call—"

"No." She twisted her wedding ring. "I won't call *him*."

"But Dan—"

"Right now I don't even want to hear that man's name."

Meg's mouth turned down. Danny seemed to be the only topic on which they disagreed. She knew Meg wanted him home.

"I'm sorry." Erin sat down again. Leaning close, she covered Meg's hand. "I didn't mean to snap. If Timmy went off as Danny did to rodeo, if he stayed away, if his son were lying in the other room . . . I understand how you must feel."

"Do you, Erin?" Meg smiled sadly. "Daniel's not a bad man."

"I know."

She just couldn't look into those hazel eyes, that slow smile, and not want to do whatever he asked of her. Anything. She couldn't live with him. Or watch him try to kill himself every weekend on some wild bull. The last time she'd seen him fly off and land in the dirt, like Timmy today, she'd sworn it would be the last time. She knew Meg blamed her, but she should have divorced him years ago.

"I just can't stand it," she said again.

"Mrs. Sinclair?"

At the voice from the doorway Erin shot to her feet.

"How is he, Doctor?"

"Doing fine," he said. "A brave little soldier."

"Cowboy," Meg corrected, joining them.

The doctor grinned. "He did tell me—in the midst of pain—that he's a topnotch bull rider. Or plans to be." He raised his eyebrows. "I guess something went wrong earlier today."

Erin worried her lower lip. "How bad is the break?"

"The x-rays show a clean separation. It could have been much worse. I've splinted it for tonight. Tomorrow you can take him to your regular doctor's office and he'll put the cast on. I've spoken with him." Perching on the edge of a chair, he scribbled on a small pad. "This prescription should handle the pain, but I wouldn't expect a peaceful night."

"He'll be glad to be in his own bed."

Clutching the prescription, Erin followed the physician and Meg down the hall to an examining room where Timmy lay on a paper-covered table, holding his favorite stuffed animal, which Meg had brought, to his dirty shirt front.

"Take it easy, cowboy." The doctor clasped Timmy's narrow shoulder. "Tell your mom and grandma to give you lots of TLC."

Timmy waited until the door closed, giving them some privacy. "What's TLC mean?"

"Tender loving care."

"Like hugs?"

"And kisses," Erin said, smoothing back his hair, "and early to bed with an extra story. As soon as we get home."

Timmy looked around as if missing something.

"I thought Daddy would be here by now."

"Oh, honey." Erin's heart clenched. "He's far away—"

"In Utah?"

"I don't know. Maybe."

"He should be in Utah if it's Saturday."

She helped him from the table. "Then I'm sure that's where he is." If there was one thing she could count on, it was Danny showing up for the next rodeo. But how did Timmy know where?

By the time they reached home, he looked exhausted and had turned cranky. The local anaesthetic had worn off, and as Erin tucked him into bed, he complained that his arm hurt.

"Your pill should help soon," she said, easing down beside him on his bed and opening a book, one of his favorites. "Rest your head on my shoulder and I'll read to you for a while."

Clutching his stuffed monkey in his good arm, Timmy frowned. "Where's Gram?"

"She's cleaning up the kitchen."

No one felt like eating the dinner that had scorched in the pans. Including Ken, who'd patted Timmy on the head then disappeared into the first floor TV room to read the paper. Or pretend to. Erin knew he worried about Timmy. He didn't like illness, though. Accidents, she thought.

"I want Gram."

Erin looked at the book. "She'll come up to say goodnight before you fall asleep."

He started to cry. He turned his head from Erin, who

seemed to be taking the blame for the pain he felt. "I want my daddy!"

"Hush now, let me hold you." When she tried to gather him close, he pushed her away.

"I don't want you! *I want Daddy!*"

She climbed off the bed and slipped into the hallway, a hand clapped over her mouth and her eyes stinging. She stayed away until he fell asleep in his grandmother's arms, the book long since read and enjoyed between them.

When Meg finally went to bed, Erin stood over Timmy in the darkness as she often did with only the hall light streaming in to see by and smoothed his hair from his forehead. She bent to kiss him, then sat in a chair beside the bed and watched him sleep.

She hadn't been raised to be a selfish woman, but she'd made a home for her son here, for them, together. She'd planted their roots deep in the land she loved and where she meant to stay. But even in sleep he held tight to the black stuffed monkey Danny had sent him soon after he was born, with its comic face and its red elastic suspenders.

Timmy had never called for Danny before; not once, through chicken pox and strep throat, through seven birthdays and Christmases. Not once.

She shouldn't have let him go this summer. Erin rested her head against her folded arms on the edge of Timmy's bed. He twisted in his sleep, crying out when his injured arm touched the sheets.

"It's okay, honey."

She whispered the words but didn't believe them. He was all she had now. She didn't want to lose him. In the darkness she raised her head, and stared through bleary eyes at the far wall, at the shadow shapes dancing across the cowboy wallpaper border. She stared at the open closet door. On the inside Timmy had crookedly tacked a poster from the Pro Rodeo Cowboys Association—the schedule for the present season.

So that's how he had known where Danny would be tonight. The same way Erin had known, all the years she'd waited for him too.

Suddenly she wished Utah were farther away.

2

The place had changed, no sense denying it.

Why should he be surprised? Danny asked himself as he drove through town late the next afternoon. Eighteen years ago Sweetwater, in the heart of Beaverhead County, had boasted nearly a thousand residents. In Montana, where just over three-quarters of a million people were sprinkled on one hundred forty-seven thousand square miles, one of the least populous states in the Union, that meant a good-sized, lively town. Lively on Saturdays at least, when area ranchers and their families made the weekly trip into Sweetwater for groceries and supplies, and to shoot the breeze with others of their kind, temporarily alleviating the isolation they sometimes felt.

But for various reasons—such as the shutdown of area mines, trouble in the timber industry, falling gas and oil prices, drought and the demise of the cattle market in the 80s—the population had dwindled. Today, the town's wide streets looked all but empty at 6 P.M. on Sunday and every other shop had been boarded up, some with siding paint peeled away to the bare wood.

The sun slanted sharply across Denton Street, the main thoroughfare, and Danny squinted against the glare off the windshield, taking stock of the place. Sweetwater looked like a ghost town.

The angled parking spaces, a classic Western holdover, on both sides of the pot-holed street held no more than half a dozen cars and pickup trucks. The Bitterroot Emporium looked abandoned, and the parking meters installed in front of it after he left Paradise Valley all showed red expired flags like handkerchiefs waved in front of a herd of bulls that had long since disappeared.

The store's scarred double front doors needed re-varnishing, and when he stopped the car for a closer look, the discreet sign—*Erin Sinclair, proprietor*—in the display window had him shaking his head.

The glass had cracked in the lower left corner. Fluttery ladies' scarves, wreaths of pale dried flowers and baby's breath, cookbooks, for God's sake, made a tidy if fussy exhibit where years ago metal pots and iron skillets, rakes and hoes had stood in proud disarray, and the sign read simply Sweetwater General Store. Accelerating, he tightened his grip on the wheel. *Emporium.* Even the name made him wince. He'd have to see Erin punching a cash register for a dozen local customers lined up, their arms loaded down with purchases, before he believed she actually ran the place.

She didn't need to. For thirty-eight years of marriage his parents had acknowledged clear-cut duties and responsibilities—his father running the ranch, his mother raising the family. Danny had inherited their traditional values. Good values, in an increasingly crazy world where love didn't seem to count. Or sticking things out for the long term.

He knew any number of guys who'd married three or four times. Some who never bothered to marry but fathered kids here and there whom they didn't bother to support.

Even Luke had struck out once, and claimed he never would try again. Luke's present notion of a relationship ended in the morning with a quick "Thanks. I'll see you around," but Danny refused to think of his own marriage as just another sad statistic.

Why couldn't Erin fulfill herself at home, with Tim, and let him earn their living the best way he knew how, for as long as he could? Call him old-fashioned, but why couldn't she join him on the circuit now and then? Or understand what the championship meant to him? At one time they'd known each other inside out; they'd second-guessed each other's thoughts and needs.

Leaving town, he turned north, toward the ranch. With such changes in the town, he wondered what he might find at the ranch, even with his father gone. Anxiety pooled the acid in his stomach. He wished he didn't have to go back just yet, without his gold buckle. He sped along the familiar straightaways and curves leading up then down into Paradise Valley, which he could have driven in his sleep even now. Like the surrounding mountains, the road never altered.

But after living near Ken so long, had Erin changed— the one person he never expected to?

Hell, he'd known her most of her life. He'd met her when she was five years old, married her right after she turned twenty to his twenty-three, and in between they'd seen each other every day. She lasted one year on the road before she left him the first time, and he thought he'd die from missing her. For four years after that they had endured a prickly, commuting marriage that added another ten thousand driving miles to his yearly hundred thousand on the circuit—and God knew how many years to Danny's life during each brief stay at Paradise Valley, near Ken and their father.

Danny had tried, hadn't he? With one hand he rubbed his side, just below his ribs. Yesterday's hard landing reminded him of another, the last time Erin stayed with him on the road at Cody where a bull gored him in the last go-round, real bad. Erin packed her bag as soon as he left the hospital. He could still remember her face then and his despair. Unless he gave up rodeo, she'd told him, their marriage was over.

Eight years later, he still wondered: How did she figure it was over? He didn't have any papers, wouldn't sign them if she sent them. How could Erin forget the love they shared, or the child they had made together?

He put both hands on the wheel and thought of Tim. Why hadn't Erin called Danny herself to tell him?

Not far from Durango last night, a call from his mother on the car phone had informed him of the broken arm. No hurry, but Tim needed him. Early that morning, full of coffee and aspirin but little sleep, he had given Luke the camper keys and rented a car to backtrack through Idaho and up I–15 into Montana. After twelve hours, the foothills outside Sweetwater blurred in front of his eyes.

He'd put pedal to the metal all the way, and his thigh cramped. As the car crested a steep grade flanked by stands of cedar, larch, and spruce and then, even higher, around a crystalline lake rimmed by lodgepole pines with the sun slipping lower in all its radiant golden glory behind them, his right foot felt numb.

Conversely, the tape around his bruised ribs seemed to make that pain only sharper, and his whole face burned. He'd avoided looking at himself in the rearview mirror since Colorado; the bruises around his eye and on his cheekbone must look like something in a full color video game—the violent kind Erin probably kept away from Tim.

Imagining her reaction to him, he pushed the car and himself harder to the top of the next hill then the last rise before beginning the descent into Paradise Valley.

No matter what changes he found there, he'd made up his mind. He wouldn't face the same battle next summer about Tim's visit. Whether she liked it or not, he was Tim's father. Erin's husband too. But he'd leave that war for later. Right now, regardless of her disapproval or his brother's, he intended to see his injured son.

He doubted Erin would like that either.

Or the fact that he'd be showing up, for the first time in eight years, right at dinnertime.

Erin dumped a can of drained pineapple into the buttered baking pan then slowly poured golden cake batter on top. Pineapple upside down cake was Timmy's favorite. She popped it in the oven. Maybe the special dessert would convince him that he had a pretty good mother after all. She wasn't to blame for Danny's absence—not really.

On her way from the stove to the refrigerator, she glanced out the kitchen window. No bike flying past today, no little future rodeo rider. Timmy lay in bed upstairs, his new cast propped on pillows, Erin's small-screen bedroom television set temporarily perched on his bureau.

She heard occasional shrieks of laughter, the irritating drone of cartoon voices. Safe, she thought. And she didn't smile at the familiar sight in the pasture opposite the house. Why blame her for the fact that they simply couldn't afford to keep a horse?

Another horse, she corrected.

Near the barn Danny's much-loved black and white paint gelding munched grass. He no longer rode it. He'd once tried calf roping to appease Erin. He leased the horse now to other riders for roping and barrel racing, and the gelding earned money, including a percentage paid to Danny. What if the horse never competed again? Why didn't he sell it?

Three months ago he'd sent it home on lay-up to recuperate from a bowed tendon suffered in competition. He'd worn her down, of course with Timmy's help, and she supposed that series of phone calls had paved the way for the boy's trip to stay with Danny. Give the man an inch . . .

•

He had nowhere else to leave the horse, he had said, promising to send money to cover feed and the vet bills. Somehow, his check never arrived before the oat bin emptied or the hay ran out. She envisioned the horse staying on, forgotten like a whim—like their marriage in Danny's mind. Through the years she'd feed it, haul it in out of the rain and snow. Timmy would become more attached to the animal than he already was. And when at last the aged gelding had stubs for teeth, or some wasting disease, she'd have to make the decision to put it down.

Erin looked away from the plumy white tail swishing flies. She could never do it. She'd grown up on this ranch, when it had been a real ranch, but she couldn't make the hard choices like those between life and death. She'd let that paint horse drop where it stood, if it lived for more than thirty years.

Besides, Timmy would never forgive her. The more pets, the better in his mind. Barn cats and kittens, wounded birds, stray dogs . . . horses that couldn't be ridden. She and Timmy nursed them all.

She slapped the vegetables for salad onto the counter.

No wonder the store barely showed a profit. She treated her customers the same way—extending credit with no hope of repayment.

Maybe Danny's brother was right.

"Right about what?"

The back door opened and Ken walked in.

Tearing lettuce into a big glass bowl, Erin didn't realize she'd spoken aloud. A quick survey of her brother-in-law brought a smile. Like the land and the house she loved, he calmed her spirit by simply entering a room. In his dependable-looking tan summer suit, Ken Sinclair fit his image as one of Sweetwater and Dillon's most eligible bachelors.

He had Danny's build, though not his height by several inches, and the bulkier muscles construction work had given him rather than the leaner definition of a bull rider.

He'd spent the afternoon conducting an Open House at his new subdivision—his first upscale housing development—near Dillon. Erin had missed it on purpose.

She suppressed a twinge of guilt. "I was thinking out loud. About the store."

"Sell it," he said as he always did, and slipped an arm around her shoulders. "We'll sell this place too."

Erin moved away on the pretext of washing the tomatoes at the sink. The uncomfortable subject had come up before, more often recently. She avoided Ken's gaze, that paler version of Danny's hazel eyes without the teasing glint.

"I'll tempt you every day until you say yes."

He sounded so sensible. She should do it, she thought. Stop telling herself she could be a successful business-woman. Stop beating herself up for the past. She could put Timmy in a real school, divorce Danny . . .

"I don't want to move. This is home."

Stepping close, Ken touched the nape of her neck. His hand felt warm, the contact pleasant, no more than that. And why should it? But how long since she'd tingled for a man, since hot blood had flowed through her veins like effervescent wine making her dizzy with longing?

Erin slipped free again. She took the tomato wedges to the table, slicing them into the salad bowl, adding green pepper then cucumber. The kitchen smelled sweet, warmed by the cake in the oven.

"I'm not making any decisions. Timmy's just back from his . . . vacation, and yesterday wiped me out. His broken arm—"

"Does he feel better today?" Ken took a beer from the refrigerator, removed his suit jacket and rolled his shirt sleeves back over his forearms. Erin heard the motions but didn't turn around; he performed the same routine every day.

She could set her watch by Ken's habits, rely on him to never have a light brown hair out of place. She counted on him to be there, day in, day out, and if he didn't have

Danny's energy or the excitement he generated with just a look, that was fine with her. She knew that wasn't fair to Ken, but he didn't seem to mind.

She managed a smile.

"He got his cast this afternoon. The doctor opened his office especially for Timmy. He claims the cast already itches, but he's looking forward to having everyone sign it, so get your pen ready." Her smile became more natural. "And wait till you see it."

"I'll take a look now."

At the table Erin tossed the salad, and kept on tossing. Ken walked from the kitchen down the hall that led to the front stairs and Timmy's room. He'd given them so much, from the moment of Timmy's birth, and other than Meg he was her best friend. But at thirty-eight he should have a wife and family of his own.

With swift, efficient motions she set three places at the dinner table. Meg had gone to Bozeman for the day with friends, on what she referred to as one of their "widows' walks," which meant touring the available shops. She wouldn't be back before nightfall.

Erin had glasses from the cupboard in each hand when a horn sounded up the driveway.

With a staccato blast that always made the hair on her neck stand up, the rural mail carrier often signaled Erin for overdue postage or large packages. But on a Sunday? With growing apprehension, she stared out the window.

"Who's there?" Ken called from upstairs.

"I don't know. I'll see. You two watch your show."

A gray late model sedan swung around the slight curve of the drive and, horn still blowing, pulled to a stop near the back door. Had something happened to Meg's car? But the car didn't belong to any of her friends.

Long shadows had begun to lay across the yard, like a man's fingers on a woman's skin. Golden light burnished the tall grass in the pasture and gleamed off the paint gelding's hide. With her heart in her throat, Erin watched the horse's ears prick. And she knew.

With the same swift sense of recognition, she felt her mouth open, and her eyes widen. The words of Meg's favorite song flashed in her mind.

But come ye back when summer's in the meadow . . .

A car door slammed.

"Hey, Kemosabe."

She heard his familiar deep voice, the horse's name on his lips, heard his familiar footsteps.

He didn't knock. Before she moved, the screen door swung back and he breezed inside, like a summer storm, bringing with him the scents of grass and car exhaust. Erin, standing frozen by the sink, had envisioned the scene often enough, but never like this.

In the early years, she'd dreamed of his return with yearning. Then, since the marriage had ended, she'd dreamed of it with dread.

He didn't smile. He didn't even say hello. He closed the door with a bang and leaned against the frame, folding his arms and pulling the fabric of his shirt taut against his biceps, his broad shoulders. Erin stared at him and he stared back.

Her heart thundered at his steady regard, but her cool gaze slipped over him too and she almost smiled, except her lips felt stiff. Timmy always said his father would come home one day wearing a straw cowboy hat, chaps and boots. But Danny held up the door frame in a plain white T-shirt, well-washed jeans, and a pair of high-top sneakers, the same outfit he always traveled in.

He removed his baseball—or should she say football?—cap. Its logo read Denver Broncos. His dark hair looked rumpled and he needed a haircut. Erin's fingers twitched, as if in some long-forgotten sensory memory of running through the shaggy, shiny depths. His hazel eyes looked vaguely bloodshot. His mouth, always sensuous and soft, turned grim and hard.

And still, something tugged at her insides. Then he spoke.

"I came to see my son."

Afraid she might drop them, Erin set the glasses on the counter. From far down the hall and overhead she heard the buzz of the TV, the drone of Ken's voice. Her safety line. Then she took another look at Danny.

His pose appeared neither threatening, nor casual. He hunched into himself, arms crossed as if protecting his middle, white surgical tape wound around one forearm and elbow as if to hold him together. And his face . . . dear God, his beautiful face.

"What happened to you?" As if she couldn't guess.

"Never mind me. What in God's name happened to Tim?"

Erin's heart turned over at his tone. Half angry, half plaintive.

"You must know," she said, "or you certainly wouldn't be here."

"Don't start on me, Erin." He came away from the door and walked toward her, obviously favoring one leg.

"He's fine," she said, taking a step back. "You didn't have to come all the way from Utah. Lose a ride and all that valuable prize money—"

Danny kept coming.

"He's my kid too, dammit."

Erin raised an eyebrow.

She meant to put the table between them but didn't move fast enough. She should have known. If Danny could still stay on a mean bull for eight seconds, he could outmaneuver her. He always had.

When he grasped her arm, she flinched.

"Why in hell didn't you call me?"

"I didn't have to. It seems someone else did."

"Mom," he admitted. "She said Tim was asking for me."

"It must have been the pain pill."

"Erin, *Christ.*" His face darkened. Up close she could

see the shadow along his jawline, see the weariness in his eyes. "Where is he?"

She fought a sense of betrayal, from Meg's not respecting her wishes.

"Don't you know?"

He'd grown up in this house.

"My room?" he said.

"His," Erin answered.

Danny resettled his cap over his dark hair, the same motion he used with a cowboy hat just before a ride. He could barely walk now. On his way from the kitchen he glanced at the table. "Set another place." His heated eyes challenged her, and he half smiled. "I drove from Durango. But how'd you know I was in Utah?"

If it hadn't been for Tim, he wouldn't have come. Danny limped down the hall and climbed the front stairs with Erin's words following, ringing in his ears like a warning, as she meant them. *Ken's up there.* He hit the landing with a grunt of pain, with Erin's face and that first sight of her still in his mind.

He had seen her only a few times, each one brief, since Tim was born, and each time she looked better than the last. She'd put Tim on a plane this summer like any other strong-willed, independent female determined to live without a man. Except for those terse calls about Kemosabe earlier in the spring, he'd talked with her by phone only a few times before and during Tim's visit—short calls full of logistics, nothing more, except the soft sound of Erin's voice.

She undid him, all right. In the kitchen he'd nearly lost it. As soon as he spotted her at the sink, nothing else had mattered. He'd almost crossed the room and taken her in his arms, almost kissed her. Then Erin's cool green gaze had reminded him of the breach between them and instead, he had plastered himself against the door. He'd never get used to that look, never accept it. And he'd wondered about her changes.

It was a good thing she didn't know he carried her picture with him, a snapshot in a cheap metal frame, taken on what he had loosely termed their honeymoon—three days during his first National Finals Rodeo in Las Vegas at a rundown motel, three days behind a closed door when he wasn't on a bull, wrapped around each other in bed until they couldn't breathe from too much loving.

She'd been a girl then, on the thin side. She was a full grown woman now, slender and willowy. Her small breasts had rounded, just the shape to fit a man's hands, and her hips, straight as a boy's once, would make a sleek but perfect cradle for a man's body now. A man's hungry body.

He fought the tightening in his groin. Some things never changed. Like her hair, which was still the same shade. It couldn't be called true red, but he didn't know what else to call its light auburn overlaid with gold, escaping every which way from that loose knot she always piled it in to keep it out of her way when she cooked.

To keep himself from going to her, he'd said the wrong thing, and watched her beautiful mouth thin into that flat line.

She didn't want him here. No surprise.

Danny inched his painful way along the upstairs hall. In the doorway to his old room, he stopped at the sight before him. He'd known a lot of moments in this room. But there lay Tim now, dark hair tousled, freckles standing out against his pale skin, that sweet baby's mouth . . . and a clunker of a cast on his thin left arm. A bright neon green cast with pictures all over it.

Danny's own arm throbbed. He felt the room spin, as if he were on a Brahma bucking to beat hell, and his rigging had slipped. His child, injured. He'd never imagined how he might feel if something happened to Tim and he wasn't there for him.

Ken was, though—scoring points at Paradise Valley, as usual.

Watching his brother and his son, Danny nudged a shoulder against the door frame. He didn't seem able to hold his own weight today. His taped ribs ached, and his heart ached with them. His face, his whole body thrummed with hurt.

"How's it goin', Ken?" he finally said.

His brother, who had been sitting on the bed next to Tim, both of them laughing at a Disney movie on television, spun around.

"What the h—"

"You're not seeing things. It's me."

"Daddy!" Tim clambered off the bed, ignoring his injured arm. "Daddy, I knew you'd come!" He flung himself against Danny's sore leg.

Wincing, Danny scooped him up, burying his face in his fragrant hair, Tim's arms clutching his neck.

Ken stood back, frowning. He must be thinking, just as he had when Tim was born. Thinking what to say that might hit Danny behind the knees and bring him down again. Danny closed his eyes, savoring the feel of his small son in his arms, his slight body pressed to Danny's chest and belly.

"The black sheep returns," Ken said at last.

"Didn't think I'd wait for your invitation."

"Might as well come. Have a good last look before we sell the place."

He hadn't prepared himself enough. The words struck home.

"Who's we?" Danny asked. As far as he knew, his mother and Ken owned two-thirds of Paradise Valley, he and Erin the rest. But in his absence even his wife had become a stranger. Did Erin want to sell?

Ken only smiled, but at the tense undercurrent Tim lifted his head. "You can't sell the ranch!" he said.

Danny hitched him into a more comfortable position.

He smoothed a hand over Tim's straight, dark hair, and looked over the boy's head at his older brother.

"Nobody's gonna sell. That's for damn sure."

Erin dished out fluffy whipped potatoes redolent of cream, garlic, and butter—Meg's recipe—and tried not to watch the three males around her table. She wasn't sure she could get through the rest of the meal.

She wanted it to be perfect. The potatoes, tender pot roast, and pineapple cake were Timmy's favorites. She wanted him back again, her own baby still, craving her cooking and bedtime stories. Last night she'd wondered about being selfish. Selfishly again, she wanted him to forget not only his broken arm but the past weeks with Danny. Now this.

Ken had been silent all through dinner. Danny and Timmy had chattered like magpies, as if to cover everyone's discomfort.

After putting a single dollop of potatoes on her plate, Erin left the table and slid the upside-down cake back in the oven to brown its sugary, coconut topping.

Then she sat down and tried again to eat.

Beside her Timmy forked a too-big piece of meat into his mouth and spoke around it. "Daddy, m'ember when we went to Texas that time you rode Daylight?"

"Remember," Erin corrected.

"Remember?" Timmy said, gulping.

"And don't talk with your mouth full."

In a gentler tone Danny backed her up. "You talk like that with your mouth full, Tim, and we'll have to give you that Heimlich maneuver. Sure, I remember." He grinned. "Stayed on too, and came in second. Eighty-one points."

"And m'ember Uncle Luke played like a bullfighter?"

"Uncle Luke is a bullfighter," Danny told him. "That's what he's called."

As a rodeo clown, Luke usually worked with a partner, known as the barrel man, while he danced around in front of an angry bull. Erin had long ago decided Luke didn't have much sense either. He must be well on his way to fifty by now.

"He's brave, isn't he, Daddy?"

"Sure is."

"As brave as you?"

Danny smiled down at his whipped potatoes. "Well, I don't know about that."

"Don't be modest," Ken said, glancing up as Danny reached for the bowl of mixed vegetables. "The boy wants to believe you're brave, let him believe."

Timmy looked curiously at his uncle.

"Don't you think Daddy's brave?"

Ken grunted. "Foolish, is more like it."

Though she shared his opinion Erin said nothing. Not knowing what else to do, she offered Ken the basket of rolls.

"No, thanks." He gave her a smile, which she could see Danny intercept with a frown. "I think I've had enough," Ken said.

He'd eaten only one helping, even though he loved Erin's pot roast. As soon as he emptied his plate Ken pushed back his chair.

"There's cake," she said, just as the scent of burning coconut filled the kitchen. "Oh, damn." Her chair screeched back and Erin ran for the oven.

Danny reached it first. Grabbing a pot holder, he yanked the baking pan out. Erin stared at the cake's blackened top.

"We can scrape off the burned part," Danny said, half smiling. When she met his eyes, they had warmed for the first time in her direction since he'd stalked in the back door. "It'll still taste good. Won't it, Tim?"

She heard a giggle.

Turning around, she caught Timmy rolling his eyes. She

supposed Danny did too, behind her back. Whirling, she grabbed the pan from him, not thinking how hot it would be. With a yelp, she dropped it on the blue-and-white tile floor. Charred cake crumbs and gooey topping flew everywhere.

Ken examined her palm. "Get some butter, Timmy."

"I'm all right," she said.

He was staring over Erin's head, at Danny. "I hope you're not planning to stay."

"What's that supposed to mean?"

"It sounds plain enough," Ken said, dabbing warm butter on Erin's hand. Then he put down the butter but held on to her hand, gently.

"Maybe I've gotten thick-headed since I left here," Danny said, bending down to pick up the cake pan. "So why don't you just say what you have to say."

"Is Mommy all right?" Timmy stood by them, peering up at the adults. "Why don't you want Daddy to stay, Uncle Ken?"

Releasing Erin's hand, Ken lightly kissed her cheek then headed for the back door through which Danny had come no more than an hour ago. He didn't answer Timmy, something he'd never done before. "I'll be out back." He turned around to look at Danny, his eyes hard. "Be sure Mom sees you before you leave."

The door shut and Danny gazed after him. "Where's he going?"

"He turned the old bunkhouse into an apartment years ago," Erin said. "He didn't want to move away from home but he wanted his privacy."

Danny looked at her. "At least the neighbors won't talk," he said.

"What does *that* mean?"

Danny didn't answer. He and Ken had more in common—always had—than either of them knew. With a sigh, she turned and began clearing the table, taking care to avoid her injured hand. There'd be plenty of pot roast for tomorrow, potatoes too. As for her special cake—

Erin scooped the pan off the counter and plopped its contents in the trash. Never mind dinner. Nothing about the last twenty-four hours had gone right. She slammed the baking tin down by the stainless steel sink.

"Mom!"

"I'll bake you another, Timmy. This one's ruined."

She stalked past him and Danny to the table, keeping her back to them. As she scraped food from all the plates onto one, then into the garbage, she heard the refrigerator door open.

"Come on, Tim." Danny's quiet tone reminded her of their first quarrels soon after they married. Like most men, he didn't seem to know how to handle a woman's anger when she finally had enough and blew. "Let's take these carrots to Kemosabe. I didn't stop on my way in. Guess by now he's real mad at me too."

The back door closed behind man and boy, but Erin didn't glance up or, as she usually did when Timmy took treats to Danny's horse, send her greetings. Until an hour ago the thought hadn't occurred to her in years that Danny might actually come back.

She wouldn't welcome him into this house—even for one night.

3

Squinting into the darkness, Meg Sinclair turned
her five-year-old blue sedan off the main road beneath a
weathered pair of gate posts and a wooden sign that still
read Paradise Valley Cattle Company. She didn't like night
driving, and in forty years of living on the ranch, as a married woman with Hank and now as a widow, she'd never
become accustomed to how black the nights could be.

She'd had a pleasant enough day but hadn't looked forward to the drive home. She didn't look forward to the rest
of the night either. By the time she reached the house
Timmy would be asleep. After exchanging news of the day
Erin would go to her room to read before bed, or think her
own thoughts, and Ken would retire to his bunkhouse
bachelor pad. He never talked to Meg much anyway. As on
all the nights since Hank had died two years ago, she'd be
alone. Utterly alone.

The car sped along the access road. Meg barely touched
the steering wheel. She let the Buick have its head, as if it

were a trusted horse—the kind Hank had always provided for her and the children.

She swallowed the sudden lump in her throat.

At fifty-six she wasn't getting any younger, but if she lived to be a hundred, she'd never forget that one other horse, that one day.

Or the look on Danny's face.

Of her three sons, she had only one left really, and Ken could be so remote. Meg thought she knew why. Ken loved Erin, who seemed not to notice—for good reason. In Meg's view Erin and Danny belonged together. If they finally divorced and Ken had his way, she supposed the family would stay as intact as it could be now; but Ken would sell the ranch and move them all to Dillon. She'd be truly alone then.

In some apartment, not too near yet not too far from Ken's new family, how would she survive? She wouldn't see Timmy every day unless she made a special effort. She wouldn't sit down to meals with the people she loved. She wouldn't hear anything in the deepest part of night except silence.

Meg caught sight of the lights of home, the only home she'd known as an adult. She and Hank had come to this place as newlyweds and had eventually taken over from his father, who had succeeded his father before that, and she couldn't bear to let the ranch go. Even her sad memories belonged here too.

The distant lights soothed her, coming closer with each spin of the tires. The gravel had thinned out over the last winter, and she kept meaning to have Ken order however many truckloads it might take to cover the half-mile private road.

Meg had no idea. She could bake the best pies in the state of Montana, soothe a feverish child, comfort a frustrated man, decorate a house on mere pennies if need be; but she knew practically nothing of what Hank used to do all those years to keep things going. A woman of her time, dependent on her man, she had only her domestic skills.

She could almost thank God that Hank had sold off all but fifteen hundred acres before he died, in order to survive after the bottom fell out of the beef market and he lost his help. He had been so angry after Danny left home, angry with him long before that, then angrier still when Ken threw up his hands and stopped ranching too. Hank never gave up entirely, but the last years were lean. Now all she had was her share of the land, the house, a pittance from Hank's insurance and social security—and whatever Erin and Ken provided, plus her piano teaching money.

Soon, her decisions would be taken from her hands.

The lights twinkled closer, and with her usual feeling of gladness and gratitude for her blessings, she guided the Buick around the slight arc that led to the house. The rest of the long drive continued on toward the now-abandoned barns and other outbuildings, the unused corrals and empty grazing pastures.

She'd lose them too, like Hank. He'd been a difficult man, as Erin always pointed out, but a good man. Like Danny. In Meg's opinion everyone had faults, shortcomings. As long as the strengths balanced out the weakness . . .

Seeing a strange car in the drive, Meg slowed. Despite the warm evening cold fear trickled down her spine. She'd tried not to show how Timmy's accident yesterday affected her, as she forced away memories of another, more final tragedy, but it brought back so much suffering. Was he having some complication now?

No, she'd never seen that car before. It wasn't the doctor's. Ghostly pale and gleaming under the outdoor spotlight by the back porch, the sedan's surface was already dew-covered. It had been here a while.

Braking behind it, Meg shut off the engine and got out.

Her legs felt weak, her heart went racing. She'd called him, knowing she would displease Erin.

But could it be . . . ? Please, Lord, let it be him.

Danny lay back against the headboard of Tim's bed, his son tucked into the crook of his arm, the one that hurt. He hadn't wanted to get too close to Tim's cast, though, while he read him a story so he'd picked that side. He smiled at Tim's bright green cast with the Power Rangers figures on it.·

He didn't want to think about Erin's reaction to their story time. When Tim begged him instead of her to read, she'd given Danny a killing look then stomped downstairs, just as Ken had stomped off earlier to the bunkhouse.

It seemed only one person wanted him here—fortunately the boy he'd come to see. He held him closer, and his smile faded.

With his dark hair and slight frame, Tim reminded him at this age of his youngest brother. He'd been only a year older then than Tim.

Turning a page, distracting himself, Danny read on about a family of bears with human characteristics. Anthropomorphic, he thought the term was, which he'd learned long ago in biology class, the year after . . . Funny what you remembered. Did he really think he could get away, in this house, on this ranch, without remembering? He stared at the book.

"Daddy, why did you stop?"

Danny squeezed him and Tim giggled. "Sorry. I was . . . looking at these pictures. The person who drew these illustrations has a gift, don't you think?"

Tim peered closer at the picture.

"I like the daddy bear best."

"He's good," Danny agreed, inspecting the drawing too, "but I think the mama bear has a lot going for her." Like Erin, with that hair, those eyes.

"Yeah, but"—Tim's nose scrunched—"I like men better. Boys," he said. "Don't you? Girls and ladies like Mom—not Gram—get grouchy sometimes."

He was referring to Erin at dinner tonight.

"Well, mares—women—are always more complex."

"What's complex?"

"Hard to figure out," he said, searching for his place in the story with an index finger. He'd broken it once in a rodeo and could still see a knot on the bone. Or had he broken it that day in the ranch corral when his little brother . . .

No, Trevor!

"Daddy, *read*."

He pressed his lips together tight, then cleared his throat and resumed the story. He should have expected not only the cool reception from Erin and Ken, but the flashes of memory too.

Through the window headlights swept across the bedroom ceiling in a dizzying arc. Danny's head still ached, and the print began to blur on the book's page. Before he realized who might be coming, he heard light, running footsteps on the stairs.

A second later his mother appeared in the open doorway, looking just the same as he remembered. Unlike Erin, she had stayed exactly the way he knew her.

"Hi, Gram!" Tim jumped off the bed into her arms. "Did you have a good time with your friends? Did you bring me something?"

She had the same light brown hair showing hardly any gray—or did she color it now?—the same brown eyes, which only the last of her three sons had inherited, the same quick smile of acceptance. It broke Danny's defenses wide open.

Reaching into her denim skirt pocket and handing Tim a lollipop, then a plastic package containing a miniature car, she smiled over his head. "Here, favorite boy," she murmured, looking at Danny.

"Hi, Mom."

"Daniel," she said.

At his name, spoken through tears, he lunged off the bed, warmth filling him like a blast of sunshine as he took her in his arms.

"Oh, my," she murmured into his shirt. "I never get used to the fact that my boys are taller than I am, bigger and stronger. I still think of you all—of you both—as being small, like Timmy."

He felt wetness soaking into him and her shoulders shook. Danny patted her awkwardly but didn't speak.

"Why are you crying, Gram?"

She lifted her head to smile mistily at Tim. "You won't know until you've raised your own family. You can't imagine how it feels to have a son come home again." She looked at Danny, who swallowed hard. "It's been so long. When your father died, I thought . . ."

"I should have come home."

He would have, if he could bear to see Hank Sinclair again, even in death. If he thought his father would want him there.

"You would have if you could have." She stroked him here and there—his shoulders, his chest, the seat of his pants. "Can you stay?"

"Not long, I'm afraid." He glanced down. "The season's under way. But thanks for calling. I wanted to see Tim, make sure he's okay. You too," he added.

Drawing back, she gave him a weepy smile that made Danny's throat tighter. "You look . . ."

She trailed off, blinking. His bruised face must have stopped her.

"Don't say I look wonderful." He held her hands in his, rubbing his thumbs across her knuckles. "I look just what I am, a broken down saddle tramp who got tossed last night clean across the ring."

"Oh, Daniel."

He shouldn't have said that. "No lasting damage. I'm on the mend. See?" He pointed at the yellowing splotch on his cheekbone. Only that morning it had been livid purple. "They tell me I'm a quick healer."

"So I remember. You have to be." She looked down at his belt buckle, the silver he'd won last season in Calgary. "How are you doing this year?"

"I'm doing all right." He needed Durango, though. The points and the money. In a day or two, he'd leave to rejoin Luke. "One of these years I'm gonna get that world championship. Wait and see."

A shadow crossed her features. He knew his mother's dream as well as he knew his own. She'd always been proud of him, but she wished he'd leave the circuit and come home for good. He knew what else she wanted, and on that they agreed.

"Where's Erin?" Giving him time to answer, she slipped from Danny's embrace to fuss over Tim's gaudy cast. "My, look at this collection of autographs—and drawings too?"

"Six of my friends already signed. We saw them at the playground near the library on our way home from the doctor. See?"

Danny watched her bent head as she read the inscriptions, admiring the artwork. He looked away, down at the wall-to-wall carpet pattern of roads and village where Tim ran his miniature cars.

"Erin didn't much like our story time," he said.

"She's gone to bed already?"

"I guess."

Meg glanced at the clock with the galloping horse motif on Tim's wall. Danny had sent it last Christmas. Erin probably hated the clock too.

"And look what time it is." Meg bustled Tim into bed. "Lights out. That arm needs rest to get well and strong."

"Daddy's needs rest too."

He and Danny had spent the first part of their time alone together commiserating over their wounds. Tim seemed to think Danny's taped ribs and elbow, his scraped face and blue-black eye were worse than his own broken arm.

"Yes," Meg agreed, "it certainly does," kissing Tim good night before she straightened to apply a smooth hand to Danny's cheek, like a healer. "Should I make up a bed for you in the—"

"I'll find a bed." He kissed her cheek then dropped back onto the mattress. "I'll just stay with Tim a while. We want to finish this book about some crazy bears on a picnic."

He wanted to lie beside his son until Tim fell asleep in his arms, for once. After that, he'd see about a place to sleep.

Meg switched off the overhead light, leaving them with a blown kiss for each from the doorway.

"'Night, Gram."

"'Night, Mom."

"Good night, favorite boy." She looked at Danny again, her voice dropping low. "Daniel, I'm so glad you're . . . here."

Their gazes held and he said, "You didn't think I'd come this time either. Did you?"

She answered with a still-dewy smile then closed the door. Tim snuggled closer in his arms and Danny rested his chin on Tim's head. He picked up the story where he'd left off but didn't really hear the words.

Erin didn't want him here. Neither did Ken, for obvious reasons, one of them an unpleasant surprise to Danny.

But his son did. And despite his long absence and what had caused it, so did his mother. Erin had just lost her swing vote, he thought. And smiled into Tim's hair.

Later that night Erin walked down the upstairs hall, wearing a summer weight nightgown and with her hair unbound. Her bare feet made no sound on the worn beige runner, which suited Erin's purpose. Timmy would be asleep by now. She'd kiss him unaware and steal back another moment with him for herself.

Erin eased the door open on the typical boy's room it always had been. Danny and Timmy, in turn, had the same taste in decor, and Erin wrinkled her nose at the cowboy wallpaper border she'd bought under duress. True, its more whimsical design, the primary colors repeated in the bedspread and curtains gave the room an updated look. But the clock Danny had sent, and the Pro Rodeo poster Timmy had brought home from the circuit could still be Danny's. Timmy must have climbed on a chair to nail it up on the closet door, a no-no on both counts. But he'd managed. Not bad.

Adjusting to the dimness, she gazed around the room, taking in the maple dresser, the mirror above it—she had her own memory of that mirror—the matching chair underneath the window. The toy box that Hank had built for Danny, Timmy now stuffed with cars and trucks, Legos, and lately, cowboy figures. One hung out below the lid, which wasn't quite closed, a plastic arm linked with that of a Power Ranger.

Then she looked at the bed. She had a memory of that too, having nothing to do with children.

Once, not long before she and Danny ran away to get married, they had made love on that bed—his bed then—languid, lustful love, the kind she had never forgotten but tried to, every night in her room down the hall. Hank and Meg had been gone that day, attending some regional fair to show Hank's prize Hereford bull, and Danny, home between rodeos, had coaxed her upstairs in the empty house.

He teased her into bed, then teased her more until Erin lay damp and desperate for him . . .

To her surprise he lay in that same bed now. Erin hadn't allowed herself to wonder where he might sleep and didn't want to look. She couldn't help herself. Dimly lit by the reflected glow from the backyard security light, the scene seemed more intimate in a very different way from that other time.

He slept spoon fashion, curled around Timmy like a human cocoon shielding him from further harm. Timmy's cast rested on top of Danny's bandaged arm, which draped Timmy's middle, his dark hair indistinguishable from her son's in the low light. Timmy's stuffed monkey peeped out from the covers on his other side, its wide-eyed grin approving in the dark.

Erin edged closer to the bed. She touched Timmy's hand and he twitched in his sleep. Then she studied Danny's face, his bruises more prominent in the yellowish light, his cheekbone hollows casting shadows toward his jaw. His mouth had gone slack, and his straight white teeth showed faintly between his open lips.

How many times had she watched him sleep? Even that forbidden afternoon, one of many in other places before they married? They had cherished each other then. If only that had lasted . . .

He'd made her laugh. He'd made her weep.

He'd made her shout with pleasure. And in love.

Taking a deep breath, Erin whispered "Good night" then started from the room. She took a single step before a strong male hand ran up the outside of her thigh to her hip and caught her close.

"Don't run off. Look all you want."

His hand felt hot around her hipbone. He had turned over in bed, and his tone sounded slow and lazy, almost drugged. Erin tugged at his hold.

"Danny, let go."

"You come spying on a man when he's asleep, especially a deprived man, no telling what might happen if he wakes up."

She should have realized it was an act. Danny had always wakened like a shot, even from sound sleep. When Erin pulled again, he drew her down. She landed gently on her knees beside the bed, their faces close together.

"Tim welcomed me back," he nearly whispered. "Mom too. Why not you, Erin?"

"You know why."

"I'd rather you tell me." He shifted his hand, snaring her wrist.

"Danny, for heaven's sake."

His thumb brushed back and forth against its inner side, its delicate blue veins. Erin felt a tingle of awareness, more dangerous than the jolt she'd felt when he stepped in the back door before dinner. He used his left hand, the one he controlled those Brahma bulls with, and she could feel raw power, as she felt unwelcome sexual attraction.

Erin stared at his hand on her wrist.

"I never should have let Timmy spend those weeks with you. Now he has a broken arm—"

"Is that my fault?"

They spoke in whispers, not to wake Timmy, but she heard the edge in his tone. He'd long ago become defensive, thanks to his father.

"*Is it*?" In the darkness his eyes looked nearly black, the pupils enlarged.

"Let go of my hand."

"Sure thing." Before she could consider his too easy answer, he had released her. But before Erin could rise on shaky legs, he hooked that same strong hand behind her neck, buried his fingers in the loose flow of her hair, and pulled her down.

His mouth hovered half an inch from Erin's.

"Now say you're glad to see me."

She didn't know where she found the strength herself. "*Like hell.*" With a quick shove at his chest, she jerked up and bolted from the room. She didn't realize Danny was right behind her until she tried to close her bedroom door, wishing she had a dead bolt lock.

He pushed it open.

He followed her inside and shut the door. The light in the room seemed harsh. The white walls brightened the square space, so did the white dotted swiss curtains riffling at the windows, and Erin had left a bedside lamp on. She'd tried for hours to read, to ignore the soft rumble of Danny's deep voice and Timmy's answering boyish one, their laughter. But the ensuing silence seemed worse, and she decided to assess the situation. To make sure Danny wasn't upstairs. To say goodnight to Timmy, she'd told herself.

She saw the futility of lying to herself now. She hadn't hoped to find Danny gone at all. She wanted to see him exactly as she found him, lying vulnerable and open to her inspection, totally unaware. She wanted to find some physical flaw, to negate the attraction she apparently still felt for him.

Danny had caught her before she did.

Now she turned from a contemplation of her pine four-poster bed and its multicolored flowered coverlet to find him stripping off his T-shirt, drawing her shocked gaze to the tape around his ribs and the washboard muscles of his abdomen. There wasn't a better sit-up than riding a bull. Then she noticed his scar below that, where he'd been gored years ago and a horn had perforated his intestine. That didn't seem like a flaw to her either but a reminder of why she'd left him.

"What are you doing?"

"Going to bed. What's it look like?"

Shirtless, he revealed the silky dark hair on his chest, more than she remembered, the thick pads of muscle. Erin stared. He undid his Calgary Stampede buckle and pulled the belt from its loops then paused with a hand on the button of his fly. She'd always been a sucker for a man in button front jeans. A sucker for Danny, period. He gazed back at her.

"Or am I supposed to spend the night coiled around my son like a calf rope? I've got enough hurts," he said. "I don't need a stiff neck too."

His glance faltered. She'd seen his bravado before.

"Then go to bed—but not in here."

Meeting her eyes again for an instant before he gave her

a slow once-over that made the mild June night seem stifling, he fixed at last on her breasts. Were they visible in the thin cotton nightie? she wondered. She didn't look at herself or at him. Erin fixed her gaze on the wooden floor, the bright rag rug by the bed.

"I mean it, Danny."

A quick upward glance showed the top two buttons of his pants undone, the stripe of dark hair from his flat belly toward his groin. He strolled toward her, but Erin stood her ground, her heart slamming. She considered picking up one of her potted plants, a heavy philodendron in a white ceramic pot, and heaving it at his head.

"You can't possibly think you'd be welcome in my bed. That you can just waltz in here—"

He cupped her cheek in one palm. She could see the pulse beating wildly in his throat. "You've never said no to me before. Not about that."

"Consider it a first, then."

"Erin, come on."

He started to draw her closer, to lower his head as he had in Timmy's room, but Erin saw his eyes flicker again. He wasn't sure of himself at all, of her. She stepped back out of reach, and saved herself.

"I said no."

Danny's hand dropped to his side, and his gaze clouded over. He let out a breath then looked at the waxed wooden floor between them.

"I thought it was my imagination," he said.

"What was?"

"You." He glanced up. "And Ken."

"Me and—?"

"When did all that start?"

She couldn't believe her ears. "Have you fallen off one too many bulls? Have you lost your mind?"

"I don't think so."

Erin fingered her wedding ring. Let him think what he

would, then. If it got him out of her room and out of her sight before he dazzled her senseless again with that bare chest.

"Why not?" she said. "You've been gone for years. Out on your own, driving farther away from me and Timmy with every rodeo. You can't have it both ways. You made your choice."

"I didn't run out on you! You left me."

"Danny, we've had this argument before—"

"And rodeo is how I make my living."

"It's not a living! It's a fantasy."

"Call it what you want." Scowling, he edged toward the door. "Whatever's convenient." He opened it then stopped. "Are you sleeping with him?"

"I'm sleeping right here." She waved at her bed, the bed they'd shared more than once during his sporadic stays in Paradise Valley.

"You know what I mean, dammit." He stood, one hand high on the door, the other cradled against his stomach. She could see pain etched in his features.

Stunned, Erin looked away, focusing on the white wicker nightstand by her bed. After all these years, she still couldn't bear to see him hurt. His scrapes and bruises had always bothered her more than they did him. And that was just the physical. She made a placating motion.

"Look, it's late. We're both exhausted. You had a long drive. You're all banged up—again—I've had a dreadful time with Timmy . . ."

She was talking to thin air. For a few seconds she stood in the empty room, feeling the force of Danny's presence still there—as he had been there most of her life. From the day she met him, when her widowed father hired on to become Hank Sinclair's foreman, Danny had been a part of her. *He's not a bad man*, Meg had said. Despite their irreconcilable differences, it seemed only natural to still feel *something* for him, even to feel his pain as well as her own.

Then he poked his head back in the open door, and all over again, she felt exasperation.

"You mind telling me where I'm supposed to sleep?"

She'd forgotten. The house had four bedrooms—long ago, one for each of the three Sinclair boys, one for Hank and Meg. Now Meg, Erin, and Timmy each had a room, but since Hank's death Ken had lived in the bunkhouse, and the fourth bedroom had become Meg's crafts room. She could just imagine how it looked: fabric scraps, ribbon streamers, bits of lace and pillow stuffing, the half-finished dollhouse Meg had started last winter . . .

"I see your point. The spare room's a mess, right?"

"Disaster."

"Ken has a sofa bed in the bunkhouse."

Danny gave her a look. "He won't want me there."

"The living room sofa?" she suggested.

"Too short. Why doesn't Mom buy a new one? The old spring's still about to poke out of that cushion."

Erin joined him at the door, unable to stop her smile. She'd made her own position clear, and she knew Danny well enough to know he wouldn't push.

"Well, you can either spend the night 'coiled like a rope,' or I can help you move some of that stuff in the sewing room and find the daybed underneath. There must be sheets around somewhere to fit. It won't be the most comfortable place, but for one night . . . "

At her emphasis on the last words Danny smiled a little. Maybe she didn't know him that well after all. He gave it one more try.

"There is another solution."

"No," she said, "there's not."

"Then come show me where to put Mom's junk."

As if it were the lesser of two evils Erin helped him make up the narrow daybed, crowded in by the dollhouse on the nearby table and a stack of ruffled aprons Meg was sewing for the town fair next week, without touching Danny. Or letting him touch her. She flipped the yellow sheets toward him over the mattress from the opposite side.

Those few moments by Timmy's bed had been enough.

When they finished, she didn't linger. Neither did Danny. He worked off his sneakers, shucked off his jeans before she reached the door, and turned out the light; he slid into bed with a heavy, heartfelt sigh then called her back just when she thought she was safe.

"Erin?"

"What?"

"One question."

She didn't want to hear it. Like Danny, the questions were no good for her, whether he asked them or she did, of herself.

"What?" she said again.

He was lying against the pillow, one arm under his head, his bandaged arm resting lightly on the top sheet. She'd seen the same pose on other lazy summer nights or on cold winter ones. Looking straight into her eyes, he smiled.

"How come you never divorced me?"

4

The next morning Danny woke up well after seven. Normally he was an early riser, but he hadn't slept well on the single daybed. When he finally got comfortable, his elbow throbbed; the second day was always the worst. He'd ended up lying awake most of the night, until first light, thinking of Erin. He couldn't have had more than two hours' sleep.

He woke up thinking of her too.

Clumping down the stairs, inhaling the meaty aroma from the kitchen, he cursed himself. He shouldn't have pulled that fool stunt last night—almost kissing her, and with Tim lying right there. The other stunt too—strolling into her bedroom, even though it had once, now and then, been theirs, and stripping off his clothes as if he had every right to bed her after eight years apart.

Wishful thinking.

Or jealousy? The image of Ken, tending her burned palm and looking as if he owned her now made Danny see red.

Yawning, he wandered into the kitchen and stopped short in the doorway.

The sight of Tim at the table, his dark head bent over his cereal bowl, the box of Frosted Flakes near at hand, grabbed Danny and wouldn't let go. For an instant he saw his youngest brother again. He saw life as it had been then, sweet and simple.

His brother at the breakfast table, scarfing down soggy cereal and slurping milk like any self-respecting eight-year-old. His mother at the stove, cooking for his father and Ken, the two of them stomping in from the barn after morning feeding, bringing the smells of animals and hay, of sunshine, rain, or snow.

"Hi, Daddy." Tim looked up and saw him in the doorway. "Want some cereal? I can get you a spoon and bowl."

"'Morning, Tim." He ruffled the boy's hair on his way past. "How's the arm doing?"

"Okay. How's yours?"

"Still hurts."

"Mine too," Tim amended, clearly relieved to admit it. "But we're still tough, we keep going. Don't we?"

"That's what rodeo riders do." Danny wondered if Erin coddled Tim, preventing him from acting like a real boy.

"Good morning, Daniel."

Meg's warm brown eyes reflected her smile of pure pleasure as she glanced over her shoulder, holding her favorite cooking spatula in one hand.

He crossed the room to kiss her. He'd had no opportunity in all the years of his self-imposed exile, and it amazed him now that she still could smile at him, without any emotion except gladness.

"You sit with Timmy now," she said, flushing, "while I finish up these eggs. Biscuits are nearly done. There's fresh orange juice in the refrigerator."

Danny's stomach growled. Only one thing—one person—seemed to be missing from the morning scene. He poured himself a glass of juice from a well-remembered quart glass container and took it to the table, sitting across from Tim who grinned at him. Danny basked in it, as he relished the sight of his mother fixing him a meal.

On the road he and Luke ate in fast food places or way-side diners mostly. When they cooked in the camper's crowded kitchenette, it was quick and simple and not very tasty: a box of macaroni with powdered cheese that turned into a sauce when you added water; a tough steak and canned potatoes fried in the grease. He wondered how many food additives riddled his liver.

"Can we go see Kemosabe after you eat?" Tim asked.

"If your mom says it's all right."

Danny glanced around again as if Erin had appeared while he wasn't looking.

"She's already gone," his mother said. "She opens the store at eight o'clock."

"She doing any business?"

"Not enough to pay her bills, I'm afraid." Meg carried the skillet to the table, setting it on a cast iron trivet with a rooster design in the center. She gently clamped both hands over Tim's ears. "The word 'bankruptcy' keeps cropping up lately."

"I noticed a lot of shut down stores in town on my way through." He served himself fluffy scrambled eggs then forked four fat patties onto his plate. "Sausage too?" His nose hadn't misled him but he grinned. "We're all supposed to be watching our cholesterol and fat intake these days."

Tim had pulled Meg's hands away.

"It's a treat, Gram said. What else did she say? While I couldn't hear?"

"None of your business. That's why your ears were cov-ered," Danny told him.

"Grown-up stuff?"   .

"Yes, sir."

Meg hurried back to the stove. "I'll make all your favorites while you're here."

So he could store up more memories? He was already on his way, not all of them good. The kitchen clock above the refrigerator read seven-thirty. He couldn't have missed Erin by that much; or had she left early to avoid him this morning?

"Ken gone too?"

Maybe they traveled together, and Ken left her in town each morning to go on to Dillon, collected her each night and drove her home. He wondered what else Ken did with her behind his back.

"Ken leaves at six," his mother said, bringing a plate of hot golden biscuits to the table. She plopped a dish of butter—real butter—beside him, then a bowl of raspberry preserves, homemade he was sure. She'd always spent her summers making jellies, canning fruits and vegetables.

Danny's mouth watered.

He wanted to ask his mother about Ken and Erin but couldn't risk it in front of Tim. Instead, he piled jam on his biscuits and shoved one in his mouth, chewing so he wouldn't be able to talk.

He swallowed. "Great, Mom."

"I suppose you're wondering . . ."

"Later," he said.

"Because little pitchers have big ears?" Tim, not his mother, had spoken.

"You got that right." He and Meg laughed.

"Hurry up, Daddy. Kemosabe's hungry and I always take him some Frosted Flakes at breakfast time."

"Frosted Flakes?" Danny shook his head at his half-finished plate of eggs, sausages, and biscuits. "Well, why not? The poor guy deserves a treat." He could understand that. "You ever had a bowed tendon?"

"No. Will you tell me what it is? Show me? Can we—"

"I'm hurrying," he said.

His mother had always cooked big meals for hungry ranch workers, especially her family. But she had gone beyond the call of duty this morning.

As she did after his brother died, she eased all the hurts for others, particularly Danny. Giving him strength now for what he sensed would come next from Erin.

Erin hated scenes, no doubt about it. And a confrontation looked imminent.

She fitted her key into the front door lock at the Bitterroot Emporium, which she'd operated in Sweetwater for the past six and a half years. If business stayed as bad as in the past few months . . . she didn't care to finish the thought as she stepped into the store with Ken right behind her.

He shut the door, snapping down the green window shade before Erin had fully raised it to indicate the store was open. Their hands met on the braided pull then drifted apart. She forced the smile.

"Could I make you some coffee?"

"I had plenty at home." Ken followed her through the narrow aisles crammed with merchandise while Erin switched on lights then glided over the worn wooden floor into her cramped office as if seeking refuge. "Erin, we need to talk."

She wished she'd been more adamant about driving herself to work. He'd stayed silent on the way to town. He didn't drop her in front of the store as he sometimes did, or lean across the car seat to kiss her good day, a ritual Ken required but Erin never quite accepted. They'd been friends all their lives . . .

She and Danny had been friends too.

Last night had he meant what he implied about her and Ken?

Turning, she leaned against her desk. Even to stall, she couldn't patronize Ken. "I suppose this is about Danny."

"You suppose?"

"I know," she corrected, feeling she'd already lost control of the situation.

"What in hell is he doing here?"

"Your mother called him."

Ken only groaned.

"Timmy apparently begged her to."

Earlier she had asked for Meg's explanation. Both women had been bustling around the kitchen before Timmy woke, or Danny, and both moving fast to hide the awkwardness they felt at having some unpleasantness between them. She and Meg were not only relatives by marriage and close friends. During Erin's girlhood Meg had acted as her surrogate mother.

"You know how Timmy's been since he came back from seeing Danny," Erin said now.

"Spoiled," Ken said.

Erin ignored his tone. She knew Ken considered him almost a son, but he didn't have the patience with Timmy she would have liked. The patience she'd seen last night at dinner in Danny.

"More demanding than usual," she agreed, "but I think that covers his real feelings." She paused. "He misses Danny."

"Do you?"

Erin looked away.

"We're talking about Timmy," she said. "I didn't want him to spend time around rodeo, but . . . " She trailed off.

It had been easy to say no when Timmy was small. Danny wouldn't have dealt easily with a toddler or pre-schooler, and he'd never asked. Behind the chutes at a rodeo could be a dangerous place, especially for a small child, and that's where Danny spent much of his time. Last summer he and Erin had quarreled regularly by phone, with her claiming Timmy was still too young to fly alone; this summer she'd had no reason to refuse him.

She wasn't happy that Timmy had gone, or that he'd played bull rider and broken his arm, or that he took a certain pride in the injury because Danny had injuries too. But after seeing them together for herself, did she have a right to keep Timmy from being exposed to his father's chosen life? They hadn't shared that much time.

"Timmy's growing up," she said. "He needs a male role model and he's picked Danny."

"What about me?"

She touched Ken's sleeve. "I guess you're feeling left out right now. So am I. But children can be fickle." She patted his arm. "I keep reminding myself that kids swing back and forth, choosing one parent at one stage, the other at the next." Or would she still lose him? Her confidence felt tissue-thin.

He smiled a little. "Well, Danny will be gone soon."

Erin didn't say anything. She swung her foot, her shoe heel tapping against her desk, a gouged and battered walnut veteran of some law office. She'd bought it at an auction, like most of the store's furnishings.

"Won't he?" Ken said.

"You know Danny. Here one day, gone the next." She smiled into Ken's troubled gaze. "I don't know what his plans are, but by Friday at the latest, he'll be on his way to next weekend's rodeo somewhere . . . unless Luke Hastings calls him before then."

"You're sure?" He stepped closer. "You don't want him to stay here?"

"Oh, Ken."

"You know what I want."

"I'm not ready to sell the store."

He touched her cheek. "It's a dead concern," he told her for the hundredth time that spring and summer. "Sweetwater's dying. The young kids are moving to the cities, the ranchers still here don't spend money."

"That I know." Ken had a habit of stating the obvious.

"Who's going to buy milk and bread or parlor curtains from the Bitterroot Emporium?" He trailed a finger to her ear, tucking stray hairs behind it. "The occasional tourist? Do you want to stay here, Erin, and become a curiosity?"

Erin pulled away. Even his light touch seemed improper somehow, wrong to her, and yet—

"I know you're right. I know I should sell." To soften her words, she reached out again, taking his hands. They felt warm and dry. "I should stop commuting from the ranch and teaching Timmy at home—"

"I wish you'd come see the new subdivision," he said. "It's damn good, solidly middle class. The property values can only go up with the years. All the designs are roomy, bright, well laid out, if I do say so myself, and the kitchens—"

She groaned, as she always did when he launched into his sales pitch. "Ken, I'm nearly bankrupt. I can't afford a house in Sweetwater or Dillon."

"We'll settle that later. Quit procrastinating."

"It's my most endearing quality."

He couldn't help grinning. "No, it's not."

"What is?" She smiled back.

"Your love for Timmy, for Mom and—I hope—for me." His smile turned friendly, non-threatening. "Your practical nature. Somehow that pragmatism has a tough time overcoming your inertia." He grasped one hand, holding up her wedding ring between them.

"I'll decide," she said, "about everything. I will."

But the often-repeated words didn't soothe him now. Not since Danny had come home last night.

"When?" Ken asked.

"Soon."

"When Danny leaves?"

"I promise."

"It's not really a decision," he added. "That's why I may seem to be pushing you. It's the right thing for you and Timmy. The house is really antiquated, needs work. If you're worried about Mom—"

"I'm not worried."

"Once we get rid of the ranch—that albatross—we can find her a place in Dillon. Believe me, she'd wonder why she didn't move sooner. She'd be able to have her own life then, closer to her friends—but she'd still get to see us and Timmy." He took Erin's hand, and she walked him to the emporium's door. "She can still baby-sit."

He lingered at the door, holding her hand and running his finger over her ring, looking as if he had more to say. Erin didn't want to disappoint him. Maybe if she did say the words he wanted to hear, he'd become more concrete himself.

"He is leaving, isn't he?" Ken asked.

"Of course he's leaving."

Erin stepped away, and took a tole-painted watering can from its place near the front windows. She busied herself watering the hanging plants there to avoid Ken's face and her mental image of the night before—Danny lying on his side on the too-small daybed, his skin burnished by the low light, his eyes seeing through her. His question scared her. *How come you never divorced me?*

She couldn't make even that decision, the simplest of all. Or so it ought to be. She should have made it years ago.

"Maybe you should tell him tonight," Ken suggested.

"Maybe I should."

That evening after dinner Danny escaped from the house as soon as he scraped his plate and put it in the dishwasher. He and Tim brought a shiny red apple and some carrots to Kemosabe, who stood munching the last orange nubbin while Danny leaned against the corral fence, waiting.

Erin hadn't said a word to him during dinner. When she glanced his way, only once, he saw what he'd expected since the night before in her green eyes—a look of impending doom.

Bored with his silent company, Tim ran back to the house, and Danny folded his arms over the corral's top rail, ignoring the pull of the tape on his healing elbow. He'd spent all day with his son, even napping on Tim's bed with him because neither of them felt that great. He'd had enough talk and didn't welcome any more just then.

That didn't mean he wanted to leave Tim, but he had to—tomorrow. If he wanted money in Durango, he had to ride first. He gazed out across the barnyard toward the mountains of the Pioneer and Beaverhead ranges that ringed Paradise Valley. The familiar sight hadn't changed at all, one of the few constants he had found.

As a boy he'd climbed this very fence at just this time of day to watch the light change over the snow-covered peaks of the Rockies and the shadows shift to gradually darken their slopes, changing colors from slate to rose to purple. In this placid, stream-fed valley for which the ranch was named, he had always found the solace it promised. Or he had then.

The narrow valley was smaller than Big Hole, or any of the larger valleys in the southwestern corner of Montana that could spread fifty miles wide. Danny wondered if, after so many years and miles away, he should have come back even for these few days . . . or after he finally won the world. Erin had said much the same in different words.

She'd changed all right, like Sweetwater and this very ranch. Danny gazed past his horse at the shabby barns and overgrown fields. Along one side of the corral fence he spied a weak spot. If Kemosabe leaned against it, the rusted wire would snap, spilling him out onto the drive, the road . . .

In his youth such a gap would never have occurred—his father saw to that—and the grazing lands beyond the corral and the nearby bunkhouse had teemed with cattle, softly bawling, restlessly moving in giant herds back and forth to the more mountainous slopes. At sunset that lowing had been his favorite sound. Gone now.

But why in hell didn't Ken maintain the place? The back screen door slammed. Turning his head, Danny watched his brother's approach—an emissary from Erin in the kitchen?

"Can I give you a hand putting your things in the car? You'll want to get an early start tomorrow."

"Some gentle hint, Ken."

"So I'm not tactful. I say what I mean."

Danny preferred things said plain himself. He considered that one reason why he and Ken always got on so well, or had when they were brothers. "Boys," he muttered.

What right did Ken have to judge him, moving in on Erin with a wedding ring still on her hand?

Maybe that shouldn't surprise him. In the years since Tim's birth, Ken ironically had been Danny's link to his child. Tim's June visit wasn't his first—just his first to the circuit. Twice a year until this summer, Ken had delivered Tim to Danny somewhere for a few days during spring vacation, a week at Christmas. Then collected him again. Danny suspected that Ken cooperated to keep him from suing for visitation rights—and to keep him away from Paradise Valley.

He studied his brother, frowning. He had Erin buffaloed all right. It made Danny's blood boil. Only last winter she'd sat, stony-faced, in Ken's car while he unloaded Tim's suitcase. Danny had stood back as long as he could then tapped on her window. She never said five words to him, just rode with Ken sometimes to say good-bye to Tim. Other times, she made some excuse and stayed home.

Finally, the window glided down and he leaned in.

"Why don't you get out of the car?"

She didn't look at him. "I don't want to talk to you."

"Then you're not over me yet," he'd said.

In the rodeo arena Danny made snap decisions. He had to if he wanted to stay alive. Looking at Ken, he made one now.

"Think I'll stick around a few days."

Ken stiffened. "Why? So Timmy will miss you more when you disappear? So Erin will wind up confused again? Or so Mom can get used to having you around, cooking and cleaning up after you as if she had nothing better to do?"

Danny ignored the part about Erin and his son. "That's what Mom's always done. She picks up after you too."

"I have my own place now." He gestured with a thumb toward the bunkhouse. "Renovated it myself, furnished it. I clean it too. Every Saturday morning."

"That's virtue for you."

Ken went on. "I stock my own kitchen with beer, Coke, and snacks, some breakfast stuff so Mom doesn't have to get up early . . ."

Danny looked at the bunkhouse. He'd look anywhere but into the corral with Ken standing near. He propped a foot against the lowest fence rail.

"Mom likes getting up for Tim and Erin."

"Well, I think it's time she had more for herself." He waited until Danny glanced at him. "Time for you to move on again." Ken let his gaze drift to the corral, where Kemosabe whickered to himself in pleasure as he chewed. "It's never been right having you here—you know that—since Trev died."

At the name, Danny's gut clenched. "Thanks, Ken. I appreciate you bringing that up."

"Dad would have said the same."

"And I keep thinking this place has changed."

"We're doing fine without you." Without a backward look, Ken walked away in the direction of his converted bunkhouse. He called over his shoulder, "Don't get yourself stomped by any mad bulls, Danny boy."

Danny felt weak. He dropped his head onto his folded arms, but he could see the corral in his mind.

He could see the dark bay gelding, not Kemosabe, its black tail switching, its eyes rolling. Trevor on its back.

He could hear Erin's shouts again.

"Danny?"

She had called from this corral to him in the barn. He tasted fear in his own mouth, felt himself running, shouting:

"Get down! Get off him!"

Danny had trained the horse himself, the first entrusted to him by his father. At thirteen he was proud of his efforts, but the horse wasn't ready to be ridden by an eight-year-old boy. Trev hadn't asked permission . . .

Danny got there in time to see the horse rise into the air, all four legs off the ground, back arched high—like the logo on all those Wyoming license plates. Except that horse had a little kid clinging to its mane.

Danny tried, but there'd been no stopping him. The horse had gone wild.

Buck him out! Ride him till he drops, head hanging, starving for air. Don't let the sonofabitch beat you. Oh, Trev . . . Christ!

Cold sweat ran down his spine again now. He looked around to see Erin coming toward him across the yard. For a moment he didn't realize she'd called to him before, and her determined stride didn't register. Then he thought, Erin too? Except he knew what she would say, what she'd been trying to say for eight years.

Dazed, he didn't move from the fence. He could still hear Trev's cry and the sharp snap of bone in his neck. He swore he'd heard that.

"*Danny?*" She stood right beside him, as she had that other day.

"Oh, God." He dropped his head back onto his arms, hiding his eyes. Why had he remembered that day? He couldn't bear to look at her while she said what he knew she'd come to tell him.

"Timmy wants you to read him a story."

"Bet that just tickles you."

She took a breath. He could feel her watching him. "What did Ken say to you?"

"The same thing you must be thinking. For me to pack my gear. It's not the first time."

Erin made a small sound but didn't speak. She weighed everything, even words. Danny wondered how long it took her at the store to measure out a pound of green beans or flour.

"He didn't mean that," she said at last.

He briefly opened one eye. "Don't try to tell me that's not your preference too."

"It was," she admitted, "until I saw you sleeping last night with Timmy. I've been thinking all day," she said. "I understand how much he needs you and that I—well, I've never denied you seeing him but I never—made it easy for you either."

An image of Trevor flashed across the screen of his closed eyelids. Trev landing hard in the dirt. That sound, like a twig breaking . . . the awful stillness.

"Maybe you were right," he said, his voice muffled by his arms.

"It's not that I want him chasing rodeo, but at dinner tonight he asked you to cut his meat and watched every motion of your hands as if they were . . . sacred or something. Lately he doesn't seem to have much use for me."

"You're a good mother, Erin."

"Thank you."

"He's a helluva kid," Danny said, thinking she'd picked a lousy time to approve of him, to communicate. "You've done a good job." He paused. "I wish I'd done as well."

He straightened, and Erin was watching him, her green eyes as dark as grass before a storm. She stood with her back to the fence, and Danny faced it.

"When I got here last night," he said, "I saw Tim with that cast—" He broke off. "I saw him, and every little thing in me started hurting. My elbow, my face, my head. My stomach turned queasy. . . . "

Erin nearly smiled. "It happens to me too, every time he cuts himself or scrapes a knee . . . and when he fell off that bike—"

Danny looked at the corral. Kemosabe had stopped munching and stood splay-legged, his head down, his prehensile lips flapping for stray bits of carrot in the dirt. He stood just as the bay had, over Trevor.

"I wasn't there for him. That's what made me hurt."

"I never thought I'd hear you admit—" Then she seemed to sense his true meaning. "Is that all, Danny?"

He didn't answer.

He could feel Erin's gaze following his over her shoulder to Kemosabe.

"You're thinking about your brother too, aren't you?" she said. "About Trevor not just Timmy?"

He'd bent over him, lying so limp in the dust. He'd lifted him . . .

"Every time I see this ranch"—he waved a hand—"this corral. It's guaranteed."

She touched his arm. "There was nothing you could have done. You know that."

"Dad didn't," he said. "Ken still doesn't."

"He said that to you?"

"Pretty much." Danny fixed his gaze on the mountains. "You know what's hardest about coming back?" He cleared his throat. "It's Mom," he said. "The hardest part is looking in her eyes, not seeing any blame at all."

He was trembling. All over. When he lifted his hands, they shook like a green kid's before his first bull ride.

"Danny," she whispered.

Shifting his gaze, he looked at her. He'd come into the house last night to learn that the girl he'd married had grown into a woman he didn't know. But now, again, he saw in Erin's eyes the old connection between them, the glimmer of need he'd glimpsed in her bedroom and wondered this morning if he'd imagined. He saw Erin. And all the sweetness they had shared.

Maybe she wouldn't say what he expected after all.

In that same instant she lifted one hand to the back of his neck, nudged her hip closer to his by the rail, and without changing their positions more than that, with Erin still facing him against the fence, she shut her eyes. Then raised her mouth to his.

Echoing her first motion, Danny slipped his hand behind her neck too, but hesitated to take what she offered. Caring, acceptance, forgiveness? He didn't know for sure. What he did know was that he couldn't leave just yet—not only to goad Ken. If he left, he would lose his last chance with Erin and Tim.

How come you never divorced me?

He leaned closer and so did she, by inches, by degrees. Like Erin, he closed his eyes against the sight of the corral, the flashback of Trevor, and took her mouth. For the first time in eight years he kissed her—open-mouthed, his lips soft on hers, then his tongue, his teeth.

"Oh, Danny."

He felt a shudder run through her, and didn't know whether to smile or cry. If Erin didn't know why she hadn't divorced him, in that moment Danny did.

5

She had suffered a momentary lapse of common sense.

Leaving her warm nest of flowered sheets the next morning, Erin tiptoed across the cool wooden floor of her room and to the bathroom. She'd also overslept. She'd open the store a little late this morning, not that a crowd would be clamoring at the doors when she arrived.

After washing her face, she grimaced at her reflection in the clouded mirror. The silver backing had begun to show through; Meg needed a new medicine cabinet, and Erin decided to give her one when the next shipment of housewares arrived at the Emporium.

Money was tight these days in the Sinclair household, at least among its women.

Coming from the bathroom, she stumbled into a solid wall of muscle. "Ohhh."

Looking up as he steadied her, she met Danny's amused gaze. He'd obviously just wakened too. His hazel eyes still looked sleepy, unguarded, and his hair stood in tufts that made Erin want to smooth it down as she'd wanted to that first night, to feel its silky warmth again in her fingers.

Barefoot too, wearing only his jeans with the fly mostly undone, he'd emerged from the sewing room—Erin could see its open door at the end of the hall—apparently headed for the bathroom himself. She shouldn't have hit the snooze alarm twice, making it impossible to avoid him this morning. Erin jerked her gaze from his abdomen to his chest, then met his eyes again. She wouldn't look below his waist.

"You might have said something instead of letting me barrel into you," she finally said.

His hands lingered on her upper arms. He smiled down at her. Even his voice sounded husky from sleep, sexy. "If I'd said I was coming, you'd have run the other way." Lifting one sun-browned hand, he stroked the tangled hair from her temples, making Erin shiver—but not from cold. "You'd have hightailed it in to that room of yours, shut that door, and slammed the bolt home just like a chute banging closed."

She wished she didn't hear the laughter in his voice now and want to answer it. "It doesn't have a bolt."

"I'll keep that in mind." Suddenly Danny had that look in his eye, the one he'd gotten last night by the corral fence the instant she had touched the nape of his neck and, as if she'd lost her mind, pushed closer to him. Comfort was one thing, her own survival another.

She eased back out of reach, and his hand dropped. His smile faded.

"You getting ready to run now, are you? Like a halter-shy filly?" Rubbing his bare chest, Danny tilted his head. "Nothing in my hands, and I'm not wearing any sleeves."

She refused to look at him. She kept her gaze fixed on the wooden floor between their bare feet and edged back another few steps toward her room. Tomorrow, if he stayed until then, she'd set the alarm early again, be gone before he woke.

"Erin, about last night—"

"I'm late for work. The bathroom's yours for the next twenty minutes." She'd showered the night before, as if to wash off the scent of her and Danny, together even for those few moments. "After I dres—" She couldn't finish the word. "After I have my coffee—"

"The usual two cups? With half a spoonful of sugar and plenty of cream?"

"—I'll need to put on some lipstick and comb my hair."

"Can I watch?"

Erin didn't answer. One more step, and she reached safety. She whirled into her room, shutting the door firmly behind her, shutting out the sound of Danny's low laugh.

"I've still got a good imagination," she heard him say.

The trouble was, so did Erin. And a lot of memories she didn't care to recall either. Last night she'd made the mistake of touching Danny, of letting him kiss her—no, instigating the kiss herself—and she vowed it wouldn't happen again

"Sure, I will," Danny said into the kitchen phone, the receiver tucked beneath his chin. He opened the refrigerator, pulled out the container of orange juice, and because his mother wasn't home, tilted it up and drank from it instead of getting a glass. The habit, Luke's practice too, had always driven Erin crazy.

After their meeting in the upstairs hall, Danny had used ten of his twenty allotted minutes in the bathroom, then tugged on a clean T-shirt and hurried downstairs. Erin was already gone, probably drinking her second cup of coffee in her room. Meg had driven to Sweetwater for an early dentist appointment.

"I know I promised to meet you in Durango," he told Luke, setting the orange juice on the table. "Hell, I planned to." He paused. "Sure, it's gonna be a damn good rodeo but there's no way I can make it now." The first go-round was today. To his relief Luke told him he'd drawn a pair of mediocre bulls anyway. "Something came up here . . ." He laughed. "No, not my di—" At the sound of scuffling footsteps near the kitchen, he broke off.

Luke growled in his ear some more, wondering when Danny intended joining him on the road again. "The camper payment's due," he said.

"Two of them," Danny corrected. "I'll send you some money." He'd dip into his savings then pay himself back next time he won. He considered his stay at Paradise Valley an emergency.

Luke groused again. "Don't you want to get to the finals? Out there in the middle of nowhere, losing rides, losing points, losing prize money, you're already in negative numbers."

"I know." He shifted the phone to his other ear. He could hear Luke furiously snapping the usual wad in his cheek. "I'm working on something."

Luke's tone turned suspicious. "You sound like a lovestruck kid. What's going on there? Don't you know marriage—especially an on-again, off-again marriage of thirteen years—can only hog-tie you? If you feel cold on the road, you can buy another blanket."

"There's a difference," Danny said.

Luke couldn't see that. "If you need sex, that little barrel racer who keeps finding you everywhere we go looks willing."

"There's a difference," he repeated. "Give me a call when you get to Cody, let me know what I drew for Saturday, okay? Save me the call-back."

He could never get through to a rodeo office about his entry when he needed to. He listened for a minute. Luke sounded like a nagging wife himself.

Tim stomped into the kitchen, grabbed the cereal box with his good arm, and poured Frosted Flakes over half the tabletop. Unrepentant, probably because his mother and grandmother weren't there, he grinned at Danny.

The sugar bowl tipped, spilling next to Tim's bowl.

Danny frowned at him but lowered his voice to Luke.

"I said, I'll meet you in Cody." The Fourth of July meant more to a bull rider than picnics and fireworks; it was traditionally called Cowboy Christmas for the number and variety of rodeos that week.

"You'd better get there," Luke said, and Danny hung up, feeling guilty. He really couldn't afford time off just now, not for the rest of summer.

He put the phone down and poured himself some coffee.

"Sometimes he's crankier than a wife," he said to himself.

"Who was that, Daddy?"

"Luke."

"He's not grouchy. He's funny." Tim and Luke had appreciated each other's sense of humor from the instant Tim stepped off the plane earlier in June. Which said something about Luke's maturity. "He makes me laugh and he even let me play in the barrel, remember?"

"Yeah, but he gets ideas and won't let go."

"You mean, about your dick?"

Danny blew coffee all over the floor.

"How'd you know about that?" Then he remembered. Tim had taken a long time to get from the stairs to the kitchen. "Your mom teach you while I was gone to listen in on other people's conversations? You know what that word means?"

"No. Yeah." Tim took a sudden interest in his cereal.

"Well, forget it. That's not what we were talking about anyway. So don't repeat that, understand?"

Tim kicked the leg of his chair.

"I won't."

"And clean up that mess you made. In the whole time you spent with me and Luke, I never saw you slop cereal and sugar like that. You'll draw ants. You expect your grandmother to wipe up after you, or something?"

Sponging the coffee-splattered tile floor himself, Danny glanced at his son's downcast face. His cheeks had gone pink. As he ate he rested his neon green cast against his concave belly. He looked smaller somehow, yet Danny saw he'd already grown this summer. The blue-striped Western-style shirt that was brand-new when Erin packed his bags weeks ago now inched above his belt, showing a strip of pale skin.

He looked so vulnerable that Danny sighed. He'd still been smarting from Erin's rejection in the hall, his body humming from the sight of her then and the feel of her mouth under his last night, when Luke called wondering why he hadn't come to Durango yet. Luke's expectation had irritated him, which irritated Danny with himself, and he'd taken that out on a seven-year-old.

"Let's finish breakfast," he said, getting a bowl from the cupboard and joining Tim. "Hand me those Frosted Flakes and the sugar bowl—what's left in it." He reached for the milk pitcher on the table.

"Daddy, soon as we're done, can we give Kemosabe some sweet feed?"

He laughed. "Another treat? That's all that lazybones needs. He hasn't had a lick of exercise all summer. Hasn't done a second's worth of work to earn his keep." Danny watched the smile break over Tim's freckled face. "I thought maybe I'd put you up on him today, see if he remembers what to do. How's that sound?"

"Me?" His eyes went saucer-round.

"Yes, sir."

"Ride Kemosabe? A real horse?"

"Just inside the fence. You've done it before, with Luke and me."

"But not with Mom around."

Danny rolled his eyes. "You mean she doesn't want you to ride?"

"Well, with Kemosabe hurt," Tim said, "and no other horses since before Grampa died, and me still being so little, she says, and her havin' no money . . . and this—" He raised his casted arm.

Excuses. Brainwashing. At Tim's age Danny had already owned his own horse, and been looking forward to his first rodeo. Erin had grown up on the ranch and loved riding then. Did she really think a simple horseback ride would hurt Tim?

Stupid question, after last night. As she had also, he remembered the corral again, and Trevor. He needed to wipe that out of his memory. Erin's too.

"Don't you worry about your mom on that one." Danny dug into his cereal. "It's not like you're riding bulls yet."

Erin had been running behind the action all day. By the time she opened the store and waited on her first customers, her blouse felt damp at the armpits and she hadn't cooled off since. Flapping the dusky green camp shirt against her front, she breezed the Jeep toward Paradise Valley at well past six o'clock that evening.

Like many Montanans, on the well-maintained road through open spaces with sparse traffic, Erin drove fast. Meg would have dinner on the table before she got home. Then there'd be Timmy's bath, a story . . .

Would Danny still be there tonight? He hadn't said good-bye that morning. But of course she hadn't given him the chance.

Still regretting her rash actions the night before, she hoped he'd left to rejoin Luke Hastings. Those two might as well be married, Erin thought, slowing for the turn onto the ranch access road. Luke had certainly spent more time with her husband than she had in thirteen years, though Danny would say that was her fault. They probably got along better too.

Without the ever-present sexual component, maybe she and Danny could have made things work, but she doubted that.

He was a dreamer clear through, and Erin had been

born pragmatic, as Ken said, or at least arrived there at an early age. Losing a mother when you were two years old did that to a person, she supposed. Then her father hadn't been the most demonstrative man. He'd done what he had to do for her, little more. When he became Hank Sinclair's foreman, she imagined he felt glad to let Meg mother his only daughter during the rest of her growing-up years.

Erin sped along the road. She loved having Meg for a stand-in mother, and she gave thanks every night for her stalwart presence in her own child's life. Meg adored Timmy, and in Erin's view, he came as close as possible to replacing Meg's youngest son.

At the driveway, she stopped at the mailbox, scooping out bills and fourth-class flyers. For a second, she nearly glanced through the stack as she drove on—a habit she still hadn't broken. In the early years Danny had sent love letters, then postcards, then only pages from *Pro Rodeo Sports News* with his standings or an article about him, as if to say, *See? I'm doing just what I wanted to* . . . then nothing. Until, since Timmy's birth, he sent things for their son.

Barreling the Jeep up the drive, she flung dust in her wake like a cloud around her thoughts of last night, and Danny.

She had to admit, he'd brightened Timmy's spirits. He had hardly complained about his cast at all. Another month, five weeks at most, the doctor had said, and his bone would be knitted as good as new. Maybe through Timmy she and Danny would at last find peace with each other.

Erin approached the rambling, white, two-storied frame ranch house, ringed with porches and topped by two stout, red brick chimneys. It looked reassuringly indomitable set on the low, grassy knoll at the curve of the drive opposite the barn. Her haven.

Then at the sudden sight before her the image shattered, and she jammed on the brakes. The Jeep screeched to a halt, and she jumped out and marched across the dirt toward the corral where she'd acted foolish with Danny . . . where Trevor had died.

Laughing, Timmy sat there now on Kemosabe, his casted arm thrust high, his knees pulled up over the horse's withers. He wore the straw cowboy hat Danny had bought him during his stay on the circuit, which Erin had finally banned from the house lest he wear it to bed.

"Danny!" she shouted. "Daniel Sinclair—"

He turned, his grin freezing in place.

Timmy waved the hat.

"Hi, Mom!"

Under other circumstances Erin would have smiled. He had his father's bravado. But he knew she'd forbidden even the thought of climbing on Kemosabe, not only because of the horse's injured tendon. That was well on its way to healing now, after the three-month lay-up Erin had provided.

"Get down from that horse. Now!"

Timmy swung a leg over in front, where the saddle horn should have been, and Erin's pulse jumped into her throat. He meant to obey her instantly, one-armed.

"Danny, help him off!"

Facing her, speechless, he had his back to Timmy, but at Erin's tone of voice he spun around. Timmy looked so lost on the gelding, which stood nearly sixteen hands, and until Danny grasped Timmy's waist, she didn't breathe.

She said nothing more until he safely reached the ground. Then she closed the rest of the distance to the corral, and Danny, whose hand stayed on Timmy's shoulder.

Standing ground-tethered near boy and man like a good quarter horse, Kemosabe twitched an ear in her direction as Erin swung the gate wide. He obviously expected a carrot. When she didn't produce one, the horse turned its head away, swishing its plumy tail and catching Erin on the arm.

She rubbed the spot, glaring at Danny. The tantalizing aroma of roast chicken and stewed tomatoes wafted from the house to Erin's nostrils, mixing with the scents of horse-hide and manure.

"Timmy, go to the house, please."

He didn't move. "Are you gonna bawl Daddy out?" Looking up at her, Timmy slipped his hand into Danny's. "We were just—"

"Now," Erin said. "You can help Gram with dinner." She kept her gaze on Danny's until she heard the gate swing shut again, and the clomp of Timmy's small cowboy boots across the hard-packed dirt.

"Thanks a lot," Danny said. "You just made me look like an idiot in front of my kid."

"You are an idiot!"

"Now wait here—"

"What else would you call it? Putting him up on a horse that size—"

"On any horse at all," Danny said. "That's what you really mean."

Erin huffed out a breath. "I suppose you call that macho, being a real cowboy. Did you by any chance happen to notice the cast on that child's arm?"

"He wasn't going anywhere. I gave him a riding lesson this morning, the fundamentals he should have learned when he was three years old."

"Hank sold off the horses soon after Timmy was born."

She saw Danny flinch. Timmy was Meg's joy, and he'd been Hank's too, their only grandchild. And for Hank, he was also a constant reminder of the boy he'd lost.

"He ought to know anyway, how to sit a saddle."

"With no hands? His legs in the air?" She pointed at Kemosabe's bare back. "That horse isn't wearing a saddle."

"He doesn't need one." A muscle twitched in Danny's jaw. "That's not how any of us learned. I led Tim around the corral a few times before lunch today." He ran a hand through his hair. "We took naps again. After that, Tim—"

"Started begging for more."

He couldn't help the half smile. "He sure knows how to make his point." Danny looked at her. "Must take after you."

"You can put the cowboy charm away. I'm not buying."

Kemosabe stamped a foot.

"You've become a real hardnose, Erin. Must be all that time you spent around Dad, the time you spend now around Ken."

"At least you're no influence."

With a disgusted sound, he rubbed Kemosabe's velvet muzzle, then fussed with the gelding's forelock.

"I thought you'd be gone by now," she said.

His heated gaze snared hers. "All right, why don't you fire all the guns at once and get this over with? Then maybe we can start talking to each other like decent human beings again. Like we did for a couple of minutes last night."

"I don't want to talk. I want—"

He turned away. "Let me guess."

"Danny, he could have been hurt. Or worse," she added, and saw his shoulders stiffen. She hadn't forgotten that upthrust arm either. "To actually teach him *bull riding*—"

"I wasn't." Danny spun around. "When you drove up, we were finished walking around the ring. I had a lead rope on the halter and never let go," he said. "The horse never went above a lazy walk, no action at all. What do you take me for, Erin? Tim's a healthy kid—"

"With a broken arm!"

His eyes blazing, he stood toe to toe with her. "Does it ever occur to you that maybe he admires his father? That he wants to be like me? Is that the worst thing you can imagine for him in this life?"

Erin opened her mouth but Danny cut her off. "Yeah, I suppose it is." Clucking to Kemosabe, he tugged the horse forward into a walk, almost knocking Erin over. "Tim was trying out his moves himself. I never told him to, never gave him any instruction." He paused. "If that comes naturally to him, as it did to me, as it does to lots of other boys his age, I'm sorry that bothers you. I'm sorry as hell you're not proud of me too."

"Danny."

He put a hand on the gelding's neck, stopping him with that small motion, waiting. His words shamed her. She had all but blamed him for Trevor's accident too. Maybe she'd overreacted.

"It's not easy raising a child," she said. "I try my best but I know sometimes I hold onto the reins too tight."

"Is that an apology?" He stared at her. "Maybe you shouldn't be holding them alone."

Looping the lead rope around the corral's top rail, he walked back to her in the softening light. From the house she heard Meg ringing the iron triangle once for dinner, then the sound died into silence. She must have seen them.

"I'm part of his life too, Erin."

"For how long? Until tomorrow morning?" She held his angry, wounded gaze. "As soon as Timmy gets to know you, you'll be gone. Rodeo's what suits you, Danny."

"It has," he agreed, not looking away.

"This ranch, your family, the store are what suit me. We both have our priorities, don't we? You wouldn't quit rodeo and I wouldn't leave here. That's why our marriage never worked."

"It worked just fine—"

"Where? In bed?"

"Not a bad beginning," he said, "but we were friends before we ever went to bed with each other. Good friends."

Erin's throat tightened. "Then maybe we should never have . . . slept together. Because we aren't friends now."

"You sent me away, Erin."

"You wanted to go."

"And every time I came back, you sent me away again."

Erin blinked. He made her sound cold, unloving. But she'd loved him too much and they had nearly destroyed each other. "Maybe that was easier than waiting for you to say you were leaving."

"I thought when Tim was born—"

"You weren't there!"

He gazed at her then glanced at Kemosabe, shifting from one leg to the other at the rail. Danny walked to the fence.

"You'd be surprised," he said, untying the lead rope and opening the gate. "If you didn't have everything nailed down tight in your mind, I'd tell you. But I think you're right after all. Talking's not what we're best at."

He led the horse out into the dusty yard.

"Tell Mom I'll be in as soon as I put 'Sabe in the pasture and throw some feed in his bucket for later."

Erin watched them go, man and horse. Both magnificent animals, she couldn't help thinking, both looking solitary and somewhat worn. Danny's slight limp told her he still felt sore, and the gelding moved gingerly.

After only a few steps Danny turned around, leading the horse in a small circle until they both faced her.

"You're not mad about Tim on this horse. You know he'd take care of that boy." His gaze darkened, sliding over her until Erin wanted to disappear. "You're mad about last night. I'd be willing to bet on that. And your own thoughts of that big bed of ours, how lonely it must feel."

Meg pressed a hand to her hungry stomach and watched Danny with his horse in the pasture opposite her kitchen window. The sight of the paint's black-and-white hide, of her son's dark head gleaming in the lowering sunlight made her forget to turn off the steamer pot of broccoli on the stove. Danny passed a hand over the horse's neck then leaned his head against it.

"Gram, supper's burning."

She hurried away from the window. At the kitchen table

Timmy bent over a crayon drawing next to his plate. He'd set the table himself, putting knives on the left and forks on the right, ignoring spoons entirely, all the while with his small face pinched pale.

"Mom and Daddy are fighting," he'd told Meg.

Resisting the urge to pry, she'd praised his table setting then given Timmy a pad of blank paper and the crayons. Now she switched off the front stove burner and set the pot aside.

Taking a serving bowl from the cupboard, she slipped the dark green vegetable into it, adding a generous dollop of butter and squeezing on some lemon juice. One question couldn't hurt.

"Did you and your daddy have a good day together?"

Timmy didn't answer for a moment.

"Real good," he finally said, dumping the crayons back into the box. "While you were at the dentist then at church with your ladies' club we read and talked and took a walk . . . and before our nap, he let me sit on Kemosabe." Timmy hesitated. "While you were cooking dinner, we did it again . . . until Mom came home."

So that was it. Just as she suspected. With three boys she'd seen her share of broken bones.

"She didn't like you riding with that cast, did she?"

Timmy shook his head. "She didn't say anything before I left, when she sent me to the house." He paused again. "But I saw Daddy from the back door taking 'Sabe to the pasture, and he looked like he got a spanking."

"Your mother's worried about you."

"Us bull riders—"

Meg touched his hair. "Timmy, I'd leave that for a bit, until your cast comes off and your arm is all better. No sense mentioning bull riding until then."

His chin jutted out.

"She can't stop me from rodeoing."

Erin could try, she thought. And Meg, who took pride in

Danny's accomplishments, couldn't blame her. It was a dangerous business, inborn, she'd sometimes thought, and needed no encouragement. Over time, it promised an even greater chance of tragedy than a small boy riding a green horse in the corral . . . a boy like Timmy now.

"Gram?"

"What?"

"Are you missin' Grampa?"

"I miss him every day," she said, "but why do you ask?"

"You look sad." His chin quivered as he peered up at her. "Are you sad because of Mom and Daddy?"

She'd been sad about Erin and Danny for a long time. If only Erin didn't expect the impossible—that a man who loved rodeo with every cell of his being would give it up. Or if Danny were willing to do just that and come home, on Erin's terms. She didn't see any other solution for those two.

"I wish your parents would look past their differences," she said, "and find the similarities again." The kitchen smelled fragrant before dinner, and she should carve the chicken. But taking it from the oven, she smiled faintly. "When they were children, just your age and not much older, they were inseparable. Together all the time," she said. "And when they grew up a little, noticed each other—"

"Like girlfriend and boyfriend?"

"Yes," Meg said. "They looked so right together, as if they were just grateful to have each other."

"Why don't they like each other now?"

"Maybe they will again someday." She left the chicken on the countertop to glance out the window. Erin was walking across the yard, her shoulders slumped, her head down. Danny watched her from the pasture as he removed Kemosabe's lead rope.

"And then Daddy would live at home with us? And he and Mom would sleep in her room together?"

"Wouldn't that be fine?" Meg murmured. The house full of laughter again, and another baby or two to spoil. Danny

might even take up ranching where Hank had left off. He'd
fix the fences and barns, raise some prize bulls . . .

It seemed too much to hope for now—until Timmy
spoke again. His earnest little face studied her too closely,
and Meg imagined he could see all her sorrows, her abandoned hopes. Her fear for her own future now, without
Hank—or any of the people she loved.

"What if we help 'em?"

"Help them?"

"Sure." He sounded just like Danny. "How could we,
Gram?"

"I don't know," she said, and then, "Any way we can, I
suppose."

Timmy wriggled in his chair. "You and me could go to
the movies to see 'The Lion King' again. Uncle Ken could
come too. Then Mom and Daddy would be here together,
and they'd have to like each other—else they'd feel lonely
without us."

Meg blinked. "Perhaps we could."

"Then Daddy would be Mom's favorite guy, like I'm
yours, huh?"

She shouldn't get the boy's hopes up, but . . .

"Yes, Timmy."

"And Mom would kiss him—" He hunched his shoulders
as if shivering in distaste "—and they'd be in *love*."

"I hope so," Meg whispered.

She heard Erin's footsteps on the first tread of the back
porch.

"Then we'd be Valentines, wouldn't we?"

Out of the mouths of babes, she thought as Erin opened
the door and Danny's boots hit the steps behind her.

Meg smiled. "Yes. I believe we would."

Tipping his head back, Timmy beamed at her.

"I already love you, Gram."

Meg passed a hand under his stubborn chin. She
couldn't say which parent he'd gotten that from, Danny or

Erin. But if neither of them knew what they needed, Timmy did. And so did Meg. Just maybe, it was possible. She planted a kiss on his cheek before he could squirm away.

"I love you too, favorite boy."

6

Erin hadn't known what love meant until she loved Danny. As she swept out the store two mornings later, muttering to herself because her summer help hadn't arrived on time—again—she brushed away the memories of a long ago afternoon in Danny's bed. The feel of his hands on her body, the two of them completely naked together for the first time after months of furtive scramblings in the barn, the tool shed, the far reaches of the pasture, the old sod house over the hill.

She'd had only one lover in her life, and even now she didn't want another. Erin flushed but blamed the warm weather. Predictions said it would be the first hot day of the season.

She swept faster. And if she didn't forget daydreaming, she'd never get the store cleaned up, the inventory started, the shelves straightened. Tonight, because of Jason Barker's lateness, which had become a habit since his high school graduation in May, she'd have to take work home. The accounts needed updating by the end of the month, and there wouldn't be time now when she had to handle Jason's chores too.

She thought she knew why he was late again, or both reasons why, which only increased her irritation. Because of his rodeo obsession and his current girlfriend, he reminded her of half the boys in the area—of a younger Danny.

Why even allow herself to think of Danny's challenge the other night and the memories it provoked?

You're not mad about Tim on this horse . . . you're mad about last night.

The bell over the emporium's door jingled as it opened, letting in a blast of hot summer air—and Daisy Chatworth, Erin's lifelong friend.

Like Erin's, the other woman's oval face glowed with perspiration, and her long dishwater blond hair stuck to her temples and neck. She flashed a smile.

"What are you sweeping for? You look like a one-woman band this morning. Where's Jase?"

Erin's smile was wry. "This is the third time in the past week he hasn't shown up. Guess where he might be? But since I'm paying slave wages, I'm not really in any position to complain."

"Spoken like a woman on her way to bankruptcy."

"Could be."

"What's this? A new air of fatalism?" Daisy sauntered among the shelves, picking up a bar of Yardley soap here, a deck of red-and-white playing cards there.

Leaning on her broom, Erin watched without answering. Obviously, Daisy had something in mind other than shopping. Which wasn't all that strange. Half her customers came in hoping for local gossip and left without getting any, at least not from Erin, or buying a thing.

"Isn't the library open today?" she asked.

"God, yes." Grinning, Daisy looked up from a display of hair ribbons.

She wouldn't buy one of those either. In her usual snug

jeans, which revealed practically no hips, and a blue chambray short-sleeved shirt that hid her all but nonexistent breasts, Daisy looked as glamorous as she ever cared to get. She looked the same as she had in high school—tall, slim and boyishly athletic, like the champion barrel racer she'd once been.

"It's summer reading club day," Daisy told Erin, "so I left my teenage helpers to listen to all those book reports about dinosaurs and Ninja Turtles."

"Oh, darn." Erin set the broom aside. In her preoccupation with Danny's presence at the ranch, she kept forgetting her real life. "I didn't remind Meg to drive Timmy in this afternoon. He read three books this week."

"One of them about rodeo."

Daisy had a photographic memory. She probably remembered what every kid in town checked out

After asking about Timmy's arm, Daisy studied her reflection in a shiny copper skillet bottom in the housewares department. "So what's this I hear about Danny being back in Paradise Valley?"

"Ah," Erin said. "I wondered when you'd come to the point. Is that why you really escaped from the library?"

"I didn't want corroboration except from the source."

"Then go see Danny."

"It's true? He's really home?"

"I wouldn't say home," Erin murmured. "But yes, he's back for a few days. To see Timmy."

Daisy glanced at her. "Still feeling the aftershocks from that visit of Tim's to Never-Never Land?" She tried not to laugh. "Have you bought him a horse yet?"

"No, and I'm not going to." But the floodgates opened, and Erin told Daisy about Timmy's riding lesson. When she finished she leaned back against the counter near the cash register with a sigh. "I know he's glad to see Danny. So is Meg—"

"Are you?"

Daisy and Erin didn't lie to each other. They'd been friends all their lives, since their first day of school, and Daisy was Danny's friend too.

"He still looks good," she said. "More than good. But I'm still basically a single parent with no illusions." She paused. "I know Luke Hastings called a few days ago. Timmy said so. If Danny doesn't take off soon, Luke will be on our doorstep to fetch him."

"Luke's a drifter. Danny's not." Abandoning the housewares aisle in which she had no interest, and probably never would, Daisy walked to the front of the store. "You know as well as I do, Erin, why he left home. Years before you married him."

"I wish he could have made peace with his father before he died."

"Maybe if you gave Danny some encouragement, he'd stay."

"Oh, Daisy. I doubt that—even if I wanted him to."

"His mother sure wants him there, I'd bet—"

"What about Ken?"

"Well, Ken," Daisy said. "What can you expect?"

Erin defended him, as she usually did. "Ken's been good to Timmy and me." She hesitated. "Lately, though, I've been noticing . . . "

"What?"

At Daisy's sharp tone Erin shrugged. "I don't know. Something. The way he looks at us, at me." She studied the floor and a dust ball she'd missed with the broom. Erin swept the piece of fluff aside. "Maybe I'm imagining things. But I do know he doesn't want Danny around. The second night he was here, Ken suggested he leave."

"Danny must have loved that."

"I found him at the corral afterward." Erin raised her gaze. "Daisy, he looked so . . . torn. Not because of Ken. I'm sure he knew that was coming and Danny's never been shy about doing what he feels like doing—when he wants to do it." She shook her head. "He still hurts about Trevor and I tried to let him know I understood, that I still hurt for him too."

"And then?"

Her tone dropped. "I didn't plan to, but—well, it just happened—I kissed him. Not in a sexual way—"

"Bull droppings."

"Well, it was and it wasn't."

"Quit while you're ahead." Daisy bent over to peer into Erin's downcast face. "This is me, remember? The friend who guided you through senior high and the great love affair of your youth? It was sexual between you and Danny from the time you hit puberty."

"Are all librarians so soft-spoken? So tactful?"

"Only the best ones."

Erin blinked. "Why do I want to get home tonight and find the driveway empty except for Meg's car and Ken's? Before that gray rental car begins to seem natural parked by the back steps? Why am I afraid at the same time that I'll find exactly that? Empty space."

Daisy didn't answer. There was no answer, Erin knew.

In the next instant she didn't need one. At least at that moment.

The bell jangled, the door opened again, and Jason Barker lunged inside, breathing hard, his dark hair flopping around his shoulders and his face red.

"You hurry in this heat, kid," Daisy said, "and you'll drop dead before you get laid the first time."

"Daisy!" Erin scolded.

Jason's blue eyes sparkled, full of life. "Hi, Miss Chatworth. Why aren't you at the library, listening to those dorky kids tell about books they haven't read?"

"I'm on my way." She mussed his hair as she passed. "Why weren't you at work on time for once?"

Erin hadn't said a word, and Jason blushed, turning his face a brighter scarlet. His gaze met Erin's.

"I'm sorry," he said. "I slept late."

"I'll give you a new alarm clock. See that it doesn't happen again, okay?"

Jason nodded. Picking up the broom, he started for the rear of the store. He'd probably had a date last night, and Erin called after him.

"I can't afford to hire anyone else."

When she turned back, she looked into Daisy's guileless expression. With a hand on the doorknob, Daisy obviously had more to say.

"Tell Danny to come see me. Maybe that'll keep him in town a while longer. We can talk about our high school rodeo days. Oh—and tell Tim I want to sign his cast."

With a wave and a sigh, Erin went behind the counter to dig yesterday's receipts from the wooden box in which she kept them. Despite her best intentions, she went back to her daydreaming, and thoughts of her lonely bed.

That evening Danny banged through the back door to be greeted by a bouquet of mouth-watering aromas and a note propped on the kitchen table.

Gone into town to a birthday party. Dinner's in the oven, enough for two. Ken's working late and has a Rotary Club dinner after in Dillon. Love, Mom and Timmy.

Danny checked out the oven that had kept dinner warm: A chili casserole with corn bread, a fresh apple pie.

"Erin?"

She wasn't home yet. Her car hadn't been in the drive when Danny drove in, but he wanted to dispel the silence in the house. Like Erin's earlier rejection, it reminded him uncomfortably of years ago, the late afternoon when his brother died.

His voice still echoing in the stillness, he went to the sink and washed up. He'd spent the morning with Kemosabe, putting him through his paces to freshen the horse after its three month lay-up. He'd have to return him to competition soon. The percentage of his winnings kept Kemosabe, but Danny had a sentimental attachment to him. Maybe some day he'd retire Kemosabe on this very ranch.

An easy retirement, at least for the horse.

Danny switched the oven off. He'd let Tim watch him that morning but hadn't put him on the horse again. He didn't want to spoil Kemosabe's focus on the job—or piss Erin off. He'd spent the afternoon in town, buying feed so she couldn't nag at him about not paying for the horse's upkeep, and shooting the bull with the locals. Everybody in town seemed glad to see him, except Erin and Ken.

He wouldn't have to look at Ken's sour face tonight, and Erin might not come home until later, but he'd miss Tim's bright chatter at the dinner table and his mother's eagerness to please.

Nobody had wanted to please him in a long time.

He loaded a plate, adding the mixed vegetables from his mother's garden that he found in a pot on the stovetop, turned to low. Then he heard a car coming up the drive.

Danny had two plates on the table, silverware ready, even napkins folded in place when Erin walked in, wearing a faint frown and the withered look of a woman who'd worked too hard all day.

"Wash up," he said. "Sit down. Supper's ready."

"Where's Meg? And Timmy?"

"Gone somewhere. A party," he added.

"Oh. Yes. I remember." Erin swept past him without looking in his eyes. Didn't want to be alone with him, he supposed. "One of Timmy's friends is hosting a pizza party at a kids' game parlor near Dillon." She raised her eyebrows. "I guess Meg must have remembered to get a gift."

"She didn't say."

"Where's Ken?"

Danny gestured at the note, which he'd moved to the

countertop near the coffee maker. Reading the message, Erin frowned more deeply.

"Come on," he said, "let's eat." When she hesitated, he sat down. "Or don't you want to eat with me either?"

"Don't be ridiculous." She didn't move from the counter.

"I can take my plate in and watch the news, if you'd rather—if you want."

"No, this is fine."

They ate in silence until Erin finally cleared her throat. "Actually, I'm glad Timmy went to that party. He doesn't see other children that often."

"Why not?"

Erin looked at him then down again. "You grew up here. Did you have a yard full of friends to play with?"

"My brothers," he said. "And you."

"Timmy doesn't have even that." Using her fork she toyed with a tiny pile of vegetables.

By now they should have had another kid or three. She might be reproaching him, but he doubted that. Her expression didn't change.

"Ken used to take him to day camp in Dillon, but he's been so busy lately—summer is always his most hectic season. Meg doesn't like the drive, and I don't have time with the store. In the summer I open earlier than I do in winter."

"I bet he'll be glad when school starts then."

Erin's gaze flickered to his, then away again.

"What?" Danny said.

"He doesn't—well, the local elementary school shut down two years ago when Timmy was ready for kindergarten, and the regional school's nearly an hour from here by bus." She paused, looking down at her plate. The wall clock ticked loudly in the silence, and Danny could hear himself swallow. "Ken used to get up at four in the morning just to plow the drive in winter so Timmy could get to the bus stop at the road. So we decided—"

"Who decided what?"

"I did," she said. "Ken, your mother. We tried home teaching his first year. We plan to do so again next fall."

"Home teaching?" Danny was used to seeing kids all over the place in rodeo; families touring together in the summertime. "Which one of you does that? And how well?"

"I do. We all do." Erin glanced up. "I teach reading and writing. Ken handles arithmetic, some science, and this fall he'll start geography. Meg will do history and she'd like to teach Timmy piano."

"What happens when he gets to high school and can't graduate?"

"He'll take the achievement tests, like every student, each year. The regional school's SATs are pretty good, but Timmy will probably do as well, if not better, than any student there."

He leaned closer. "Why wasn't I asked about this?"

"Oh, Danny." Erin shoved her plate aside, her dinner mostly uneaten. They couldn't even eat together, he thought, without battling.

"Because I wasn't here? Or because you didn't think I'd care? Which, Erin?"

"Since we—not you—had to deal with his education, I thought we should make that decision."

Danny slapped his palms down on the table. He shoved back his chair, carried his plate to the sink, rinsed it off, and stacked it in the dishwasher. The dishwasher looked full, so he added detergent and flipped it on, not asking Erin about her plate. Then he stalked to the back door, carrying a small pail of vegetable parings for Kemosabe. He didn't know if he could even speak.

"I'd appreciate it if you three would stop making all the decisions concerning my son without me."

"Fine," Erin said as he slammed the door, "as long as you come home to plow the drive and get him to school."

Danny stayed outside until dark. He'd rather talk to his horse than to his wife, who seemed to think he was the

Invisible Man. She expected him to abandon the work he loved, and come home to a place that didn't even want him. To a woman who wished him gone as soon as she saw his face. Or so she tried to tell herself.

When he entered the house again, most of the lights were out. The kitchen looked spotless. Walking through the empty rooms, following a faint, flickering glow, he discovered Erin in the darkened first floor television room, which had once been the ranch office and his father's sanctuary.

Another change he didn't care for. The deep walnut bookshelves that had once held the ranch ledgers now housed the television set and VCR.

"What are you watching?" he asked.

"'Sleepless in Seattle.'" Erin didn't look up, or sound interested. "Your mother probably rented it."

He'd been in Washington State lots of times. He liked it. He'd won a first, bull riding there last fall. Danny dropped down beside her on one of two small, red-print sofas with dark wooden frames—love seats, his mother called them. His look dared her to get up and leave the room now that he was there.

"You're interested in a love story?" she said.

"Not in the last eight years."

She stiffened but stayed where she was. Danny worked off his boots, dropping them on the flat-weave beige carpet, scrunched down on his tailbone in his usual viewing position, and rested his head against the sofa back. Hands behind his head, he watched Meg Ryan and Tom Hanks try to find each other, and love.

The room grew very still. Danny became more and more aware of Erin on the seat beside him, a foot away but close enough that he could sense her body heat, her reactions to the romantic movie. After a while, Danny began to smile.

"You realize something, don't you?"

"What's that?" Her gaze stayed fixed on the screen, her foot swung lightly to the background music.

"Mom's playing matchmaker here."

Erin sat up, gaping at him.

"Sure," he said. "It's obvious. The dinner in the oven—your favorite chili and my favorite apple pie—this movie we're both not watching. She planned all this. It's a shame to waste the evening arguing, don't you think?"

"How on earth did you arrive at that conclusion?"

"About fighting?"

She made a sound. "No, about Meg."

"You've lived with my mother longer than I have. You think I'm wrong?"

Erin's gaze swung back to the screen.

"Do you?" he said.

"I suppose not."

"Well, then?" He watched her until she stopped pretending to watch the movie and looked at him again. "Why don't you go fix us some popcorn? I'll stop this thing and back it up to where we can both get interested." When Erin didn't move or stop staring, he added, "Or are you going to keep blaming me for that kiss the other night by the fence? And picking fights with me to cover up your feelings?"

"Picking fights—? You started about school—" She subsided against the sofa back, her spine relaxing for the first time since the tape started. On screen Meg Ryan looked dreamy, and desirable. His mother must know she was one of his favorites too.

Erin being his first choice.

"You mean act like decent human beings?" she said.

"I'm sure Mom wouldn't mind."

"I suppose," Erin said under her breath and, without looking at him, went into the kitchen.

Danny hit the Stop button on the remote control. He was grinning. Let Luke lecture him every other day about points for the nationals. Let his own guilt keep growing that he'd stayed long enough. Slouching on the sofa with Erin, tossing popcorn into his mouth and watching Tom Hanks kiss Meg Ryan to the strains of a syrupy love ballad suddenly seemed like the best way to spend an evening. His elbow didn't even hurt. And neither did his heart.

Across the yard Ken opened the bunkhouse door then shut it behind him. He ought to put a lock on it. If he could, he'd fence in the whole ranch, including the half mile driveway, and lock that too. With a great big padlock to which only he had the key. Danny's rented car still sat like some alien intruder by his mother's back porch, and as he'd driven past the house Ken had the feeling that with any invitation from Erin, his brother would stay for good.

That would be Ken's worst nightmare.

Laying his keys on the coffee table made from a tack trunk in front of the green gingham-upholstered sofa, he emptied his pockets: assorted coins, a packet of tissues, a roll of breath mints. He took out the small notebook he always carried from his inside jacket pocket and dropped it with the rest. Then, remembering that he'd seen lights on in the house, he sorted the coins and stacked them—nickels, dimes, quarters. The twelve pennies he wrapped in a fist, taking them from the airy, cedar-beamed room into his bedroom and the brass tray on his dresser.

The clock radio beside his double platform bed informed him it was after midnight and he frowned. His mother's car was still gone, but Erin always went to bed before eleven. That left Danny.

Apparently he hadn't gotten the hint several days ago. But then, it had taken Danny years to realize he wasn't wanted at the ranch, that Hank wouldn't forgive him for Trevor's death, and Ken couldn't either. Had Danny forgotten the lesson after all this time? And not that long ago, when Timmy was born? He imagined so. At an age when he should know better, he was still riding bulls, convincing Ken that he'd gained no sense over the years.

Maybe he thought their father's death erased the past.

Shrugging off his blue seersucker jacket, Ken loosened his tie, then hung both in his closet just off the black-and-white bathroom. He'd worked late without accomplishing much. At the Rotary dinner he'd eaten little of the tough steak, and his stomach growled. He didn't feel like cooking in his small kitchen off the main room. He'd go over to the house, fix himself something substantial to eat—his mother always had leftovers—then talk to Danny.

This time he'd get his message across.

By tomorrow, Danny would be on the road again, chasing his dream of a world championship. Hell, Ken hoped he got one. If he did, Danny would never give up, never come home. He was too competitive.

Crossing the black yard, he stepped into the circle of light cast by the security globe over the back door.

Inside, the small kitchen light shone above the sink and he thought of Erin, loading the dishwasher there sometimes with the light gleaming in her hair, turning its unusual pale auburn a frosty red-gold.

He'd been thinking about her lately, too much. More than normal. He'd been on the verge of asking her to dinner or a movie without Timmy, for a change, when Danny blew in, lighting up her eyes again when she thought no one could see her.

Rifling the refrigerator, Ken pulled out a platter of vegetables and meat. After removing the fat from the roast beef, he piled a plate and slipped it in the microwave.

Then he heard a sound.

Cocking his head, he could just make out the soft murmur of voices, one male, one female from the television room. A light ripple of laughter. He'd loved that sound since he was ten years old.

Ken dropped his hand from the microwave control pad.

With his pulse thudding, he walked through the kitchen, down the hall.

And there they were, or what he could see of them from behind the sofa.

The two of them, together, watching a movie. It had been Erin's laughter he heard, and the on-screen voices.

He saw Erin's pale hair flowing across the sofa back, the darker shag of Danny's next to her, their heads not touching—not quite—but both of them looked relaxed, intimate.

Erin had rejected Danny before she became a mother. With a bit of help from Ken and their father, Danny had relinquished her. In Ken's mind Danny had no right to be here now, in this room.

No locks, Ken thought, but he had other ways. He stepped closer, clearing his throat.

Erin and Danny jumped.

"Ken," she said, sitting straight and turning around as if he'd caught them doing something they shouldn't. The kind of thing they'd done often enough as kids, thinking they fooled him.

Danny's eyes met his. "Grab yourself a beer and join us. This movie'll be over in a minute."

"Think I will." But he didn't bother with the beer or his food. "I'll just watch the late news with you."

"That'll make Mom real happy," Danny said, gazing at Erin as if they shared some secret.

7

Dumping quarts of plump blackberries into a white enamel pot the next morning, Meg smiled to herself. Nothing gave her more satisfaction than keeping her hands busy in the kitchen—nothing else except her family. Normally Erin would have helped prepare the fruit, sorting and washing berries, but she'd had business at the store. Her smile broadened at the mere thought of her daughter-in-law.

Meg had always wanted a daughter. In Erin, after three difficult pregnancies produced three healthy, boisterous boys, she'd found one.

That spring, nearly twenty-eight years ago, Hank had increased his cattle herd, some by births, some by purchase at the livestock sales. After the last threat of snow, he turned them out to graze on the lush Montana spring grass that covered the undulating hills of the valley they both loved like a waving ocean of plenty. For the extra work he decided to hire extra hands. The boys had been too young to be much help—Ken at ten, Danny eight, and Trevor three. Meg recalled seeing a dozen men or more before he settled on Garrett Brodey as his new foreman, but she'd had her misgivings.

Garrett had been a hard man, tougher than Hank, but Hank didn't object when Garrett drove into the ranch yard that first afternoon towing a rusted house trailer, with his young daughter perched beside him on the dented pickup's seat like a surprise package just for Meg. Hank too took to Erin right away, and Meg always wished Garrett would do the same.

Before the truck slid to a stop, five-year-old Erin flung open the passenger door and jumped down, practically into Meg's lap. Surprised, Meg laughed. Green eyes sparkled at her, and an unruly mane of the most amazing pale auburn hair, looking frosted over by sunlight, swung around Erin's narrow shoulders.

She hitched up baggy jeans, and Meg's heart turned inside out. She had a sudden itch to take needle and thread to the little girl's torn plaid shirt, to immerse her in a bath full of flower-scented bubbles, then to dry her long hair and braid it with ribbons.

The sight of another female, even one who stood three-and-a-half-feet tall, on Paradise Valley land seemed an unexpected blessing. Meg felt she'd discovered a treasure.

"Are you my new mom?" Erin asked.

Garrett slapped a dusty straw hat against his thigh. "Erin, mind your mouth. This is Mrs. Sinclair."

"Call me Meg." She held out a hand, first to Erin then her father. "You too, Garrett. We don't stand on ceremony here."

"It doesn't seem right," was his answer, and Meg would have sworn on a Bible that was the longest sentence she heard from him in the eighteen years he worked for Hank—or the most emotion. He'd never called her Meg either.

"He misses his wife," Hank would say. "Doesn't know what to do with a little girl on his hands. Garrett's at his best on a good horse, dropping a loop over some balky calf's head."

"He could give that child a smile now and then." At the dinner table where Garrett as foreman and his daughter took meals with the family, Meg's glance would always drift toward Erin and she'd tell Hank later, "Thank heaven the boys have taken to her. She's like their mascot." Or a baby sister.

"She's your mascot, mostly," he said, running a hand through thinning dark hair. "I'd think you'd tire of sewing dresses for her, 'specially since she has no occasion to wear them other than Sundays to church. I heard the reverend's wife last week, saying Erin Brodey will grow up with ideas beyond expectation if someone doesn't take a firm hand with her."

Meg had scoffed at that notion. Did the woman think life wasn't worth reaching for with both hands?

Now she wondered whether she had ideas herself that would never be realized.

She measured sugar into the large pot filled with blackberries, heating on the stove, and her smile faded. She and Timmy had launched their plan the night before.

Ken had spoiled things.

She had come into the house with Timmy, both of them snickering over the obvious signs of dinner consumed, the two wedges of apple pie missing from its tin, then shushed him down the hall to the den—where they discovered Ken watching a television sports recap with Danny.

She fought her disappointment without success. No romantic interlude between Danny and Erin over "Sleepless in Seattle." No heads close together, no hands entwined. She looked around. No Erin at all in fact.

"She went upstairs before the news," Danny informed her without turning around. "She brought some work home."

"Said she preferred her own company," Ken added.

Using a wooden spoon Meg stirred the berries and sugar for jam. Clearly, she and Timmy had their work cut out.

∘   ∘   ∘

Danny couldn't imagine working indoors, spending his days stuck behind a counter like Erin at the Emporium—or Daisy Chatworth at the Sweetwater Public Library. It seemed he'd been born with the wind in his hair, the sun on his face, the feel of a good horse or a bad bull between his legs. He never felt quite at home on his feet and he sure didn't like being tied down—though Luke might have disagreed. But like Luke and most rodeo riders, Danny called himself an independent man and didn't care for the notion of calling another man "boss."

Stepping into the hushed, high-ceilinged main room of the library, he removed his baseball cap. He glanced around but didn't find Daisy where he expected behind the curved mahogany counter. Instead, she was sitting squat in the middle of a group of kids in the far corner of the main floor under the sign proclaiming that the children's area. A hand-painted placard on an easel told him about a summer reading club.

Tim belonged to the club, he knew. He had chattered to Danny about it only the day before, proudly showing him a rodeo book.

Daisy looked up, her face brightening when she saw him. She gave him a wave then went back to listening to a pudgy boy about ten years old recite some story. Waiting for her to finish and feeling closed-in, Danny wandered the library, then watched a young clerk at the front desk check out a little girl's books. The library wasn't computerized, which didn't surprise him, and the clerk punched a card from each book into a clunky machine that printed the due date.

Sweetwater was dying all right. Not keeping up with the times. Considering the memories he carried, he didn't know whether that was a bad thing, except he'd loved Paradise Valley until Trevor died.

Danny was hunched over a rodeo magazine at the periodicals rack when Daisy wrapped her arms around him from behind.

"Hi there, bull rider." She gave him a squeeze. "How you doing?"

Turning, he hugged her to his chest and grinned. "I'm a little out of my element here, but Erin told me you'd be out of joint yourself if I didn't stop by." He held her off, gauging the effect of the several years since he'd seen her. "D.C., you look just the same. Broken any records lately on the local circuit?"

Remembering too late the accident she'd suffered several years ago, he felt her turn rigid under his hands.

"I'm not riding any more."

A wave of sadness passed through him. Daisy was a top rider, and her palomino mare one of the sweetest horses Danny had ever known except for Kemosabe. And one of the best professional barrel racers. Daisy had trained her. She'd trained her first horse too, competing during their high school days and winning blue ribbons on such a regular basis that even Danny, the state's top teenage bull rider three years in a row, sometimes felt jealous.

He knew she'd taken a bad spill during training a few seasons back, but he'd never imagined she might give up completely.

The children chattered nearby, demanding attention from Daisy's teenage assistant. "Let's get away from my library page and the reading club." Daisy led him to a soft-cushioned, fake leather sofa in a more quiet corner of the reading room. They sat next to each other and Danny waited for her to speak.

"I'm leaving all the glory to you. As you can see"—she waved at the card catalogue—"I've taken gainful employment and I must say it's handy having a regular paycheck."

"What about your horse?"

"Out to pasture," she said, looking down at their hands joined on the cushion between them. Her palm felt cool, a little clammy in his. "She's so fat and sassy, I can hardly get a girth around her these days." Her glance fell short of meeting his eyes. "I wouldn't want to work her that hard."

Danny didn't believe that for a minute, just as he refused to consider Kemosabe permanently out of competition.

"Actually, she's not just fat, she's newly pregnant. I looked at her one day and decided she shouldn't stay a maiden lady, like me. She's bred to another palomino—a big, good-looking stallion from Helena." Daisy smiled. "I thought she should have some fun while she can." She stared at the far wall of shelves. "I may sell her and the foal . . . I'm not sure."

"Mom mentioned your accident at the time, but, hell, I thought—"

She removed her hand from his. "I hurt my back pretty bad. It still hurts when I move wrong." Daisy's smile quavered. "Must have been the good Lord telling me to slow down, to try another way of life."

She'd lost her nerve, Danny thought. "Don't you miss competing?"

"Danny, you know. We all compete against ourselves, really," she said. "I had some good times in the ring, a few records—as you say—a wonderful horse that made me look better than I was. What more could I ask?"

"Except the nationals."

Daisy shook her head, her dishwater blond hair moving on her shoulders. "Have you seen those young girls with their fifty-thousand-dollar horses? Nugget's got a champion's heart, I'd hate to see her break it trying to keep up with them. No," she said, "we're both better off now."

Then why couldn't she meet his eyes?

Danny took her hand again, running a thumb over the smooth ridge of one knuckle. His gut felt tight, as if he'd drawn a good bull but hadn't shown up to compete. If he couldn't ride, he'd die.

"Nugget could still give 'em a good run." His gaze lifted, locking at last with hers. "So would you, D.C."

"My competition days are over." Her grin took him by surprise, like the change of subject. "What about you, Mr. Sinclair? Thinking of settling down before some bull stomps your chest in, or are you still trying for that brass ring?"

"That gold belt buckle," he said.

Fingering his baseball cap, he frowned. He'd had another call from Luke and knew he wasn't doing himself any good in Sweetwater or Paradise Valley with the season in full swing. Every day he lost possible money on the circuit. If he'd drawn rank bulls—decent bulls—for Durango, he would have gone. If he stayed much longer . . .

"How are you and Erin getting on?"

"Like two bears with sore paws."

He looked away from Daisy's probing gaze. Hell, he didn't know what he was doing here, now that Tim's arm was on the mend. His mother's easy acceptance made him feel peaceful and at the same time jumpy, never mind Erin. And Ken watched him like a hawk.

As if Danny had waved a wand over a magic hat, the library door opened, admitting a blast of hot air, and his brother walked in.

Danny did a double take. Tim followed Ken, carrying a stack of thin children's books and wearing the straw hat Danny had bought him last month. Daisy freed her hand and stood up.

"Hi, Daddy." As Tim ran up to Danny, two books started to slide from the stack. "What're you doing here?"

He helped his son fumble the books back into place. "Talking to Daisy."

"I have to give my report." Tim glanced at her. "You wanna hear it now?"

Daisy put an arm around his narrow shoulders. "Come on, little britches. Let's hear what you have to say about that rodeo story."

"Mom said you want to sign my cast too."

Danny's stomach tightened another notch, as if he'd cinched his belt too snug. Why didn't anyone at the ranch tell him Tim needed to come to the library today? Erin knew Danny was going. Why did Ken take his son everywhere, with her blessing?

Holding Tim's hand Daisy paused. Danny watched her cheeks turn color and felt as if she'd betrayed him too.

"Ken, nice to see you. We won't be long." She touched Danny's arm. "Come visit me again before you leave. Come to the house and see Nugget too next time."

Ken said nothing. His gaze tracked her across the library, Daisy's sneakers making no sound on the shiny black tile. He should be happy she'd quit. Ken had never approved of her rodeoing either. A woman had no place in the ring, he said.

"She's as bad as you are, encouraging him in that nonsense." Ken brushed past Danny, heading for the children's department. "I'll pick him out some books this time myself. Something useful to read when you go."

Moments later, jamming his baseball cap on his head, Danny left the library and stalked along Denton Street. Before he'd swung through the front door, he'd stopped to pick out two books on rodeo and one on horseback riding for kids. He had his new library card stuffed in his wallet.

Let Daisy give up but he'd be damned if he would. Luke was right. He belonged back on the circuit, away from Sweetwater and Paradise Valley most of all. Yet his steps veered to the opposite side of the street toward the emporium. He could manage any mean bull he drew. But how in hell had his personal life—his wife and their child—gotten so completely out of his control?

"I won't stand for it," Erin said, thumping the broom down against the emporium's counter. "I can't even remember how many times Jason Barker has been late. As soon as he gets here—"

"He's a good kid, Erin."

She glared at Danny who'd been prowling the aisles like a bull in a holding pen since he entered the store. She'd seen him of course, stalking along the sidewalk in her direction. Erin had peered out the front windows for the hundredth time looking for Jason, and seen Danny with that look of fierce concentration he assumed before a ride, when he practiced his moves in his mind to calm himself.

He plucked a plastic scouring pad from a bin, then instantly flung it down again. He wound the stem on a chrome-and-white kitchen timer and let the buzzer ring.

Erin refused to be distracted. She looked away from the play of muscles in Danny's arm, the shift of tendons in his strong hands. She could tell he wanted to have it out with someone, and she must seem as good a choice right now as any. But she already had a fight going, without him for once.

She'd been warring with herself since she opened the store that morning and swept it out again herself.

"Jason could be Future Farmer of the Year—" she began.

"From what you tell me, he's more interested in winning enough rodeo money to get his Professional Rodeo Cowboys Association card."

"I didn't ask you about his PRCA chances. He's either chasing rodeo or that girl he sees. I don't care. If he can't get to work on time, this time he's out of a job."

"Tough talk."

She jammed the broom's handle against the floor again for emphasis. Erin shared Jason's parents' view that he should go to college in the fall. "I mean it."

"Okay, but why get riled? There must be someone else willing to work regular hours, on schedule, for modest pay."

Erin avoided his gaze. Those direct hazel eyes saw too much, made her feel things she didn't want to feel again, like that other night when they'd watched that movie. And she certainly knew his views about the rodeo circuit. Of course he'd defend Jason. Suddenly fascinated by the arrows of sunlight striking near her feet, she spoke to the wooden floor.

"Most kids around here would rather drive into Dillon and work at McDonald's. Or deliver pizza. The pay's better."

"So is the company, I bet." Danny wound the timer again, its clamorous noise shredding her nerves.

She grabbed it from him, their hands brushing. A thrill raced through her, repulsing Erin.

"Will you stop that?"

"Hey, don't take it out on me."

"You're being deliberately irritating—which shouldn't surprise me." Setting the timer on the shelf, she whirled around.

She'd tried avoiding him, but each morning they met in the upstairs hall at the ranch, and she experienced the same despicable weakness. At night she swore she could hear Danny breathing from the sewing room as if he were beside her again in bed, his breath warm on the nape of her neck as they slept curled together like cozy kittens in a hayrick. She couldn't take much more of him at Paradise Valley.

"Just when are you planning to get back to business so Luke Hastings will stop calling the house every day?"

Danny didn't answer. He snatched up her broom, muttering something about "witches," and began sweeping the aisle at the rear of the store, his movements strong and energetic, but still under a tight rein.

"I just had a run-in with Ken," he finally said, "or he had one with me. I didn't get to respond the way I wanted to—which was to smash a fist in his face for saying much the same thing you just did—so leave me to my irritations, will you?"

The doorbell jingled and Jason Barker entered, looking shame-faced. His uncombed hair dripped water to his shoulders from an obviously hasty shower. His mesh athletic shirt hung loose over a pair of cutoff jeans, and his running shoes were unlaced. Erin crossed the last off to teen fashion these days, but the rest made her boil.

"Don't tell me you overslept." She'd given him the new alarm clock with the expectation he would use it.

Jason didn't seem to hear. He'd spotted Danny and his eyes lit up as he ran through the store to pump Danny's hand. "Oh, man. Danny Sinclair. *Wow*. I saw you ride last summer at Cheyenne—"

Danny grimaced. "And come in fourth?"

"You were great! That bull—"

Erin short-circuited his gushing. "Jason, you're fired."

Danny resumed sweeping but she could feel his interest just as she'd felt that tingle when their hands brushed.

"I simply can't run this store," she said, "without help, and your lateness in the past few weeks is no help at all. There's stock to be unpacked, shelves to be loaded." Reminded of the two phone calls she'd had within half an hour, she took a breath. "I promised Mrs. Eady, whose legs are bothering her again, that we'd deliver her order. If I have to drive ten miles south of town, the books don't get done, and a million other things."

Jason's face turned sullen. "I have a life."

"So do I. And I'd like to enjoy it before eight o'clock every night. I don't know where we went wrong but—"

"I went to Jackson Gulch last night. Me and my girl-friend." Jason's gaze challenged her and Erin saw him flick a glance at Danny. "She didn't like seeing me get dumped once, but I won second in a rodeo, bull riding."

He couldn't keep the pride from his voice but Erin only groaned. Jackson Gulch was in the northeast quadrant of the state. He'd probably driven all night. And she certainly understood his girlfriend's misgivings.

"Oh, fine." She glared at Danny.

"Don't look at me," he said, applying the broom to a corner.

Erin rounded the counter to the cash register. She punched No Sale on the old machine, a bell chimed, and the drawer rushed open, ramming her in the stomach before she thought to step back. Erin yanked out several bills.

"Here. This should cover your entry fee for the next one. Don't come back when you get thrown in the dirt."

"Erin." Danny had paused and was staring at her, hard.

"No big deal," Jason told him. He took the money from Erin then stalked stiff-legged to the door. "I don't need this job. Or a woman picking on me like my mother. Or my girl." He held the door open, letting in the hot air. "Rodeo's what I want anyway. Think I'll take off for the circuit full-time. See you there, Danny." With that, he slammed the door behind him, setting the bell clanging.

"Great," Erin muttered. "It'll take an hour for the ceiling fans to cool this place again."

She stormed around, righting things on one shelf, snatching half a dozen bottles of outdated salad dressing from another. She didn't realize Danny had stopped sweeping. Then she felt his hand on her forearm, and jumped.

"Why are you still here?" she said.

"Damned if I know." He shook his head. "Right about now I envy Jason Barker his freedom. Hell, he'll see me all right. He'll prob'ly wipe my butt in the ring someday."

"Nobody's keeping you here."

Danny's eyebrows lifted. "Is that why you raged at that kid for being late a few times?"

"A few?"

"You and I showed up late to things plenty of times when we were his age."

At Danny's meaningful look, the darkening of his eyes, another quiver ran through her. They hadn't been rodeoing.

"I should have had my head examined."

He fought a smile and lost. "Erin, thinking was the last thing on either of our minds." He came closer, his tone dropping low. "Remember the rides we took in the hills on hot summer afternoons like this? Remember the sod house where we first—?"

"Stop."

She didn't want to remember.

"Jason's got his dream. We had ours."

"Different dreams," she said, looking away from the dark intensity of his gaze. "I learned how different. And I learned the world—my life—can run without you."

He didn't miss a beat, though his tone hardened. "What do you plan to do about getting help?"

She hadn't thought that far yet and the question, as Danny's usually did, took her by surprise. He always seemed to think faster than she did.

"I don't know. Run an ad in the paper, I suppose. Stick a sign in the window. Charge up and down Denton Street begging people—" She threw a hand in the air. "How do I know?"

When she looked at him, Danny nailed her with that darkened gaze again. And another smile. It turned Erin's knees weak, but she locked them, like her resolve.

Danny said, "That's what you get for being hasty. You always tell me I'm the impulsive one. What's happened to that thoughtful way of yours? Turning everything over in your mind a thousand times before you come to a decision?"

In spite of herself she smiled a little too. "It must be the heat." She shook her head. "No, I've been stewing about this for weeks. You just stepped in my path." She paused. "Lord, I hope he doesn't get himself killed."

"Jason's young. He'll bounce." Ignoring the fact that his own brother hadn't, he showed her the broom in his hand. "I had a real yen to take Ken out myself a while ago. Maybe we're both substituting here."

"Maybe we are," Erin agreed.

Danny's smile disappeared. Then, as if surprising himself too, he asked another of his hard questions. This time he looked as puzzled as Erin felt, as troubled.

"So what are we gonna do about that?"

"I don't know," she said, "but I have the feeling you're about to tell me."

"Tell you what." That night Danny rapped at the bunkhouse door, stepping inside before Ken answered. He needed the upper hand. "I'm going to relieve you of some responsibilities here, give you some breathing room."

Lowering the TV's volume, Ken sat up. He'd been lying on the green gingham sofa with the remote control on his belly next to a bottle of Coors, and the bottle tumbled to the carpet.

"What responsibilities?"

"Tim. The summer reading club. Teaching him to ride." Danny leaned a shoulder against the screen door jamb. "Making all those decisions about his schooling. Erin," he added, as if she were an afterthought rather than a preoccupation.

"For how long?"

Erin had asked the same thing, though he hadn't dared include her among the responsibilities he'd discussed with her. Ken needed everything spelled out.

"I figure you're busy enough over in Dillon with that new housing development." He folded his arms. "Dad would sure be proud of you."

"He was," Ken said, his gaze turning dark.

Danny watched him mop spilled beer from the rug with a snowy-white handkerchief.

"I envy you that, but never mind. I've decided to stay and help Erin at the store until she can find someone." He smiled without letting it reach his eyes. "I felt guilty when she fired Jason Barker for wanting to rodeo more than he wants to load baby-food jars on a shelf all day."

Ken took a step, his eyes flashing. "What the hell's your game?"

"Game?"

Erin had fought him, but she'd had to give in. She needed help. Even more, Danny needed to give it. He figured the close proximity, working together every day, might accelerate his plans. That meant not only missing Durango but Cody and Cowboy Christmas. He could almost hear Luke yelling, but . . .

"What is it you want?" Ken said.

"Besides my wife, you mean?" Dropping his arms to his sides, Danny held his ground, letting Ken come to him across the width of the softly lit room, the drone of the television announcer the only sound.

Ken grabbed his shirt. "You think a piece of paper makes you man and wife? She may have thought so when she was twenty years old, but you were never a husband to her, not that much of a man either—"

Danny gripped his brother's wrist. "Who are you to talk? Shagging somebody else's woman behind his back!"

Ken's other fist clenched in front of Danny's nose. "Shut your mouth! Erin's a decent woman and if I had my way . . ." He trailed off, his gaze angry but his fist falling.

"If you had your way, what?"

Ken shook his head.

"Say it," Danny coaxed.

With a disgusted sound, Ken put distance between them. From the center of the neat living room, he said, "I'd marry her myself. I'd adopt Timmy and give them a real home of their own—our own—a real family life."

Folding his arms again, holding himself tight, Danny watched his brother straighten the sofa cushions, pleat the evening paper, and lay it on a stack in a rattan basket. Ken probably never left anything lying around, had never kicked a pair of dirty socks aside on his way to the bathroom at night. Had never drunk orange juice from the container.

"Christ," he said. "You know damn well why I've stayed on the road. Because you and Dad made anything else impossible after Erin left. Long before Tim was born, you poisoned her mind."

"Is that what you tell Erin over there in the house at night when you're trying to crawl in her bed again?" Ken emptied the change from his pockets onto the tack trunk coffee table and began sorting them by denomination. "I was here the same as you the day Erin came to live on this ranch—and I was here the day she came home from the circuit, broken-hearted."

Danny flinched. That still hurt, like the verbal beatings he'd taken from Ken and their father. Like the goring he'd taken in the ring before she left him.

"Why would she stay to watch you get your brains kicked in some day? And end up raising Timmy on her own anyway?"

"Not if you have anything to say about it."

Ken inclined his head, then went on counting his change. Quarters, dimes, nickels. He set the pennies aside. His tone sounded weary.

"Why don't you go back on the road? Erin was just about over you when you showed up again." His gaze met Danny's.

Danny felt his spirits lift. She must want him still. He'd thought so.

"You want one thing," Ken said, "she wants another. Where's that ever going to lead except divorce court?"

His stomach clenched. "Did she say that?"

"Not in those words." He looked at Danny for a long moment. "You and I once had an understanding."

Of course Danny remembered. Years ago, when he'd wanted Erin so badly he couldn't stand up for the wanting. He still felt the same way.

He eyed Ken. "We agreed you'd look the other way when she and I went off together somewhere, if that's what you mean. That you'd cover for me with chores . . . keep Dad from finding out where we'd gone."

"That old sod house," Ken said with disgust. "Dirt and darkness, smelling of mold and old mice. God"—he shook his head—"I wish I'd stopped you then."

"You couldn't have stopped me then." Danny held his gaze "I don't know why I ever let you stop me, you and Dad, when Tim came." But it had been Erin's doing by then too.

"You're feeling guilty a bit late, aren't you?"

"Tim needs me, Ken. He needs his father. Whether she knows it or not, Erin needs me too."

"To push a broom at the store?"

"I'm staying," he said. "Like it or don't, it doesn't matter to me." He opened the screen door to a starry summer night and the chirp of crickets in the pasture. The grass smelled fresh and sweet. "That's what I came to tell you."

He reached the narrow porch before Ken swung him around. "Let me tell you something. You make that woman—or that boy—the least bit unhappy before you finally leave, you'll answer to me." He flung Danny's arm away but Danny kept his balance on the step and fought the impulse to hit his brother.

"Does that include Mom?"

Ken followed him into the yard, in the circle glare of the security light. "You damn bet it does." He pushed a finger into Danny's belt buckle. "It means everyone on this ranch."

Danny gave him a thin smile instead of a fist in the belly, then went on his way. Ken called him back.

"One more thing," he said, his voice falling rather than rising on every word, "I don't want you sleeping at the house. From now on, the sofa bed in the bunkhouse is all yours."

Danny kept walking.

"Use it, Danny boy."

Like hell, he thought.

He meant to help Erin. But he meant to have his wife again too. As soon as possible. And he didn't need Ken's permission.

8

Danny wouldn't get under her guard, Erin decided. As long as she kept reminding herself of that, she'd be fine. And so would Timmy.

He sat beside her on the back seat of Ken's Taurus station wagon as they started for the Fourth of July fair in Sweetwater. Swinging one foot and humming to himself, he admired his shiny new black cowboy boots. Timmy wore crisp jeans, a red plaid Western style shirt with pearl snaps, also new, and for the first time since he'd come back from his stay with Danny, his hair lay neatly if wetly combed to his shower-fresh head. Erin smiled. She'd rarely seen him that clean.

"Mom, can I go on all the rides this year?"

All the rides meant half a dozen, none of them particularly dangerous—except in Erin's memory, one. There was a small merry-go-round. A few Dodge 'em cars. A children's roller coaster. And usually, as there had been years ago, a Ferris wheel. The Sweetwater Women's Grange Auxiliary Fair each year was just a warm-up for the larger county and state fairs of late summer, but Timmy looked forward to it. At his age so had Erin, before another July night. . . .

"I suppose you can," she said.

"Because I'm seven now?"

"Almost grown up, I'd say." Ken spoke from the driver's seat next to his mother. Meg held her home-sewn aprons stacked on her lap, as if something might happen to them stowed in the trunk. "I'll throw in a dollar for some cotton candy," Ken added.

"Whoopee!"

The car rounded the curve at the bottom of the driveway onto the paved access road, and she saw Danny in the field. Erin shifted her gaze but not quickly enough. He stood along the broken fence line, a pair of wire cutters in his leather-gloved hands. A post hole digger lay near a fresh roll of barbed wire.

Stringing fence could be a nasty job, even hazardous, and Erin felt a twinge of guilt.

She had to admit, Danny worked hard when it pleased him. He'd spent the holiday afternoon at the store, stocking shelves according to Erin's instruction—given before he left the ranch. She'd avoided going with him. For the past two days he'd competed at rodeos, first in nearby Ennis then in Livingston, a PRCA-sanctioned rodeo outside of Bozeman. Erin had resisted the urge to ask him how he'd done.

She still couldn't believe she'd missed the ad deadline at the local paper for the week and had to accept his help.

"Daddy!" Timmy waved a hand out the window, stirring up the warm, end-of-the-day air. He leaned forward to tap Danny's brother on the shoulder. "Uncle Ken, stop!"

Ken barely took his foot off the gas. "He's busy. Leave him to his work."

Timmy thumped him on the shoulder again. "Nobody's too busy for the fair."

Ken sighed, and the Taurus's tires crunched to a halt on

the loose gravel. Without turning around Danny lifted a gloved hand in greeting.

"C'mon, Daddy."

Danny climbed over the broken-down section of fence wire and strolled toward the car. Bending, he braced his forearms on the open rear window and grinned at Timmy.

Erin pressed her spine into the seat back, even though she sat on the far side. She and Meg had left dinner for him at the house. She didn't owe him more.

Danny ruffled Timmy's hair. "You folks headed to town?"

"To the fair," Timmy said.

"I saw a lot of activity there. You planning to watch the Jaycee fireworks at Lynch Park over in Dillon later?"

Erin threw him a look. "We can't do everything," she said, which seemed to reprimand Danny for his busy weekend commuting to rodeos and working at her store. She fixed on the wire cutters he held.

"Don't you wanna go, Daddy?"

Erin looked away. Danny's ever-present baseball cap, its bill low over his handsome features, his clear hazel eyes, so full of life, his smile . . . all seemed to chide her for not wanting him around any longer than necessary. To her surprise he had moved into the bunkhouse with Ken the day after he agreed to help her at the emporium.

Ken revved the car's engine. "Mom needs to get to the fairgrounds," he said, inching the Taurus forward.

Danny walked with it. With a sharp rap of his knuckles on the car's roof, he said, "Hold on." He skirted the wagon's rear end, opened Erin's door, threw the wire cutters on the floor, and slid in beside her, forcing her toward the middle. He pulled off his leather gloves.

"Hooray!" Timmy drummed his booted heels against the seat. "You and me can go on the Tilt-A-Whirl together."

Erin was already tilting, her senses spinning with the scent Danny brought into the car. Even with all the windows open she could smell him: a lingering, fresh soap smell overlaid with fresher sweat, all male, and not offensive as she might have wished. He smelled like . . . Danny, close to her in the night.

He pressed closer, or so it seemed to Erin, with every mile, his jeans brushing her white-shorted thigh, his white T-shirt sleeve rubbing against her bare upper arm and along the side of her breast, the thin green cotton top she wore, until her pulse centered low in her stomach, and warmth flowed along her inner thighs.

When they reached the fairgrounds on the other side of Sweetwater, Erin kept away from him. As she'd been keeping away from him for eight years.

Timmy might need him, she told herself, but she didn't. The sooner she hired someone at the store, the sooner Danny would leave. And this time, she'd summon the nerve to divorce him.

As if keeping that decision in mind, Erin stayed close to Ken. Holding Timmy's hands, they toured the tents filled with homemade crafts and baked goods, watched a craftsman burn personalized letters into wooden signs for people, felt the warm day linger into sunset. As soon as they had reached the fairgrounds, Meg had hurried off with her aprons to her assigned booth in one of the tents, and they wouldn't have time to make the Fourth of July fireworks in Dillon. She wished Danny hadn't mentioned them. Those fireworks had been a family tradition.

"Here, get started." Coming back from a refreshment stand on the midway, he plopped a bright red lollipop in Tim's hand. He dropped a green one into Erin's palm. "Matches your eyes." He tore the wrapper from a lollipop the same color as hers.

Erin turned away but opened her lollipop and defiantly stuck it in her mouth. Danny gave Ken a yellow one, which he put in his shirt pocket. Then Ken strode off to buy ride tickets, refusing Danny's money.

Danny bought tickets himself. Working on his sucker, he trailed behind Ken, Timmy, and Erin, his cap pulled low over his eyes, his free hand shoved in a back pocket. As the sun slid below the horizon, Erin let Ken slip an arm around her shoulders, protecting her, his other hand resting on Timmy's head.

She barely noticed the rides. At each one she held herself increasingly rigid, watching Ken with her child, feeling Danny hovering nearer each time. At the Dodge-'em car ride, she stood with her back to him near the metal railing around the enclosure, ready to cheer on her son and his uncle. Pretending she was alone.

As she had feared Danny edged close beside her, and after one quick glance at the tight set of his mouth, she looked down. The rail had been painted red but was scaling now, with rusted bare metal showing through.

"Is this what you want, Erin?"

She focused on Timmy with Ken in one of the cars, whipping around, banging into other drivers, and laughing. "For Timmy to have a good time? Of course."

He moved closer, the heat of his body nearly touching hers, his voice low. "Ken didn't want me to come along. He's muscled Tim into every ride without me. Look at him," he said, poking a thumb toward Ken and Timmy, at the sparks jumping on the enclosure's ceiling and the cars gliding, crashing. "The other day at the library, now tonight . . . He acts as if he's Tim's father, not me."

"He's been more a father to him than you have."

Danny muttered a rude word and moved away. Erin didn't look at him, but she could feel him still standing there by the rail, could feel his anger. It was his own fault, she thought. But her throat tightened as if she'd swallowed the lollipop whole.

Erin let another Dodge-'em ride go by, then the merry-go-round before she eased toward Danny, her voice low. The calliope music nearly drowned out the words. "You can't just come back again, and think to wipe out all the years without you in his life."

"Or yours?" he said. "What about 'till death do us part? For better or worse? In sickness and in health?'"

"I am not going to watch you kill yourself!" Erin turned away. "Can't you get that through your head?"

"I guess not."

They would never agree, even on divorce.

"Come on, Mom." Exiting the merry-go-round, Timmy tugged at her hand. His pleading tone, his impish face made her smile in spite of herself.

"You and me and Daddy." He pointed.

Erin hung back. "No, Timmy. Not the Ferris wheel."

"Why not? Does it make you dizzy?"

"Yes," she said, glancing at the huge wheel silhouetted against the darkened sky and the reflected glow of midway lights that had just come on.

Danny's tone goaded her. "She's afraid of getting stuck on top."

"We'll hold on to you." Timmy tugged again. His smile challenging, Danny caught her other hand, but when Ken would have stepped between them, Timmy put up a hand like a traffic cop.

"Not you, Uncle Ken. There isn't room."

"Timmy," Erin began.

"He can ride in the next seat."

He peered up at Danny, who held their blue tickets. She hadn't been on a Ferris wheel in years, and Erin hesitated, staring at them. Fifty cents. Good for one ride. They'd been cheaper then.

"I'll wait on the ground," Ken said, then walked away.

Before she knew it, Erin, still looking back at his stiff-shouldered frame, was seated in the red and yellow Ferris wheel compartment, the safety bar across her lap, the car swinging gently as it rose another notch to let the next people on.

"I didn't want to do this," she said, with Timmy between her and Danny.

Come on, Erin. I won't let you fall. Come on before Ken finds us and says you can't go.

She'd been fifteen that night, so young that first summer Danny competed professionally, so innocent when the car rose into the starry sky, high above the midway, far away from Ken and the simple friendships she'd always shared with him and Danny.

She didn't sense the change right away.

She leaned back against the seat, tipping her head and letting her hair, longer then, flow backward. She stared up into the nighttime splendor, picking out constellations and hearing laughter float up from below, the shrieks of girls on other rides.

Then the car swayed to a stop at the apex of the wheel, and she sat trapped. Suspended.

Danny, get me down. I don't like it up so high.

You're okay with me.

But like all young men with their girls, Danny had a mischievous streak. He teased her, lulled her, while the car stayed on top, then gently started it swinging, back and forth in the cool night until Erin felt giddy and flung both arms around his neck. Their bodies pressed together, hers still girlish, her breasts small and soft, his body leaner, harder. Then she felt his hand at the nape of her neck, his fingers stroking her skin at the hairline.

She'd looked at him, into the face of desire for the first time. A man's desire. He had looked as consumed, as frightened by it then as she.

Oh God, Erin.

"Mom, look!" Timmy's voice drew her back to the present. The car had stopped in midair. "Look! We're almost to the moon!"

It hung like a golden Christmas ball in the sky, as it had that other night. Erin's gaze met Danny's and she knew.

He'd been remembering the same Ferris wheel ride, the same night. Those same feelings.

I think I'm gonna teach you how to kiss.

She would never forget his words. Moving even closer, he'd wrapped his arms around her and lowered his head.

Timmy separated them now. His boot heels bumping against the seat, his head flung back, his eyes closed to savor the light swaying motion. Erin realized Danny had set the car moving, and he smiled over Timmy's head.

"I haven't done this in years," she admitted, captured by her own memories, by the smile on his lips, and the seriousness of his eyes.

"Done what?"

Erin lifted one shoulder. "Acted like a child."

"Had fun, you mean?"

He had a point. She didn't take much time these days to play. As if to smooth over their earlier harshness, she said, "How did you do this weekend?"

Then she realized the words might sound like an accusation.

"At Ennis? I took second." Danny leaned across Timmy. "Got a fourth in Livingston. Brought home some money— believe it or not, I do that on a fairly regular basis."

But it wasn't the lack of a paycheck she hated; Erin was self-employed herself and was used to not relying on a steady income. It was the bulls. The danger.

"I didn't mean . . ."

"Shhh."

Angling his head toward Erin behind their son's shoulders, Danny edged closer, and she stared at him, at the faint smile on his lips, remembering.

Ah, Erin. That night he had dragged his mouth across hers, lightly at first, then again. His lips felt warm and pliant, soft, molding hers as he dipped his head a third time, whispering. *You taste good, you feel . . .*

He'd kissed her before. A quick, stolen kiss or two in the

barn, behind the house. With lips closed at ten or twelve, that had seemed harmless, exciting only because of the danger of being caught in a first experiment. They'd even thought it funny.

But that time . . .

At eighteen Danny had probably kissed lots of girls. He certainly knew how.

Open your mouth . . .

And she'd learned ecstasy. She'd learned that trouble was named Danny Sinclair and that life would never be the same for her again.

"Erin," he whispered now.

His mouth was a few inches from hers, and still lazily smiling. His eyes looked hot but with a touch of humor in them. Then she saw why and came to her senses.

Drawing back, Danny pointed over Timmy's head.

He had fallen asleep, tipped back and basking in the starlight. The midway sounds drifted up. Laughter, talking, the far-off calliope trill. The smells of popcorn and hot dogs, of rancid cooking oil and the day's lingering heat. Someone set off a firecracker and Timmy jerked awake.

The Ferris wheel lurched into motion, sending them over the top of the world into a stomach-dropping plunge toward earth, and reality. The entire interlude had lasted no more than a few minutes.

A moment ago Danny might have kissed her, tasting of lollipops and cotton candy. He had kissed her then, but she didn't need the memory. She didn't need Danny. Damn if she did. Damn.

Danny had lost track of time. He knew he should meet Luke and, having missed Durango then Cody for nearby Ennis and Livingston, head for Laramie, but time got away from him somehow—in that sky top view of stars, Sweetwater and Erin's eyes from the Ferris wheel—and all at once it was Wednesday. In mid-morning he glanced up to see his pickup camper bumping along the ranch driveway. He leaned on a post until the truck stopped in a cloud of dust beside Danny and the latest patch of broken fence.

With his usual chaw bulging out his cheek, Luke Hastings leaned out the driver's window into the hot day. "What the hell you doin', trying to put your eye out with that fence stretcher?"

Danny noted Luke wasn't smiling. "Sorry. I got delayed."

He'd been daydreaming just before Luke pulled up, looking out over the pasture, toward the hills. Thinking what it would be like when he finally came home for good and everyone welcomed him. He'd fix all the fences and nail the barns back together. Ever since he'd driven between the Paradise Valley gateposts himself, he'd been dreaming up ways to make rightful use of the ranch again some day. He'd finally settled on a plan. It wasn't perfect, but he thought it might work.

Luke scowled at him. "You missed a real dogfight on Sunday. Couple of young boys from Texas went way over the top on points. Good money too."

The bottom of Danny's stomach dropped.

"How much?"

Luke told him and Danny whispered, "Shit."

"Can't win if you don't show up to ride."

"You knew I wasn't going to be there."

"Planning to miss Laramie too, are you? I thought you should tell me to my face."

"No," Danny said, winching the last strand of barbed wire tight. Even through the thick leather gloves his hands felt as raw as a calf's hide looked after branding. "But now that you got all twitchy as a mama cow and came to pick me up, I'll save some time."

Luke had driven from Wyoming and would turn around to drive back. He wouldn't save time or distance at all. He tossed his dusty black hat onto the passenger seat, shut off the truck's engine, and climbed down.

"Damn you, Sinclair." Then he bear hugged Danny, dirty gloves, sweat and all. Pulling back, he grinned. "How's that boy doing with his broken arm?"

"Doing fine." Gathering his tools, he gave the new fence section a cursory look and, satisfied it would hold, got into the truck. "Come on, let's see what kind of leftovers Mom's hiding—maybe a piece of pie and some of yesterday's ham."

"You are goin' to Laramie?"

"Hell, yes."

They rolled up to the house in silence, the only sounds the faint drum of thunder in the distance, the pickup's engine—which would need a tune-up, Danny noted, before the trip to Wyoming—and from the pasture, Kemosabe's whinnied greeting.

"I'll be damned." Luke put his hat back on. "That guy still getting fat on grass? Saving his hocks for some other season?"

Danny grinned in the horse's direction. "'Sabe's on the mend. I'll start thinking about sending him back to work pretty soon."

The two men left the truck in the shade of the maple tree near the back porch. Talking, laughing, punching each other on the arm or shoulder in turn, they ambled up the steps into the ranch's blue-and-white kitchen. Luke stopped dead in the doorway.

"What's that smell?"

"Not leftovers," Danny assured him.

At the stove, his mother bent over the oven in her jeans and a checked blouse, inadvertently showing off her youthful, trim hips. Barefoot, she pulled a pie tin out, hefting it onto the marble block on the counter to cool.

"Mom, get your head out of that stove. We have company. Come meet my partner, Luke Hastings."

Meg straightened and turned, her cheeks bright pink.

Luke whipped the black Stetson off his head. The back of his neck looked suddenly sunburned, and he flicked his darkish blond hair from his eyes.

"'Morning, ma'am. I've heard so much about your baking, I had to come see for myself."

"Well, a pie's not just for looking at." She waved at the kitchen table, still flour-covered. "Welcome, Luke. Sit yourself down—you too, Danny—and I'll cut you a slice."

"Or three," Danny said, clearing the table.

Because her latest blueberry pie was still too hot, Meg cut them each a generous piece of last night's strawberry-rhubarb, not Danny's favorite but apparently Luke had no preference. He dug into his pie with all the enthusiasm of a man who hasn't seen home cooking in years.

In ten days, Danny had forgotten his own lack. He could feel his jeans getting tight around the waist, one reason he'd been mending fence.

Meg didn't join them. Busily scrubbing the stainless bowl she used to mix pie dough, cleaning off measuring spoons and the crescent-shaped pastry blender with which she cut shortening into flour, she dropped first one implement then the other. Softly cursing, "Oh, sugar," she washed everything twice.

"Mom, sit down."

She turned around, nailing Luke with the no-nonsense look she'd given Danny as a boy. She'd obviously singled him out as the troublemaker.

"I suppose this means you two will be leaving."

At the bruised look in her eyes, Danny said, "We've got a day or two yet."

Luke stared at him, his fork poised, berries dripping. "You blow this one, you might as well hang up your riggin' till next year. We—"

"I'll make some calls. Find out what stock I've drawn. We can be in Laramie in ten hours," Danny said. "Stay until

Friday. I can use a hand with that fence and Erin still needs me at the store—this afternoon. You could help me. We tacked up some ad posters, and she's had a few people for interviews already." Luke gaped at him, and Danny dragged the pie tin across the table. He dumped another piece on Luke's plate, like a warning to shut up. "Till Friday," he repeated. "What's your hurry?"

So he'd miss another round. He'd still be there for the weekend.

"I'll have to call in for a replacement then. But I'm just a bullfighter," Luke murmured into his pie. "What do I know?"

A week later, unconvinced by Danny's latest argument but determined not to let him under her skin, Erin folded her arms and leaned against the emporium's front counter. What did he know about the mercantile business? For six years she'd been making it on her own, and in Sweetwater a small profit could be called a good one—if she made a profit this month.

She wouldn't admit that aloud. Whether she did or not, she doubted Danny could turn her business around.

"It's not Sweetwater," he said, stacking canned green beans on a shelf. "The town's had its day, maybe. But there'll always be enough people here who need groceries. The beef industry's coming back. Too late for Ken and me to take advantage—though he seems happy doing what he's doing and so am I." He paused, letting that sink in. "It's not the town, Erin."

"Then what is it?"

In her opinion he knew how to rodeo, and how to flirt. Period. Why hadn't Luke dragged him off somewhere? Erin made a mental note to hire the older woman she'd interviewed the day before. Or did she want to risk another teenager?

"For one thing," Danny said, gazing around him, "those curtains."

"My curtains," she repeated, frowning.

He'd been eyeing them, his lips quirked in a smile, ever since she'd fired Jason Barker and he'd come to work for her. Temporarily. She supposed he rarely saw refinements, like curtains.

"Those little flowered things." Danny pointed at the blue-and-green pattern trimmed in lace at the front windows. She'd splurged on the material and made them herself, with Meg's help. At the look on Erin's face, he apparently decided not to mention the hanging plants. His gaze lit on them in the window, then snapped back to the two large cans he was still holding. He set them on the shelf.

"What's wrong with Laura Ashley?"

"Not a damn thing," he said, neatly rearranging the beans so the cans lined up at the front of the paper-covered shelf. Erin tried not to notice that vulnerable-looking nape of his neck.

"Laura Ashley," he went on. "Prettiest damn fabric I ever saw. But the men around here—"

"The ranchers," Erin supplied.

Turning, Danny looked through the front door glass. A pickup rumbled past, two overalled youngsters hanging off the tailgate. "A man walks in here, he feels like he stumbled into a beauty parlor or something. He half expects someone to walk out of the shadows and start giving him a manicure."

"Danny, really." She should never have agreed to let him help out at the store. She should have known, after that night at the fair, she wouldn't be able to stop looking at him.

"I'm serious."

"You're saying that's why I'm losing business?" She waved a hand. "Just because I painted this place eggshell white to look brighter, and hung a few curtains?"

"Nice ones—for a kitchen."

"And some *plants*?"

"That's how it seems to me."

"Well, you're wrong."

He eyed her without flinching. He looked her up and down. "I am a man, you know. Or had you forgotten?"

Erin's frown slipped; she almost smiled, except she had the distinct feeling she'd lose ground again. "I haven't forgotten," she said, thinking about those fragile moments on the Ferris wheel. "I noticed."

"Did you now?"

"How could I help it, every morning in the upstairs hall?" He had an uncanny sense of timing, as if he knew just when she'd emerge from her room or when he should come out of the bathroom. "I shouldn't," she admitted, "but I have."

"Why don't you tell me," he said.

Erin cleared her throat. Had she completely lost her senses? She flashed him a cheeky smile.

"I notice the scars. The one on your stomach, the one on your knee, the one on your leg where the doctors put in that pin . . . "

Danny grinned. "What else did you notice?"

He *was* teasing her. And she was teasing him. But she wouldn't let things go any farther.

"Never mind. I'm not one of those buckle bunnies." She watched Danny's gaze darken, and backed off a little. Her muscles, her bones felt fluid. "But I am a woman. You know perfectly well, you're a magnificent . . . male specimen."

He took a step away from the shelves and Erin did too, away from the counter. His tone dropped, becoming husky.

"Why do I suddenly feel I'm at the livestock auction in Dillon?" He walked to the door, flipped the Closed sign around, then came back to her. He edged her toward the stairs. "Why don't we discuss it while we unload the rest of that stock down in your storeroom?"

She knew her mistake as soon as she touched the basement door. She remembered the name for trouble the instant she went down the first step, with Danny behind her, closing the door after them, switching off the light she turned on, into the dampness of the old cellar. It smelled faintly of mold and mildew, of potatoes and onions, and in Erin's memory of sexual experiment.

Long ago she and Danny had ridden to the old sod house up in the hills. The original Sinclair homesteader dwelling, it had been dark there too, familiar but at the same time forbidden. It smelled the same here and was just as dark.

He crowded her down the stairs. At the bottom his voice turned her knees to water.

"How much would you bid for me, Erin?"

Her voice shook. "Turn on the light."

"We don't need any light."

She turned, finding him right there, and knew he spoke the truth. In the windowless dark, she could sense him, every nerve and muscle; she could smell him, clean skin and Danny.

Erin spun, blindly heading away from the stairs.

"These boxes in the corner . . . you'll need the razor knife. Cereal," she said. "Cheerios on the top shelf with the other basics in that section. Upstairs." She kicked a carton. "Bran flakes and granola in the middle."

She dropped her head low, another mistake. That quickly, Danny put his arms around her and nuzzled her neck, bending his body to hers, pressing near.

"Stop fighting. You came down here with me. You kissed me by the fence that night. At the fairgrounds you wanted to again."

"Don't tell me what I want." She struggled but he only held her closer and Erin stiffened. "No, don't tell me what *you* want and hold me responsible."

"I'm not. I want to kiss you. I need you to kiss me back, like you did that first time on the Ferris wheel. Like you did in the sod house when we . . . "

"What are you trying to prove?"

Gently, wordlessly, he turned her, framing her face in his hands, in the dark and damp. Erin's nostrils quivered at the scents around them, at the scent of Danny.

She wet her lips. "All right, you've proved I'm still attracted to you, but . . . "

He didn't acknowledge her protest. He didn't release her. Danny drew her to him until their bodies—hers taut and unyielding, his loose and fluid—touched from thigh to shoulder, and she was tucked once more into the shelter of his embrace. He held her there, his cheek against her hair. His voice stayed soft.

"Erin, I've been riding bulls for a living since I was eighteen years old and I'm still walking around." He paused. "Why doesn't it ever occur to you that I'm good?" His tone coaxed, seduced. "I've always made money, I've always paid my bills." He sifted her hair through his fingers. "I'm not a rich man but I could support you and Tim. You wouldn't need the store."

"I love the store."

"I love bull riding. I finished sixth in the world last year, thirty-five years old then. Doesn't that tell you something?"

Erin moved her head against his shoulder, savoring in spite of herself the feel of her hair sliding through his hands, against his shirt, the warmth beneath it.

"I never said you weren't good. Does it occur to you that I'm capable at what I do too?"

She felt his smile. "You'll go out of business, clinging to those fancy curtains."

"And you'll run out of luck some day." Putting space between them, she felt close to tears. "It won't matter then how good you are."

"Stubborn woman." He pulled her back into his arms.

"Stubborn man."

But he didn't argue any more. He lowered his head, angling it just so, as she felt certain he'd been about to do the other night in midair, and when his mouth sought hers in the darkness, she felt weightless, lost in sensation.

"That's my girl," he whispered, backing Erin to the wall. She felt its coolness through the thin cotton of her shirt, felt the hard stone meet her hips, as Danny did, sliding his hands from her shoulders to the curve of her waist to settle on her hipbones. "You know you've wanted to since I walked in the back door at the ranch. I sure have." Lightly, he kissed her, shutting off further protest, and pressed himself against her, sounding shaken. "Close your eyes, Erin. Enjoy it. Enjoy us . . . together."

She couldn't trust that enjoyment, the strong pull and tug between them that never seemed to weaken. It couldn't change anything. She pushed at his shoulders, breaking the kiss when he cupped her breast in one hot palm.

"Danny, *don't!*"

She shoved him away. He fought for balance, and, like the athlete he was, found it without touching her. He stood, his chest heaving, his head down. Erin could barely make out his features in the all but nonexistent light, but she saw the glitter of his eyes, the wounded look. She held out a hand to ward him off, and Danny's gaze settled on her wedding band.

Then turning aside, he shouldered the first carton and with heavy footsteps carried it upstairs.

Erin watched him go. Once she hired help, she wouldn't have Danny minding her business, turning her inside out— or Luke Hastings shooting her looks that could kill. He and Danny, having missed Laramie after all, could get on their way before, as Luke threatened, the season went completely to hell and he lost his bullfighting contract.

Eight years ago she'd left Danny because she had to. As a result, because she still wanted no one else, she dreaded spending the rest of her life alone. When Timmy grew up, like Meg she'd have no one. Erin raised a shaking hand to her lips. Even so, she couldn't regret her painful decision then.

Now, she dreaded something worse than Danny never coming back—which she'd brought upon herself—or her own reaction to him in this darkened cellar.

Ironically, what she dreaded most had already happened. Danny had come home.

"You're my wife, Erin. Dammit, you're still my wife."

9

Late that night Erin sat in the darkened kitchen, staring at her hands folded on the table top, remembering the raw expression in Danny's eyes.

That look triggered another memory she'd been trying to avoid since he'd walked back into her life and set it spinning like a Ferris wheel gone mad.

He hadn't said a word to her since those moments in the store cellar. After closing for the day, she'd driven home as she usually did, but with Danny trailing behind tonight in his camper. Sometime that morning he and Luke had returned Danny's rented car to the franchise in Dillon before Danny went to work at the emporium.

She didn't know how Luke had spent his afternoon. He didn't appear to like her much, which was nothing new. As far as he was concerned, Erin felt sure, she'd always been a road-block—a closed chute gate that wouldn't open when it should.

It had been hard in the early days of her marriage to feel like an obstacle, to feel shut out herself. Well, Luke had won. He and Danny made a pair all right. And tomorrow or the next day, they'd take off again. Why resent that? She led her life and Danny, with Luke, led his.

She hadn't meant to hurt him, though, before he left.

Erin shifted the salt and pepper shakers around on the table in the dark. They had all seemed divided during dinner: Danny, Luke, and Timmy on one side of the table reliving their month on tour in June, laughing and cueing each others' jokes. Ken, Meg, and Erin on the other side saying "Pass the broccoli" or "How was your day?"

Maybe Meg didn't trust Luke's influence either. Ken sure didn't, she knew; he'd told her Luke was another overgrown kid, like Danny.

Pushing the shakers away, she propped her feet on the opposite chair under the table, remembering another mostly silent meal. With Meg out playing bridge tonight, Danny and Luke with Timmy at the movies—a rodeo film, of course—and Ken in Dillon because of some problem at the building site, the house felt empty, the way she'd felt inside so many years ago . . .

At thirteen Danny had already been tall and strong, full of himself that day, and still high on his amateur ride the weekend before. He'd boasted of his victory, which Erin wanted to cheer, but his father put him in his place.

"You ought to spend more time at home, helping Ken with the chores. He and I get stuck while you're off somewhere grabbin' the gusto."

"I do my share." Danny slouched in his chair, avoiding his older brother's smug glance and the grim set of her own father's mouth. Ten-year-old Erin tried to tell him with raised eyebrows that he should sit up before Hank found something else to complain about.

"And another thing"—his father scooped more mashed potatoes from the bowl onto his plate—"You're burning up your mother's time and a lot of gasoline. If you mean to keep rodeoing all over this state, you better find a way to pay for it."

"I'm glad to drive him," Meg murmured.

Hank quelled her with a look. "Glad or not, it isn't right. Next Saturday and Sunday I want to see some work around here from you, Danny. Is that understood?"

"I've been workin'! I did all my chores this week and I trained Trev's horse for him, didn't I?" Danny nudged his youngest brother, who had just turned eight and was tickled to have a horse all his own rather than an aging hand-me-down. "I trained him as good as you could," Danny told Hank.

Hank's fork clattered on to his plate. "That horse isn't finished by a long shot." His gaze swung to Trevor's slight frame, his dark hair and brown eyes. "Don't let me hear you've been on him."

Erin had lost her appetite. Glancing at her own father, who kept shoveling food into his mouth, she pushed her plate away, her meat loaf half eaten. She tried not to look toward Danny or Trevor. But the younger boy caught her eye, a grin lurking on his mobile mouth. Trevor had a rebellious streak, she knew. And she had a bad feeling in the pit of her stomach.

After dinner Erin stuck close, helping Trevor feed Meg's chickens while Danny silently fed hay to the horses and filled their water buckets. She could hear him in the barn, murmuring favorite phrases to each horse. Hank's reprimand didn't seem to bother him—she supposed he had a thick skin after living with his father for thirteen years—so Erin felt the sting for him.

Danny had taken first place in that rodeo last weekend. Erin admired his blue ribbon as she admired him. Hank was a tough man to know, Meg always said, a worried man because Montana's beef market was struggling to survive, but she thought he loved his three boys as best he could. Erin wasn't that sure.

She tossed corn to the squawking chickens pecking the ground near her ankles. When she looked up, Trevor was gone.

Calling him, Erin heard him answer from the corral nearest the barn. By the time she reached him he was flinging a leg over his new horse's back, pulling himself up by its mane.

He laid a finger across his lips.

"Don't tell," he said. "I'm gonna show Dad I can ride as good as Danny. Better than Ken." He patted the horse's neck, and the bay gelding turned an intelligent, kind brown eye on Erin.

What could happen? She'd watched Danny in the ring, working the horse through its gaits. She was there the first time he saddled it, the first time a human being—Danny—had settled on its back.

Trevor kicked the bay into a snappy trot, and in the hot, early evening Erin climbed onto the fence rail to watch. Maybe she'd get a turn too. But shouldn't he have put a bridle on at least? The horse didn't even wear a halter. She glanced toward the open barn door, wondering if she should call Danny.

In that instant the horse whinnied sharply. The harsh sound snagged Erin's attention. She looked back at the corral and felt the blood drain from her face.

The horse seemed to shriek again, as if in pain. It bolted suddenly, and clinging, white-faced, to the horse's neck, Trevor screamed.

"Danny!" Erin called.

From inside the barn she heard the hose drop into a bucket, then running, booted footsteps.

Erin leaped down from the fence. She waved her arms, hoping to attract the horse's attention but it thundered past, narrowly missing her.

"Danny!"

The horse veered away toward the center of the ring. Its hide shivering, it slowed for a moment and Erin prayed it would stop.

"Get down! Get off him!" Danny yelled, vaulting over the fence. He'd come out the other door, not to spook the horse even more. Erin didn't see what happened next. He pushed her out of the way, blocking her vision, but she knew Trevor couldn't safely dismount, and the halterless horse couldn't be caught.

"Buck him out!" she heard Danny shout but lost the rest of what he said. Then she heard hooves striking the ground, a sharp cry, the sickening thud of a body landing hard in the corral dirt.

"Jesus!" Danny cried. "Trev!"

Inside the corral all was silent. Danny moved and she saw Trevor's new horse standing over his fallen form, switching its tail and quivering.

"Take him to the barn, Erin." Danny didn't look around. He knelt over Trevor. Afraid, she didn't respond and he said, "Leave him in the crossties. Then bring some water. Trev's out cold."

Erin's bad feeling grew. She'd seen people fall from horses plenty of times. She'd fallen herself. But never had she seen someone lie that still and boneless. And Trevor's head lay at the strangest angle. She wanted to think he was joking, but he didn't even twitch.

The horse snuffled at her outstretched hand, like a well-trained dog. Erin fetched a halter, left him in the barn, then pelted back with a bucket of tepid tap water.

"Has he come to?" she said.

Danny shook his head. "He hears me, though. He has to. He'll come around any minute." But the water didn't produce the eye opening or coughing Erin expected. She knelt beside Danny, looking first into Trevor's grey-white face, at his bluish lips, then into Danny's pale features. "We better take him to the house," he finally said.

"Is he . . . breathing?"

Danny's gaze snapped to hers. "Of course he's breathing, dummy. Haven't you ever got knocked cold?"

"Sure I have." But not like that. Couldn't Danny see that Trevor hadn't moved at all?

Danny lifted his brother, which Erin had always heard was the wrong thing to do. But the fierce look on Danny's face kept her quiet all the way to the house. He'd never called her a name before.

Hank and Ken weren't home. They'd driven into town to a ranchers' meeting about some coyotes that had been killing calves no one could afford to lose. The local men wanted to organize a hunting party.

Meg would know what to do.

"Mom!"

Erin dogged Danny's heels through the back door past the washing machine and dryer on the enclosed porch, the big sink where the men washed up for dinner, and on into the kitchen.

"Mom! Come here quick!"

Meg hurried down the stairs, probably from her sewing. She wore a red pincushion with an elastic band around her wrist. "Do you have to slam doors like that and holler so, Daniel?"

Then she saw Trevor.

"He . . . took the bay without asking," Danny explained, his brother's limp body seeming to spill over his outstretched arms like water from a bowl. "The horse dumped him. Spooked and bucked."

Meg's face grew even whiter than Danny's. His eyes looked desperate, haunted.

"Bring him into the living room," she said, "and lay him on the sofa. He'll have a goose egg tomorrow for sure." She turned with empty eyes. "Erin, please call the doctor. His number's on the list by the kitchen phone, dear."

Erin kept staring at Danny, who hadn't moved. Their gazes locked and with Trevor still in his arms, which were trembling, she saw that he knew the truth too. But oh, his eyes . . . She watched him for a second longer then ran for the kitchen phone.

"He'll be fine in a minute," she heard Meg say.

At the kitchen table now, Erin dropped her face into her hands, as if to hide from the sorrowful memory she couldn't avoid.

She'd been Danny's shadow, his friend from the day she arrived at Paradise Valley. But on that terrible, fateful evening she had known for the first time how much she loved him.

From then on she'd been his champion, through the years of Hank's blame and Ken's rejection. She'd held him when he couldn't bear to see Meg's unchanged love in her eyes any longer. She'd vowed never to hurt him herself.

Today, she had. And now, the same terrifying feeling ran through her in the kitchen, alone again. Despite her determination not to, she cared for him all over again—as if she'd never stopped.

The next night after supper Meg abandoned her watching post inside the back screen door and pushed it open. From the corral she heard Timmy's happy shouts and Luke's answering, deeper voice as he guided her grandson on Kemosabe in a circle around Luke as pivot with the lunge line in his hand. Meg crossed the yard.

She had her blessings, even now.

Erin's friendship, Ken's presence and quiet support, and for a time, Danny again. But Timmy, she thought, through Danny and Erin was God's special gift.

Meg never walked toward the corral without feeling a twinge of past grief. For years, until Timmy was born, she hadn't been able to look in that direction. Now, she could even smile at the sight of a seven-year-old boy on the big black-and-white paint gelding. And give thanks for the healing passage of time.

She'd lost Trevor when he was only a year older than Timmy. How young he'd been, and how small Timmy looked now.

Meg folded her arms, resting her chin on them along the top fence rail.

"Hi, Gram!"

"Hold on," she called, keeping the smile on her face. He looked so proud. Maybe she and Erin had been wrong to keep him on the ground all this time. Perhaps they needed to rein in their tendency to protect him.

Luke Hastings led the horse in a wide arc around him, flicking the long whip to maintain Kemosabe's pace and keep his mind on business. Luke had control and Kemosabe was a gentle horse. Still, Meg's throat tightened.

A lot of things had died in that ring one early evening. Not only her youngest son.

She'd hoped that with Danny home again, he'd stay, that he and Erin might patch up their marriage, become a unified family for Timmy's sake—and for their own. Luke threatened that uneasy peace, and she wanted to dislike him.

She had reason. That chawing habit, for sure. It made her teeth grind.

Yet she had to admire Luke's rangy form, his taut muscles, his straight, dark blond hair and warm brown eyes. To her continuing surprise, he'd stayed at the ranch for more than a week, and grew ever easier on the eyes, especially to a woman who'd been a widow, and celibate, for two years.

Straightening, Meg chided herself. How could she be attracted, even mildly, to a man like Luke? A rodeo clown who usually wore baggy britches or silly tights, white greasepaint, and wanderlust as plain as the dark lines around his mouth? Rodeo had destroyed Erin's marriage, and Meg had cried her tears over Hank too.

She had her place here, as long as she could keep it, and like Erin she didn't yearn for anywhere else.

"You ever seen a boy sit a horse better than this?" Shifting the disgusting wad in his cheek, Luke called over the cloud of dust rising from the ring and Timmy laughed.

"I'm a born rider—bull rider too, Gram!"

"I never saw your father do it better," she said.

Luke began reeling in the lunge line, slowing Kemosabe to a loose-jointed walk to cool him down and Meg turned away. She had pints of berries waiting to be processed, poured into jars then wax-sealed. She'd come to see Timmy, not to moon over some stranger passing through.

"Ms. Sinclair?" Luke shouted after her.

She stopped but didn't turn. "Yes?"

"That was mighty good apple cobbler tonight."

"Thank you. I'm glad you liked it."

"Great pie the other day too." Leading Kemosabe with Timmy still on board, he walked over to the corral fence. At his silence, Meg finally turned around to find him watching her. His warm gaze ran over her, up then down and back again before he said, "A man could get used to such fine cooking. To a woman's touch—curtains and such."

"Tell Danny that," Meg answered.

She crossed the yard to the porch again, climbed the steps, then paused.

"Mr. Hastings?"

"Yes, ma'am?"

"That tobacco chewing habit," she said, "is most unwholesome. Unhealthy, too. If I were you, I'd try to give it up."

Luke laughed. He took the wad from his cheek, holding it up. It was not the brown mess she expected, but a pinkish lump.

"Gum," he said. "That's all it is. Just gum."

Embarrassed, she went inside, letting the screen slam bang behind her. Surely that look in his eye wasn't attraction? For her?

She normally didn't believe in second chances, except with Erin and Danny. She'd been a good wife to Hank Sinclair; she made a respectable widow. In Meg's mind she was still married to him and always would be. *Great pie . . . apple cobbler.* She should thank Luke for the reminder.

She was a grandmother now. With luck, she'd become a grandmother a second time or third. She went into the living room to her piano, seeking refuge. That's what life had in store for her. No foolish daydreams need apply. She'd be happy with that.

She would.

At the battered spinet, she sat down and began to play.

In the hot, airless claustrophobia of the camper he normally shared on the road with Luke, parked now under the maple tree by his mother's back porch, Danny lay sprawled on the front double bed in the alcove above the cab—the door shut, the lights out, no air moving, one arm over his eyes.

He'd heard Luke earlier with Timmy in the corral but didn't feel like taking part himself. He heard his mother join in, then fade back into the house. Now, he heard the familiar strains of "Danny Boy," wafting like the scent of ripe roses from the living room windows.

But come ye back when summer's in the meadow . . .

He must be crazy.

Erin had driven off with Ken hours ago, before dinner, the two of them chatting and laughing, Erin's hand on his brother's forearm at some comment, the sparkle in her green eyes that she once reserved for Danny.

Hell.

He guessed they could battle forever, but Erin would still hold to her opinion that she was all but single and Danny would hold to his, that they were still married.

What good that did him, he couldn't say.

He shouldn't have come back. With a sigh, he rolled onto his side. After Ennis and Livingston, it ached again—a sure sign of age, not injury. God, what he wouldn't give to be eighteen again and kissing Erin at the top of a Ferris wheel on a hot July night like this one. To ride double with her to the old sod house once more, and close themselves in the darkness as he had in the cellar at her store, to have her come willingly into his arms . . .

Danny swore.

Damn if he'd lie here, hard with wanting any woman he couldn't have. No, wanting Erin. Luke had been goading him about leaving ever since he arrived, and he'd put him off long enough. Why Luke stuck around, he didn't know either. If they didn't get back to work soon, Danny would lose his savings if not the camper as well as the season. Tomorrow, he thought; they'd leave tomorrow.

Before she left with Ken, Erin had announced that she'd hired an older woman and wouldn't need him at the store. She didn't look at him when she said it.

Flipping over again, he pushed himself up on an elbow, looking out the alcove's small window at the empty driveway. Damn if he'd hide out in the bunkhouse tonight, waiting for Ken to come home.

Danny had been sleeping on his brother's sofa bed since the night after he'd offered to work at the store, the night after he and Ken had quarreled, but he wasn't obeying Ken's orders to move out of the house. The daybed in his mother's sewing room was too narrow, and the mattress made his back ache. He knew Erin didn't want him in the house, where Danny might try to "crawl into her bed" some night, as Ken had said. In Danny's opinion Ken had no right to keep a bed check on him while he chased Danny's wife, but Danny had spent too many nights imagining the lush warmth of Erin's body in her bed just down the hall. He'd made his own decision. He slept at Ken's to remove himself from temptation.

But not tonight, not until Erin came home.

When headlights swept over the camper bed later, he sat bolt upright, his heart pounding. His mother's music had long since ended, and all he heard was the car's engine and a few crickets. Like a kid spying on his baby-sitter with her boyfriend, he stared out the window, watching Erin and Ken linger on the back porch steps.

He heard Erin's soft laughter. Then Ken leaned close to kiss her goodnight. The kiss went on too long, but he couldn't stop looking. Was Erin enjoying herself, or trying to push Ken away? They moved out of his line of vision, deeper into the porch shadows. Silence. Several long minutes of silence.

In the rodeo arena Danny never let anyone, man or animal, get the advantage—not if he could help it. He debated storming out into the yard, pummeling Ken with his fists. Though that would incur Erin's wrath again, he didn't have much to lose. He'd just come out swinging, making his moves.

He didn't get one leg over the bunk before the camper door opened, and Erin stepped inside.

"Oh! I thought you were Luke," Danny said.

Looking guilty, Erin stayed by the door. "Luke went into Dillon to see that movie about the bull rider again."

"Must make him homesick."

"He wanted to take Timmy, but Meg said she thought the later showing let out too late." She must have talked to his mother in the house then. Erin wiped her forehead. "It's stifling in here. Why are you all shut up on such a hot night?"

He'd soaked his navy T-shirt. "Is it hot? I didn't notice."

"You're sulking," Erin said.

Danny didn't answer. For a few seconds—a minute or more?—she stood near the door. Then she made her way across the small space, around the built-in table and past the kitchenette. At the raised double bed, she leaned her arms against the mattress and stared into his eyes.

Danny stared back. "Where'd you go tonight?"

"To a library board meeting."

Their gazes held in the darkness.

"Ken always kiss you goodnight after a board meeting?"

"Most always, yes." Erin glanced toward the small

window in the bunk then back at Danny. "Were you spying on me?" She took a step back. "I came to apologize. Now I'm sorry all right—sorry I ever thought of it."

Danny caught her arms but said nothing.

"My God. You're jealous—of Ken?"

He'd implied that before, but there was no use lying. "Since the first time I noticed you were a girl—not a little girl anymore but a big girl—I haven't been the same." Danny sighed. "But after the other day in the cellar, hell, maybe you're right—you and Luke. We ought to get on the road again. I never meant to stay this long," he added. "Now that you have help at the store . . . "

Erin studied his expression for a moment.

"Danny, about yesterday . . . I'm sorry I shoved you away."

"Well, I've been hurting ever since." He didn't mean his heart, exactly.

"I meant to apologize last night, but you were in town seeing that movie, and I . . . I guess I needed to gather my thoughts, decide what I wanted to say."

He smiled. She rarely acted on impulse. "Well, these things take time."

Erin's gaze softened. She stepped closer, smoothing sweat-damp tendrils of hair off his forehead. Her fingers trailed from his temple along his cheek to a soft earlobe. When she touched it, arousal raced straight to his groin.

He grabbed her hand. At the contact her fingers slipped into his. Her mouth quivered, and Danny took a chance, pressing a finger against her soft lips.

"I don't know what I feel," she said.

"About Ken?"

She shook her head. "With you."

The motion drew his finger across her bottom lip, and he wanted to groan. He imagined the greater softness of her breast, remembered its weight in his hand for only a second in the darkness of the cellar.

She leaned against the bunk again, her gaze holding his. "I didn't want to hurt your feelings. That's what I came to say. I know how hard it's been for you to come back here at all, even for Timmy, to be reminded . . . "

Danny tensed. "Erin, I don't want to talk about Trevor."

"Maybe you should," she said. "I can't help thinking too, remembering. That day in the corral and how you carried him to the house and Meg couldn't believe he was . . . dead." He turned his head away and she paused before continuing. "I knew right away. But maybe it hurt too much for her to know." She waited a heart beat. "And you."

She touched his cheek, and he turned his head toward her again. He didn't want to discuss heavy topics—except him and Erin. He tugged on her hand.

"Come on up here."

"No, Danny." She pulled back and he let her go. "There's one other thing I have to tell you." She fiddled with the ring on her fourth finger. "What you said about my being your wife. I'm not," she murmured. "Or if I am, it's in name only until—"

"Climb in this bunk, and it won't be."

Erin didn't quite roll her eyes. They'd been talking like civilized people—whether she realized it or not, like married people. Danny played his trump card.

"All right, tell me that's male bullshit, but this is your last chance to say what's on your mind. Luke and I are pulling out in the morning."

"*Tomorrow?*"

Danny half smiled at the widening of her eyes. "I thought you wanted to get rid of me. Cheyenne starts the twenty-third, little more than a week from now. I shouldn't miss any more good rides or money before Frontier Days."

He thought she would back away, reject him again, but before he could feel the pain, Erin slipped off her shoes then hoisted herself onto the bunk in a rustle of fabric, sitting on its edge beside him. Moving to give her room, Danny lay on his back, looking up at her. She wore a short-sleeved dress of some printed material, dark and light, with a scooped neck and a row of little buttons marching down the front. His fingers itched to undo them.

After a long moment, she reached out, tracing the path of moonlight over his face, touching his lower lip as he had touched hers.

"Oh, Danny." He nipped her finger, then kissed it, and watched her eyes darken. "What am I going to do with you?"

He looked at her for another second.

"I don't know, but while you're making up your mind . . . "

He drew her head down, raising up to meet her halfway, her hand dropping to his chest, to his tight stomach muscles under the damp T-shirt, their mouths blending in a kiss that threatened the rest of his sanity. Erin groaned, giving him courage. He pulled her onto him, their bodies aligning all the way, then melting into each other. After the next kiss, he couldn't tell where her mouth, her body, left off and his began.

"Let me get rid of this."

He pulled off his T-shirt and tossed it to the floor. Erin pressed close again, as if she couldn't wait, her lightweight dress hiking up, her fingers against his bare chest—his damp skin.

"Now you," he said.

Between kisses, he worked the enticing opening of her dress, then the front closing of her plain white bra. Erin's breasts fell free into his waiting hands, and Danny groaned into her mouth.

God, he couldn't believe she'd let him . . .

"Yes, touch me," she pleaded, guiding his fingers to her nipples.

He caressed her left breast, his mouth fastened on the other rosy aureole, his tongue teasing it into hardness. In the next minutes he alternated, his mouth on her breasts, then on her lips, kissing, teething, suckling. His breath came fast, and shaken.

"*Erin.*"

She had her hand poised on the hard ridge of his fly when she stopped. Lost in the growing ecstasy he'd missed so much, Danny involuntarily lifted toward her, his body begging for more, but she had already left him.

Dazed, he held out a hand as she scrambled to the camper floor.

"Come back here."

"I can't. I'm sorry," she said, her tone thick. With the words of denial, she moved close again. "I didn't mean to go this far. We're not the same."

"In some ways we are." He grasped her fingers, which felt cold in his. "I know I am—about this." He tried to drag her hand back to his jeans.

"It's not right," she said, her head down.

He pressed her palm to him. "Feels good enough from here."

Erin snatched her hand free.

"Danny, that's just—physical!"

Catching the nape of her neck, he drew her near and lowered his tone, all but whispering in her ear, knowing as he said it that he'd gone too far.

"Fits me like a deep seat on a good bull. How about you?"

She reared back. "Don't you try to reduce everything to eight seconds on some mean animal—or an hour with a woman you don't care about!"

"Where'd you get that idea?"

"I've lived with it every day for eight years," she said. "No, make that thirteen. All the reminders, and now . . . this"—she waved a hand—"and Trevor. They only make things worse. I was feeling sorry about everything that happened." She struggled with her clothes, fought against Danny's hand, his frustration. "What was I thinking of? You already said you're leaving in the morning." She blinked furiously. "What am I *doing*?"

"Making love with your husband!"

That was the wrong thing to say too, but he said it anyway, like the desperate man he was. Erin backed away as if he'd slapped her. She bumped into the table but didn't seem to notice the hard knock on her hip.

"You're not my husband, Danny."

Taking another backward step, she slipped out the camper door, leaving him to compose himself. To subside.

He knew he had to leave; he'd known that before she entered the camper. He wasn't being fair to Erin, but he called after her anyway as he slumped back onto the bunk.

"Then why are you still wearing my ring?"

$\overline{10}$

Erin put her wedding band in her dresser drawer that night. The next morning she didn't need her alarm. She hadn't slept and at the first gray light in the east she gave up trying.

With one ear cocked for the slam of the camper's doors and Danny leaving, she pulled on wheat-colored cutoff jeans and a black tank top. The early morning was already too hot and surprisingly humid for Montana to wear more. By the time she reached the bottom of the stairs, she had her latest speech rehearsed.

At the kitchen table Ken was drinking coffee and scanning yesterday's newspaper. Erin had seen the headlines: *Ski Industry Expands Toward Sweetwater*. Except for Ken, the kitchen was empty. She glanced around, standing for a moment in the faint, hot breeze coming through the open screen door.

Reaching for a mug from the cabinet, Erin craned her neck to see out the window where the camper had been parked.

It was still there.

"He's sleeping at my place. Like a six-week-old baby," Ken informed her, glancing up from the newspaper. "Came in the middle of the night after Luke got home. My shower didn't wake him this morning. Slamming the bunkhouse door didn't either."

Erin tried not to feel relief. Caring for Danny frightened her, and she'd pulled back, giving in the night before to Ken's insistence that she attend the library board meeting. She felt safer with him, comfortable. Then couldn't let it go at that. She and Danny had come close last night to making love— too close—and where Danny was concerned, she didn't believe in happily ever after. She'd tried that twice. This morning, even the thought of having sex with him terrified her more than caring for him did, or all the memories. The narrow escape last night should have taught her something.

Instead, she meant to apologize again.

"I don't suppose that gypsy caravan of his has air conditioning," Ken added. "They say the temperature may hit ninety today."

Taking a chair across from him, she sipped at her coffee. The hot liquid seared her sensitive mouth. She wouldn't apologize for leading Danny on, because sex only confused her determination not to get hurt by him again. But she and Danny, joined by Timmy, owed each other certain things.

She couldn't send him away thinking she didn't care at all when she did. She just couldn't live with him—sleep with him, Erin corrected.

"Soon as I finish," Ken said from behind the paper, "I'll send Timmy over to jump on his stomach. He and Luke will be off the property by noon."

For weeks she'd been waiting to see the red wink of Danny's taillights. Now that he was going . . .

"You don't look pleased."

Ken's comment made her flush.

"Of course I am." But she rose from the table on the pretext of fixing some toast, not to let him see her eyes. "What's worse than an ex-husband—"

The back door opened and a sleepy-eyed Danny, wearing only his jeans, paused on the threshold.

"You tell me," he said, his gaze fixed on her bare hand.

Turning to the counter, she jammed the toaster knob, watching the red coils light up. Like taillights glowing.

"I meant—"

"I can guess." With a yawn Danny crossed to the refrigerator, pulled out the orange juice, and drank from the glass bottle.

"That's disgusting," Ken murmured.

"At six-thirty in the morning I'm disgusting. You ought to remember. So were you." He glanced at Erin as if to remind her too. "While you're there, pour me some caffeine, will you?" He looked away. "Maybe if I drink enough, I'll keep my eyes open on the trip."

"Danny," she began.

Pushing past her, he sank down at the table.

"*Danny*, I need to—"

"We'll be out of your way before nine," he added as if he'd heard Ken's earlier comment too.

Setting his coffee beside him, Erin stared down at the crown of Danny's thick, dark hair. She almost wished he had a balding spot, or a thickening belly. Anything superficial that could dampen last night's lust, that might make her want him less even now.

"Make that eight-thirty," Ken said, "and I'll spring for a tank of gas." He scraped his chair back. "If you need help loading up, let me know. The offer's still open."

The back door closed behind him. In the silence, the newly created privacy, Erin bit her lip. "He's not awake either," she said. "He didn't mean what he said."

More silence.

Erin turned toward the counter then back again to find

Danny watching her, his eyes dark and brooding, the coffee mug halfway to his mouth.

"Sure he meant it. Why keep telling me he doesn't? He's meant it since Trev died. If Dad were still alive, he'd be saying the same thing."

Danny sounded as if he didn't care. Erin had heard that tone before, had seen that impassive expression. Sometime during the night, his pride had taken hold, and he wouldn't readily accept an apology from her now. She stumbled into it anyway.

"Danny, I'm sorry about last night in the camper."

He glanced again at her bare hand.

"I'm sorry it didn't turn out better. Did you mean what you said?"

"Yes," she admitted, "but I—"

"How about this morning?"

Erin rubbed her finger, which felt oddly naked the longer he looked at it.

"I didn't really mean . . . that is, Ken had just said—"

"Home sweet home. No wonder I never missed it much."

His eyes said otherwise, but in the face of his colossal pride and her thoughtless, flippant comment to Ken, she kept quiet. His gaze flicked over her, as if to memorize her bare feet, snug, worn shorts and tank top. Her face. She could almost sense his struggle not to look once more at her ringless hand.

"Who are you trying to convince, Erin? Ken?" he said, scraping back his chair. "Me, or yourself?" At the door he held it open. "Let me tell you something. I've been meaning to mention it. Don't even try to keep Tim from coming to see me on the circuit next summer, or later this year some place or other."

"Danny, I never said—"

"Your toast is burning."

When the door banged shut, her words seemed caught in her throat like the charred bread she pulled from the toaster and Erin was blinking. She knew it was better that he left. How many times could she say she was sorry? If he stayed around any longer, she'd be wearing a proverbial hair shirt for penance and hating herself.

Danny stomped out to the bunkhouse. He could hear Ken shaving in the bathroom. He flung his clothes in his sports bag, zipped it shut—and caught a shirt sleeve. Freeing it, he cursed until the heavy morning air should have turned blue.

He hadn't slept worth a damn. Earlier, he'd faked sleep for Ken.

He and Luke had a roughly four-hundred-mile drive ahead, from Sweetwater down through Idaho to Elko, Nevada where Luke would bullfight and Danny had entered the rodeo, hoping for his share of the nine-thousand-dollar purse. That much more toward his gold buckle.

In the growing heat he stalked out to the camper with his gear, hammering on the metal door before he opened it. He gave the frame a rap on his way in.

"Goddammit, Danny!" Blinking, Luke twisted in the sheets where Danny had lain too briefly with Erin hours before. "You get up on the wrong side of bed, don't take it out on me." He flinched as Danny's bag sailed across the kitchenette table and slammed against the bunk. "Hell, just because I overslept—"

"*Shut up.*"

He almost wished Luke would fly at him, fists raised and ready, but Luke knew Danny too well. His tone stayed mild.

"Who do you think you're talking to here? Your brother? Or your ex-wife?"

"She's not my ex-wife, dammit!" That sight of her bare hand still smarted.

Luke sat up, running his fingers through his silky hair.

Like some runway model's, it fell perfectly into place as he stared at Danny.

"You had a fight, didn't you?"

"Not so you'd notice. Let's get the hell out of here. You can have take-out coffee and—if you hurry your ass before they stop serving—a sausage and egg McMuffin."

Luke slid off the bunk. "A quick shower too?"

"No."

"Danny—"

"Just get dressed, will you? The rest of my stuff's in Mom's sewing room. It won't take me five minutes to pack."

"All right, all right."

"You can stop dreaming about my mother's apple cobbler too. She's sure to have more around. I'll even wrap some up for you for later."

Having made his magnanimous offer, he slammed out of the camper, hating himself, leaving Luke to figure out his mood. Damned if Danny wanted to. All he wanted now was to hit the end of the driveway and keep going.

"Daniel, you're not leaving here without a decent breakfast in your stomach," his mother told him minutes later, stepping in front of Danny at the kitchen door before he could get outside again. "I'll fix you and Luke some eggs and bacon. Another pot of coffee too."

"Ah, Mom."

By the time he downed another two cups of her special brew, he felt mean as the devil. Even Tim's bright chatter, which ordinarily would have matched Danny's, couldn't brighten his mood. It made things worse. With a glare for Luke, who seemed inclined to linger in the kitchen with Meg, he stomped outside and across the yard. Tim jogged after him, his smaller legs pumping, his cowboy boots clomping.

"Daddy, wait!"

He didn't slow down. He kept his eyes trained on the ground. "I don't have time, Tim. Luke and I need to make Nevada by evening and pay my entry fee for tomorrow."

"I want you to see me ride Kemosabe."

"Next time," he said.

"What if you don't come back?"

His tone sounded thick and Danny missed a step. "Then you'll come see me next summer. The whole summer now that you're old enough. I'll put you on a good horse."

"'Sabe's good. He's great," Tim insisted, still trying to match Danny's stride. "He's almost better now. Luke said so too when I rode him yesterday. 'Sabe doesn't limp at all."

"Yeah, so don't get attached to him. I'll be sending him back on the circuit soon. He's cost me enough money this season. It's time he earned his keep."

"But—"

"Ride him while you can."

When Tim fell behind Danny kept going. If he turned around, he'd catch his son up in his arms, bury his face in Tim's sweet neck, and disgrace himself. If he saw tears in Tim's eyes, he'd start bawling too.

He'd known from the start there would be no easy good-byes. Just as he'd known he couldn't stay.

He caught Ken coming out the bunkhouse door. His brother's scowl didn't put him off. Neither did the yellow hard hat he carried under one arm or the steel-toed work boots he wore. Danny could kick ass himself.

"Can I see you a minute before I go?"

At his station wagon Ken threw the hard hat onto the back seat. "Make it quick. I'm due for a site inspection this morning."

"Five minutes."

He'd go but he'd make himself clear before he did, not only to Erin.

Ken turned and started walking along the fence line by the driveway. "What's on your mind?"

"Erin and Tim," Danny said. "The future."

Ken looked at him.

"Future?"

"I've seen how you look at Erin. I know your intentions. She's not wearing her wedding ring this morning." Danny studied his sneakers as he kept pace with Ken. Around them the morning sun glanced off a metal downspout at the house, glinted off a row of snapdragons in Meg's garden, bathed the pasture in hot golden light. Danny could smell freshly mown grass. "I guess the next thing on her mind will be divorce papers."

"It's about time."

"I want you to know I'll fight her as hard as I can."

Ken glanced at him. "Don't be a damn fool. You and Erin never really lived together in thirteen years. You think a few nights in bed, one of them to create Timmy, makes you husband and wife? Get smart, Danny boy." Ken kicked a stone. "She should have shed you long ago."

Danny paused, frowning. Kemosabe trotted across the pasture and up to the fence, but Danny barely touched his velvety muzzle before walking on. "Erin's a bit strung out about her feelings right now. But she'll come around."

Ken made a sound of disgust.

"I love her. I love that boy too," Danny said. "Just so you'll know where we stand, you and me. I gave up long ago trying to be friends with you or even brothers, but I'm not giving up my family."

"You haven't got a family. You squandered Erin—Timmy too—for the sake of climbing on some smelly bull to prove God knows what except you can hang on for eight seconds on a good day." Ken swung around. "I can offer both of them a lot more. You never grew up, Danny. You probably never will. But even if you do, it'll be too late."

Danny rubbed the back of his neck. "I know I have to quit pro rodeo sooner or later—sooner, probably, the way my bones are aching." He met Ken's angry gaze. "I'll be back. And when I get here"—he swept a hand at the surrounding acres, the new fence—"I'll put this place right again."

"What are you talking about?"

"Stock contracting."

"Stock contracting? You crazy bastard—"

In the past weeks he'd thought it through. He'd started fixing fence, then envisioning other changes in his mind until the plan had formed, solidified. Good changes for the ranch too.

"This land needs to be used, Ken. And I'll need work when I'm done rodeoing. Erin might not take to the idea at first, but I think I can make a good living at it and it's not as dangerous as she'll probably think."

"You're out of your mind."

Ken's opposition didn't surprise him, but he didn't need his brother's acceptance. "With Mom's one-third share of the ranch plus mine and Erin's, we hold the majority."

"Yours and Erin's," Ken repeated. He started to smile. "You should have come home for Dad's funeral and the reading of his will."

Danny hesitated. "Mom told me he left the ranch in thirds."

"She couldn't bring herself to say whose thirds, I guess. Because one of them's not yours."

Danny's breakfast turned in his stomach.

"He left a third to Mom, a third to me, and a third to Erin—in her name only, not jointly with yours." Ken's look was gloating. "I thought you'd never ask, Danny boy."

"Why?" he said, barely able to say the word. "Because of Trevor? Did Dad blame me right up till he died?"

"What do you think?"

He thought he might be sick. Taking deep breaths of warm Montana air, smelling of grass and wildflowers and sunshine, he swallowed twice.

"If you have any notions about stock contracting on this land, forget them." Ken's voice seemed to come from far away down a long tunnel. "There's no future for this land except possibly development. According to last night's paper, the growing ski industry—downhill and cross country—

may move this way soon, and when it does I'll convince
Erin to sell out. Mom too."

"They'd never do that. They love this place."

"It's dead land, Danny. Who do you think's putting food
on the table here and paying the upkeep? Erin's store
barely makes a profit. Neither do Mom's piano lessons." He
waited a second then said, "I don't see much money coming from your direction."

"You know Erin won't take much, except now and then
for Tim." He paused. "I was the only one of Dad's sons who
ever wanted to ranch someday."

"Someday didn't do him any good. Like you running off
to rodeo."

Danny shook his head. He always meant to come back, to
make amends. "How could he cut me out like that, even after
Trev?" His tone sounded hollow too. "How could he hate
me that much?" So much he'd deny Danny his birthright.

He didn't expect an answer, didn't want one. Whatever
Ken said would only hurt more. They'd been so close once,
brothers and friends. In those days "Danny boy" was an
affectionate nickname and Ken's laughter rang with his.
They'd scuffled and fought, but they'd loved each other.
Now Ken hated him too. He already had the land. He wanted
Erin. He wanted Tim.

Damn if he'd get them.

Ken turned away, toward his car.

"I'll be back," Danny called. "As soon as the season ends,
I'll be back."

He knew Erin better than Ken did. He'd have her support and his mother's too.

The land shimmered in front of him with the heat, and
he scuffed along in Ken's wake. He took his time now. He
had reached the end of the pasture nearest the barn before
he realized Kemosabe was no longer there, and the sick
feeling in his stomach lurched into swift panic.

Ride him while you can.

•   •   •

Erin had decided not to wait around, or to say good-bye.
She would let Meg hug Danny; she'd let Timmy cling to
him.

In her bedroom, dressing for work, she tucked a cream-
colored blouse into her denim skirt, slipped into her beige
canvas shoes, then checked her appearance in the mirror.
If she didn't hurry, she'd be late. Again. She wanted to tidy
up before her new helper started on Monday.

Glancing out the window, Erin saw Ken's car pulling out.
He passed Danny coming up the driveway on foot but
Danny didn't look up, or wave, and Ken didn't toot the horn,
which didn't surprise her. He'd been waiting for him to leave
since Danny arrived.

At first Erin had felt the same.

She ran a comb through her hair even though it looked
neat enough. Then flung it down. She wasn't stalling. But
her gaze strayed toward the window, and she froze.

In the yard she saw Danny suddenly running, his long
legs covering ground, and shouting, but she couldn't hear
the words. He was headed for the corral.

Cold fear clutched Erin's heart.

"Tim!" she heard Danny call through the open window.

And then a child's scream.

"Oh, dear God." Erin dashed down the stairs and outside,
and hit the yard running. "Timmy!"

In the corral she saw Kemosabe first, his hide a black-
and-white blur as he galloped madly around the large, dirt-
floored ring. The reins dangled from his bridle, all but
touching the ground. As she watched, horrified, Timmy
slipped sideways on the horse's bare back.

"Hang on, Tim!" Danny shouted.

She wanted Danny to do something. To stop the horse's
wild flight, to bring her child safely down to level ground.

"Stop him, Danny!"

Yelling, she reached the corral gate, which was closed and latched. Danny didn't bother with it. Like last time, he climbed the rail and vaulted over the fence, dropping to the dirt near Timmy and the paint gelding. The horse swerved, narrowly avoiding Danny then swung around the far turn, heading for the next straightaway on the other side of the ring.

Timmy's arms had clamped around the horse's neck, holding on for dear life. Exactly that, Erin thought. She reached for the gate latch.

"Stay outside!" Danny didn't turn to see her.

He crossed the ring, obviously hoping to intercept the horse and grab its bridle. Kemosabe darted in the opposite direction, and Timmy slid toward the horse's off side. Miraculously, he righted himself again.

"Ride him!" Danny yelled.

Opening the gate Erin ran after him. She'd stood back before but not this time. There was no way Timmy could gather the reins or ride Kemosabe into a corner, a technique he wouldn't yet know.

Danny tried to herd him toward the fence angle. His first attempt failed. So did the second, as Erin formed another barrier, trying to catch the horse between them. Kemosabe raced on, his ears laid flat, his nostrils flaring, his big body weaving each time Danny and Erin got near.

"*Goddammit!*" Danny shouted.

Timmy's terrified voice filled the air.

"Daddy, stop me!"

"Whoa, you son of a bitch!"

Kemosabe's ears pricked. His master's voice reached him at last, however dimly, and Erin realized she was praying again.

Dear God, please save him.

The horse slowed a fraction. Danny jumped in front of him with Erin right there too. Kemosabe slid to a stop as if he were competing in the rodeo arena and some barrel racer had spun him around one of the three obstacles. Quivering, the horse hung his head, blowing hard and splaying out his front legs.

With a cry Timmy landed in Danny's arms. He buried his face against Danny's shoulder and burst into tears.

"I thought I was gonna die."

"You did just fine, Tim." The words came between gasps.

Erin could see Danny's chest heaving for air the same as hers.

She heard the gate latch open and behind them Meg flew across the corral from the house, crying too. "Is he all right? Oh God, Danny. Erin. Is he—"

"Okay, Mom. He's okay."

"Give him to me," Erin said.

Danny's gaze met hers over Timmy's small form.

"He's all right."

"I'll decide that for myself." Her voice sounded shrill in her own ears and Danny looked away, patting Timmy's back before easing him into Erin's arms.

She hugged him tight enough to cut off his breath—what little he had left. In her embrace he wheezed and sobbed.

Meg crowded close. "Poor baby."

Like Erin, she ran her hands over him, touching, testing, reassuring herself that he was still alive, still hers. Erin felt weak all over. After a moment she drew back enough to see his tear-streaked face, his wide hazel eyes. His legs wrapped around her waist, he tried to smile.

He propped his casted arm on her shoulder. "Did I ride him good, Mom?"

"Oh, God."

"My favorite boy." Meg stroked his hair.

"Take him to the house," Erin said, giving him to her mother-in-law, "and wash his face and hands."

Meg cradled him close. "How would you like a nice big glass of lemonade too? And some sugar cookies?"

"I would, Gram."

Danny hadn't said another word. When Erin glanced his way, he stood where she'd left him. His damp hair clung to his skull and a stray tendril flopped over one eye. Like Erin, he was still breathing hard, his shirt sticking to his chest with every movement. His eyes held that look again.

Erin stared down at the dirt between them.

Only a few feet, she thought. But the gap seemed like a thousand miles. She tried to control her tone.

"You have a good barrel racer there."

He scuffed at the dirt. "It was my fault," he said. "Tim wanted me to watch him ride before I left. I—I couldn't stand to be around him just then." He told her about promising a better horse, next summer. "I told him to ride Kemosabe while he could."

"And he thought you meant right then."

"I guess he must."

She steeled herself against the look in his eyes when their gazes met. "Well, you're absolutely right, this is all your fault!" Erin advanced on him. "You encourage him. You throw out promises you don't mean to keep—"

Danny swung around toward Kemosabe.

"Keep your voice down. You'll spook the horse again."

"I didn't spook him the first time."

He ran a hand over the gelding's hide. It quivered and Kemosabe stomped a foot. When Danny hit a spot on his withers a second time, the horse turned his head, nipping.

"He's bee-stung." Danny soothed the welt on the horse instead of swatting him for the nip. "There's probably a hornet's nest in the barn eaves—like most summers. It needs taking down."

"That's not the point."

"What is?" He patted Kemosabe's neck then turned to her. "What's the point, Erin? Except you didn't stay where I told you to, outside the fence."

"I don't want you teaching Timmy to ride. I don't want you putting him on a better horse—or any horse at all. I don't want him spending summers with you on the circuit. Above all, I don't want him practicing his moves and day-dreaming about pro rodeo some day."

"I told you before, he's a normal kid," Danny said.

"So let him ride his bike."

"He broke that arm riding his bike, dammit."

"Pretending he was just like you! Risking his neck—for what? A belt buckle?" She spun away, furious and frightened.

Danny touched her forearm, his hand clammy. "You've seen runaways before. You've been on a few yourself. Tim didn't get hurt. If he wants to rodeo some day, you're gonna have to let him."

"Never. Not in a million years."

"Listen to me."

She flung his arm away. "No! You and Luke were packing that camper, so do it! You have your life and I have mine—"

"What the hell's this really about?"

"What's it about?" she asked, incredulous. "It's about seeing my little boy on a horse gone crazy—"

"The horse got stung, for Christ's sake!"

"—and feeling all over again that the same thing would happen as it did to Trevor. He'd land in that dirt, his neck would snap and he'd never get up again—"

"Stop it, Erin."

"And by God, I don't intend to lose him!" Turning, she shoved a hand, hard, at Danny's chest. "So get out of here, away from me—away from Timmy—and take your crazy ideas with you! I don't want him near that horse again, do you hear me? And I don't want him near *you*!"

"Erin—!"

"Kill yourself if you want to—I won't have to see it—but don't you even think again about risking my son!"

"He's mine too. Dammit," Danny said hoarsely. He took two steps backward up against the fence, turned and fumbled with the gate latch. Flinging it open, he strode out into the yard, leaving Erin to deal with Kemosabe. "He's mine."

She was still standing inside the corral, holding the paint's reins in her trembling hand, when the camper doors slammed and the pickup shot down the driveway as if being chased by all the ghosts of Danny's past—by Hank Sinclair's blame and, now, Erin's too.

11

Danny took another deep breath, then let it out slowly, but his usual routine wasn't working. Around him other men warmed up for their rides—ran through their moves like Tim on his bike, traded gallows humor with other riders, slapped themselves to get the adrenaline flowing, or prayed. His heart pumped audibly in his ears, and his stomach wouldn't settle.

"Cowboy up, Sinclair," a voice said from the chutes.

Out front he heard the crowd roar. The eight-second horn bleated. Hooves pounded the dirt arena at Elko as another cowboy escaped a bull's horns and climbed the fence to dust himself off. Nearby a gate clanged shut on a defeated Brahma.

He swallowed hard, checked the tape around the wrist of his deerskin glove, adjusted the chaps over his tight Wranglers, stamped his feet to make sure his boots had seated properly but felt loose enough to come off easily if necessary, then swung up onto the splintered fence.

From its top rail he assessed the day's ride—eighteen

hundred pounds of ornery Brahma bull. Scruffy gray hide, one horn split, the other curved and pointed like a dagger, a humped back that would feel like a sliding board between his legs. A damn good bull, headed for the money.

He felt a tap on his seat. He glanced around and down into a shiny white face and coal black–outlined eyes, the black streaks that defined Luke's wide, red clown mouth. The ridiculous sight didn't register.

"Forget about her," Luke said, "forget Paradise Valley. Get your mind on business, or you know what happens."

He could still see Erin's face two days ago in the corral. He could hear her anger and her blame.

"Sometimes it happens anyway."

But Luke had his own theory. Danny swung a leg over, coming down onto the bull's back. It twitched, trying to turn its head, but the narrow chute confined it. Even so, the chute could be dangerous, and he used caution. He picked up the flat, braided rope—his own rigging—that girded the animal just behind its front legs. From the rope a metal bell dangled, an irritant to the animal once the gate opened, meant to increase bucking action.

He adjusted the rope's tension, and the bull stamped its feet with a bellow.

"He's a stubborn cuss, Danny," one of the stock contractor's men said.

Danny settled himself deeper along the bull's spine. "So am I."

The man's laughter didn't make him smile. He hadn't smiled since he left the ranch. All around him, voices buzzed, and the scent of animals, of manure rose in the air.

He laid his gloved left hand, palm up, on the bull's back then carefully aligned the rope across it. Fisting the rope tight, he used his right hand to pound the left-hand fingers around it, into the sticky resin coating. The grip didn't feel right and he frowned.

Tim's freckled face flashed across his mind.

"Give it up." Climbing up, Luke leaned over the chute rail, trying to catch his eye. "You want to win the world or don't you? You're gonna get hurt riding with your mind full of junk."

"I'm okay."

Tim had cried when he said good-bye. He wound his little boy legs around Danny's waist, his arms, one of them in the neon green cast, around his neck, and the hot flow of tears scalded his skin. "I didn't mean to take Kemosabe without asking. I didn't mean to be a bad boy."

Despite Danny's gentle hand rubbing his spine, he was still crying in Meg's arms when he and Luke left. Through the open windows of the camper he'd heard Tim shout in a furious, tearful tone: *"You better come back or I'll be mad at you—forever!"*

The rodeo announcer called the next rider over the public address system.

"Come on down here," Luke advised, "and call Erin. You're not going to be much good until you do."

"I'm not calling her."

With a derisive snort, Luke scrambled down from the fence. "Then you deserve what happens out there today."

Maybe he did.

The negative thought made Danny queasy. He'd based a long rodeo career on positive imaging. He never entered the ring without checking his gear and giving himself a talk—plain, commonsense talk, not the Zen rodeo some guys practiced. He envisioned the nationals, that gold buckle. The money that would buy his foundation stock for the ranch.

The ranch he didn't own.

Sometimes the images fell apart.

" . . . now Danny Sinclair on Rough 'n Ready. Danny hails from Sweetwater, Montana."

It would be his call next, not the announcer's. Tightening his grip, Danny told himself he could be a pretty mean bull himself when he had to. With his right hand, he clamped his straw Resistol hat lower on his head.

"Do your worst, old man."

He wasn't sure he was talking to the bull.

With a single nod, he indicated his readiness and in a flash of a second the chute gate slammed open.

Danny didn't hear it. His father's words, like the bull exploding out the gate, blasted him again.

You killed my son, his father had said when Trevor died. *It's your fault for not doing right by that horse. Call yourself a trainer? Not by a long shot. Call yourself no-good at all.*

Over the next five years until he turned eighteen and went on the road, he heard the same message. Hank had never even acknowledged the silver belt buckle Danny sent him—his first. He might as well have kept it.

"Danny, nail him!" Luke shouted from his waiting stance near the gate, a flash of baggy dark pants, red-and-white striped shirt, and snappy green suspenders in Danny's peripheral vision.

His right arm high and moving, his chest out, his chin tucked, he had his hands full now. Bull riding had few rules. You rode one-handed and tried to stay on. But Luke would have added another: Don't think. In Luke's opinion Danny's occasional mental lapses kept him from winning the world.

The bull bucked first to the left, just as Danny had been told it would, landing hard on four straightened legs. The impact jolted from Danny's seat up his taped elbow to his brain. He felt the pull in his shoulder and his arm muscles bulged.

Erin, he thought, that first time at the sod house, her arms around him, her mouth soft and warm. She'd grown up, it seemed, comforting him.

The Brahma snaked toward the center of the ring like a sidewinder, far more agile for its bulk than most people might expect. Danny's head snapped back and forth like Trevor's on the bucking horse.

Ride him, he'd told Tim.

The bull spun in a circle and the crowd went wild.

Unlike Trevor, his son was safe, and Danny knew he wasn't really to blame for Tim's mischief. He'd provoked it, though. Had he lost his little boy's faith in him? He'd lost Erin's long ago. What about her comforting him, then, in the camper? Had it been a thin veneer because she knew he wouldn't stay?

He'd stay all right. Here, for eight seconds in the middle of this ring, or at Cheyenne, and the arena after that . . . where he belonged. Winning buckles, and showing them how it was done.

His renewed determination came too late. The Brahma cut to the right. Danny slid to the left.

He heard the crowd roar its fear as he took flight. The arena turned upside down. He cartwheeled over the bull's shoulder. And six seconds after the chute opened, with a whoosh of air that emptied his lungs, he landed flat on his back in the dirt.

No score.

"Are you hurt?" Erin asked him that night.

He hadn't answered the phone right away, and Danny's explanation sounded weary through the line, his words full of background static. Years ago, he would have leaned a shoulder against the outside wall at the usual bank of public telephones at any rodeo, his other hand clapped over his ear to hear at all. Now, he and Luke had a car phone.

"No broken bones," he said, and she heard the far-off rumble of an announcer's voice. "Rodeo's still going on, a few more rides in the final round," he commented. "I'm out on my ass, but my head's on straight, more or less, and I can still walk." His tone lowered. "Just your everyday aches and bruises."

He offered nothing more. The silence unnerved Erin.

She'd worked up the courage to call on Sunday night, two days after Danny left Paradise Valley. Now she didn't know what good talking to him might do. He didn't seem receptive, and she couldn't blame him.

"What do you suppose Danny must have thought," Daisy had said, "when you lashed out about Trevor?"

"It wasn't about Trevor. It was Timmy."

"Not the way I hear it."

Daisy was right. In the corral Erin had been afraid for her child, but before that, she'd felt more afraid of her confused feelings for Danny, which she couldn't seem to sort out. She had chosen a convenient, if very painful, topic to distance herself. She didn't tell Daisy that Timmy blamed her too.

In her son's mind she had two strikes against her. Erin had refused to let him ride with Danny to Ennis or Livingston during Fourth of July weekend. He now said it was her fault Danny went away, and he wouldn't see him again all summer. But what if Timmy had gone to those rodeos, and Danny fell as he did at Elko? What if he'd been badly hurt? Timmy would have been alone, and traumatized. For Timmy's sake, she could endure her son's displeasure and his father's prideful silence.

"Danny?" she said, hearing the background murmur of other voices, male laughter.

"Why did you call, Erin?"

"To apologize—again," she said.

"No, I shouldn't have told Tim to ride that horse. I should have known he'd take me literally. He's never been much good at waiting. I suppose patience will never be his strong suit."

Erin fought a smile. "He takes after you."

"Is that another accusation?"

"No, a fact. Genes," she said.

"Jeans?"

"The reproductive kind. Heredity."

"We must have a bad connection here." She heard a smile in his voice, but he still sounded pained. "Though I never thought so, you and me. This conversation is getting real interesting."

His silky tone went through her like a laser.

Lying across her bed, she said, "Danny, I don't blame you for Trevor. You know that, don't you?"

"Hell, I thought maybe it was catching, like a virus. Ken, my father, now you."

Through the phone line someone hooted and someone else hollered back. With the rodeo ending, people would be packing up, heading for the next go-round, or for nearby bars and cold beers. Or a woman for the night.

"Well," she said, "I'm glad I caught you." Erin fidgeted with the phone cord. "And I'm sorry you got thrown today."

"How'd you find me anyway?"

"I had the number for your car phone." She'd never used it before. "I didn't know where you and Luke might be staying, so I thought—"

"In the camper," he said. "Helluva way to run a business, isn't it?" He paused. "Helluva business."

Helluva a way to run a marriage, she thought.

"Where do you go next?"

He hesitated, as if not certain she cared. "Cheyenne."

"The big blowout, hmm?"

It was always a giant party, a hundred thousand visitors and more to a town that normally boasted half that many residents—still, a big town by Sweetwater standards. In the early days of their marriage, when Erin still believed they could make a go of it, she'd gone with him to Cheyenne. Rooted for him, celebrated. Partied all night. Made love until dawn . . .

"You wanna come?" Danny asked, startling her.

"Come?"

He laughed a little. "To Cheyenne. You and Tim."

She heard the challenge in his tone, the certainty that she'd say no. Erin plumped her pillow, then cozied up against her headboard.

"That would thrill him, wouldn't it?"

"Thrill me too." His lazy voice made her ache, as it always had when he called at night after a rodeo, sounding tired and lonely. "How about you, Mrs. Sinclair? I didn't plan to ask, but it's a good idea."

Erin rubbed her empty ring finger but ignored his reference to her as his wife. "I might consider sending Timmy."

"I meant both of you." He paused. "There'd be no one to watch him while I ride." Just like Ennis and Livingston.

She'd made her apology. It ended there.

"I—" The word no eluded her. "I'll think about it."

"Sleep on it."

"I didn't say yes," Erin said.

"Dream about me?"

"Nightmares maybe," but he had already pushed the disconnect button. Gently, she imagined, the way he always touched her in the night.

Meg's excitement, like Timmy's, proved difficult to ignore.

"I think you should go," she said.

"Daddy felt sad when he left." Timmy toyed with his Frosted Flakes at the breakfast table the next morning. "He wants me to come. We could make him feel better if we went to see him ride."

When she swallowed, Erin's coffee felt like a brick in her throat. But she made no promises. She shouldn't have told them about Cheyenne until she'd made up her mind.

"We'll see."

Timmy kicked the leg of her chair. "You always say that when you mean no."

Meg joined them at the table, bringing a platter of eggs, sunny-side up, ringed with crisp bacon.

"I'll come along, Erin. I haven't had a trip since Hank died." She warmed to the subject. "Remember when we used to tour the fairs all over the state and into Wyoming? Utah?"

They had traveled in a big Carryall that Hank bought secondhand, the boys and Erin sleeping in bags on the rear seat and the back floor, parked outside the motel room where Hank and Meg stayed, "to keep away from the kids' fracas all night," Hank had said. Meaning, Erin knew because Danny had once told her so, that the elder Sinclairs wanted privacy.

"I remember," she said. They'd been good times.

Meg told Timmy the story. "Garrett—your other grand-father—would drive the pickup and stock trailer. Hank and the boys would show cattle with him. If there was a dance, we'd go that night."

"Did you dance, Mom?" Timmy's spoon dripped milk over his cereal bowl.

"She certainly did," Meg said before Erin could respond. "She learned to dance from your daddy and Ken." Meg laughed. "My, they whirled that little girl around so, I thought your skirts would fly right off, Erin."

"I always thought it was misplaced sibling rivalry. A sanctioned chance to show me who was boss in their minds."

Timmy grinned. "Is Daddy a good dancer?"

"He sure is." Meg scooped eggs onto Erin's plate. "I imagine there'll be a dance at Cheyenne."

"Gram, there's a dance every Saturday after rodeo," Timmy said, a veteran of his June tour.

"A big one—more than one—at Frontier Days," Meg agreed. "And that's not all. Every night there's a concert, with famous celebrities, country music—"

"Will you two stop?"

Erin concentrated on her breakfast, but when she looked

up again, both Meg and Timmy were grinning. She couldn't help laughing too.

"You might have some fun, Erin."

Timmy examined his cast. "Yeah, Mom. You and Daddy could have fun together." His face changed expression with comic speed. "Ouch, Gram. Why'd you pinch me under the table?"

Erin rolled her eyes. Then she stood and carried her plate to the counter, rinsing it and placing it in the dishwasher before she spoke. "I said I'd think about it."

"Think fast, Mom. And say yes."

"I'll think later," she said. "Right now I'm going to be late for work."

"I'm telling you. They won't come," Danny told Luke, driving the pickup late that same morning across the state of Utah not far from the breathtaking spectacle of the Great Salt Lake. He and Luke were bound for Wyoming but taking their time. On the way, because Cheyenne—Luke's next scheduled clown stint—didn't start until the end of the week, they planned to buzz a smaller rodeo or two.

Erin's call the night before had soothed Danny's ruffled feathers, giving him hope, but he still felt certain she'd refuse about Cheyenne.

"Maybe your mother will talk Erin into coming," Luke said. "Tim too. That's a pretty formidable pair."

Danny laughed. "They spent enough time throwing us together at the ranch. I suppose they might wear her down."

But he wanted Erin to decide herself, to come because she wanted to. The thought didn't soothe him. Knowing Erin, she might dither until Cheyenne was over.

Luke unwrapped a chaw of bright pink bubble gum and stuck it in his cheek. "It'd be nice if Meg came."

Swinging the camper around an uphill curve against a robin's egg blue sky, Danny glanced at him.

"What's this?"

"What?" Luke looked innocent.

"You and my mother," he said. She had kissed Luke's cheek when they left and told him to come back. Nothing more than she'd tell any welcome visitor but . . . "You haven't left off talking about her since we turned out of the driveway at Paradise Valley."

Luke chewed the gum. "It's been a while since I ate good home cooking, that's all."

"Hell," Danny said. "Are we talking about blueberry pie and apple cobbler? Clean sheets for the camper bed? Your jeans hung out to dry in the fresh air? I don't think so."

"What the hell are *you* talking about?"

"I don't think I ever had a more ridiculous thought than the one about you turning into my stepfather some day."

Luke snorted. "Erin pushed you over the edge, has she? You gone nuts, Sinclair?" He worked the gum furiously. "You better not ride this week before Cheyenne. Your mind is gone."

"Maybe. Maybe not."

"What would I want with a woman"—his gaze lifted—"except, say, some young barrel racer? Like the one keeps chasing you down everywhere we go? A female for a night or two?"

"She chases you too. I'm just not usually as short with her as you are."

"I can't be bothered, except on my own terms."

Danny didn't know whether to smile. His mother was still a looker, and he swore he'd seen Luke give her the once-over several times, including the day he arrived at the ranch. But Meg Sinclair and Luke Hastings?

She was the most married woman he'd ever known. Luke was the opposite, a horse who'd never been branded. And Meg was Danny's *mother*, for God's sake.

He settled his Broncos cap farther back on his head. "How long ago was your divorce?"

The gum snapped in Luke's jaw. "Fifteen years. Which you damn well know. Why?"

"A man gets lonely."

"A man gets horny too. Doesn't mean he wants to marry some woman who'll tie him down to the bedpost. Spend the rest of his life craving the smell of greasepaint and bull sweat."

Danny grinned. "I caught her looking your way a time or two. If she and Tim ever get on your case, you better watch out."

"Damn you, Danny."

The camper crested another hill then dropped down a long, sweeping arc of scenic road that took his breath away. He was glad to be on the move again.

"I'm looking out for my mother, that's all."

"I'm a free man and plan to stay that way. So are you— unless Erin changes her mind."

Danny wished for that, prayed for it. But goading Luke, he suddenly felt like Ken. Which reminded Danny, never mind his invitation to Cheyenne, that he was not only all but divorced, despite his own convictions; he was a man without a home to go back to some day.

Erin rode away from the ranch, letting Kemosabe pick his pace through the green valley up into the higher hills. Since Danny had been gone, since he'd left her to handle the horse on her own again, she and the paint gelding had come to an agreement.

Erin would feed him—with Timmy's help—and Kemosabe would stop looking at her with that placid, blameful expression. The horse hadn't moved a muscle wrong since those few moments in the corral.

If only she could erase the memory of that haunted look in Danny's eyes so easily with a few carrots, an apple, a soft pat on his silky hide.

Clucking, she nudged the horse into a lope. Danny planned to have him trailered soon to some rodeo where Kemosabe would re-enter roping competition, leased to one of Danny's acquaintances for a share of the winnings. When the horse left, Timmy would be heartbroken.

The trail wound upward into the thinning mountain air, but even on this warm July afternoon she breathed easier. In the higher mountains, it was said, the air could be so clear photographers often used filters to avoid overexposure. Her element, and long ago, Danny's.

She still didn't know about joining him for Frontier Days. Did she think to find the answer here, alone among the hills and deepening shadows before dusk?

Inhaling, Erin caught the scents of pine and wildflowers, of water from the small, clean stream that ran through the hills like a silver ribbon shining in the sun. Near sunset, it looked silver-gold, as if she'd discovered a long-neglected mother lode in the mountains that might solve all her problems. Pay her bills. Save the Bitterroot Emporium. Cool her spirit whenever she thought of Danny.

Suddenly, she smiled.

As children she and Danny had often ridden double on his favorite mare along this same trail.

"Look, Erin!" He'd twisted one day in front of her and pointed. "The stream's a river of gold. We're rich!"

"That's only the light."

"No, it's pure gold." He kicked the mare into a canter, nearly making Erin lose her seat. She wrapped her arms more tightly around his waist. "I'll buy you the world."

Now Erin urged Kemosabe faster. His tendon had healed completely, and she had to admit she'd miss him when he went. It felt good to be outdoors, with the flex of a horse's back muscles beneath her, away from the store and her worries, the wind blowing through her hair, the mountains coming ever closer.

When she reached the sod house, the place where she'd

felt closest to Danny, she let Kemosabe graze on the lush grass, and slipping off his bare back, allowed the place to call to her once more.

Like their love then, a century before Montana had been new. Danny's forebears settled this land, claiming it as their own, and preparing for a first, harsh winter, had built the sod house into the side of the hill.

It still looked the same.

How many times as a girl had she come here, alone or with Danny, though not often with Ken? This was her hiding place, her playhouse, her dreaming space. And then one day she wasn't a little girl and Danny wasn't a growing boy. He'd kissed her one night at the top of a Ferris wheel, and afterward light kisses wouldn't do.

Reaching the house, she ran a hand over the half broken window frame—the only window—then pushed at the creaky door. It opened on rusted hinges, and she stepped inside.

Darkness. Dampness. Like the cellar at her store.

She sniffed the scents of mold and mildew, and heard the scurrying of tiny feet across the dirt-packed floor but didn't run outside.

Dad says not to play in here, Danny had told her the first time she brought him. *He says it could cave in. You can help me shore it up.*

Through the years she'd carried discarded plates and glasses here, a worn red-checked tablecloth that Meg had put in the trash, a blanket . . .

Erin rubbed her bare arms against the chill air inside the sod house. Her small home with Garrett had never felt as cozy. This was hers, and Danny's.

Standing in the open doorway, letting in the light of late afternoon, she could almost see the two of them, Danny, tall and lean at eighteen, at twenty, Erin, slim and budding at fifteen, at seventeen . . .

Up the hill riding double, bareback, they talked and

laughed, or sometimes said not a word. In sunlight they came and in rain and, once, that all-important time, had nearly been trapped in the hills by the season's first snowfall.

We should go back, Danny said. *If Dad finds us both missing, he'll be mad as hell that we came here. I think Ken knows too. If we—*

Hush, Erin told him, spreading the Hudson's Bay blanket she'd borrowed from Meg's linen closet while Danny laid a fire in the old hearth.

Intimacy happened slowly, one touch—at first accidental—one kiss at a time.

Now she turned back inside, reassuring herself that the blanket was still there on the makeshift wooden shelf along one wall; that the glasses they'd used last still stood on the metal counter. She picked one up, fingering its rim, imagining Danny's mouth there. Imagining his mouth still wet from drinking, then at her breast.

Just let me kiss you. Hold you. With his arms around her, he'd lowered her to the blanket, lying with her instead of sitting beside her to talk and eat the snacks they carried from home. *Just a while longer.*

As it began to snow outside, unbeknownst to them, his kisses grew, teasing, then tempting until Erin's breathing sounded harsh, like his, and she couldn't deny him.

For two years Danny had been on the road during the season, making a name for himself in rodeo—roping events and occasional bull riding, which frightened Erin but increasingly exhilarated him. They'd had their first quarrel about it. He'd been rodeoing since childhood; what was different now, at twenty? The bulls, Erin said, instead of steers. The danger. If she didn't approve, as Hank didn't, she feared he'd stop coming home at all.

His hand sought her breast, his thumb caressed her nipple through her soft cotton shirt.

Show me, Danny, she'd whispered in his ear. *Show me what it's like.*

She set the glass on the counter, folded the now-faded blanket and put it on the shelf. Then she went out into the lowering sunlight.

Sitting with her back against the sod house front, she remembered the color and feel of his skin by firelight, his weight, the first, piercing pain and then the first, fierce pleasure. She remembered his loving words of praise and entreaty. And finally, her own words of shattering satisfaction.

I love you, Danny. I'll love you always.

She had lost her virginity in this place of darkness, dampness. She'd loved Danny Sinclair that snowy afternoon with every fiber of her being.

What had happened to the love they shared? To Danny's promise to buy her the world with a river of gold?

Erin called to Kemosabe. She gathered the horse's reins and swung up onto his back. Then she rode down from the hills into the valley, the sun at their backs raining golden fire.

She would go to Cheyenne. She'd give Timmy some healing time with his father, who needed him too. She would watch Danny ride again—fear for him again. In the process, she would stop wondering about the love they'd lost.

Then at last she could resettle her life.

12

The state of Montana appropriately took its name from the Spanish word for mountain. Rodeo in that language meant round-up, and Erin wished exactly that—that the ordeal before her in Wyoming would corral itself neatly, and end.

Cold panic curled in the pit of her stomach. The city of Cheyenne, a dusty mix of modern and Victorian, tried in vain to welcome her. All around her the crowd in Frontier Park's arena clamored for action under a cloudless summer sky, though Erin didn't notice. A vendor passed, his cardboard tray set with cones of cotton candy like rings in a jeweler's case, but the sugary scent only increased her nausea—as did the sulfer smell of a nearby oil refinery—and whetted Timmy's appetite.

"Can I have one, Mom?"

"You had one during the bareback bronc riding." She leaned close to his ear. "If you don't ask until after Daddy rides, I'll reconsider."

Until then her nerves, already splintered from the rocket burst above the park that had signaled the afternoon's rodeo start, would shriek as if to drown out the crowd's excitement for the ten-day extravaganza known as "The Daddy of Em All." Of course, traditionally, bull riding would be the last event. A crowd pleaser, a man's test of bravery. People loved to be vicariously scared out of their wits at the very thought of a Brahma bull getting loose in the crowd.

Erin frowned at her program, which invited her to "Live the Legend," to be part of the largest outdoor rodeo in the world with more than a thousand contestants and a purse approaching half a million dollars. She tried to be impressed. Twelve to fifteen thousand onlookers filled the arena on this first day of competition, and she'd heard there wasn't a bed available in Cheyenne.

Erin, Meg, and Timmy had been lucky to get a room—two of them. Finally, Danny's contact in the rodeo office had located an inexpensive motel on the far outskirts of town surrounded by area ranches. Erin barely noticed the room when they checked in the night before. Clean, neat, and spartan, it would do. Intent on surviving the sight of Danny on a bull again, she noticed nothing more.

That had been Friday, a week after Danny left Paradise Valley. All evening, while they toured Cheyenne, its newer shop front windows gaily painted with such slogans as, "Ya-hoo!" and "Welcome, Cowboys!" while Danny and Timmy glued themselves to each other during dinner, Erin dreaded the arena's familiar smells of horseflesh and cattle, which she'd always loved; but most of all, she dreaded the bulls themselves.

Shifting on her seat, a prime location in the lower level center of the East Stand above the bucking chutes, she tried to push away the fluttering in her stomach. She wished she had listened to Ken.

"Stay home," he'd said as he helped Meg and Erin pack

the Jeep. "You've seen him ride before. Too many times."
She couldn't disagree until he added, "What's the point?"

"Unfinished business," was all she said.

Eight years ago she'd sat ringside at a rodeo in Cody,
hunched in her seat as she felt like doing now, waiting,
praying. *Please, God, let him be all right.*

Danny hadn't won at Cody. If he got tossed today, and
hurt, how would she comfort her little boy? Why didn't he
understand how she had felt when a huge black bull with
enormous horns spiraled into the air, making her young
husband lose his balance and his grip? In front of her eyes,
not thirty feet from Erin's seat at the rail, that bull had
flung Danny as if he weighed no more than Timmy's
stuffed monkey, slamming him to the ground. The back of
his head had hit the dirt first.

She could still hear the collective gasp from the crowd as
Luke Hastings raced in to distract the bull. Luke's clown
role was critical. A bucking horse simply wanted a man off
its back; but a bull wanted revenge, not with just anyone,
but with the rider who tried to tame him. Erin had seen
more than one bull single a man out of half a dozen. Before
Luke reached Danny, the Brangus—half Brahma, half
Black Angus—butted him, lifting him into the air on one
curved, sharp horn.

Erin put a hand now to her mouth, as if to stop her
scream then. The bull riding at Cheyenne was just beginning, and as usual before each ride, the crowd fell quiet.
In the ring one of the newer riders on the circuit—a boy, in
Erin's mind—shot from the chute on a dark red bull with
scraggly horns.

The audience, always frozen at first as if uncertain how to
react to the bull riding spectacle, came alive a few seconds
into the ride. The longer a cowboy stayed on, the greater
the noise—unless something went drastically wrong as it
had for Danny.

Her mind slipped back again to his motionless form in

the dirt at Cody. One of the hazers had tried to throw a loop around the loose bull but missed, and the black bull, bellowing, went rampaging about the ring until someone else managed to herd it back into the chute.

By then, Danny was being carried on a stretcher from the arena, the crowd cheering his bravery.

He hadn't lasted five seconds on that bull. He'd suffered a bad concussion, dislocated his shoulder, and barely escaped serious internal injuries. A few days later, as soon as he gained his feet again, Erin had packed her bags for Paradise Valley, not knowing she was already pregnant.

"Mom?" Timmy tugged at her arm. "When's Daddy's turn?"

On Erin's other side Meg consulted the program.

"Two more," she said. "Excited?"

"Yeah! He's gonna win!"

A gun signaled eight seconds, and the young rider in the ring slid from the red bull's back to the ground.

Erin let out her breath. Safe.

"It'll be all right." Timmy patted her. "If Daddy knew you worried, he'd worry too. And he might fall off."

He made sense, but Meg didn't look that certain of Danny's victory either, and Erin herself wished she hadn't come. She hated the shouting, hated even the light shining in Luke Hastings's eyes as he turned from clowning in the ring to give them a thumbs up sign. The entire show seemed barbaric, like bearbaiting or throwing Christians to the lions. Or was Luke peering only at Meg?

Erin studied her.

"What?" Meg asked.

"I guess you're glad you're here." Distracting herself, she nodded toward Luke, trotting around the ring in the few seconds between bull rides, imitating a horse, and releasing one by one a series of brightly colored balloons from the rear pocket—or so it appeared—of his baggy pants.

"I guess I am," Meg murmured.

Erin started at the next explosion of bull and rider from one of the chutes. This was why she had come, for the last time, to prove to herself how sensible she was making a life for herself and Timmy far away from such brutality and danger.

The rider, a man high in the standings, flew off a mangy tan bull named Sneaky Pete, and Erin's mouth went dry. She couldn't stomach this life—Danny's chosen life. He'd always loved rodeo more than he loved her.

The next rider just before Danny was in and out of the ring before she blinked. At Cheyenne, probably because of the number of entrants, the fast action often seemed to coincide. At times two or three riderless bulls could be seen ambling around the arena.

"There's Daddy! I see him—See him, Mom? In the chute!"

Not that far from them Danny climbed on to the bull he'd drawn for the first round. Mozart, she remembered. She had long before committed the name to memory. It sounded harmless enough. Whimsical, almost.

Danny looked all business. His eyes hard, just beneath the downtilt of his straw hat. His mouth set. One fist pounding the other hand tight around the gummy-coated rope rigging. The same routine, the same concentrated expression she'd seen a hundred times.

Timmy stood on his seat, waving his arms and yelling. Meg rose too, one arm around her favorite boy and calling to the other. "Go get 'em, Daniel!"

Before he nodded the signal to open the chute gate, Danny glanced around. He looked up—Could he really hear and see Timmy and Meg? Could he see *her*?—and grinned around his white mouth guard.

The gate opened but Erin didn't hear. Meg lasted two seconds before her faith seemed to collapse along with her courage, and she pushed past into the aisle. Erin stayed in her seat, biting hard on her lower lip, and prayed.

Keep him safe.

Danny's own mental litany colored the already dusty-blue air in the arena. He'd drawn killer stock. He needed points and money. He needed a chiropractor.

Determined to win after his fall at Elko and another at a small rodeo on the way to Cheyenne, he focused his mind, shutting out everything else. Most bull riders fell most of the time. It was part of the sport. He just didn't intend to get dumped this afternoon in front of Tim.

His bull damn near twisted his head off on the first spin to the right. Mozart tipped Danny so far off his center that he had to fight his way back. His muscles screamed, the tendons in his wrist stood out, his veins bulged. He had himself balanced, his form close to perfect again, when the big Brahma snapped him around like the Tilt-A-Whirl ride at the Sweetwater fair.

Cursing, Danny hung on, praying for the eight second gun and a clean, safe dismount. Praying he wouldn't get hung up now, in front of Erin.

Dull-roweled spurs digging in, he thumped the bull, anticipating its next move by instinct.

The big Brahma spun counterclockwise, throwing Danny left then right again, as if sensing his own moves to compensate. By sheer grit and experience, he clung, feeling the exhilaration; the bull rope tight exactly as it should be; his legs in position; his weight balanced—his hat still on.

Stomach muscles clenched, he rode that bull to the gun, feeling pride sweep through him when it cracked loud enough to wake the dead who'd perished in this same arena.

He started to grin. Another half second, and he would have avoided falling into the "whirlpool," the hooves and horns of a spinning bull stomping a man into the dirt. He'd be home free without a nasty wreck. He grinned too soon.

The dismount was all-important, like the getaway afterward to safety. But where were the rodeo clowns? That easy slide from bull's back to the ground?

Another bull roamed the opposite end of the arena, being chased by Luke and the barrel man, and a rider had just burst from the chute. Cowboys scattered atop the surrounding fence like ornaments on a saddle.

A split second passed, no more. And Danny didn't think so much as exist on his adrenaline high. But in that brief time before he could jump and make a run for the fence, the bull snaked underneath him like water flowing beneath the sand.

Too late, Danny felt its muscles bunch. Mozart leaped high into the air, swiveled his hips like a bad rock musician— and dumped Danny in the dirt, his bull rope slipping free, the bell clanging. Unable to manage the fall, he came down hard on one hip, and pain shot through his side.

Eighty-eight points!

Meg huddled near the back door of Danny's camper in the Cowboy Campground parking lot outside the arena. How long before Erin came looking for her and discovered her cowardice? She swallowed again, the bitter taste at the back of her throat still there. Shaking, she reached for the door latch.

"Come on in."

A deep voice from the camper's interior startled her into withdrawing her hand. She thought the camper would be empty. She had turned to go when the screen door swung open and Luke Hastings lifted her into the dark interior.

"I was looking for Erin," she lied.

"She's still at the arena. So's Tim." Luke gazed at her. "Couldn't take it anymore?"

The first thing she saw was the bed. Avoiding even a glance in that direction, Meg settled onto the off-white, plastic-upholstered table bench he indicated with a sweep of one hand. The once-white glove in front of her face made her blink. Then her gaze traveled upward over his baggy pants and bright green suspenders to his striped shirt. It had a tear at one shoulder, and dirt streaked the red-and-white fabric. What could be so strangely intimate about sitting at a plain table in such a small space talking to a clown?

"I followed Daniel to rodeos most of his boyhood," she said. "I patched him up for the ride home more than once. Why would you think I can't take it, Mr. Hastings?"

Leaning an elbow on the Formica table, she rested her head on her hand. She was too old for this. Her heart wouldn't last. Danny on that bull . . . and she had looked forward to the trip, thought she could handle seeing him ride.

Luke sat across from her. The air in the camper seemed stifling, as if all the oxygen had leeched from it into the summer-hot day outside. Not a breath of a breeze stirred, and Meg's head began to pound.

"Why?" Luke said. "I imagine the paper-white look of your skin, that sweat beading your upper lip made me think some." He cocked his head. "You a white-knuckle flyer too? Or you just like gripping the seat in that arena?"

"My son is a professional. He's made his living from bulls for almost twenty years."

"You're scared to death for him."

She wouldn't let him know he was right.

Meg glanced into Luke's face and nearly laughed. His white greasepaint, the darker rays around his eyes, the streaks bracketing his mobile mouth looked ridiculous. Those black lines made his mouth appear soft and vulnerable.

"Your makeup's running," she said.

"Yours has up and gone already."

Unconsciously, she raised her hand, touching one eye and then her mouth. It felt dry, parched. She couldn't have a trace of lipstick on, or the thin eyeliner she so rarely used either. She didn't know why she had bothered.

"I must look a mess."

Luke's gaze settled on her lips. "You look fine to me—a bit pasty, that's all." As if he couldn't sit any longer, he jumped up to prowl the tiny kitchenette. Opening a frosty Coke from the half-pint refrigerator, he handed her the can then took one for himself. "Drink up. You need the caffeine. Wish I had something stronger to offer, which might relax you instead, but I don't. Me and Danny drank the only six-pack last night. After he dropped you, Tim, and Erin at the motel."

"He's hurting, isn't he?"

Luke took a swallow. "Plumb through, I imagine. Tomorrow he'll feel worse. Don't expect him to say so."

Meg didn't mean his injuries from today. "If he and Erin weren't so much alike in that—both stubborn—they might have mended things years ago." She paused, glad to have changed the subject. "I'm not sure they ever will now."

"Some things aren't meant to be."

"And that suits you?"

Luke leaned against the counter in stocking feet, those baggy pants, still wearing the grimy white gloves like some disheveled maitre d' in a fancy restaurant gone bad.

"You and Daniel have been together for a long time, practically since he left home and you got divorced."

"What are you saying?" The faint smile that always lingered, expanding the wide clown's mouth, had become a grim line.

Meg twisted the Coke can between her hands.

"It's to your benefit that Danny and Erin stay apart. That you keep him as single as you are yourself."

"A man doesn't live with his wife for eight years, he might as well be single."

That was Erin's view too, but Meg felt differently. She'd spent nearly forty years with Hank, and married in her book would always be better than single.

"What about you, Luke?" She met his gaze. "Do you like

being on your own that much? Without anyone to care for you?" She smiled faintly. "To bake you apple cobbler?"

"My wife didn't know a stove from a pickup truck."

She knew nothing about him. But she'd seen the lost look in those warm brown eyes the instant he stepped into her kitchen. He wasn't as footloose as he sounded.

"Did she travel with you?"

"No, ma'am. She stayed at home—in Oklahoma—on my daddy's ranch." He shifted his weight, arms folded across his chest, gaze fixed on the small hole in the toe of one sock. "Where she fell for his foreman. Dumped me flat to marry him," he said. "They've got four kids."

"Do you have any—"

"None that I know of."

Meg felt her cheeks warm, reminiscent of the hot flashes she'd suffered over the past few years.

"You rough and tumble cowboys," she said in her best scolding mother tone. Pushing the soda can across the table, she stood, feeling weak—from the heat, she supposed.

"I had three mischievous boys, Mr. Hastings, any number of untutored hired hands over the years, an insensitive foreman here and there . . . and a husband who, despite his flaws, never embarrassed a woman in his life. I'm not that easy to shock"—she glanced at his clownish attire before turning toward the camper door—"and I doubt you're that much of a ladies' man."

"Mrs. S—Meg," he said, coming up behind her as she twisted the screen door knob. "I don't have much call for manners on the road. Me and Danny, we tolerate each other's rudeness. Machismo, you might say. Part of the game. But I do apologize."

"I guess I came too close to a raw place."

"Maybe you did."

She didn't turn around but felt his closeness, the heat transferring from his body to hers, Luke Hastings's front against her spine. Nearly touching. He stood taller than

Hank had, his surprisingly broad shoulders all but blocking out what little light filtered through the front alcove window across the camper's bed.

When he said her first name again, all but whispering it, she didn't answer. Didn't know whether the slow drumming in her blood was his heart beating, or hers.

"There'll be a dance tonight. Save me one," he said. "I promise to behave myself."

"I'm not sure there's anything to dance about."

"Danny's okay. Don't you worry."

She hadn't waited to see what happened. The chute gate opened, the bull burst into the arena, her son—her youngest son now—fought, not for eight seconds of glory, but for his life. And she ran like an untrained horse.

"I wasn't worried. I—the heat in the arena made me feel faint, that's all. Too many people breathing at once. I came outside for some air of my own."

"He landed on his butt but he didn't break nothing."

Still holding the doorknob, she felt it slip against her wet palm. She was a rancher's wife and would be till her dying day. She'd seen Danny fall before, saw them all get thrown. Hank, Ken …

"I don't want to lose him," she said.

And feeling foolish that she'd let Luke Hastings see into her heart, she blindly stepped out into the hot, dry summer air.

"Don't lie to me, Danny Sinclair. You *are* hurt."

"I'm fine, I tell you."

With Erin and Tim on either side, Danny led the way from the arena through the same exit he saw his mother use an hour before.

Gritting his teeth against the cramp in his leg, his own need to limp a little, he kept his strides long and steady. Tim gripped his hand, and Danny fought the urge to crush it against the sharp twinge in his side. He'd fallen hard the first round but damned if he'd let Erin, or anyone else, see how much he hurt.

He wanted her and Tim to cheer him, to applaud his scores, not to pick at him or put him to bed with ice on his wounds.

"Where are you going?" she asked.

"To the camper for a cold drink. To take off my boots before my feet swell in this heat."

"The drink can wait. Your boots too."

"To collect my winnings," he added.

"Your prize money will be there. Nobody's going to cash your check." He'd won second place that day, but Erin didn't seem to notice. "You belong in the medical tent, Danny. Right now."

"Bull—" He broke off, glancing at Tim. "Blame it all, Erin. I'm okay." He looked at her and grinned. His jaw ached. "Nice of you to care, though. Sometimes I wonder."

She made an exasperated sound, which Tim overrode.

"You did great, Daddy! You really showed 'em!" He looked around. "I wish Gram saw you. Where did she go, Mom?"

"Probably to buy you that cotton candy you keep screaming about," Danny said. He tightened his hold on Tim's hand and, taking care not to wince, slung an arm around Erin's shoulder before she could protest, or move away. "Your grandma's got the right idea. Come on, you two. In eight seconds that last round this cowboy made eighty-two points on one nasty bull with a bad attitude. That money doesn't happen every day."

"That's the truth," Erin said.

"Eighty-eight points the first round!" Timmy crowed.

"Pretty good," Danny agreed, "two rank bulls," not willing to let Erin dampen his second-place victory. "I'll do better next time. Let's celebrate."

He had his own plans for later.

13

In any rodeo town cowboys choose a favorite watering hole, their preferred gathering place to drink beer after a thirsty ride, hear some music, and listen to each other's tall tales from that day's performance, or any other. Erin had always likened these informal yet strictly prescribed evenings to fraternity bashes, its "brothers" just as uniformly dressed as those on any university campus. Cheyenne proved no exception to either the dress code or the night's choice of entertainment.

At the Hitching Post/Best Western, she sat in a corner with Timmy and Meg while Luke and Danny joined the others of their kind stacked three-deep at the bar to order drinks. Timmy had requested a Shirley Temple, hoping for a paper umbrella with it, but Erin could tell he was fighting to stay awake. It had been a long, nerve-wracking day, including a late afternoon thunder shower, and she craved sleep herself, but Danny and Luke showed no signs of tiring. They could run on adrenaline for days. Even Meg, her gaze straying to the bar, didn't show fatigue.

At the bar Luke, in civilian clothes, blended in with a score of men in boots, crisp jeans, tautly tapered shirts without wrinkles, and hats. Like them, he stood medium height with broad shoulders and a well-muscled frame that seemed to belie his years. Only Danny, who was tall for a bull rider, and a few timed-event cowboys known for their size and brawn stood out from the rest.

Danny outshone even them. He had star presence, she couldn't deny that; in a room filled with a hundred men exhibiting the rodeo athlete's standard charisma, she easily picked him out, his back to her as he waited for their drinks. Erin stared at the gleam of dark hair, the straight line of it at his nape, the sweet, vulnerable back of that neck, which could so quickly be broken in a fall from some bull. She noted his erect posture, the hint of muscle at either side of his spine barely discernible through the fabric of his blue-striped Western shirt; the slim waist and trim seat of his de rigueur Wranglers, scrawled with that telltale W across both rear pockets; his best black tooled boots polished to a mirror shine.

Timmy pulled at the sleeve of her jade-green cotton sweater. "Aren't you glad Daddy won today?"

"I'm glad he left that ring in one piece."

Meg's smile seemed a reproach. "Second place," she said, "at Cheyenne. That's something to feel proud about."

"Danny knows how I feel."

Meg bit her lower lip as if to keep from saying more. Timmy kicked the leg of Erin's chair. Feeling guilty, she looked away, her gaze colliding with a stranger's.

The girl was young, no more than twenty-two or -three, and blond, perhaps not naturally so. She didn't have an ounce of fat, no softened belly or violin-shaped hips from childbearing. Her earrings and the necklace dangling into the cleft between her firm breasts were liquid silver studded with turquoise, in an Indian Ye–figure motif. Her skimpy teal-blue top left inches of sleek skin bare between ribs and slender waist, and her dark jeans clung to her like shrink-wrap.

Erin suddenly felt plain in her green sweater and simple tan chino skirt. As she watched, the younger woman's gaze drifted from hers toward the bar, homing in, Erin felt sure, on Danny. She had to admit, he was the best-looking man there. The sexiest.

"Mom." Timmy tugged at her arm again. "Why does that lady wear a shirt that doesn't fit?"

Meg answered, hiding a smile. "It fits too well, favorite boy." She tried to turn Timmy's chair to face her. "And you're too young to notice."

Timmy swiveled back. "Why is she looking at Daddy?"

"I think we should go," Erin said, but her words got lost in the blare of music from the bar's stereo system, a song of Chris LeDoux's that she'd heard when she and Danny first married. He'd played the cowboy singer's tape to ribbons then bought another copy. "It's getting late, Meg. If you want a beer with the men"—with Luke, she meant—"I can take Timmy back to the motel."

"I wanna stay here. Daddy said we can go to the dance."

"Think you can two-step with your grandma?" Danny came back to the table, carrying Timmy's Shirley Temple complete with paper parasol, and two beers, one for himself, one for Erin.

"I'm not really thirsty," she said without looking up, afraid she'd find Danny staring over her head at that blond buckle bunny. The kind of girl he saw every week, every night after a rodeo.

"Loosen up, Erin." He slid onto the chair beside her and, bringing drinks for himself and Meg, Luke sat next to her mother-in-law. "Besides," Danny said, "you promised to save me a dance."

"I promised no such thing."

"It's either that," he said, grinning, "to keep me loose

after that fall, or spend the rest of the night icing down my muscles."

"In your dreams," Erin told him, smiling in spite of herself into her beer glass. Icing his wounds had always led to other things.

Danny drank from his bottle. He always said beer tasted better that way. "I guess you've forgotten how to dance."

"You taught her," Timmy piped up, twirling the tiny paper umbrella. "Gram said so. You and Uncle Ken showed Mom how to dance."

"Uncle Ken's had more turns than I have lately."

"No one's had a turn," Erin said.

She hadn't danced since her honeymoon in Las Vegas—at another rodeo—if she could call that a honeymoon. The story of her married life, beginning to end. She looked at the tabletop but didn't move her hand in time. Danny covered it with his, and his body heat warmed her like a wood stove on a winter night.

"That so?" he said, sounding pleased. "Then everybody drink up. Let's go dancing."

Before he could rise from his chair, another bull rider came over. Not waiting for an invitation, he sat down, regaling them in turn with that afternoon's anecdotes, then those from another rodeo—one Danny had missed.

"You should have seen 'im, Sinclair." The tow-headed cowboy tipped back in his chair, laughing at his own story. "This kid's on board, the chute flies open, that bull blasts out six feet in the air from the get-go. The kid looks like 'what the hell's happening' and then he's sailing, his bull rope with him like a streamer, that bell clangin' like hell—heck, excuse me, ma'am"—he looked at Meg—"then he's on his britches in the middle of the ring. He and that Brahma never touched ground until his but—bottom—went thud in the dirt."

Danny's hand twitched on hers but he laughed with Luke, and so did Meg. Timmy giggled appreciatively at the man's story.

"Where were you then?" the man asked Danny.

"In Montana . . . home."

He glanced at Erin. "A woman needs tending now and again, I guess. You'da been in the points for sure, though, Sinclair. You missed Rancho Murietta too, didn't you?"

"Yeah," Danny said, his voice quiet.

The California site was part of the Bull Riders Only tour. For top riders, with bull riding the only event, it provided stiff, exciting competition and good money. Erin studied her hand, laced with his.

Danny was currently ranked high in the national standings. She'd read about him in *Pro Rodeo Sports News* before leaving the ranch.

The man scraped back his chair and stood. "You been headin' for the finals this year. Hope you don't miss out."

"I'll try not to."

"Gonna get you a gold buckle one of these days, Danny," he said, "if I don't get mine first."

"Good luck."

Danny watched the other bull rider rejoin his friends at the bar, then no longer smiling, he drew Erin to her feet.

"Let's find that dance."

Erin didn't have the heart to refuse. When they reached Frontier Park's fairground and heard the first strains of a ballad, she went into Danny's arms as if she'd never left. That seemed bad enough, betraying herself. His newly somber mood seemed worse. Barely moving to the small live group's plaintive rendition of "I Will Be Your Man," she sighed.

"Why do I feel it's my fault that you missed Rancho Murietta?"

"It's not your fault."

"I needed help at the store and you stayed."

"I wanted to, Erin." He turned her lightly, bringing a flood of memories—other dances, other songs—all of which she wanted to avoid. Like the thick, molasses-warm flow of her blood in her veins and the growing heaviness low in her body pressed too close to Danny's.

"For a while," she said. "But that man made you yearn for the open road again, didn't he? For another eighty-eight points, another good check?"

"That's how I make my living."

"It's more than that." She raised her head from his solid shoulder, where she hadn't even realized she was resting. "It's your way of life."

He pressed her cheek back again, his tone dry.

"That's what you hate most, isn't it? Not that I rodeo full-time, which not many men can do, or leave you and Tim alone." He moved naturally, in rhythm with the song, the bittersweet cry of the background violin. "You hate that I love what I do, not that I'm good at it."

"Danny, I—"

"This afternoon, how did you feel when I was riding? Not when I got dumped after the gun but before that when everything was working just right. You've seen enough bull rides to know," he said. "You can recognize a textbook-perfect thing when you see it. How did you feel, Erin?"

She lifted her head to meet his gaze.

"Afraid," she murmured.

"Hell, I'm always afraid."

But his adrenaline rush carried him through. She'd always thought it was easier to ride than to watch someone else. She didn't imagine Danny would agree.

"When I stop being afraid, that's when I'll worry. You weren't only scared today."

"I didn't know you could read minds."

"Erin."

"All right," she said, raising a hand from his shoulder. "I felt proud of you. For Timmy's sake," she added.

Danny only smiled, sadly. He guided her head back onto his shoulder, fitted his body to hers, and hushed her when she would have spoken. His gait developed a slight hitch, but he kept going.

"You can tell yourself more stories than that bull rider tonight," he murmured.

To the sultry beat of the band and the summer night, in his oh-so-familiar arms, she lost track of time, of who she meant to be, of where she meant to remain. How did it happen? One beer at the Hitching Post. The warm, late July air smelling of barbecue and someone's perfume as a couple in red gingham and blue denim danced past, the stars overhead, visible over Danny's shoulder through the fairground tent flaps. Another beer or two, drifting to the music in Danny's arms once more, and somehow she lost the slim hold she kept on her life, and Timmy's.

When she lifted her head the next time from Danny's shoulder, it was after midnight and the music, which had alternated between dreamy ballads, classic country-western, and the lively square dancing that would go on every night, had turned even slower, sweeter.

A few feet away she saw Meg, to her astonishment dancing with Luke, his one arm around her waist, the other hand buried in her hair, both their eyes closed as if they'd been swaying there a while.

"Danny? Look." She pointed and felt him tense.

"God almighty."

"I think they look nice together."

"Luke's younger than she is . . . he's a wild man."

"If anyone could tame him, Meg could."

He frowned. "Nobody will ever hobble Luke Hastings. Least of all, my mother. I think I'll have a word with him."

Erin drew him back before Danny could take a determined step toward Luke.

"Leave them alone. It's harmless."

"I guess you're right." He worked the frown into a smile again. "Tomorrow morning Luke'll put on that greasy white stuff, stick another chaw of bubble gum in his cheek, and forget all about dancing—with my mother or anyone else."

She let him think what he would, but glancing at Meg's dreamy expression, at the contented half smile she wore so rarely since Hank's death, Erin wasn't that sure.

Then Danny jerked a thumb toward the far corner of the tent where Timmy lay curled into a tight ball on someone's buckskin jacket, thick fringe trailing across his cheek.

"He's worn out," she said. "I should take him home."

"Not yet."

Pausing here and there to speak to friends, Danny waltzed her outside, into the cooler night. Erin's cheeks felt heated and the idea seemed a good one, putting distance between them.

With an arm draping her shoulder, his step unsteady, Danny walked her toward the Cowboy Campground near the arena where he and Luke had staked out a place for the camper that week.

Erin matched her stride to Danny's, which seemed slower with every step, more halting.

"You're hurting, aren't you?"

"Feeling a little stiff." He smiled in the darkness. Fireflies winked from the rustling grass, and a distant owl hooted its lonesome call. He squeezed her shoulder. "My leg too," he said.

Erin faltered. "I should go. Timmy—"

"Mom will watch him."

They reached the darkened camper, but Danny didn't open the door or urge her inside. He sat down on the metal step, grunting with the effort, and pulled Erin onto his lap.

"What's your hurry? Going back to that motel room on a night like this?" He waved at the stars. "Getting into bed by yourself, that's a real waste."

His mouth covered hers, not hard, not abruptly, but with a sense of rightness, as if it were his still to claim. Soft, hot, pliant, his lips moved over hers until Erin thought he just might have that right. She opened her mouth, letting his tongue inside to taste and savor. Then without her realizing, he slipped the top button on her sweater, slid a hand inside onto her warm flesh, and down to a sensitive breast. Her nipple tightened in a flash and she moaned into Danny's mouth.

Seizing his advantage, he held her head in both hands, holding her still for his kisses, those kisses heating more with each sliding motion of mouth across mouth, each change of angle, each deepened penetration of his tongue, mimicking the act of love so long absent in her life.

Two more buttons, a clasp, and he had her free, both thumbs caressing the nipples that had hardened like the undone buttons on her sweater.

"Danny."

Pulling back, he held her gaze, his breathing harsh, his thumbs still circling. "You tell me this isn't good, or right. You tell me if you can. Tell me you forgot this—dammit—that you don't want it anymore." She could feel him under her, the back sides of her legs pressing down on his thighs, his erection pushing upward against her bottom.

She leaned her forehead against his neck. "I can't."

"Can't what?"

"Tell you."

"Tell me what?" he insisted.

"That I—don't want you."

He took her mouth again, murmuring the words into her moist darkness. *"Say it, then."*

"Mom? Daddy?" Timmy's sleepy voice came out of the blackness, startling Erin to her feet. "Are you at the camper? Where are you?"

"Over here, sweetheart." She held out a trembling hand, the other grasping her sweater shut. "I'm right here."

"Me too." Danny rose slowly from the metal steps and scooped Timmy into his arms before he could see Erin's rumpled state. "Did you wake up alone and wonder where we were?"

"No, I woke up and Gram and Uncle Luke said we should come get you. The dance is over. Are we all gonna sleep in the camper?"

Danny's laugh sounded more like a groan. "No way."

"You and I are going back to the motel." Erin rubbed Timmy's hair, her hand grazing Danny's on the back of Timmy's head. "Let's find Gram or you'll be grumpy tomorrow."

"I wanna see Daddy ride again."

Erin looked at Danny. "You will."

Nothing was going the way she'd planned. She had come to cure herself of Danny and his dreams. Now she felt feverish, restless, incomplete. Empty.

Luke emerged slowly from the darkness. "We interrupting anything?"

"Everything," Danny said over Timmy's head.

Meg followed Luke, a step behind, her hair glowing in the starlight, her eyes wide when they met Erin's. "It's time for bed, isn't it? Time to go to the motel, I mean."

Erin swore Meg's cheeks would be flaming red if it were light enough to see. Surely nothing had happened between her and Luke, with Timmy there.

She patted her tan skirt pocket for her keys.

Danny took them from her. He handed them to Meg.

"You and Tim go find the Jeep," he said. "Luke can walk you through the lot. Erin's staying here."

Meg stared at her, and Erin ran a still-shaking hand through her hair, mussed from Danny's fingers.

"We have two rooms," Meg said.

In Danny's arms, Timmy leaned close toward her, his gaze conspiratorial. "Gram, you said I could sleep with you tonight, taking turns." He'd slept with Erin the first night. "'Member? You promised."

"Yes I did."

Luke gave her a smile. "You got two rooms over there?"

"Yes," Meg said.

"Don't worry about me. I'm no sleepwalker." He gave Danny a once-over, lingering below his belt, then glanced at Erin. She could have sworn he saw right through her sweater to her unclasped bra. "Meg and Tim can have her room, I'll take Erin's." He paused, looking back at Danny. "Unless you'd rather move?"

"I can't."

Luke grinned. "Fresh sheets on the bed up front."

Erin's mouth fell open and Danny closed it with a kiss. "You're staying right here."

Before she knew it, he handed Timmy into Luke's arms for the walk to the Jeep, and opened the camper door. She and Meg exchanged a look. Then Meg, like a traitor, turned away, looping an arm through Luke's and blending into the darkness.

"Moms and dads are s'posed to sleep together. Aren't they, Gram?"

"They certainly are, favorite boy."

Erin stood by the camper's rear door, speechless. She hadn't agreed to anything, but even her seven-year-old son seemed to have made the decision for her. Meg too, and even Luke.

"Come on inside. This woman needs tending," Danny quoted the other bull rider earlier. In the open screened door, he held out a hand. "It's not too hot. There's a good breeze, and we can leave the door and windows open."

He'd tried his bull rider bravado the first night in Sweetwater. She wanted to tell him now, again, it wouldn't work; that she'd known him too long and too well. But that was just it. Climbing those three steps seemed natural, and so did turning into Danny's arms just inside, finding his sweet mouth with hers.

"What just happened here?" she asked when the kiss finally broke. Danny only flung his hat in the direction of the camper's table and opened his mouth over hers again.

"You know what."

"I guess I do." She tensed in his arms. "I imagine this is common practice on rodeo nights. I feel like one of those buckle bunnies."

"Erin, you know why you came here—to Cheyenne, the dance, this camper. And before you slap me, I don't mean simple sex."

"Oh," she said.

Breathless, she went back for more, then more after that. In the next moments, together they shed Danny's pearl-snapped, blue-striped shirt, then Erin's half-buttoned green sweater. His black boots, her low beige heels. His blue Wranglers, her tan skirt.

The dangling bra sailed onto the kitchenette bench with his briefs, her panties, then warm, scented flesh met warm, scented flesh. Erin pressed her breasts to his chest, her belly to his, her thighs to Danny's. She felt the hard jut of his arousal nestle into place, like a homing pigeon.

"Erin, Erin."

In the closely held darkness, in the small, private place they'd made, with the soft midnight breeze fluttering his hair and hers, he ran his hands over her, lightly at first, then with increasing ardor, lingering on a breast, finessing a nipple, sleeking over the outer edge of a thigh then up its inner, softer side. His hands, callused but gentle, felt like a teasing butterfly. One man in her life, she thought, just one. And couldn't imagine anyone better.

"You feel the same," he whispered, his mouth on hers.

"So do you." She breathed in. "But Danny, we aren't—"

"In all the ways that matter, we are."

With kisses, touches, he edged her toward the bed, lifting Erin onto the double mattress in the alcove and raising a faint scent of flowery fabric softener to mingle with the nighttime smells—moonlight, starlight, sultry summer air. She caught the scent of roasting marshmallows from someone's grill not far away, heard laughter float in through the screened window by the bed.

Danny followed her, smoothing his hands over her hair, his gaze silvery, intent.

"Touch me now."

They rolled together on the bed, centering themselves, facing each other, eyes on a level. Erin did as he asked, her fingers trailing whisper-soft over his sleek skin, like warm water over the hard muscle just beneath. She kissed his shoulder, his chest, the bud of a flat nipple that instantly rose in her mouth.

"God," he said.

In for a penny now, in for a pound, she wouldn't question the decision she hadn't quite made. Growing bolder, re-exploring, she moved lower on the bed, her hair brushing over Danny's washboard belly in the wake of her busy fingers, over the rise of his hipbone . . .

"Oh, Danny," she whispered, pausing.

He raised his head to look where she was looking. "It's nothing. Just a bruise."

"You get them all the time," she said for him.

But the contusion, appearing purple-black in the dim light through the window, made her blink. It was the size of his hand, or more, covering most of his right hip and flank, streaking across the hipbone. She'd felt such fear that afternoon. If he'd come off that ornery bull and landed wrong again . . .

Pressing moistened lips to the mottled spot, she closed her eyes, feeling the pain for him. The lesser of two evils. Another, thankful reprieve.

"Do you want some liniment?"

"Uh-uh. Just keep doing what you're doing." He moaned at the next graze of her mouth over his wounded skin. He twined a hand in her hair. "Erin, it's all right."

"No. No, it's not." Her hair sliding against his palm, she turned her head to look at him through the screen of her eyelashes. "It's just better than . . . the other."

"I wish I had you around after every ride." Half smiling,

he pointed at his ribs and a fainter bruise nearly as large. "If you want to kiss me better, keep going. There's plenty more."

Erin didn't smile. In that instant she would have done battle with the bull herself to spare Danny.

"I know," he said, his smile fading. "Come here."

Wrapping her tight in his arms, he rocked her until Erin's tears blinked dry without falling. He wiped her cheeks anyway, slow and gently, then rolled her beneath him, aligning his lean, hard body with her smaller, softer one. He dropped his mouth to hers, his knee opening her legs.

"There've been no women to speak of," he said.

"No men," Erin answered.

"Not Ken?"

She shook her head.

"Tell me, then."

Erin didn't need prompting. He deserved an answer to his earlier question. She couldn't hold back, or lie. The hollow ache inside her needed filling, and the only man who could ease it was lying over her now, waiting for the words.

"I want you, Danny."

He sighed, his breath rustling past her cheek.

"Remember that one song tonight at the dance? While we were both stepping close, pretending not to catch on fire?"

She thought she knew but kept silent. She couldn't trust her voice.

"From the day I met you, I've loved you," he said, his tone husky. He touched her ringless hand. "I never even thought of marrying anyone else. You know that, don't you?"

"Yes." She could hardly say the word.

His tone was fierce. "Erin, you're my woman." He nudged her legs wider, fitting himself to the empty space prepared for him. "I'm your man. I always have been." In the same half second it took to lower his mouth to hers, he slipped inside her, after eight long, empty years. "God. I always will be."

She stroked the bruise along his ribs, the other across his hip, but didn't mean only his wounds when she said, "Danny, please. Stop hurting."

She meant Trevor and all the years he'd felt unwelcome at Paradise Valley. She meant herself. Closing her eyes, kissing him, she lost herself again. As they began to move, together, to find the rhythm they had all but lost, she wondered why she'd fought it for so long.

Then she wondered, soaring with Danny to completion, what might happen if she trusted the feeling. The love.

14

In the middle of the night the air through the camper window blew gently over Erin's flushed skin as if Danny were still over her, breathing against her breast. Curled into the curve of his body, their legs intertwined, Erin came drowsily awake, the hot rise of body heat off his bare chest, his belly a surprising aphrodisiac countering the cooler night breeze.

She couldn't make herself get up and leave.

Her left hand trailed once over Danny's stomach before his stronger grip closed over hers.

"Is it morning yet?" His voice sounded lazy, even deeper than usual, bringing with it another rash of memories.

"Not quite." She squinted at her watch. "It's just after three."

"Time, then," he said. "I promised Tim we'd watch slack at seven."

Four more hours. She smiled.

"Time for what?"

He rolled, taking Erin with him deeper into the tangled

sheets onto a cool spot kissed by the predawn breeze. "Making love to my wife."

"Danny."

Opening his eyes, he caught her hand on the downswing, ready to graze his belly again, or lower, and held it to the streaming moonlight.

"I don't care whether you wear my ring or leave it in a drawer at home. It's only a symbol anyway to please the folks in town and at the Beaverhead County courthouse. What's between you and me doesn't need a marriage license—divorce papers either—and it sure as hell doesn't need a shiny ring."

She answered lightly but her pulse rate sped at his serious tone. "What's between us is elemental all right."

She groped with her other hand in the small space between their bodies, Danny lying half over her, swelling as they spoke, his penis stretched along the crease of her thigh. He grunted as her warm hand closed around him.

"That too," he said.

He dropped a kiss on her mouth, then one on the damp curve of her neck. He licked the spot, murmuring about her salty taste and how he'd missed her skin, how he would bathe her again with his kisses, with his tongue.

She didn't try to ease away. She let her heart race on as if she, not Danny, were on some lusty bull in the arena, trying to make the wonder, the power of it, last this time. When he moved over her, she was still holding him, warm and moist.

Outside she heard another couple drift past near the camper, heading for their own space, she supposed, in the Cowboy Campground. A bull rider or bronc buster, with some buckle bunny for the night? Their low, intimate laughter teased Erin's aroused senses like the breeze through the window. Farther away a dog howled.

"Baying at the moon," Danny said into her ear. "I know just how he feels. Sooner than I expected."

"Me too," Erin admitted.

He buried his face in the curve of her shoulder, his hands roaming her sides, coming to rest on her hipbones.

"It's good with us, Erin."

"It always was."

"I mean tonight too," he said. "When we started making love, I didn't think I'd last. It felt almost like the first time when we rode up to the sod house and made out and couldn't stop. Remember?"

"Yes." A woman never forgot that first time, that first man. She wished she could go back there vicariously in this bed, wipe out all their mistakes, make things—them—go right this time. "I remember."

He stopped nuzzling her neck.

"Then don't sound so sad." Braced on his elbows, he looked down at her, his hazel eyes as silvery in the moonlight as one of his prize buckles. "I didn't hurt you, did I? After all this time—"

He'd hurt her with hundreds of empty nights.

"No," she said.

"There really hasn't been anyone else?"

"I said there wasn't."

"I'm not trying to insult you, I just—well, I mean, if you're sore now . . . "

"I'm not sore." She stroked his hair. "I haven't been sore since the sod house—and Las Vegas, the first week we were married."

Danny smiled at her. "Remember my scores there?"

Erin groaned. "You drew a bad bull, an eliminator, for the first round."

"And got dumped twice after that. Know why?"

"I distracted you?" She should have stayed home, stayed single.

"I couldn't concentrate," he said, "for thinking of you. I couldn't wait to get off those bulls and back to that motel, that bed." He paused. "I know that wasn't much of a honeymoon, but it wasn't so bad. Was it?"

Erin felt his hips flex experimentally against hers. She couldn't help smiling at how wrong she'd been.

"I won fifty dollars in the slot machines."

Danny's gaze darkened. "I won more than that."

His hands slid down her ribcage, brushing the side swell of her breasts, before settling on her hips once more. The cradle of her pelvis seemed to have a mind all its own, as it always had near Danny.

"You're not sleepy, are you?" he asked.

Erin smiled into his earnest expression. "Not with you on top of me, after that prize-winning performance."

"Yesterday afternoon?"

She should have known he'd refer to his bull riding again, his scores and the money he'd won. She was jealous but not for the reasons Danny might choose; she was jealous, insanely so, because rodeo—the sport he loved beyond all else—threatened his very life. She held him closer.

"No, not yesterday." Then she saw his grin. "Oh, you know what I mean."

"Sure do, Mrs. Sinclair."

"Well, I suppose," she said as he dipped his head, softly laughing. "For old times' sake."

"Don't kid yourself." He sought her mouth.

In harmony with the kiss, her breasts tingled, her lower body ached, warmed, softened. Readied itself. Finally pleaded for his. With a small cry of frustration, of surrender, Erin wound her arms around him, running her hands over his naked back and feeling the muscles roped beneath his hot, smooth skin.

"You may be right."

She lifted to him, and Danny groaned. Kissing her, he leaned his weight on one arm, sliding the other between them, closing a hand over her breast. The taut nipple stabbed his palm and she blushed, making him laugh again.

"Sweetheart . . ." He teased her opening with his arousal.

"A good man is hard—"

"Oh, you bet."

Erin gasped. "—*to find*!"

The camper bed creaked. Except for that and the light raggedness of their breathing, the night grew still. And Danny, with Erin's guidance, settled into her. Again. Once more.

She was lost. But never mind tomorrow.

Or the day not long from now when she would return to Paradise Valley. Alone.

She didn't care. God, she didn't.

Meg greeted that Sunday morning with a silly smile. Lying in one of her motel room's two king-sized beds, she heard the shower next door running full blast and a man singing "Home on the Range" badly off-key at the top of his lungs.

Luke Hastings wasn't shy.

After leaving Erin with Danny at the fairgrounds the night before, he dropped her and Timmy at the motel then went back to the Hitching Post for a nightcap. Tucking Timmy into bed, she didn't have time to wonder about his drinking or the available young women he might meet. She hadn't pondered her own jealous twitch at the thought, or even called it that.

Then Luke had returned, tapping at Meg's connecting door and gesturing her into his room, bringing her a Seven-Up, a bucket of ice, and a can of Coke for himself.

"Speedballing," he told her with a grin, holding one finger to his lips. Timmy was snoring lightly and wouldn't miss her, but she left the door ajar in case he woke, or she needed an escape.

"I've had my quota of beer for the night," Luke said. "Never does kill my thirst. I'm working tomorrow so I need my wits about me."

He ripped the plastic wrap from two motel glasses and poured soda into each then handed Meg one.

"Drink up." Shifting the usual wad in his cheek, he sat on the edge of the bed and eyed her over his glass. "I didn't ruin a good dream, did I?"

"No," she said, taking care to sit in one of the two orange-and-brown upholstered tub chairs nearest the door between their rooms. "I always have trouble sleeping after a rodeo."

"Mother hen," he said. "You still worry about Danny."

"Not only on rodeo days."

"You worry about him, you're wasting your time. He's six feet tall, maybe a bit more. Most of that bone and muscle." Luke downed the rest of his Coke. "He's nearer to forty than he is to thirty these days." He looked away from Meg's gaze. "Besides, Danny Sinclair's one of the best bull riders I've ever seen—and I've worked with most of 'em. He missed the world last year by a few hundred dollars, missed the finals the year before that by fifty."

Meg couldn't help but be impressed. She knew Danny was good—he'd shown his talent early—but she didn't follow the standings. The finals, she knew, included the top fifteen riders for that season in each event.

"And this year?"

Luke frowned. "You know where he's been most of July. Expensive time off."

"He should spend more time with Erin and his son."

"That's for them to work out."

Meg set her glass down and stood. She and Luke Hastings would never agree. "You'd just as soon they divorced."

"I never said that. But you've implied it twice now." He rose from the end of the bed and came toward her. "And the day I arrived at Paradise Valley to fetch Danny, you fed me real good, but the way you looked at me was like you'd dumped that bucket of ice on my head. Or down my pants."

"Mr. Hastings—"

"Don't go all mother-like on me. I don't need a scolding." Inches from her, he towered over Meg, taller than Hank had been, broader, every bit as much a finely tuned athlete as her son. She pictured Luke in his clown makeup, and stepped back as he said, "I suggest we avoid talking about Danny and Erin and concentrate on ourselves."

Meg's eyes widened. "Ourselves?"

"You and me."

"Don't be ridiculous, Mr.—"

"You call me mister once more, I'll have to show you why you shouldn't."

Glancing over her shoulder, she located the connecting door. Fifty-six or not, she was a woman alone in a place she had no business being. If Hank knew . . .

"Meg, I won't hurt you."

"You most certainly won't."

But his big, solid bulk blocked her retreat, and he reached out to gently close the door between their rooms.

Her pulse jumped. "Is this why you invited me here? To amuse yourself by coming on—that's the term, isn't it?—to a woman old enough to be your mother?"

Luke looked offended. "How old do you think I am?"

"Danny's age, or close."

"I'm forty-eight. So unless you were to give birth before you were ten years old, I don't see how the term mother could apply. It's certainly not how I see you, Meg." He paused. "It's not how you look at me either."

She gaped at him, fighting the ludicrous urge to pat her hair into place.

"I married young," she told him, standing sandwiched between the door and his taller, stronger body. "I was sixteen but ready to make Hank Sinclair a good wife. I loved that man for thirty-eight years before he died. I'm not looking for another."

"Did I say anything about marriage?"

She swallowed. "Then what did you have in mind?"

"There's the rest of rodeo week here, then we'll see. If I'm welcome at Paradise Valley, I'll come visit when I can."

She couldn't seem to breathe properly, or to look away from Luke's warm brown eyes. "I'll be happy to bake you another pie. The elderberries will ripen soon. No more frozen ones. Of course you're welcome. Anytime."

"You bake a fine pie and I'm partial to it, apple, blue-berry, whatever." Moving so swiftly yet easily that she failed to note the motion, as if he were hemming in an errant bull, he crowded her against the door. "But I had something in mind besides working on a middle-aged spread."

"Luke, I don't think . . . "

Turning aside, he removed the pink wad from his mouth. Keeping his eyes on Meg's, he stuck the gum to the wood-work. He braced both hands by her head, and she realized he had backed her right against the door panel.

"Try it, you might like it."

With that, he closed in on her astonishment, dropping his head low while she stood paralyzed by his audacity and her own foolishness. When he nearly reached her mouth, he stopped. His brown gaze lifted to hers, but she said nothing. And she didn't move.

Satisfied, Luke smiled a little. Then he bridged the last gap between them, but only with his mouth. He touched hers once, lightly, as if expecting her to scream. When she didn't but only opened and helplessly closed her hands, he tried another kiss, a bit more pressure, but still, gently, so gently it brought tears to Meg's closed eyes.

She didn't open them, or her mouth. Oddly chaste, the exchange seemed more friendship overture than imminent seduction. His body never touched hers and his tongue stayed where it belonged.

It was Meg who nearly kissed him back and asked for more.

In the utter stillness, Luke lifted his mouth and stepped away from her, his arms falling slowly to his sides. He stared at her for a moment, his brown eyes darker, twin dots of color on his cheekbones, his mouth slack. She didn't know who seemed more surprised, but the same heady rush of blood seemed to be in his veins too.

"Something you might think about," he whispered.

Then he had reached behind her, opened the connecting door, and turned Meg into her room.

Lying in bed the next morning, with the shower running in the next room, she allowed her smile to grow. It had been so long since she'd heard that sound, knowing a virile man stood naked nearby, and Hank had never sung. It had been a long while since she'd been kissed, tenderly or at all. Except by Timmy.

The thought sobered her, and she looked over at the other bed. Her grandson lay awake—wakened as she had been by the lusty singing from the other bathroom?—and looking around him at the unfamiliar room. His green cast glowed in the early morning light.

"You're with me, Timmy," she said. "Luke's next door."

His thoughts apparently focused and he grinned.

"Mom stayed with Daddy."

"Yes, she did."

"Do you think they like each other now?"

Meg remembered the heated looks between them last night, remembered Erin's earlier fear for Danny and the pride she didn't want to show. "I think they might."

He leaped from his bed onto hers. "We did it!" Flinging himself at her, he smacked a wet kiss still smelling of cotton candy on her cheek. "We're Valentines!"

"We just might be."

The shower shut off, the singing stopped. So would her own fantasies about Luke Hastings.

Giggling, one-armed, Timmy pulled her upright.

"Watch your cast," she said.

"Get up. We gotta make sure of it. Then me and Daddy are gonna watch slack after breakfast." He was already scrambling for his clothes. "Can we have pancakes, Gram?"

Gram. After last night, again, she needed the reminder.

Forget it, Danny told himself the next Friday. Hours after Tim dragged him to the last of the three pancake breakfasts Cheyenne offered, his gut felt heavy. Rising from the dusty arena, he retrieved his hat, which had landed twenty yards away along the rail, and slapped it hard against his thigh. He didn't feel the sting through his embossed leather chaps, but he'd heard more than one person say a cowboy wore a hat in the first place to give him something to do during that embarrassing walk from the ring after a bad ride.

He didn't blame the pancakes. He'd made his eight seconds. He even landed practically on his feet, in time to glance up at the grandstand, to see Erin cheering next to Tim and his mother. But he'd drawn a "dink," a lackluster bull not known for its action. He spurred it high—not on the shoulders but the neck, which impressed the judges more—and kept his center. It didn't matter.

Danny vaulted the fence, dropping down on the other side. The no-win side. He should have stayed within the wire-fenced ready area under the bleachers reserved for riders and the press. Just sauntered past the guards then inside, loosened up with his bends and stretches, and shared tall tales with the other guys, not wasted his time.

From the two judges, who scored bull and rider separately, a hundred points—fifty each—made a perfect score. There'd only been one perfect ride in rodeo history, and he was nowhere near that today. His closest competitor, a twenty-five-year-old hotshot off the Texas circuit, would ride soon. Danny didn't want to hear his score either.

Not looking back, he tried to tune out the announcer's

voice. Danny's bull, a grisly black-and-white Braford cross, trotted meekly from the arena into the chutes.

"Slow up." Luke was right behind him.

"A score of sixty-nine for Danny Sinclair," the announcer yelled.

"Goddammit." Carrying his bull rope, he stalked past other entrants, most of them mentally preparing themselves. One reached out, tapping his shoulder in commiseration. "I needed a money bull, bad."

"You're still in the money," Luke pointed out. "Did you hear that announcer? 'Nice ride, beautiful ride, great dismount.' Third or fourth, prob'ly."

"Maybe."

His side hurt. Every morning Erin had spread liniment over his skin and the yellowing bruise on his hip that felt bone-deep. He'd ache for a week. He could still feel the bruised ribs he'd suffered in Utah. He didn't heal as fast as he used to. The kid from Texas had the edge, no matter what bull he drew; over the next years, anyone would.

"Danny! Hey, Sinclair!"

At the young male voice, he turned, giving Luke a high sign as he headed back to the ring to help his barrel man, and saw Jason Barker bearing down on him from the grandstand with a young woman in tow. At first he didn't recognize him. The boy had cut his shoulder-length hair into a neat, trim style.

Danny forced a smile. "Jason, how y'doing?"

"I've been all over since I quit working at Erin's store. Even won me a buckle down in Oklahoma."

"That's great. Keep it up." He glanced at the brown-haired girl holding Jason's hand tight enough to turn her knuckles white. She eyed Danny without Jason's apparent admiration. "Next year you'll probably be riding bulls here yourself at the 'Daddy of Em All.'"

"Naw, I'm like the kids who come to the emporium to stare through the candy counter glass, that's all."

Danny looked the dark-haired boy over, from his spotless straw hat and smaller, leaner frame to his brand new boots. "You're even built like a bull rider."

Jason's gaze shifted to the girl at his side. She edged closer to him and he said, "There's more to it than that. More than my wanting a PRCA card or even a world championship someday." He smiled down at the girl, who flushed prettily. He didn't look at Danny. "My folks brought us down here to Cheyenne as a treat—a belated graduation gift, they said—before I start—before we both start—college in September."

"College? But I thought—"

"I tried the circuit, Danny." Jason kept looking at his girl. "I know it's only been a few weeks, but I never expected the travel to be so hard. I never thought I'd get so lonely. I started thinking. My mom worries about me and—"

"So do I," the girl murmured, her gaze never leaving Jason's.

"She's right, my parents too." He glanced at Danny. "I mean, I could rodeo until I'm as old as y—" He broke off. "Until I'm too old to ride and maybe never get to the top. I took a bad fall last weekend in Nebraska, got a slight concussion . . .and nobody was there to care about me when my head felt ready to split in two."

Danny gripped his bull rope. "Part of the business, Jason. You know that."

"But I'm not as tough as you, and I know I'm not as good as you were at my age. How many times have you been hurt, Danny? I sure don't want to wind up broke or crippled in the end—or as my dad says, find I've squandered all my other opportunities." He squeezed the girl's shoulders. "I sure don't want to lose what I already have."

As if he'd said too much, he flashed Danny an embarrassed smile. When Jason held out a hand, Danny put all his strength behind his grip.

"I'm glad to see you again," Jason said. "Bad bull today but a nice ride."

"Thanks." A shit ride.

All of a sudden, Danny felt like a has-been for sure. His score, that kid's from Texas. He could hear the announcer call out, "Ninety-one points!" And now, Jason Barker, who sounded young, maybe a bit tactless, but all too rational. He made Danny seem foolish, irresponsible. As if his chosen way of life had been one big mistake.

"Jason!" Erin came toward them behind the chutes, threw her arms around his neck, and kissed his cheek. "Look at you—growing up by the day. And who's this?" She turned to his girl and Jason introduced them, including Danny.

"Did you find someone to work at the store?" Jason asked.

"An older woman, a widow. Part-time," she said. "I left her in charge this week, but Daisy promised to supervise."

Jason's blue eyes sparkled. "You'll be lucky to have a store when you get back."

She and Jason chatted on as if they'd never exchanged harsh words, but Danny stopped listening. In his mind, he inverted his numbers into a winning ninety-six, thousands of dollars, and a buckle.

When Erin said good-bye to Jason, the boy clapped Danny on the shoulder, like one veteran cowboy to another, fading one, before walking away. Danny immediately spun her around into his arms.

He kissed her, hard. Cheyenne was one of the top four rodeos in the world, every season, and Danny usually liked it better than the Calgary Stampede, the Salinas Rodeo, or the Pendleton Round-Up. He'd done all right this year. But what if he was wrong about rodeo, had been wrong all along?

The kiss broke, and Erin smoothed hair from his damp forehead. "What was that for?"

"Come on," he said. "We're going home."

She looked toward the parking lot.

"To your motel. To your room."

Erin's visit had been the best part of Frontier Days this summer. The new glow in her face assured him she was enjoying herself, enjoying him. She'd been abandoned, passionate beyond his memory in Danny's bed—or rather, Erin's motel room—the last few nights.

He might finish out of the big money or relinquish his place soon to someone younger, but he was still a man.

"My room?"

"For the rest of the afternoon and evening."

Her hand in Danny's, Erin didn't say another word. Finding Meg, she made sure Tim would be taken care of. Meg and Luke promised him dinner after Luke finished clowning, then an evening at the carnival midway instead of the Alan Jackson country music concert they'd planned to attend. Luke was using the camper again after that one night, so Erin's room would be free. Tim and Meg would get back late, his mother assured them, assessing Danny's expression.

Like his impatience now, his need of Erin seemed to grow rather than diminish with every bout of lovemaking, every mind-blowing climax. He supposed they were finally getting that honeymoon week he owed her.

On the way to the motel the usual afternoon rumble of thunder suited him. He kept silent but could feel her watching him, wondering at his mood—which only made him harder, even if he didn't like himself for behaving like a mad bull.

Inside the room he yanked the draperies shut, turned off the overhead light Erin flipped on, and tumbled her on the bed. Her surprised shriek didn't faze him. He had his mouth on hers, his hands divesting her of clothes before she took another breath.

The adrenaline still pumped through him from his ride.

If he'd drawn a rank bull, a spinning, whirling, jumping, twisting, spiraling son of a bitch that could have made money, he might not feel so bad. Or ornery himself.

Tempering his strength, he warned himself to go easy. But the madness drove him. The smell of the bulls, the roar of the crowd, the feel of his rope sticking to his gloved hand, Jason Barker and his girl . . . all became Erin, underneath him, around him, in him. Riding out the wildness.

"Jesus"—he gasped as he came—"let me!"

Afterward cold shame spilled through him.

Still lying on her, unaware if she'd experienced her own release, he closed his eyes. He could be a selfish bastard. No wonder she'd thrown him out years ago.

At least she didn't sound angry, or afraid, simply bemused.

"And what was *that* all about?"

He buried his face in the hollow of her neck.

"It's a good thing we're still married," he murmured.

"Sort of."

"You mean good sort of, or sort of married?"

"Both." She rubbed his back in lazy circles, sending arrows of fresh desire through him. "Are you all right?"

"I'm okay." She was asking *him*? Withdrawing, he raised on his elbows. "Sorry, I had the devil in me but I wanted you real bad."

Her finger kept stroking. "It was a good ride, Danny."

He snorted. She saw right through him. Always had.

"At Frontier Park, or just now?"

"Well," she admitted, smiling, "both."

He waited a second. "Did you come?"

Her eyes sparkled. "You saw me in the stands."

"I mean here." In another minute she'd tease him out of his mood.

"You didn't hear me? Yes," she said.

"Scale of one to ten," he murmured.

"Eight and a half."

"Not perfect?"

"I didn't know what was going on with you. It distracted me—at first."

They lay in the darkened motel room, far enough from the arena for him to forget. The week in Cheyenne, like Frontier Days, was ending, an interlude to remember despite his crude, macho display just now.

He even smiled to himself. On Monday Erin had dragged him and Tim to the annual Governor's Art Show, and in return she joined them to tour the Old West Museum with its collection of wagons and western memorabilia. Erin earned a few hours the next day at the Old Town Mall before he and Tim drove her out to the Indian village along the roads edged with wild sunflowers on Wednesday. Tim just had to see the parade the morning before—quarter horses, Arabians, paint ponies, tricks, a finale with a high noon–style shoot-out—one of four that week.

Cheyenne was a circus, all right. The Air Force Thunderbirds flying over. The free chili cook-off Erin couldn't resist. And yesterday afternoon, the three of them had walked around the Wyoming State Capitol Building, taking in its gilded dome, marble floors and stained glass, its lifesize wildlife display. And always, each day, there was the rodeo. This time, he hadn't been alone.

He needed a shower but didn't move. Erin's hand on his spine held him in place, though her thoughts had gone elsewhere.

"No buckle bunnies?" she said in his ear.

"I didn't say none."

She tensed and he cursed himself.

"Do you want to hear that I haven't had another woman in eight years? Or are we being honest here?"

"Honest," she said.

Jason had made a good point. "Erin, I got so lonely away

from you. Like I said, it was damn close to no other women.
Nobody special. I can count them on one hand."

"Count."

"A girl in Idaho during the Pocatello round-up, probably
almost eight years ago—right after you tossed me out. I
can't recall her name or what she looked like. I'm not proud
of that." He sighed. "A typical bunny like the ones you saw
the other night at the Hitching Post—a couple of years
back. That's all."

"I don't blame you."

Her tone said otherwise. "But you're kind of angry,
aren't you, that I asked about other men—about Ken—
before I said what I'd done?"

She didn't answer that. "What did you do the rest of the
time?"

He couldn't help smiling. "Uh-uh. You first."

She laid her head on his shoulder so he couldn't see
her eyes. "The same as you," she murmured, sounding
embarrassed.

Danny laughed.

"Cold showers?"

"It's rarely warm enough in Montana."

He laced their fingers together. "Your hand hasn't fallen
off yet?" His thumb traced a pattern in her palm. "You
aren't going blind, are you?"

"Not that I know of."

He felt something light skim through him.

"Did you—think of me when you—"

"Stop," she said.

"Did you?"

"*Yes!*"

His tone dropped low. "I thought of you. Nearly drove
myself crazy." He hesitated. "Still, it sounds like a reason-
ably healthy solution to me, especially in this day and age
with so much disease around. You don't know what's safe,"
he said, "except that supply of condoms we've been going

through so quick these past few days. Did you wonder why I had them?"

"I didn't let myself ask the question."

"I bought them for you—for us. Though I do wonder how long we're gonna go without another baby. Tim's already seven, that's quite a big gap."

"Danny, we can't."

His gut clenched. He didn't want to lose what he'd shared in Cheyenne with Erin and his son. Oh, he could keep seeing Tim two or three times a year, and each time, as Tim grew older and needed him more, they might become closer. He might even convince Erin to see him now and then. But Jason made him wonder: Was that enough? Had he sacrificed Erin for his dream long ago?

He'd always thought of winning the world, then going home and having everything turn out right. But nothing seemed that simple now, and he was just beginning to think about his future after bull riding. Yet if he told Erin his notion of stock contracting at Paradise Valley, she might not take well to that idea either. To her, it would be another dangerous undertaking. Working with bulls, raising them for rodeo, might seem as bad as riding bulls. Maybe he'd better ease into it.

"What do you think this means?" he asked.

"Having a baby?" She frowned.

"No. That we both took the same route for the last eight years," he said. "That I didn't end up traveling with some buckle bunny instead of Luke? And you didn't crawl into Ken's bed some lonely night?"

She stayed silent, as if holding her breath.

Wrapping his arms around her, he laid his chin against the top of her head, the silk of her hair. He breathed her through his pores, the scents of woman flesh and some light, sweet-smelling shampoo. She always smelled fresh. To a man who spent much of his time around animal excrement, Erin seemed wholly clean.

He couldn't say the wrong thing now.

"You haven't filed for divorce either, and until I mentioned it, you didn't take off your ring." He rubbed his cheek against her hair. "I think we both still care, Erin. About each other and what we almost had once. We threw that away," he said, "before we really got started."

"We had our reasons."

"I don't think we're that different. I saw you in the stands today. You might be scared, but you're proud—and today you got excited, even with that lousy score." He listened to the far off sounds of traffic, imagined he could hear the distant trill of a calliope at the fairgrounds. "I miss being in Tim's life," he said, tightening his embrace around Erin, "but I miss being part of yours even more."

"Oh, Danny."

"So what are we gonna do about that?"

She sighed but nestled closer. "There's nothing we can do. Yes, I cheered for you today. It's hard not to. But I still want a peaceful life at Paradise Valley, running the store, raising Timmy where he can breathe fresh air and feel secure." She brushed a hand over his cheek. "You still want to get on board some bull named Twister or Bad Business and risk your neck."

She had a point too. He had spent most of his adult life in rodeo—an adolescent pursuit, Ken thought. Even Jason had said as much. What if he stayed, and lost Erin for good, lost Tim? *What if he never won the world?*

"Maybe I don't want to risk it as much as I used to."

She looked at him in disbelief. Neither of them found compromise easy, but even the way they'd chosen the sights to see with Tim in Cheyenne proved they could do it.

"I'm not getting any younger, Erin. There's only a handful of guys on the circuit older than I am now."

"You'd consider quitting?"

She seemed to be holding her breath.

"Slowing down," he said. "I have some plans for the

ranch." If he could get around Ken and gain Erin's acceptance. "We need to talk about that."

"When?"

He raised her chin to kiss her mouth. "Not tonight."

"When, Danny?"

He had her interest anyway. He didn't intend to blow it,
so he slid lower in the bed, taking her with him into the
sheets still warm from their bodies, still fragrant from their
earlier lovemaking. He'd be tender this time. The most
tender lover she could ever have. She'd never be able to
send him away again.

"After Cheyenne, I'm gonna drop down to Kansas. There's
a pretty good rodeo coming up there, but I can be in
Sweetwater afterward, mid-week. We'll talk then."

"Mid-week, meaning on the way to the next rodeo?"

"We'll talk," he promised.

15

Still knotting his tie, Ken crossed the yard from the converted bunkhouse to his mother's back door. For Montana in early August the late afternoon seemed warm without any air stirring, and a few low-hanging, dark clouds promised rain. He hoped it held off until he and Erin came home, until he said what he had to say.

He found her in the kitchen, smoothing her hair into place without quite looking in the oak-framed mirror near the door. She wore her hair loose, falling over the shoulders of her white knit top. A denim skirt stopped just at her knees and her legs were bare. As he watched she slipped into a pair of navy flats on the multicolored rug his mother instructed everyone to use when coming in from the yard. Erin had obviously been barefoot, a sensual gesture that he couldn't appreciate.

He was afraid he knew what it meant.

Erin glanced at the wall clock. "I thought you said six." He was fifteen minutes early, like a boy on his first date.

He cleared his throat.

"Let's stop for dinner on the way."

"On the way where?" Her smile landed beyond him, near the kitchen cabinet that held his mother's china cups.

"Secret," he said, feeling the slow thump of his heart.

Erin, his mother, and Timmy had come home from Cheyenne nearly a week ago. Ever since he'd been trying to ignore the new radiance Erin wore like a special dress, the lighter spring to her step. He hadn't seen her smile or heard her laugh so easily in years.

Even his mother and Timmy seemed to know why.

On the way to Dillon he made conversation, but each time he tried steering it toward the personal, Erin changed the subject.

At the restaurant she picked at her fried chicken, then pushed her coleslaw aside untasted. When she handed Ken her biscuit, dripping butter and honey, he caught her wrist.

"Is something wrong?" he asked.

"No, I'm just not hungry."

"You're not ill?"

"I feel fine." She beamed at him, her green eyes more clear than he remembered, even from childhood. "Except I hate secrets and you won't tell me."

In Dillon he drove by Western Montana College then near Vigilante Park where a baseball game was in progress, past his offices on Montana and finally, along quiet streets lined with older houses to the town limits.

What if she didn't like his surprise? Wouldn't accept him?

Turning in at the brick gateposts that read Wooded Creek, he kept his gaze trained on the newly paved road that snaked through the ironically treeless subdivision.

"This is where you've been working," Erin said. "I recognize the raw earth that cakes your boots every night."

He laughed. "Caught me. What do you think?" He waved a hand at a Georgian-style house, its many windows still showing brand-name stickers and workmen's fingerprints.

"There are six basic plans." He pointed to the left. "Victorian's popular right now."

"Mmm," Erin murmured.

He knew Victorian wasn't her favorite; he should have driven past it. Seconds later, Ken drew up in front of a brick-and-stone transitional on the right at the apex of the horseshoe-curved street that comprised the development.

Erin shot him an inquisitive glance, but he said nothing. Opening his door, he came around to her side.

"Let's take a look. I think it's my best work."

He ushered her into the house, which couldn't have been more different from the ranch house at Paradise Valley. Three thousand, five hundred square feet of well-planned and -executed space. Two tons of rock artistically stacked and mortared into an award-winning fireplace. Ceramic tile floors in all four bathrooms. Polished wood, its grain perfectly matched and gleaming, on all the other floors. A state-of-the-art kitchen.

"Ready for the twenty-first century," Ken told her, encouraging her to run a hand over the gray granite countertops that cost over six thousand dollars but would last a lifetime. "This stuff's impervious to stains. Timmy could beat on it with his metal trucks. I can set a hot pan right here"—he touched the countertop's center—"without leaving a mark."

"Beautiful." Erin's gaze widened. "Ken, what is this?"

"The new house," he said, as if his intentions were also obvious. "Wait till you see upstairs." One staircase flowed up from the front entry, the other wound down from the bedroom hall into an enormous family room off the rear glassed-in porch and open deck. "Timmy can have his own room and bath."

"And Meg?"

He looked away. "Mom needs her own place. We need privacy." He jingled the change in his linen pants pockets.

"Is this what I think it is?" she asked.

Hell.

He'd planned to take her on a full-scale tour, every nook and closet, the central vacuum system, the Jacuzzi in the master bathroom, the view from the bedroom overlooking the new golf course. In a few months she wouldn't miss Paradise Valley. And Ken could stop worrying himself to sleep each night, as he'd stopped hearing Danny flip over on the sofa bed for hours.

Walking around the counter, he took her shoulders.

"I've never been good with words, Erin. I meant this to go more smoothly, though. I meant to wait until you fell in love with this house before I proposed."

"*Marriage*?"

"Have I made that much a secret of my feelings?"

He'd loved her since he was a boy; he watched her fall for Danny, watched her leave. He saw her come back with her heart in pieces, and he was there when her son was born. He'd always been there for her.

Erin stood still, and silent.

Taking her in his arms, he dropped his head low, seeking her mouth, kissing her without protest. He could have groaned at the soft, moist contact of their lips, and when he explored with his tongue, she nearly let him in. Then her mouth closed tight, like a vise around his heart, and she yanked away, running her hands over her arms as if he'd chilled her. His own flesh felt hot, needy.

"I want us to be a real family," he said. "I'm the only father Timmy's ever known. I'm the one who's taken care of Mom and you too. Didn't you know how I felt? Didn't you guess that I love you?"

"Oh, Ken."

She sounded shocked. Easing farther away, at the green-house window she looked out at the barren expanse of dried mud, the deep ruts like scars from construction vehicles. "I don't know what to say."

"Say yes. We'll work everything else out later." Behind

her, he slipped his arms around her waist. "Divorce him," he said, his breath stirring the fine hairs at the nape of her neck. "It's never going to work between you two, Erin."

She shivered at his touch, and Ken's heart sank. The glow about her, the easy laughter, the clear green eyes. He'd seen that before, when Erin was fifteen, then seventeen, then twenty . . . and gone. His tone hardened.

"Had a good time in Cheyenne, did you?"

"Yes." She gestured helplessly at the immaculate kitchen, gray and white and sparkling in the early evening light. "I learned I still care about Danny. I shouldn't have come with you tonight. I never thought—Ken, he's coming home in a few days."

"Paradise Valley is not his home."

She turned. "How can you say that?"

"You heard the reading of Dad's will when I did."

"The will was wrong."

"You know Dad didn't want Danny near the ranch."

"Or near me?" she said, looking down.

"He felt as I do about that. Neither of us ever hid it."

"No one uses the land. Danny has plans for it."

Ken studied her bent head, the lowering sun, the lengthening shadows turning its frosted auburn to a deeper, rich russet.

He shouldn't have waited this long. After the library board meeting, when he kissed her and Erin pulled away, he should have spoken. Instead, he'd watched her minutes later, entering the camper. Then Danny had spoken to him about the ranch and Erin, but still Ken said nothing to her. He'd watched her leave—again—for Cheyenne over his objections. Now he saw his chance.

"Oh, he has plans all right."

At his tone Erin looked up.

"You don't know?" he said. "That's Danny, holding his bull rope in his teeth. Having a good time at your expense. Erin, he's using you."

"What do you mean?"

"He wants the land all right—for a stock contracting business."

She went pale. "Stock contracting?"

He waved a hand. "Bulls, horses . . ."

"Producing rodeos too, I suppose."

The flattened tone of her voice told him to keep pressing. It was Danny's fault he hadn't told her. He deserved whatever happened.

"If he wants real money, I'd guess so."

Her face looked even whiter against the darkened red of her hair. "When does this take place?"

"I doubt Danny has a schedule. Some day, I suppose, like everything else. It's always some day with him."

Her eyes had turned a dark green, like marble. She ran a hand over the granite countertop he'd lovingly designed for her; he had even supervised its installation. Thinking, dreaming, planning for himself, and Erin.

"I can't stay here," she said.

With a blind look, she marched from the kitchen to the front entry.

"Erin, wait."

He'd gambled and lost. Obviously, she and Danny were sleeping together again. But how long could that last?

"Erin, talk to me." He followed her through the house. "I did this for you. What can he give you? You need a place for Timmy, a solid marriage—"

"I need to go home!"

The next morning at the store Erin drifted through her duties in a red haze of anger. She checked the change supply in the cash register, swept the aisles, flipped the Closed sign around to read Open, but didn't notice Meg unpacking baby food in the rear aisle.

Later, Timmy, who was at the library, would dust

shelves—his first job, for which Erin had agreed to pay him fifty cents an hour. Timmy had already declared himself "rich" before he'd picked up a dust rag.

He needed a job. Danny had told him he was coming home the middle of next week—four more days—and Timmy wouldn't stop pestering her. *What day is it now? How much longer, Mom? Is he sleeping in your room?*

Erin still couldn't comprehend her shock at Ken's proposal. She had discounted Danny's inferences that his brother was interested in her. Why hadn't she seen that herself? She'd considered Danny's statements to be part of the lifelong competition he and his brother had waged. But marriage to Ken?

She loved Danny's brother, platonically, and knew she'd hurt him, but his proposal—the new house he'd obviously built for her—seemed as hard to believe as Ken's conviction that Danny meant to begin stock contracting at Paradise Valley.

"Erin, where should I put the strained meat?" Meg held up a jar.

"You decide. Or no, next to the canned vegetables."

Erin had come home from Cheyenne to find her new helper's resignation on the emporium's counter. The woman had taken another job in Dillon for more money. When Meg offered to fill in, at first Erin refused.

"You have plenty to do at home. Once Timmy begins his schoolwork in the fall, and I'm at the store all day, you'll be more than busy."

"I've been thinking," Meg said. "Timmy's old enough this year to spend time at the store and do his lessons in your office. He might help too, moving boxes and cleaning up. Among the three of us we should be able to handle any heavy work."

"I couldn't impose. You do far too much for me as it is."

"Ken's always telling me to get more interests away from Paradise Valley—and maybe he's right." Meg had paused.

"There may come a time, **Erin**, when I'm not needed to bake and sew." She clinched the job by adding, "Besides, you hired one older woman with time on her hands."

But in the few days since Meg had started working at the store, her mother-in-law's normally high spirits seemed to have dipped. Did she find the work too tiring? Meg barely seemed to stop for breath from opening until closing time. Or did she miss Luke Hastings? In Cheyenne she had seemed so alive, looking even younger than she usually did.

As Erin stood on a stepladder to take the Laura Ashley curtains from the front display windows, she frowned. Removing the curtain hooks, she wondered what could have happened between Luke and Meg. If something had, she knew whom to blame. Luke would tease and flirt, then disappear, not understanding or caring that he hurt someone. Meg. She tossed the curtains to the floor then clambered down, asking herself the same question: Had *she* somehow led Ken on?

She had hurt him, but she couldn't blame Ken for wanting to get back at her or Danny by telling her about his plans. And to think, she'd nearly trusted Danny.

She couldn't envision the grazing lands at Paradise Valley dotted with Brahmas or rank horses. Danny might be a fine bull rider, and Erin admitted his performances at Cheyenne thrilled even her in the end, but rough stock could be unpredictable. Tragic.

Erin couldn't keep still. She put the curtains in the Jeep to take them home for laundering, then brought Timmy's favorite stuffed monkey from the car into the store for fixing. Its head kept separating from its shoulders in places, and she'd already sewn it half a dozen times, but she'd promised Timmy to finish mending it by the time he got back.

Timmy had skipped off to the library wearing the buckskin chaps and vest Danny bought him at one of the truck stops outside Cheyenne their last day. With his jeans and clumping cowboy boots, he swaggered across the street with his father's boyish bravado. In a few more years he wouldn't cherish the comic-faced monkey as much; and she would find it harder to control him. One day, if Danny's plan became fact, Timmy might pick a horse for himself, or a bull to practice on. And his harmless ride on Kemosabe would become her happiest memory.

Old sorrow surged through her, then fresh anger. No wonder Danny had wanted to avoid talking in Cheyenne. She stabbed a curved mattress needle through the hole at the juncture of the monkey's neck and shoulder.

"Erin?" Meg said. "I've finished stocking. What should I do next?"

The empty store told her it wouldn't be a busy day.

"You could fix us some coffee."

"You don't have to pay me, dear, if there's no business."

"Of course I'll pay you." Again, she assessed Meg's down-turned mouth. "You work harder than Jason Barker ever thought of doing." She paused. "Meg, has something happened since we came home?"

"I might ask you the same."

She managed a smile. "I need to discuss something with Danny, that's all." She didn't elaborate for fear of worrying an already-troubled Meg, and she wouldn't mention Ken's proposal.

"Is he coming home alone?" Meg asked.

"Luke and Danny are Siamese twins," she said. "Is that a problem?"

"I just wondered how much food to plan. It's not as if we can afford to feed extra mouths—especially mouths like that rodeo clown's. That man eats enough for three men."

Meg always prided herself on fixing meals men couldn't resist; her biggest boast had always been that Hank ate enough for two.

"I see," Erin said, trying to sound noncommittal. She

bent low over the monkey, taking care with her stitches. So it was Luke. "I thought you and Luke were fast friends. Would you like to talk about it?"

Refusing, Meg picked up the dust rag Erin had left for Timmy on the front counter. She swiped at the nearest shelf, and a bottle of rose toilet water fell to the floor, shattering. Its smell quickly pervaded the small store.

"How clumsy of me!" She scurried for a sponge and water.

As Meg scrubbed the spot, Erin abandoned her sewing to open the front door and prop it wide, airing out the store, and giving her mother-in-law time to regroup.

Meg finally said, "Am I that transparent? I've called myself ten kinds of fool, Erin. And what would Danny think about my chasing Luke?"

"That's Danny's problem. But I doubt you chased him."

Erin leaned against the open door. Meg sat back on the floor, braced on her arms, the slim line of her still-firm body all the more noticeable for the unconscious pose. Even showing her recent unhappiness, she could have passed for a woman fifteen or twenty years younger.

"I . . . let him kiss me. Once," she added. "The night you stayed with Danny at the fairgrounds." She held Erin's gaze. "I hadn't been kissed like that since long before Hank took sick, and I can't tell you how good it felt."

"I think I know," Erin said ruefully. She still blushed every time she thought about the night in the camper, the nights in her motel room after that. The feel of Danny's skin, his whispers in the dark. His mouth. "What's wrong with a single kiss or feeling good?"

"The morning after," Meg admitted. That Sunday she had dressed with care and taken Timmy to the fairgrounds to meet Danny to watch slack, the overflow session for timed-event riders. There, she'd seen Luke. "He was talking to a girl half my age, or less. Pretty, dark-haired, not an ounce of extra flesh. All decked out in fringe and boots, riding a palomino horse."

"A buckle bunny," Erin said.

"No, one of the rodeo committee. But it was clear he knew her from other seasons, other places. Knew her well."

"So?"

"It made me realize," Meg said, staring at the forgotten sponge in her hand, "that I'm an aging widow. I haven't been on a horse in years, and I'm too old for romance, especially with a man like Luke Hastings."

Erin didn't share Danny's objection to Luke, which had probably been a knee-jerk reaction about his mother anyway.

"So what if he's younger than you are?"

"He certainly hasn't marriage on his mind—which, I'm ashamed to say, I blurted right out."

Erin didn't think Meg would remarry if she could. But then, she'd always assumed Hank Sinclair would live forever.

"Luke was probably horrified," Meg said. "Oh, Erin, I'm Timmy's *grandmother*. If you and Danny would patch things up, I'd like to have another grandbaby or two." She forced a smile. "Wouldn't that solve my problems? Luke Hastings, what to do with the rest of my life . . . "

She was obviously trying to change the subject.

Erin left the door propped and walked over to Meg. She took her hands. "There's nothing wrong with happiness—at any age."

Meg let Erin pull her to her feet and smiled more broadly.

"Then take your own advice."

Happiness? She wasn't sure about those nights in Cheyenne, no matter how good they felt. She knew how she felt about stock contracting, though. Pretty much the way Meg felt about Luke Hastings as a marriage prospect. There was no way she'd let Danny destroy Paradise Valley's tranquility with a bunch of bulls.

While Meg washed the emporium's front windows,

claiming she needed the work as therapy, Erin finished mending Timmy's stuffed monkey, until the next time it fell apart—like her marriage, and her faith in Danny. She hadn't taken his advice—removing the hanging plants from the store or getting rid of the Laura Ashley curtains—and she would keep tending her own business, literally, at the ranch and right here. She would make the Bitterroot Emporium support itself, and her.

"Men," Erin said. "The ultimate confusion."

"I am in love!"

Daisy Chatworth's laughing voice carried to Erin, standing along the fence, from inside the corral. Erin had invited her to dinner to thank her for helping at the store while she was in Cheyenne. After the meal, she had offered Daisy a ride. Dismounting, her lanky friend ran an assessing hand over Kemosabe's gleaming black-and-white hide.

"Look at this coat. He has a lovely bloom," she said. "A little overweight but he's obviously recovered from that bowed tendon. Why hasn't Danny shipped him back to the circuit?"

"He spoils his horses. Always did." Erin looked around to make sure they were alone. "He keeps saying he'll trailer him soon. But I think he's worried about Timmy. So am I. He's taken such a shine to Kemosabe that when that horse leaves, I'll have real trouble on my hands."

"Timmy's not ready for a horse like this."

Erin had to agree. The gelding was gentle as a kitten, but too specialized for a seven-year-old boy. "He's trained for barrel racing as well as roping," she said, "but hasn't done any barrels in years."

Daisy's gaze clouded. She patted the horse's neck then laughed again as 'Sabe pulled a carrot from her back pocket. "Did Danny teach him that?"

"Timmy did."

"Well, when Danny gets back, you can all go looking for a beginner horse. I'd be happy to give this one a home."

"And go back into competition?"

Daisy rarely talked about that topic. A car door slammed across the yard, distracting her. Leading Kemosabe over to the rail she stood near Erin, watching Ken leave the bunkhouse with a pile of clothing on hangers.

Daisy threw Erin a questioning glance.

She gnawed her bottom lip. "We had a misunderstanding the other night, and this morning he announced he's decided to live in Dillon."

She told Daisy about the house there, then about Ken's surprising proposal.

Daisy stroked Kemosabe's muzzle. "What brought up the subject of marriage?"

Erin looked away, at Ken who seemed to be arranging the clothes in the rear seat of his serviceable station wagon. Slamming the door he went back into the bunkhouse. He didn't once glance their way, though he must have seen Daisy's car and the activity at the corral.

"I wondered the same thing," Erin said. "I doubt I've ever given Ken the impression I was interested in him, romantically."

"Apparently you must have."

Erin looked at Daisy, whose gaze stayed fixed in the distance upon the bunkhouse door. She could hear Ken come out again and then shove some more clothing into the car.

"He never said anything."

"Men seldom do."

"Daisy, I feel guilty enough. I can't believe you'd accuse me of teasing Ken."

"Maybe he thought your buddy act—which has been going on since you and Danny split—covered something else. You've certainly leaned on him enough since you tossed Danny on his ear like some bad-tempered Brahma."

Erin's mouth fell open.

"You know why I left Danny. As for Ken, I never—"

"Quit kidding yourself!" Daisy's eyes flashed. At the tone of her voice, Kemosabe laid his ears back. "Left him, kicked him out—what's the difference? You couldn't look beyond yourself and what you wanted to what Danny needed in his life. So you high-tailed it back to Sweetwater. Some encouragement that must have been for Danny, out there on the road by himself—"

"He has Luke."

"Some consolation. That man loved you, I never saw a man love a woman so hard—I'd sure as hell give my arm to find one—and you just pushed him out, like a kitten no one wants from a speeding car. What amazes me is, he keeps coming back for more." She took a breath. "What excuse will you use this time to make him leave? To keep things your way?"

Kemosabe stamped a foot, as if in agreement.

Erin turned from the fence. Her heart beating fast, she started walking toward the house. Then she whirled around and went back to the rail.

"Stock contracting," she said through gritted teeth.

Daisy looked blank.

"That's his latest. To turn Paradise Valley into a way station for mean broncs and meaner bulls! If you think I'll sit still and watch my son get trampled some day—"

"Like Trevor?"

She bowed her head. "Like Trevor."

"That kid had a bug in him sometimes. The horse that threw him was no meaner than Kemosabe. Trev shouldn't have got on him that soon, that's all. Hank said so, Danny told me." Daisy paused. "That accident could happen to anyone."

"Not to Timmy!"

Across the yard the station wagon's trunk thudded shut with finality. Erin glanced up and, as Ken looked toward the corral at last, Daisy lifted a hand.

"Hi," she called in a challenging tone. Ken hadn't come in to dinner either, and he frowned.

"What are you doing out here? Trying to get your face rearranged in that corral dirt?"

Saying no more, he turned and went back into the bunkhouse.

Daisy whirled on Erin.

"You and Ken Sinclair have something in common. No wonder he thinks he's the right man for you. You're both half alive sometimes. Believe me, I know. Like Danny I've seen the other side, when you're completely alive in that arena."

"You're not seeing it now."

Daisy didn't answer. Her eyes turned cool. Clucking to Kemosabe, she led him from the corral through the barn's side entrance, avoiding the main door between the fence and Ken's station wagon. Too angered to care, Erin left her there, talking to herself.

Let her defend Danny, as she always did. She didn't need anyone's advice about stock contracting, or marriage. Especially from someone who, like Daisy, was lying to herself.

"True," she heard Daisy murmur. "Too true."

16

Danny crept in the back door late one night the next week. He left his duffel bag in the laundry room and his sneakers on the rug by the door, then walked through the kitchen, noting the quarter wedge of devil's food cake in the center of the table.

His mother must have left it—probably for Luke, not him. On sock feet Danny went through the dining room and hall to the stairs. He'd dropped Luke in Scottsbluff, Nebraska to catch a bus; he had a clown stint at a kids' rodeo not far from there and would meet Danny and the camper in Belle Fourche, South Dakota for next weekend's round-up.

He rubbed the back of his neck. Halfway to Paradise Valley, the camper had blown a radiator hose. The long drive from Kansas had worn him down, and he missed Luke's company after Nebraska. But he missed Erin more. The second step creaked in the stillness, as it always did. He hoped she would be as glad to see him as he would be to see her.

After checking on Tim, who was burrowed into his covers like a prairie dog down a hole, with only his monkey and the tip of his cast showing, glowing in the dark, Danny tiptoed down the hall. The bedroom door was shut, as if to keep him out. He should have called.

Nudging the thought aside, he pushed the door open. He heard the gentle rasp of Erin's breathing before he saw her in the bed, and felt his lower body tighten. After eight years of sleeping alone, he'd become used to her beside him, around him again in the week at Cheyenne.

Shucking his clothes, he climbed naked into bed.

With a sigh, trying not to feel disappointed, he scooped Erin's warm body into his arms, fitting himself to the flow of her curves, then nuzzling the nape of her neck. He'd hoped she'd wait up for him, not only to talk about the ranch.

He slipped one hand beneath her to touch a breast. It felt warm and soft. Danny groaned. "Erin, I'm here."

"Get out of this bed!"

The covers flew back. Cool night air rushed over his bare skin like cold water, dousing his desire. Erin lunged up, her eyes shooting sparks like tracers in the dark.

"You have some nerve!"

He reared back as she stumbled from bed, dragging on a robe to cover her cotton nightgown.

"I said I'd be home Wednesday." He glanced around but saw no calendar like the one he and Luke kept in the camper, with rodeo dates filling the squares. "This is—"

"Thursday morning, to be exact."

He explained about the radiator hose, and leaving Luke at the bus in Scottsbluff. Erin switched on a lamp, flooding the room with harsh light and making them both blink. Her gaze looked furious and so did every inch of her body. He could have run a plumb line down her spine.

His spirits drooped. The last fifty miles of road, he'd all but counted every rotation of the tires toward

Paradise Valley. Why expect a warm reception when he got there?

"Okay," he said, the wounded husband. "What'd I do now?"

With her back to him, she said the words that had stuck in his throat not long before. "Stock contracting."

She said them as he knew she would, like curse words. Danny sat on the side of the bed, his elbows resting on his spread knees. He studied the floor.

"Who told you?"

Few people knew. He wouldn't talk up his plans at a rodeo—didn't want anyone to know before he actually decided—he hadn't told Luke, and he'd never mentioned it in Tim's hearing. Then Danny went cold.

"Ken," he guessed, looking up.

They'd quarreled before Cheyenne. He wouldn't have been happy that the week there turned out so well.

She whirled to face him. "Why didn't I hear it from you, Danny?"

"My mistake."

Her gaze stayed carefully above his waist. "You knew all along. When you came home because of Timmy's broken arm, while you worked for me at the store, because I thought you wanted to—"

"I did, dammit."

"You mended all that fence line and I thought how good it was to see you working here again—" She broke off, flinging a hand out in frustration. "Does Luke know?"

Shaking his head, Danny stared again at the floor.

"That comes as a surprise," she said. "What about Meg?"

He hadn't told his mother either. Didn't want to see the light in her eyes before he actually committed to the idea.

"No," he said.

Her mouth twisted. "Why not? If you'd told her she would have believed in you. She would have encouraged contracting—turned the whole ranch over to it if she could just to have you home." She tied the robe's belt with quick, jerky motions. "You knew I'd oppose you." Leaning down, she grasped his shoulders. "Didn't you? That's why you didn't tell me."

He flattened his tone. "I guess it is."

"How dare you try to take away my right to that decision!"

"Erin, you can't make a decision."

"I've made one now. How dare you bring danger into my front yard!" Her nails bit into his skin.

Danny looked up at her. "Near Tim, you mean?"

"It's never going to end, is it? You're not slowing down, changing your life. Everything you said in Cheyenne was a lie. They don't call rodeo the suicide sport for nothing. And after that comes *stock contracting*?"

"Will you give me half a chance? Erin, in the last twenty years, since before I started riding bulls, there've been roughly a dozen deaths in sanctioned rodeos. Thousands of go-rounds but that's all and not all of those were bull riders. Most other sports with any danger to them sure couldn't say the same."

"And in no other sport would a man *pay* for the privilege of competing—and trying to kill himself. A few deaths," she said, "but how many broken bones, broken people? Young men who are old before their time, *crippled* for the rest of their lives. But that's just part of rodeo, isn't it, Danny? And so are they." She stepped back, as if disgusted. "Break an arm, break a leg or a face, so what?" Her eyes filled. "Break a *neck*—"

He got up to stalk around the room so he wouldn't touch her, shake her. "You have to be a little crazy to compete. I never said I wasn't."

In the silence he heard his own breathing. He felt cold, shaky. Abandoned.

"I guess you're right," he said. "I was afraid to tell you, afraid I'd get the reaction I did, but stock contracting's not the same as rodeo." He reached the end wall of the room, spun and paced again. "I promised we'd talk when I got back. I wasn't lying. I meant to tell you everything."

"That won't be necessary."

The cold became ice in his veins as Erin, not meeting his eyes, explained in a shaking voice about the house in Dillon, and Ken's marriage proposal, as if it were a done deal in her mind. Ken offered her a better, more peaceful life. He offered Timmy security. Was there any reason she shouldn't take that instead?

"Paradise Valley," he said.

Erin's gaze shadowed but she clamped her lips tight. Her words still buzzed in his brain as they stared at each other, clearly at an impasse.

"I guess Cheyenne didn't glue us back together as much as I hoped." He stopped pacing to sit on the bed again. Weakness pervaded him, as if he'd gotten thrown hard in the dirt. "I guess you don't think I know what I'm doing."

"You're a good bull rider, Danny. Superb. I know that. I can even accept it in saner moments." She stood at the window, looking out into the dark night. "What I can't understand is, why you do it."

Long ago, he'd told her it was his dream. Weeks ago, he'd admitted it was a way of life. He'd even told her it was how he made his living, and she sure as hell knew he loved what he did, what he'd worked so hard for to get even this close to winning the world. He'd be damned if he'd sit there now with his head in his hands, his heart in spasms, and let her tell him to go sleep on the daybed in his mother's sewing room. Or that she'd said yes to Ken's proposal.

He got up and walked past her to the door.

Welcome home, he thought. Just like always.

"Why do I do it?" he said without turning. "Because it's the only thing I know."

* * *

Meg was at the stove, pushing fluffy scrambled eggs around in the skillet, when she heard Danny's footsteps on the stairs. The first thing she'd seen that morning was his camper in the drive, the second his overflowing duffel bag full of dirty clothes.

"Good morning, Daniel," she said, hearing him come into the kitchen. She waited for Danny to come up behind her, wrap his arms around her middle, bury the point of his chin in her shoulder, and kiss her cheek. When nothing happened, she turned. "Or should I ask, bad night?"

He gave her a wan smile, the kind she'd seen too often in his teen years before the rodeo claimed him. Saved him, she had thought, from Hank's censure.

Meg trained her gaze on the skillet. She'd done enough looking out the window at the camper, her pulse in her throat.

"Luke's in Scottsbluff on his way to South Dakota," Danny said.

She resisted the urge to express her disappointment. She knew it was best. He belonged with that dark-haired girl on the palomino, or one like her. So much for his wanting to come visit when he could. "I was going to say he could stay in the bunkhouse. Ken's moved out."

"Do you miss him?" Danny asked.

She suppressed her uneasiness at whatever had happened to make Ken leave. "He wanted his privacy, he said. I don't see that much of him anyway. He's been so busy with the new subdivision in Dillon."

"I meant Luke."

"Oh. Well, we—had some pleasant times." Which were obviously over, as they should be. "In Cheyenne," she added.

Danny glanced around. "Is Erin gone?"

Meg stirred the eggs again. Apparently, he hadn't been in Erin's room last night, in her bed.

"She went out early, on Kemosabe." At his surprised look she added, "She's been exercising him. I think the rides do her good. She said she had thinking to do."

She ignored his shaking hand when he poured himself a mug of coffee. She'd make small talk. She was good at that; at covering up the hurts.

"Timmy's still out like a bear hibernating for winter. He'll have to shift his clock for school lessons in a few weeks. We keep a schedule the same as in Dillon."

Danny stared into his coffee until Meg couldn't take any more.

"I don't mean to pry"—she served his eggs, adding crisp bacon from the microwave Ken had bought her for Christmas—"but Erin said you were going to talk about something, together. Did things go badly?"

"About as bad as they can get."

"Want to tell your old mother?"

He grinned weakly, giving her the once-over.

"You're never gonna be old. When you're eighty, you'll still look thirty-five. Forty, tops."

Meg flushed. First Luke, now her own son telling her she hadn't lost it—when she knew she had. And shouldn't miss it.

She sat across from him, sending meaningful looks when he picked at his food. "Eat. You need your strength." She paused. "You made a fine picture in Cheyenne. Some beautiful rides, Danny." She'd managed to watch a few.

"And Dad would have been proud?"

He looked at his full plate. "In his fashion," she said. "What did you and Erin discuss? And argue about?"

"No argument. She already had her mind made up."

"What about you?"

He shook his head but couldn't stop the smile.

"Got me there, Mom. I have my plans too."

Meg waited but he said nothing more.

She laid a hand over his larger one. It was deeply tanned,

and sinewed, the tendons visible, strong blue veins standing out—the hand he gripped his bull rope with.

"You're a good man, Danny." She squeezed his hand lightly. "And you know how I feel. When you and Erin ran off to get married, the only thing I regretted was not seeing the ceremony. In Cheyenne I thought I hadn't been wrong in believing you still belong together. I saw it in her eyes, and yours."

"Erin would say that's just sex."

"Part of any good marriage." Willing her cheeks to stay cool at his bluntness, Meg stroked his hand. "It took your father and me years to learn, but each one has to give a little ground to get where you want to go. You're not giving up now, are you?"

He shrugged. "No, but I—"

A small whirlwind blurred across Meg's peripheral vision as Timmy burst into the kitchen.

"Daddy, you're home!"

He threw himself at Danny, who caught him just before Timmy landed in his coffee. "Whoa there, mind you don't dip that arm cast in my breakfast." He gathered Timmy close, kissing him. "How you been, anyway? I missed you for a whole week and a half."

"I missed you more."

"Wanna arm wrestle for that?"

"Don't even think about it," Meg said with a smile. "He has a bit longer in that cast."

She fought her own distaste at its now grimy, neon green surface covered with signatures and drawings. Timmy hooked his good arm around Danny's neck. "Mom'd break my other arm—yours too—if I got hurt again. Wouldn't she, Gram?"

"You can count on that. It's a mother's duty."

Brushing a hand over Danny's dark hair, she went to the refrigerator for Timmy's orange juice. "The Sinclairs don't give up. Boy or man."

"You talking to me, Gram?"

"No," she said. "I'm talking to your father." Over Timmy's head she sent Danny another significant look. "I think you know where to find her."

Erin rode Kemosabe up the hill in the early morning light. Thanks to Meg's new habit of opening the store for her, the daily ride had become habitual, therapeutic for her and the horse, she thought; but she'd never gone to the sod house except that one time, to make up her mind about Cheyenne.

Had she made the wrong choice? As she crossed the outer pasture then wound through the scrubby woods, emerging higher up the trail amid a stand of stately lodgepole pines, she heard birdcalls—a Steller's Jay, for one—and the far-off burble of the clear-running brook. The water ran over her thoughts, as if to cleanse them.

After a brief stop to water the horse, they finished the climb and, tucked into the side of the hill, the sod house emerged. Erin could see sunlight glinting off the lone window in front. She ground-tethered Kemosabe, leaving him to munch lush virgin grass, before she pushed open the sagging wood plank door beneath the grass-covered roof and went inside.

All over again the darkness, the stillness enveloped her. The scent of damp earth prickled her nose.

Just let me kiss you . . .

Danny, show me what it's like.

Oh, God, in Cheyenne, how he'd shown her again. To rid herself of the feelings he roused, had she deliberately let him think she might marry Ken last night—as if a house in Dillon could be her talisman? She felt mean-spirited.

Taking the old blanket from the shelf, Erin carried it outside, shook it, and then spread it on the grass near

Kemosabe, whose coat glistened. Stretching out, she basked in the sunlight herself, needing its warmth.

She should have known she and Danny couldn't find common ground. They hadn't since he first left Paradise Valley. Or was Daisy right, and as Danny had said, that she never gave him a chance? That she stubbornly only wanted things her way?

Exhausted from their quarrel, Erin finally dozed. She didn't know how much later a sudden sound woke her and she started, sitting up on the blanket. A pebble had landed beside her, and she shaded her eyes against the sun.

Someone had thrown the stone at her.

At first all she saw was a man's tall form cresting the hill some yards away. Then the shape resolved itself into a battered Broncos cap, a pair of broad shoulders, and a lean, familiar, well-muscled form, a well-worn pair of high-top sneakers.

Danny.

Her mouth went dry. Her thoughts scattered.

Despite their argument, he'd always done that to her simply by coming into view.

"Now I know why Dad always kept horses—in the plural," he said. At Kemosabe's nicker, he ran a hand over the gelding's withers, then dropped down onto the blanket. He picked his spot at the very edge, not touching Erin. "That's a helluva climb up the hill. Must be a mile and a half."

"You're an athlete. You're not even puffing." She looked at him then away. "How did you know where to find me?"

"I knew where to find you," he said, "and why."

She fiddled with the blanket edge. "Well, we talked. It didn't change either of our minds. As usual." She glanced up. "You're right about Paradise Valley, though." She remembered what Ken had said about Hank's will and Danny using her to get the ranch, though in Erin's view Danny had more claim to it than she did. "I love it here, but I can't condone your bringing trouble to this land on purpose, whether or not you intend anyone getting hurt."

"Including me?" he said.

Erin looked at him blankly.

"What do you think brought me up this hill on foot? I spent most of last night awake on that damned daybed, going over what we both said." He leaned back on his elbows, raising his face to the sun. "Maybe we'll never really forget what happened to Trev. You, me, Mom or Ken. But it seems you were as concerned last night about me getting hurt as you were Tim."

"I don't want anyone hurt."

"More than that, Erin."

"Yes, I'm including myself." She shook her head. "Danny, don't you see? It's not just this new thing about stock contracting—as much as I hate the idea. Cheyenne was an interlude, away from reality here. Maybe Ken made me see that. You and I . . . we never last long . . . " Her throat tightening, she couldn't continue.

Danny sat up, his eyes darkening. "You're the one who left me in Cody eight years ago with my belly stapled together and my cheekbone busted. You're the one who zipped back to Sweetwater because you couldn't stand being married to me."

"I came home pregnant," she said, but in some perverse part of herself, she had still needed him with her. Yet she could never bring herself to ask for his help, as if admitting she'd been wrong to leave the painful situation—him—after all.

"So you think I just turned my back, and kept on going to the next rodeo with Luke? That I might do that again?"

"Yes," she said, "that's exactly what I think."

She'd end up feeding broncs and bulls by herself, alone.

He looked at her in disbelief. "You think I didn't wonder

how you were for nine months carrying my baby—or, rather, the six months I knew about him? Didn't wonder how long your labor lasted?" He leaned closer. "That I didn't worry whether Tim would be whole, and healthy? Or want to know how you felt the morning after you gave birth? How you looked in that blue-flowered nightie?"

Erin stared at him. How did he know she wore that?

"Mom called me," he said, "just like she did when Tim broke his arm." Danny's voice turned husky. "She said, 'I thought you should know. Erin had the baby tonight. At two minutes after midnight.' I could hear the smile in Mom's voice." He met Erin's gaze. "She told me you were determined to deliver after twelve, so the hospital wouldn't charge you for the whole day before in the nursery."

"Where were you?"

"Santa Fe." Danny held her gaze. "As soon as I hung up, I started driving, hell for leather. I reached the hospital around noon, I remember. The sun was high, the birds singing." He smiled a little. "I talked my way past the reception desk, then the nurses' station on the maternity wing. I said we were separated, but I needed to see you."

"You charmed some nurse."

Danny half smiled. "Guess I did."

"And then?" She was fascinated in spite of herself.

His gaze softened. "Another nurse led me to your room and I saw you. Lying there in that flowered gown, fast asleep, the sun beaming on you, your hair shining like fire. Looking so exhausted, so . . . productive."

He didn't wake her. She'd never known.

"I asked to see Tim, and she took me to the nursery. Someone held him up at the window." He paused. "I didn't even help name him, but I had to touch him myself."

Erin blinked. Once she and Danny separated, she hadn't heard from him often. His reaction to her letter about her pregnancy had been a stilted note in reply, wishing her well. If there was anything she needed . . .

Erin pressed her lips together. She'd never imagined . . .

"I held him, me wearing one of those ugly gowns, sitting in an old rocking chair, feeling too damn big for that place. All these other babies squalling around me." His gaze slid away. "Erin, he was so small. I held him, and he didn't feel as if he weighed any more than a horse's halter. He almost seemed to fit in the palm of my hand, and I felt all thumbs." He shook his head at the memory. "He smelled like innocence itself."

"I thought so too," she murmured. No scent compared with that of a newborn baby, and like certain songs the memory nearly made her cry.

"I held him for ten minutes, then gave him back and stood outside the window while a nurse fed him a bottle of water."

"My milk hadn't come in."

"He fell asleep in that little plastic crib with his name on the end. 'Timothy James Sinclair. 7 lbs., 8 ozs.'" He frowned. "Then Ken came along, like the proud father himself, carrying an armload of yellow daffodils with blue streamers."

She remembered the flowers, those from Meg and Hank too. She remembered the stuffed monkey from Danny, for his son. Ken had never said a word about his visit.

"He told me to get out of Dillon, out of Montana, out of your life." He paused. "I told him I'd go—because that's what you kept saying you wanted. And I had rodeo calling me." Sitting cross-legged, he plucked at the grass. "I didn't know what else to do. I had to see him, Erin. Had to see you too."

Her eyes filled with tears. She could barely speak. "If I'd known . . . We weren't together, Danny, but he was still your child."

He made a sound. "That wasn't my impression. All the times I called that first year. The times you told me in clipped words how Tim was developing—and by your tone of voice that you didn't think that was my business."

Had she been that cold? That fearful of contact with him? Afraid even of his caring? Afraid she might want him again?

"Danny, you make me sound so . . . stubborn."

"You still are stubborn."

He meant last night.

"And you're too proud."

On her knees Erin crawled to him across the Hudson's Bay blanket that scratched her legs, her lips quivering, the tears overflowing. She couldn't fault Ken after so much time. She had taken those first moments of their son's life from Danny herself. Yet Ken had lied to her with his silence. And in all her memories of him, sweet or sad, Danny had always been honest.

"So where are we now?" He grasped her hands, and rubbed the bare knuckle of her third finger. "In Cheyenne you sure didn't reject me. But is what I do—what I want to do—or who I am going to separate us for the rest of our lives?"

Erin could barely see him through her tears. Blindly, she freed her hands, cupping his face in them, stroking his cheekbones, his dark hair.

He said, "I know you don't like the idea of stock contracting here. But what else can I do when I'm done bull riding? Have you ever thought of that, Erin?" He gazed into her eyes. "I confess, I didn't, maybe until Tim broke his arm and I came back to Paradise Valley again." He took a breath, steadying his voice. "I never went to college. Do you know these kids today—kids Jason Barker's age—get scholarships? They have rodeo *coaches*, for God's sake, just like football and basketball."

"I'm so used to you competing that I never considered what you might do after you quit."

"You didn't have to. We weren't living together." He rested his hands on his thighs. "I'm thirty-six years old, Erin. How do I make a new start?"

"I don't know," she said.

"And what in hell are we fighting about?" He stared at his hands, while Erin stared at his muscled forearms. "Ken tells me I don't have a share of the ranch. So stock contracting's probably just another dream. If I can't convince you or Ken . . ."

Erin sat stricken by his words. In her own way, she had pushed him out, like Hank and Ken. As Daisy said, she'd given him no other choice. Keeping his arms at his sides, his head down, he closed his eyes, and Erin whispered the words she'd kept from him so long. They spilled from her like her tears.

"Danny, no matter what . . . Danny, I love you."

She wound her arms around his neck and kissed him, her tears wetting their mouths, turning slick and salty. Erin wasn't sure she was the only one crying. She squeezed her eyes shut and held him until she felt his arms tighten around her, heard his voice shake.

"I need you, Erin. *Now*," he said.

The sun radiated off her skin. She opened her eyes and found him watching her, briefly tipped her head back, and smiled through tears at the clear blue sky.

"Outside?"

"Or in the sod house, if you like."

His eyes pleaded with her. Wordlessly, she slipped from his embrace, gathered the blanket when he stood up too, and carried it inside. The darkness seemed total for an instant before her eyes adjusted, but the rich earthy smell welcomed her. Welcomed them. Then on the threshold, Erin paused.

Behind her he settled his hands on her shoulders, turning her to him.

"I want this—you," she said, "but I'm afraid."

In Cheyenne she had felt need, powerful and sharp, that only seemed to grow with every joining. It had become its own reality, threatening to consume her in tenderness. Now desire had a new and even gentler, stronger dimension.

"You weren't afraid the first time."

Holding the blanket between them, she whispered, "I didn't know then what could happen if I loved someone too much."

"Don't be afraid."

He took the blanket from her, letting it billow to the earthen floor. When he drew Erin down onto it, she felt its sun-kissed warmth soothe her now-chilled skin. Lying over her, Danny looked deep into her eyes, unsmiling, so that she wondered if he felt the same fear but wouldn't admit it.

"It's like those bulls you're so wary of. You just have to get on and ride. There's nothing to be afraid of—not when I love you as much as I do."

In the darkness, with only the sounds of soft breathing, of Kemosabe's snuffling nearby in the grass, heard through the open door, of the sweet bird calls from the valley, they undressed each other in the place where they had first come together, and gave each other all they had to give once more.

Danny sought her bare breasts; he touched her lips.

In turn, Erin stroked the crisp, silky hair on his chest; she teased the corners of his mouth.

They shared sweet, grazing kisses, then long, drugging explorations that made Danny groan, and Erin beg.

"Please."

"You don't even have to tell me." Danny settled himself closer between her legs. "You're not gonna marry Ken."

"No," she said, and soon, words failed them completely; they didn't need them now, needed nothing but each other.

At last, with agonizing slowness, his gaze on hers never wavering, Danny pushed into her, seating himself deep, then deeper still until she knew he'd reached her very soul.

"Feel me inside you," he whispered in the fertile darkness of the sod house. "Erin, feel the love."

"*Yes*." She clutched him tighter, rising to him, seeking and finding. "*Yes!*"

"Another beginning," he told her. "We can work the rest out. We can."

17

Like a bittersweet love song, Danny's promise played itself in Erin's mind the instant she awoke each morning. Lying beside him in the bed they had shared so rarely in thirteen years of marriage, she closed her eyes again.

Not quite two weeks, she thought. As planned the first weekend, Danny had met Luke in Belle Fourche. He had placed second and won reasonable money. He'd come home again on Sunday night in high spirits, but the previous weekend he "just had to go to Gordon, Nebraska" where he took first and on the way back, third place at a smaller rodeo that paid for the trip. The following Wednesday Erin was already waiting for him to leave again.

When he was at Paradise Valley, he continued to fix fence and had started on the barns, but the latest issue of *Pro Rodeo Sports News* ranked him fourteenth in the world standings. If he stayed there, he would make the cut for the National Finals, which included the top fifteen riders.

If this was Danny's way of "working out the rest," she

didn't know how much longer she could tolerate the arrangement. They hadn't discussed stock contracting again, had avoided all issues that might cause an argument.

She turned to ease an ache in her shoulder from sleeping curled into the curve of Danny's body all night. She could take sleeping with him forever. But they had tried commuting marriage before and it hadn't worked.

When his arm went around her again, settling at her waist, she opened her eyes and found him peering over her shoulder, smiling. His sleepy eyes met hers and she groaned inwardly. Another second, and she'd be lost again.

Erin inched away, focusing on the white wall opposite the bed.

"What?" Nuzzling the nape of her neck, he didn't sound concerned. "Am I losing my charm?"

"You have a lifetime supply." She rolled onto her back, pushing down the flowered coverlet, knowing her mistake before he shifted his weight to thread one hard thigh between her legs. "But, Danny, I need more."

His morning smile turned into a puzzled frown.

"Not enough? You've been wearing me out." He kissed her lightly. "I'm not quite awake. So consider that a warning that this isn't the best time for serious discussion of any topic—except one."

His leg stroked hers. She ran her fingers through the thick hair edging the top of his ear, then followed his hairline to his neck, and moaned softly.

"See?" He pushed his leg higher between hers. "This is working just fine." He cut off her protest with a longer, sweeter kiss, finally coming up for air. "I'm here just like I promised."

"Luke called again last night."

Danny swore softly.

"He left a message with Meg," Erin said. "Something about a rodeo in Utah." She paused, trying to ignore Danny's mouth at the sensitive juncture of her shoulder and throat. Inhaling the breeze through the dotted swiss curtains, she was tempted not to tell him. "He thinks it's a sure winner but entries close today."

Danny nudged closer.

"I'll call him after breakfast."

"And tell him what?"

He eased her cotton nightie higher over her hips, leaving a trail of heat behind on her skin. "No discussion. No argument."

Pushing away, she sat up against the pillows.

"What will you tell him, Danny?"

He dropped onto his back, a hand flung over his eyes.

"No decisions either, this early in the day."

"I suppose when you make one, I'll be the last to know."

Never mind his mother's transparent joy that Danny was home again, at least half the time. Meg had been cleaning and cooking for a week. The day before Erin had caught her slumping at the desk in the emporium's office, half asleep over an order form she was supposed to be filling out.

Never mind her own joy, Erin added to herself.

Danny spoke from behind his arm. "Are we going to make love this morning, or am I going downstairs to wake up?"

At that instant the bedroom door flew open. Timmy charged into the room. Seeing his mother and father, he launched himself toward the bed with a happy shout.

"Wake up, you guys!" Miraculously, he landed between Erin and Danny, scrunching himself on his stomach into the sheets, wiggling his narrow bottom and propping his chin on his good hand. "Gram says waffles and ham in ten minutes, but coffee's ready now."

"She a pretty good cook, is she?" Danny traced the line of freckles across Timmy's nose.

"She's a great cook. And you know what else?"

"She's a barrel-racing queen headed for the nationals?"

"No, Daddy." Timmy giggled. "She's pretty too."

"She sure is."

"Danny," Erin said.

Timmy had distracted them, and Danny reached over the side of the bed for his jeans on the floor. She knew it was now or never.

"Tim, tell your grandmother I'll be down in a minute."

His serious tone stopped Timmy in mid-motion. His hands were poised, ready to pounce and tickle Danny's midsection, a game they played each morning when Danny was at Paradise Valley. Timmy's hands fell to his sides, his eyes rounding.

"Are you guys gonna fight?"

Danny's gaze met hers. "No, but I need time with your mom. Alone."

"Oh, *that*." Timmy slithered off the bed and raced for the hall, calling Danny's request to Meg before he reached the stairs. "Hurry up!"

"We're not, are we?" Danny tugged on his jeans and worked his fly. He was still morning-hard, and Erin looked away, fighting herself. Danny wanted to be part of their lives again. She wanted him too, but not part-time.

She slipped out of bed, and with her back to Danny, put on a pair of white shorts and a navy blue top. Barefoot, she brushed her hair without looking at him in the mirror. She could feel his gaze on her, part thwarted desire, part growing anger.

She set the brush on the dresser. "I keep remembering Cheyenne. I saw that you were not only competent at what you do but special. I went with you to collect your check." She smiled a little. "I helped you spend it too."

The last night Danny had taken her, Timmy, Meg, and Luke to dinner—prime steaks at Cheyenne's priciest, and overbooked, restaurant. Danny's rank, his obvious reputation as a rodeo star, had gotten them a choice table and a complimentary bottle of expensive wine.

"It's half yours," he said now.

She hesitated. "When we talked at the sod house I

tried to believe in your coming home and working things out."

Danny said nothing. His hand still at the top button of his fly, he seemed unable to move. His hazel eyes looked watchful.

"You don't think we can?" he said. "Why? My mother's happy enough. Tim's beside himself seeing us in bed together every morning—"

"Not every morning."

He stared at her.

"I need more than a few days a week, Danny. I thought it might not matter, considering the years with nothing, but it does." She looked at the floor between them. "You get home Sunday night late, or Monday. By Wednesday or Thursday you're either champing at the bit or already on the road again."

"I need the money, Erin. There's a good chance I'll make the finals this year."

"I know," she said. "I read the standings."

He looked pleased by her interest. "If I get to Vegas, that's possible cash in the bank."

Cash to buy a bunch of bad bulls and badder broncs.

"And then you'll start stock contracting?"

He tugged on his boots. "Look, I know you don't like the idea—but it could make us a good living, with enough to send Tim to college. Enough for any other kids we might have too," he added. "What's so bad about that? I'll put in as many safeguards here as I can. I'll lecture Tim about staying away from the bulls until he's blue in the face from listening to me. But I don't know what else—"

"I can't live with halfway measures, Danny. I've tried but I can't. It's too hard watching the driveway for the camper, telling Timmy you'll be home tomorrow or the next day. You call this slowing down? And when you get here, we start waiting for you to leave again."

A muscle jumped in his jaw.

"You want me to leave, for good?"

"No."

"You want me to quit." It wasn't a question.

She nodded. "I guess that's what I'm saying."

Danny pulled open a drawer in the pine chest, took out a fresh T-shirt, and slammed it shut. "You want me to just hang up my bull rope in the middle of one of the best seasons I've ever had? You want me to lose my best chance at a world championship when Lord knows I've only got a few years left in me? And my bones already creaking, muscles aching?"

Erin said nothing. He wasn't really asking her but himself. She waited, holding her breath.

He held her gaze for a long moment, as if remembering the last time she'd walked out on him, but she didn't look away. Twin dabs of color abraded his cheekbones. His mouth became a straight line. Finally, he exhaled the words.

"All right. I quit."

He turned away from her, stalked to the open door, and strode along the hall to the stairs. She heard the heavy clamber of his footsteps going down, heard Meg's morning greeting and Timmy's glad cry for Danny to sit next to him, to have some Frosted Flakes.

She'd won. After thirteen years, she had won.

Victory didn't feel as it had in all her dreams. In the pit of her stomach it felt small, and bitter-hard. Like an unripe apple stolen from a tree.

After Meg left for the store, and Erin took Tim into town to play with a friend, Danny returned Luke's call. Like the breakfast he'd picked at, his last cup of coffee rolled in his stomach.

The heavy words he gave Luke provoked a queasy silence.

"*Quit*?" Luke finally said. "How the hell can you just quit? In the middle of the season?"

"It's what Erin wants. What Tim needs." He waited a beat. "I know how she thinks. To Erin, the rest of the season's a gamble, long before I get to Vegas. It's that many more chances to break my neck."

"She convinced you of that, did she?" Luke snorted. In the background Danny could hear male laughter, someone calling out about the day's draw. "Just like a woman. Hammer and nails always ready, poundin' down the coffin lid."

"Luke, I've been gone a long time. Tim's half grown already, and the only male influence in his life has been Ken, who isn't exactly my cheerleader. What else can I do?" he said. "I love my boy and I love Erin."

"That doesn't mean she has to get her own way."

"Maybe I've had mine long enough."

"You sound real happy about that."

He ran a hand through his rumpled hair. "I have to own up to my responsibilities for a change."

"What about your stock business?" He'd told Luke last weekend about his ideas.

"She didn't give me a flat no this time." He said he thought he'd eventually bring Erin around. "I'll start slow, let her see the benefits outweigh the disadvantages, the danger. One day at a time."

"Kill your dream," Luke said, "you kill yourself."

"Is that why you haven't been back to Sweetwater to see my mother? Because you're afraid she'll tell you to stop playing games and grow up too?"

"I've been married. Once was once too many. Anything less wouldn't please Meg Sinclair, as she pointed out. Besides," he said, with a smile in his tone, "I'd have you and probably Ken on my back if I came courting."

Danny wasn't that sure. He didn't think his mother belonged alone. As he spent time at Paradise Valley, he found he didn't like her relying exclusively on him and Erin, on their child, to make up her life without his father. The first thing he'd done was encourage her to work more hours at Erin's store. He could watch Tim, he'd told her. But he'd watched on his own schedule, taking off for Belle Fourche last Thursday at dawn, leaving Meg and Erin to watch Tim at the store.

He heard hoofbeats in the distance over the phone line, the bleat of an announcer's voice. "Maybe you'll change your mind about women some day," he told Luke.

"Maybe you will." But like the good friend he was, Luke didn't try to change Danny's decision. "Guess I'd better go buy myself a pickup truck now that I'm traveling alone."

When Luke hung up, Danny held the dead receiver against his thigh, as if to shut off his last words. Leaning against the kitchen counter, he could almost smell horse-flesh, dust rising from the arena, even the pungent aroma of bull droppings. How could he miss that? Already?

He finally hung up the phone and turned to lean his elbows on the counter. He stared out the window at the empty yard, at Kemosabe in the pasture. He'd been smelling the gelding, the dust from the corral. He'd imag-ined the bull but gave it an image—short, squatty, sweet. A real twister. A money bull. Waiting for him in Grand Forks, or Fort Worth, or nearby Dillon for Labor Day.

He wouldn't even get that far now.

Danny jerked upright as a familiar station wagon appeared on the drive, raising clouds of dust. He poured himself an unwanted cup of coffee and carried it outside before Ken stepped from the car. He'd be damned if his brother—always in the superior position because of his age if nothing else—would pin him in the house with no escape.

He felt hemmed in enough.

"Ken." Settling his Broncos cap on his head as he walked, Danny met him halfway across the yard. "You forget some of your clothes?"

"Mom said you were here again."

"Nice of you to come visit." He sipped the lukewarm

coffee, which turned his stomach. "I'd offer you some coffee, but I just emptied the pot. What's on your mind?"

"I'm selling my share of the ranch."

Ken smiled a little, as if he'd savored the announcement all the way from Dillon.

Danny's breath rushed out. His brother never wasted words; he didn't believe in subtlety. Danny felt as if he'd been gored in the gut again.

"You can tell them for me, if Erin and Mom want to keep their shares, that's up to them. Once I stop contributing here—I can't run the house in Dillon too—they may not have any choice. I've just come from a Jaycees meeting," Ken said, "and the word's out. There'll be a buyer before you finish that coffee. Good money too."

Ken named six figures that made Danny's head spin.

"For five hundred acres of dead ranch land? You're bluffing," he said.

"I saw headlines in the paper here not that long ago. The town council met last night. There's expansion all around, radiating out from Maverick Mountain." Ken's smile grew. "It seems the snow bunnies will be heading for Sweetwater in the not too distant future. Entertainment people too from LA and New York. They're buying up Montana, and a place like Paradise Valley even sounds good."

Danny said nothing.

Ken grinned. "Maybe Erin's been right not selling out. Land values will keep rising. But then, she could turn her business around now too, so maybe she still won't want to sell her share of the ranch, Mom's either, although you'll have neighbors close by from my share who may not like smelly horses in their backyard." He paused. "At least she'll be able to support you when you get your ass busted riding bulls–or get too old to climb on one."

Danny dumped his coffee on the ground between them. The dark liquid splashed over his old boots and Ken's newer ones.

"Word travels fast. I only quit rodeo ten minutes ago. Erin doesn't even know yet, and you're circling around like some vulture."

"You *quit*?"

Danny nearly smiled. It had been years since he'd shocked Ken.

"From now on, I'm a full-time family man."

"How long will that last?"

He bristled. On that statement alone, he'd make a go of stock contracting, of his premature retirement.

"It's permanent," he said.

"You must have been making better money than I thought."

Not nearly enough, he thought. "I have a few bucks."

Ken's smile disappeared. A hard light came into his eyes. "You want to buy out my share of the ranch? Dad'll roll over in his grave—but if you're going to hang around, you'll have to do something halfway useful." He paused. "Of course when that something horns you in the belly or the groin, sends you flying into the air and landing back down on your head, I'll be there. To pick up the pieces, so to speak."

"Erin's not going to divorce me or marry you. Whether I'm here or gone, dead or alive."

"We'll see."

Danny dug his bootheel in the dirt.

"You been sitting over there in Dillon, have you, brooding about that new house Erin didn't want?" He looked at Ken. "She loves Paradise Valley with all her heart."

"Then you'll want to see she keeps it."

Danny's blood pressure kicked a notch higher. "Ken, I'll need all the grazing land I can get—including yours. But I can't meet your price. Not right away." He stared into his empty mug. This wasn't turning out to be the best day of his life. "I'll pay you twenty per cent down now and count on you accepting—because of Erin and especially Mom. It would kill her to leave here." He thumbed his Broncos cap back. "I'll get the rest somehow."

"A builder can have condos up before the first snow."

"I'm your brother, for God's sake!"

"Not as I see it."

"Goddammit." Danny dropped the coffee mug, reaching for Ken's jacket lapels. The Broncos cap fell off.

"You're getting desperate, Danny boy."

"You're taking advantage!" He jerked him once, then pushed him away. "I can get you the damn money." He held Ken's gaze with his. "I'm asking you to wait a while longer, that's all."

"Until when?"

He swallowed. He could see Erin's taut face earlier, see the hope in her expression when he gave in. He didn't know what else to do, except to beg Ken.

"After the finals—Las Vegas. For Tim," he said.

The ranch would be his son's one day. Danny would see to it. The only way he knew how, despite the objections Erin would surely have.

When Erin drove in that night, she saw Danny in the corral with Kemosabe. The gooseneck horse trailer waited nearby. She stopped the Jeep and switched off the engine but didn't get out. With her hands laced on the steering wheel, she settled back in the seat to watch.

She couldn't tell whether he saw her, but he kept to his business—twitching the long, thin whip at Kemosabe's hocks, sending the black-and-white paint around the ring at the end of the lunge line, head high, circling Danny in perfect, graceful cadence.

She'd have the opportunity now to watch this same sight as often as she pleased. Danny was staying home. She'd see to it that he was as happy about that as she and Timmy.

"A man has to do what he has to do," Meg had told her that afternoon at the store when Erin expressed her guilt over the morning's quarrel, and Danny's decision. "Do you think he's ready to give up bull riding?"

Erin couldn't answer that. It was Danny's decision; all she'd done was give him a snap of the whip, as he did with Kemosabe, to keep his mind focused. She supposed Luke Hastings had a name for that.

Danny finished schooling the horse and slowly reeled him in at a walk. Patting Kemosabe's nose, he produced a carrot. Then unsnapping the lunge line, he adjusted the stirrups and swung into the elaborately tooled western saddle he'd bought with his first winnings after they married.

Erin walked across the yard to the corral and leaned her arms against the fence rail.

"Nice evening," Danny said, continuing to put Kemosabe through his paces. "Mom and Tim went to church. There's a covered-dish supper tonight, and the kids are scraping old paint in the sanctuary. Next weekend the men's group is scheduled to prime and repaint." He half halted, then nudged Kemosabe into a loose-jointed but spirited walk. "Mom left supper for us. You go ahead if you want." His eyes didn't meet hers. "I'll be in as soon as I finish here."

"He looks good," she said, squinting against the sinking sun. "I think he feels good too."

"In part because you've been riding him every morning. But he's had his vacation." Danny jogged past, the horse's long mane and tail flying in a breeze of their own making, stirring the warm late afternoon stillness. "I'm finally sending him back on the road. A guy I know from Lubbock's interested in leasing him the rest of the season."

"Timmy will be crushed."

"I've been thinking about that," Danny said over his shoulder. "When things settle down, I'll look for a nice horse for him. Kemosabe's a showpiece. He likes the crowd, the applause. He belongs on the circuit winning money."

Erin gnawed at her lower lip. Danny's tone sounded wistful. Or did she imagine it did?

"When things settle down?" she repeated.

"We need to talk."

He made no move to join her, and he'd told her to eat alone. He kept pushing Kemosabe through his gaits, up then down and all over again. Erin's arms ached. She straightened from the rail.

"Let's talk, then."

"Later."

"Now," she said.

Throwing her a sullen look, he gave the horse a loose rein, kicked his feet from the stirrups and let them hang. Crossing his arms over his chest, he rode over to her, his whole body in rhythm with the horse, his back straight but relaxed, his seat deep. He was a born horseman, and she suspected Timmy was too.

"You make quite a sight on that horse."

He didn't smile. His gaze fixed on the fence at Erin's chest level, then he slid off Kemosabe's back. At his serious expression, she couldn't breathe properly.

"I'm going back, Erin," he said. "For the rest of the season. Until Christmastime."

She couldn't speak; she couldn't form the words.

"But I thought—this morning—"

"Something came up."

"Luke Hastings?" Leading Kemosabe, he edged past her through the gate and headed for the barn. Erin pursued him. "What? You called Luke and he called you pussy-whipped? Is that all it took for you to turn your back on us again?"

She stalked after him, knowing better than to follow so closely at Kemosabe's rear, but not caring. A coarse, white tail slashed across her shirtfront, flicked the corner of her eye like a warning.

"Let's have it, Danny. What do you want from me? A convenient roll in the hay three nights a week? Someone to cheer you when you make points?" She touched his upper arm, feeling hard muscle. "What do you want from *us*? You haven't been here a month and you're taking this horse away from Timmy—who's pampered him while you were on the road and couldn't be bothered—you're patting that little boy on the head and promising—*what*? To come back again in another week, another month?" Her breath came in harsh gasps. "When he breaks his arm again?"

Danny snapped the horse into the crossties just inside the barn. "When you're finished, let me know."

"And when will you come back for me? After you've left me pregnant, and you decide to see what your new son or daughter looks like this time?"

"Ken's selling the ranch."

She didn't think she'd heard right, his tone stayed so quiet. He turned to stare at her.

"There's some developer coming into town from Denver, bent on putting up condos for the folks who ski over at Maverick Mountain and Beaver Creek Run. Ken says we're sitting on prime land here—for that at least— and he's selling his share."

"He can't do that."

"I hope you're not surprised. How long has he been trying to get you and Mom out of here? Why do you think he built that fancy house in Dillon and asked you to marry him?" Danny turned aside, stroking Kemosabe's nose. "Ken hasn't wanted this place since Trev died. I bet every morning he walked from that bunkhouse to his car, he cursed this ranch."

Danny was right. Ken's dislike of Paradise Valley had seemed to grow with the years, her own love expanding to fill the gap.

"What can we do?"

Danny didn't seem to notice she'd said *we*.

"He offered me the chance to buy him out. I don't have the money right now."

Was Ken getting even with her? She reached out to touch his arm again, but Danny moved, putting the horse between them. "I have until December to raise the money to pay him."

"Bull riding," Erin murmured.

"I know I promised you," he said, "but the only way to get that money is to finish this season—and hope I make the finals. Not only make 'em," he added, "but win. With that, and what I have put by, I might get him to settle, or hold him off a while longer. Or maybe I can get a mortgage somehow for his share."

Anger surged through her. Hank Sinclair had denied his middle son the land that should have been his; now Ken would do the same.

"I could sell the store," she said.

"No." Danny shook his head. "You've worked too hard for it. Mom's all excited about helping out there. Ken's right, when business starts booming around here, you're sitting in the catbird seat." Erin could see him smile faintly. "Laura Ashley curtains, hanging plants, and all."

She slipped under the crosstie, coming close to Danny. For a moment she watched him sweep a brush over the paint's hide. "Danny, I'm sorry I jumped in without waiting to find out what had happened."

"You do have that tendency where I'm concerned." He flicked a glance at her. "Unless," he said, "you're putting off acting at all, which is usually more your style."

She raised her eyebrows. "True. But in all the years we haven't seen things the same way, I've always known you loved Paradise Valley too." She cleared her throat before going on. "We've always had that in common."

"What are you saying?"

"If you need to keep on riding to save this place, I'll try not to mind—or to worry so much."

"I kind of like you worrying about me." He frowned. "If I can keep the ranch together, Erin, you know what else that means."

"Ornery bulls and broncs running all over Paradise

Valley?" She covered his hand on the brush, stilling the motion. When his eyes met hers, she said, "I guess that's better than looking out our bedroom window every morning and seeing cedar shake condos everywhere."

The brush fell to the cement floor. Kemosabe stomped a hoof. Turning his head, the gelding pushed Danny who took the hint and stepped closer to her. He framed Erin's face in his hands.

She could feel her pulse beating against his fingers. Or Danny's heart pulsing in his fingertips? She couldn't seem to separate them.

"I guess watching for you every night is better too."

With an answering smile, Danny bent to kiss her.

"I'll make sure of it."

18

Labor Day had come and gone, but a month later, in the first week of October, with the autumn foliage of aspen and larch glorifying the hills surrounding Sweetwater and Paradise Valley, Meg still watched the driveway each night and morning. She jumped each time the emporium's front door opened, jangling the bell above it to announce someone's presence. Luke, she always hoped.

Earlier that day the bell had announced Mrs. Eady, one of Erin's most loyal customers. Meg spent an hour with the elderly, white-haired widow, commiserating about her poor circulation and finally sending Mrs. Eady away with a brighter blue in her eyes, happy with the new elastic stockings Meg sold her and a home remedy for pain.

Briskly, she counted money in the cash register, satisfied with the tally. Late afternoon sun slid through the display windows, and she couldn't say business was—Ken's word—booming, but several local women seemed to like the aprons she stocked on consignment; they'd bought half a dozen, the last of those she'd sewn for the Labor Day bazaar in Dillon, part of the Beaverhead County Fair.

Danny had won first place there bull riding in the annual two-day Jaycees rodeo, which attracted both local and nationally top-ranked riders, but he'd also landed on his face after a bad dismount, and Erin's white complexion made Meg wonder about her own advice to let Danny follow his dream if he must.

Luke didn't fare much better. Amid the holiday hoopla including a parade, dances, a barbecue, and a wild horse race, on the last day he stepped in front of a mad bull to save some young cowboy, and had the bruised ribs to show for it. Reluctantly, she was sure, Luke had spent several days at the ranch, healing—and eating Meg's home cooking. She hadn't seen him since.

When the bell jingled, she whirled, furious with herself for caring, then disappointed when Ken walked in.

With a quick greeting for her son, Meg glanced at the other customers in the store—a young rancher buying baby food for his new daughter, a pair of teenagers giggling over the hair ribbons. At least the store wasn't empty these days.

"I stopped at the ranch to give Timmy his math assignments for the week," Ken said. "We scheduled a quiz, but nobody was home."

"Erin must have forgotten to call." She'd left the store early that afternoon, distracted by her errands and the fact that Danny was due home later. "She took Timmy to the doctor for his checkup." He'd already had his cast removed weeks ago, and the bone looked strong, though his one arm appeared thinner than the other. "The doctor says he's fine. It's not like Erin, though, to forget to leave a note."

"She's not herself these days."

Ken toured the aisles, scowling at the teenagers who laughed when he passed, selecting a can of shaving foam, some razor blades, then a carton of milk and a TV dinner from the dairy/frozen food coolers at the rear.

To Meg, Erin seemed perfectly herself. Only that morning she had caught Erin singing while she rinsed off the breakfast dishes. Both she and Danny looked happier than Meg might have dreamed a few months ago.

Ken set his purchases on the front counter, lining them up by size.

"In a few weeks or a month, when winter sets in, she'll come to her senses," he said.

"Kenneth Sinclair, you have been avoiding your church commitment and it shows. I raised you to be more charitable, especially toward your brother and his wife." She emphasized the last word. "I'm a Christian woman but I'll speak plainly. I know you asked Erin to marry you." Erin had finally told her so, not to Meg's surprise, and Danny had added the rest. "I know you thought to bribe her with that house in Dillon."

"Any other woman would be overjoyed to live in a house like that."

She turned the TV dinner around to read the price sticker, keeping her voice low. "You are nearly forty years old. I suggest you begin looking for a more suitable marriage prospect and stop waiting around for Erin and Danny's relationship to crumble."

Meg cut off anything he might have said with angry jabs at the cash register keys. She didn't know what had come over her; she never made harsh statements to those she loved. She announced the total without looking up. She loved Ken too, but like Hank he could be pigheaded, and she felt certain he'd always envied Danny—not only because of Erin, but the fact that Danny had a dream.

Who knew better than Meg Sinclair that life didn't always work out according to some neat design? She wished Ken realized that.

"I suggest you rethink your intention to sell part of the ranch—"

"*My* part. Unless you think I should hand that over to Danny too."

He counted out bills and change, placing them on the counter between them rather than in Meg's hand, and arranging the coins in small, precise stacks.

"Your father never meant for that ranch to be cut in slices like a rhubarb pie. You know he didn't, Kenneth."

"He never meant for Danny to have it."

"I wouldn't be that sure."

Ken glanced around, at the girls coming along the aisle to the front of the store. He nearly whispered the words.

"You'd say anything to keep Paradise Valley intact, wouldn't you?"

"Yes," she said, scraping the money off the counter into her open palm. "I would. Just in case you meant to try to 'convince' me to sell."

"Don't count on Danny, Mom. If he doesn't ante up for my share, I'll sell it to the first buyer. I'm sure as hell not going to keep paying expenses on that godforsaken piece of dirt!"

"Don't swear at me! They'll carry me out in chains and auction off my share before *I* sell." Meg slammed the money into the open register drawer. Ignoring the girls with their chosen hair bows, she shoved it closed, then rounded the corner before Ken picked up his change and started for the door. "I raised you to be a God-fearing, decent man. What kind of vileness has taken over your mind?"

He towered over her, as tall as Hank had been, nearly as tall as Danny. His eyes blazed but she didn't back down. A mother of three boys learned early to hold her ground. What had happened to her tongue, she couldn't say.

Ken dropped his packages into a string shopping bag.

"I'm a grown man. I say what I please, I think as I please. And I damn well do as I please." He swung away toward the door. "I'm not your boy any longer. Don't treat me like one."

"You'll always be my boy," Meg said but didn't try to

touch him. Ken had never cared much for coddling, or hugs. "All three of you will."

"There's two of us now. And if Danny keeps on, there'll probably be just one."

Her lips pressed tightly together, Meg let him go.

The door banged shut, the bell jittered loudly. He reminded her of a sturdy oak that would try, unlike a willowy birch, to withstand every storm without bending.

"Kenneth," she murmured, "Kenneth."

For a long time she'd thought she had lost Danny along with Trevor. Now Ken was gone, and she wondered whether she'd lost more than she ever imagined long ago.

"What you need, my boy, is a woman of your own," Meg said. Then she turned to the register, beaming at the giggling girls, who were all wearing too much makeup. After she chatted with the rancher about three-month infant colic and wished him well, she tidied up the store, closed out the register—and tried not to look through the front windows for a glimpse of any of her missing men.

She even tried not to count Luke Hastings among them.

A week later Danny pulled in from a long haul to Texas for two rodeos, yanked his gear from behind the camper's front seat, and started for the house. At one in the morning Paradise Valley looked black as hell itself, and sounded silent as the grave, without even a familiar whinny from the corral. Kemosabe was on the road too, with a calf roper named Wes Turner, about whom Danny had growing doubts, which he wouldn't mention for fear of setting Tim off again. After sending Kemosabe away, Danny wasn't Tim's favorite person just now.

He glanced up at the darkened house. He doubted Erin would be waiting for him either, half awake like a few times since he started spinning wheels all over creation to maximize his season earnings. A smaller go-round here with a smaller purse but a bigger chance of winning, a big show there with tougher competition and stock but big money too. He'd broken even the first time this trip, won two thousand bucks the second. Probably spent half that—or so it seemed—on gas getting back.

Carrying his gear bag, Danny rubbed the back of his neck with his free hand. He'd always liked the open road. Tonight, he felt bone-weary. He thought his travel buddy had gone to the bunkhouse until he heard Luke's footsteps dogging his.

"I'm half starved. Think your mother might have some dessert hanging around from dinner?"

"What do you think?"

Danny continued into the house, from the back porch through the laundry room, then into the kitchen. He didn't stop or turn on any lights.

Luke nearly stepped on his heels when he paused to pull off his sneakers. "Maybe a cup of coffee left over too? By now it ought to be standing in the cup just the way I like it."

"See what you can find."

"Danny?" He heard the uncertainty in Luke's tone and turned in the doorway, surprised. Luke stood in the dark, and all Danny could make out was the gleam in his eyes, and the fact that he was already setting his shoes near the door. Pretty eager to please, for a man who didn't want to be roped by a woman and hog-tied.

"Yeah?" he said.

"I don't want you to think I'm freeloading here, between jobs, using your mother's hospitality . . . "

"What are you doing then?"

Luke laughed. "Damned if I know."

"Saving us separate travel expenses?" he suggested. "Don't rattle the plates. Folks are sleeping. My mother too." He fought a smile. "And just so you'll know, I can hear anyone who passes my room on the way to hers. Even a man in his sock feet. That might save us both some trouble."

He heard Luke's snort but didn't look back. At the moment Danny had his own woman on his mind.

With a grateful sigh, and holding Erin's present, Danny crawled into bed after stripping down to his briefs. She claimed Tim was old enough to be aware of his parents' nakedness in bed, and she thought it better to practice modesty. He slipped one hand underneath her, around to her breast. Tonight modesty meant a softly worn cotton pajama top of Danny's, probably from his boyhood, and— he explored lower—a pair of silky panties that didn't appear to cover much at all.

"You are a sinful woman," he murmured, nipping at an earlobe.

"You're late." Erin curled against him. "Seven thousand rodeos offered in a year"—she quoted Danny earlier that week—"and you have to go all the way to Texas?" She wiggled closer. "Did you win lots of money?"

Danny opened his other hand, and released piles of tens and twenties to flutter over her from belly to breast. Then he covered her shriek with his fingers.

"We had a flat coming up I–25 through Wyoming. A blowout," he added.

"Are you all right?" Erin's tone was hushed. She knew the saying about rodeo as well as Danny did: If the bulls don't kill you, the traveling will. Not to mention that tire, exploding . . . "Was Luke—"

"We're both fine. He's with me." Danny smiled against the sweet curve of her neck and shoulder. "He's in the kitchen wolfing down Mom's pie or cake, whatever." He snuggled her deeper in his arms. "Miss me?"

"Missed you," she whispered.

She brought her mouth to his, then before he could wallow in the kiss, moved fast, rolling over to straddle him, pinning his arms at either side of his head. Grinning, Danny let her have her way, giving silent thanks that he wouldn't spend the night in some wayside motel or the back of the camper. He loved her new playfulness. He loved Erin.

He couldn't remember their last quarrel, though of course they still had some, only that they resolved their differences more readily. And afterward . . .

"Wipe that smile off your face, pro rodeo man. You have just met your master—I mean, mistress."

"Shame on you, Mrs. Sinclair. And here I thought you were a happily married woman."

"I'm working on it."

"Why don't you show me?"

She lowered her head to his, making him groan. It had been a long week away from her. How had he stayed away for thirteen years, or even eight? Or until tonight?

"You know, this commuting's not so bad," he said.

"It has its advantages. Like homecomings."

"You think so too?" He thumbed a soft nipple, feeling it turn hard as a cherrystone between his fingers, and Erin moaned. Danny's voice turned husky. "God, I haven't felt this good since I left home at eighteen, when I decided to 'go hard.'"

Erin laughed softly at the double entendre, a rodeo term that meant to compete professionally, with serious purpose, if possible toward a championship. She pressed her lower body to his, which felt anything but soft, and chose her own interpretation. "You're still the man you were then . . . better. Believe me, you haven't lost . . . a thing."

Later, when their lovemaking ended and they lay in each other's arms, with the flowered coverlet kicked off and the cool October night air whisking over their heated bodies, Danny sighed again.

"This bed creaks."

"It's an old bed."

"We should buy a new one."

He felt Erin's smile against his bare chest. "That depends on how much use you plan to give it."

"*We* plan to give it."

"Umm, I think I like the sound of that."

All his muscles relaxed, his bones settled into their proper niches, and his eyes finally stopped seeing the white center line on the dark road through Beaverhead Pass. He was here again, with Erin. She still didn't wear his ring, but she would. He only had to love her enough, to make her believe in them again.

"I'll tell you something," he said, stroking her sleek hair, fanning it across his belly. "I already know I'm a happily married man."

The lowdown warmth spread sweetly through him at the same time, becoming hot once more in seconds, and he rolled Erin again onto the sheets. He thought he just might not mind it when his last season ended.

"Is Luke coming home tonight?"

Erin asked her mother-in-law the question casually as she stacked boxes of hair color on the third shelf in the center aisle. Meg had seemed half hard of hearing all day, and Erin kept asking her things twice. Not long before, she'd almost given a man the wrong change for a twenty-dollar bill.

Meg had chattered about the man long after he left the store. A man from the West Coast, she'd said, who was building a house in the mountains. New people were trickling in to the area, a good sign for business.

"Luke? I wouldn't say coming home."

Meg zipped around the end of the aisle, toward the sewing notions area.

"He's come with Danny every time in the past two weeks."

"Since the night he ate that entire lemon meringue pie after the Texas trip?"

"Maybe he likes more than the food."

Erin could almost hear the startled silence. Then small drawers in the notions department opened and closed one by one.

"I thought we had more of that olive green thread. I need to hem that pair of pants for Timmy." Meg paused. "What did you say, dear?"

"Try the last drawer."

It snapped open then shut. "I should have known."

"You should have," Erin agreed. "You know this store better than I do these days. You've certainly worked more hours."

"I enjoy working."

"And I'm glad to have more time with Timmy. He's reading really well—"

"Despite the fact Danny still thinks he should go to school in Dillon?" Meg peered over the shelf with a grin. "I heard you two last week. The plaster walls aren't that thick."

Erin flushed. If Meg heard her quarreling with Danny, she also heard them make up soon after. There hadn't been any animosity left then, any disagreement. Nor any energy, Erin added to herself.

"I suppose if Danny stays the winter, we'll have to think about building our own house."

"Erin, I love having you there. All of you." She smiled slyly. "In fact, if you wanted to give a fine mother-in-law a perfect Christmas present, I do think that sewing room might make a nice nursery. If Danny insulated the porch, I could use part of the laundry room for my projects. It might be more convenient."

Meg joined her in front of the hair color display, holding the spool of green thread, a slight frown creasing her forehead. "What did you mean, if Danny stays the winter?"

Erin had seen the wanderlust in his eyes often enough to wonder if he'd make it through from December to April in Paradise Valley.

"You didn't see him packing on Wednesday morning before he and Luke left on Friday last time?"

"No," Meg admitted.

"I imagine you were too busy pampering Luke to notice."

"Erin Sinclair, that is not true."

She arched a brow and Meg's face turned pink.

"That's a becoming color," she said. "You should try some of the new NaturGlow blusher that just came in. Then you'd have that radiant, stars-in-your-eyes look all the time."

Meg bit back a laugh.

"I'm not sure it's a good idea, Danny being home so much. You're turning into a very outspoken person on private matters."

Laughing, Erin grabbed her mother-in-law and hugged her.

"Admit it. These men may confuse us, but you're smitten, Margaret Sinclair."

"Me? That's—"

She didn't say the rest. Erin pulled back and pointed. In one hand Meg still held the green spool of thread for Timmy's pants; in the other she clutched a box of hair color.

Erin read the label. "Sunset Gold?"

"I've never dyed my hair. Hank would have had a fit."

"Lots of women color their hair." She patted Meg's soft brown hair, showing a few faint strands of gray. "If you think Luke would like it, go for it."

"Erin, not another word about Luke Hastings!"

Erin hid her face not to burst into laughter as Meg surreptitiously read the back of the package, then put it back only to select another, slightly darker shade.

"I won't tolerate matchmaking," Meg murmured.

"Why not? You and Timmy threw Danny and me together all last summer."

"We did not—we—" Helplessly, she threw up a hand. "All right, but that worked. There's nothing you could do to Luke that would turn him from the rodeo circuit and his freedom." She added, "As if I'd want him bound here."

"Hmm," was all Erin said. Then, "Did he say what time he and Danny might get home?"

Meg studied the box of hair color even more intently. "About midnight."

Erin couldn't hold back the snicker. "That should give you time to try that new look."

"Erin Sinclair! I'm a widow. A grandmother!" She wagged a finger.

Then they both broke up in laughter.

"Will you help me?" Meg asked. "And stop giggling!"

By the end of October Ken had stopped fuming about his quarrel with his mother, but he hadn't talked with her since and didn't intend to. He carried out his teaching duties with Timmy, avoiding Danny when he could, and spoke briefly each time with Erin about school matters only. But he wouldn't apologize to Meg and ignored the Sunday dinner invitations she left on his answering machine.

She and Erin would come crawling to him when Danny took off again. Playing house, that's all his marriage meant. There was no way he'd spend a winter snowed in at Paradise Valley, Ken told himself, casting a glance at the darkening sky which portended a coming rainstorm. The weather, though cool that day, had stayed too warm to snow.

Driving along Denton Street past the library, Ken switched his headlights on. He'd had a meeting at the bank in Sweetwater that day. He caught sight of a long, leggy figure striding along the sidewalk with squared-shouldered purpose.

The sight irritated him. Daisy Chatworth always did. He

remembered her drawing attention to him as he packed his car to move after Erin said no to his proposal. No doubt about it, he and Daisy rubbed each other the wrong way. Still, watching her long denim skirt alternately pulling, clinging around those willowy legs, he felt a lowdown tug inside. Ken tried to imagine her legs bowed out around the belly of a barrel racing horse.

He slowed the car anyway and drew alongside her. "Want a ride?"

"No, thanks." She didn't even look his way, a sure sign she'd already seen and rejected him.

"Your house must be another mile from here."

"I need the exercise."

He glanced at the threatening clouds. "It's going to rain in another minute."

"I like rain."

The sky rumbled. "You like thunder too? Lightning crashing all around?"

Daisy missed a step. "Are you telling me to stand under a nice, big tree on a hill and hold up my metal key ring?"

"Why don't you just get in the car."

Daisy quickened her stride.

Ken kept pace with her as thunder rattled overhead, then the first drops of rain started to fall. The storm broke with predictable suddenness. Within seconds a torrent had drenched Daisy to the skin and was streaming sheets down the windshield.

"Open the damn door!" she shouted, her figure a blur through the glass, even as he reached for the passenger side handle. She wrenched the door open and squished onto the seat, kicking off her wet shoes. They were navy blue with two-inch heels, and he shook his head, wondering why a tall woman would try to look even taller. No wonder she never married. He tried not to notice her feet—long, narrow, high-arched, they started another dance of desire in his gut.

"Satisfied?" She glared at him.

He couldn't help smiling. "You are a sight."

"I've been wet before."

The words hung like another cloud between them, and even Ken's face warmed.

"Don't say a word," she warned him.

She'd never been the elegant type. For years, he'd seen her only in jeans. Still holding her ugly denim hobo bag, she swatted him with it, splattering water all over his gray suit.

Ken brushed at it. He slipped the car into gear and Daisy stared straight ahead. He could barely see the street, but he'd drop her at her house if he had to float every inch of the way. The street ran with water, overflowing the storm drains, and wet leaves made the asphalt slick. A loud crack of thunder startled them into glancing at each other.

"Maybe you should pull over," Daisy said.

"Maybe you should get a backseat driver's license."

The station wagon crept along the flooded streets. Another car passing from the opposite direction sprayed dirty water over his window, making Ken flinch.

Daisy shivered, and he flipped the heater/defroster on high.

"I suppose I have to thank you for rescuing me."

The words sounded like dirt in her mouth. Ken only grunted.

"And here," she said, "I thought the only time you'd ever notice me would be if I were face-down in the corral and you felt obligated to call 911."

"Anyone who makes her living running a horse around a bunch of barrels has to expect that."

"I make my living as a librarian."

"Sure," he said, "and Danny's going to come home for good one of these days and become a stock contractor."

He could feel Daisy studying him, could almost feel the blaze of anger from her gaze. She held her shoes up, letting the water drip on to his rug, then zipped them into her bag.

"I don't imagine that goes well with your plans." She paused. "Erin told me about that big house you built over in Dillon. It's a nice house. I hope you enjoy it by yourself."

"How do you know it's a nice house?"

She kept her tone light. "She told me where it was. I got curious. I drove by. I didn't know exactly which house, only the street and the house's style, but I knew it right away as yours."

Ken waited. What had possessed her to spy on his new home? He felt unaccountably glad the landscapers had finally laid sod and planted a few trees.

"There's not a blade of grass out of control," she said, "and every flower bed is lined up just so—as if the flowers next spring wouldn't dare to bloom except in perfect rows, all the same height and color." She smiled. "I could have eaten my dinner off the slate walk to your front door."

"Is there something wrong with a man who's neat and clean?" He didn't smile back. "Or have you spent too much time around guys like Danny? All sweaty and mud-caked?"

"I appreciate a man who's clean. I have trouble with one who's so tidy he must store his broom up his—"

"Isn't that your house?" Cutting her off, he pointed through the smeary passenger window, his right hand grazing the tip of her nose.

Daisy nodded, her eyes flashing.

"As if you didn't know. I know why you have such a problem with us rodeo types," she said as he guessed where the driveway began and turned the station wagon off the street. "Don't think I don't."

"Because none of you have any sense."

He reached across to the door handle, the back of his arm brushing too close and connecting with a soft breast. He yanked it back, tingling.

Getting out, Daisy let in a gust of rain. "Thanks for the ride—and the philosophy."

She didn't look back but ran to the house, the denim

hobo bag over her head like a sodden umbrella. He could barely make out her form and the clinging denim skirt, her bare feet.

Feeling that tug again, he tore his gaze from her retreating form, glad she hadn't asked him to come inside and sit out the storm. He'd rather drive through a flash flood—and he just might, heading home.

Her disapproval of him seemed clear enough; she thought he was a fool to ask Erin to marry him, and not to give up when she said no. She'd always liked Danny, though. Two of a kind, he thought. Besides, he'd never had any use himself for Daisy Chatworth.

He'd stop taking Timmy's books back to the library.

He wouldn't let her irritate him again.

He wouldn't think of her surprisingly pretty feet, her long, leggy stride in the wet denim skirt, or her soft, warm breast.

Plowing back along Denton Street through Sweetwater and on to Dillon, he reminded himself to be patient. One snowstorm, a few days trapped in the house, and Danny would go stir crazy. He'd abandon his notion of stock contracting. He'd leave Paradise Valley, Erin and Tim, as he always did.

Leave them to Ken.

19

On December first Danny checked into the Four Queens, the Las Vegas host hotel for bull riders at that year's National Finals Rodeo.

He'd kissed that gold buckle half a dozen times but never claimed it in the end. Having finished the season in thirteenth place, he meant to win his title.

Flopping on the king-size bed in his room—Luke was staying at Bally's for the ten-day event with an old barrel man friend—Danny looked forward to the evening, before the competition began, when Erin and Timmy would arrive.

As the sky darkened outside he kept one eye on the television set across the room, its sound muted. That morning by phone Erin had reported snow in Montana, six inches and still falling, which probably meant a foot or more sifting into Paradise Valley. The televised map showed him a drifting weather system in the Bitterroots, heading slowly east. If Erin and Timmy hadn't caught their scheduled flight in Butte, he probably wouldn't see them before the fourth or fifth round, if it didn't snow more.

In balmier Nevada he wore a black short-sleeved T-shirt, and his jeans felt too warm even in the air-conditioned room. Danny kicked off his sneakers. His mother was coming too, and though Luke hadn't said a word, he must know. Danny had reserved two adjoining rooms, one for Timmy and his mother, this one for Erin and himself.

Thinking of Ken, he frowned.

His brother's telephone call on a bad connection from Dillon had taken Danny by surprise—if not shock.

"Think I'll come south to see the Finals," Ken said. "That way, if you win, you can hand me the money for my share of the ranch as soon as the check's in your hands."

Obviously, Ken didn't think he could win.

"You'll be talking out of the other side of your mouth when I'm wearing that gold buckle."

"You lose," Ken added, "and I'll be on the phone that much quicker to my Realtor. I can have my land sold before you and Erin get back to Paradise Valley."

Danny watched the weather channel.

His blood thumped. He'd show Ken, prove himself at long last. He tried to feel glad that Ken would be there for those ten straight performances. Two point eight million dollars in prize money. And as for each bull rider, for Danny, ten prime-quality, tough-as-steel, top-of-the-line bulls, the finest bred. Cadillac bulls. Money bulls, every one of them. They were the kind of bulls a man dreamed about, the way a jockey must dream about riding a horse like Secretariat.

He glanced at his watch. In another few minutes, he'd leave for the airport to meet Erin and Timmy. He needed them there, just as they needed him at Paradise Valley. With their support he'd win, he promised himself, or, speaking in the figurative sense, die trying.

o   o   o

Cheyenne had been a ten-day long party, with the usual overlay of tension surrounding the competition. Las Vegas to Erin seemed an entirely different world, orders of magnitude removed from the smaller town, its easier atmosphere missing completely—at least in Danny. And now, Erin.

By the fifth round of competition she had bitten her fingernails to the quick. Danny won twice and placed high enough the other two previous rounds to keep him within breathing space of his title. His rides were strong, exciting to see. As the announcer said, "That's one sticky bull rider," which meant Danny didn't easily get dumped. He stood third highest in overall points. But Erin was a basket case.

She'd never believed in being able to cut tension with a knife blade, but changed her mind. First, there'd been the nerve-wracking drive north to Butte's airport in a near blizzard—they'd survived half a dozen such storms already that early winter—then a turbulent, stomach-clutching flight full of air pockets to Las Vegas. Danny seemed glad to see her and Timmy, but distracted.

She knew why when Ken arrived the next day just before the first round. It wasn't like Danny to get so nervous otherwise, even at the Nationals, which she'd attended with him once, the first year of their marriage.

That night, after Timmy fell asleep in the next room with Meg, Danny held Erin close.

"Sure, I'm worried," he admitted. "I promised Ken the rest of that money by December. Guess what?"

"It's December."

He stroked her back. "Beyond that, I think he'd love to see me fall on my ass in that arena. Or worse."

"He's never made peace with himself about Trevor."

"Who has?" he said. "So he'd punish me—and through me, you and Mom and Tim—and turn everything Dad worked for all those years into a bunch of upscale condos next door for a bunch of city slickers on fancy skis?"

At his taut tone Erin remained silent.

"Or is it because of you?" he said. "I'm not blaming you, but Ken had his mind set on marrying you, and he's like a bull going after the man who rode him." He shook his head, the movement a whisper of sound in the darkness, against the pillow. "My own brother. I kept thinking he'd come to Vegas, get caught up in the excitement the way he used to when I rodeoed not much older than Tim. I hoped he'd root for me, clap me on the back when I won . . . "

Wordless, Erin touched his cheek.

"Forgive me," he added in a whisper. Danny had turned his face into the warm hollow of her neck. "I won't let you down, Erin."

She blinked now. Didn't he know that she'd love him if he never earned another point or another dollar bull riding, if he never went near another rodeo? In fact, that was her preference. And if he couldn't pay Ken for his share of the ranch . . .

"Mom!" Timmy's excited voice somehow reached her from the floor of the arena—or did she only imagine it did?

The Grand Entry had begun, competitors, local saddle clubs, rodeo officials, a sprinkling of celebrities, parading into the arena, but the music, the roar of the crowd, the rhythmic beat of hooves on dirt didn't capture her until she actually saw her small son riding high and proud with Danny on Kemosabe.

Next to her, Meg said, "He looks wonderful!"

She meant Timmy, but Erin remembered what he'd said upon seeing Kemosabe once more in the stabling area.

"He looks like a king!"

And so he did—so they did, horse, man and boy.

Like Meg Erin leaned forward in her seat. Timmy's eyes shone with wonder at the spectacle of horses and riders circling the ring. The glistening black-and-white gelding pranced past, wearing a black, silver-tooled parade saddle and gleaming silver-studded bridle, and Danny looked handsome, magnificent, in black boots, jeans, a black western shirt with pearl trim, and his new black 20X-beaver Resistol hat. Erin's gift to him for the finals had cost her four hundred dollars, worth every cent. In boots, jeans, denim jacket, and straw cowboy hat, Timmy looked like a miniature version of his father and every other cowboy in the arena.

"'Sabe's not ours right now," Timmy had told her too many times since Danny leased him to Wes Turner, a calf roper, for the rest of the season. But he cheered when Danny told him that Kemosabe had also made the finals.

Erin knew that Timmy still feared the horse wouldn't return to Paradise Valley afterward.

"Daddy promised I can ride him again," he said.

"You will. Next week."

"Even if it's still snowing at home?"

She gave silent thanks to Danny for asking Wes Turner if he and Timmy could ride Kemosabe in the Grand Entry just once during the finals. The treat was common practice among cowboys with their children, and her throat tightened as the parade swept along the far side of the arena and out into the barn area. A pair of clowns, one of them Luke, immediately tumbled in, chasing each other and maneuvering in front of a bull fashioned from a wheelbarrow, making every child in the arena laugh, and more than a few adults.

The laughter died during the traditional recitation of the Cowboy Prayer, which always made Erin swallow tears.

Heavenly Father . . . We ask that You be with us at this rodeo . . . and guide us in the arena of life.

Then the rodeo began, and she rubbed her bare ring finger through each event: Bareback bronc riding. Calf Roping, in which Kemosabe failed to place that round. Saddle Bronc Riding. Steer Wrestling. Barrel Racing. Team Roping. And finally, Bull Riding.

She glanced along the row at Ken. His face looked set and stern, deepening the lines around his mouth. He would turn into a bitter old man before his time if he didn't make his peace with Trevor's death, with Danny. Erin tried to see it as a good sign that he'd come at all, but she also wondered if Danny's eagerness to heal their rift might make him careless in the ring.

Concentration could mean the difference between victory and defeat; between life and death.

Danny won his fifth round on a dark gray Brahma cross called Redhot Salsa, securing third place going in to the sixth round. He felt deep affection for that bull, an unusual reaction. His aggressive ride, those eighty-five points, made his blood hum. Like many bull riders, in a sport that happened shockingly fast, he had no memory of the ride itself. He'd tried to focus on staying on, on a perfect dismount. No straying thoughts this time; no failed concentration. He'd won good money, and felt as much on top of the world as possible with four rounds before the championship round . . . before he could pay Ken off.

Walking behind the ring after his ride, he coiled his bull rope, the crowd's cheers still ringing in his ears. More people watched professional rodeo than NFL games, which never seemed more evident than at the finals with every performance sold out. He could imagine only Ken sitting on his hands in the jam-packed arena amid whistles and applause.

Passing a couple of college cowboys, saying hi to one of the rodeo jet set, last year's world champion who now traveled by private plane, he smiled to himself. Although Danny usually fared far better, most riders counted themselves lucky to earn ten grand a year, at least early in their careers, to break even at most rodeos; but there must be justice in the world.

Danny bumped head-on into a woman.

"Pardon me, ma'am."

She flung her arms around him. Her white hat fell backward into the pounded-down dirt leading to the stable area, and a kiss landed on his dusty cheek.

"Danny Sinclair, that was the most beautiful bull ride I've seen here! Congratulations!"

Danny held her off, grinning into Daisy Chatworth's shining face. Taller than Erin, she stood almost eye level with him. She looked happier than she had for years.

"Am I seeing things? What are you doing here, D.C.?"

"Watching you win the world."

Danny told her about Ken being there, then about the money he owed. Her smile disappeared like the sun plunging below the horizon. Her eyes dimmed too. "Ken's a fool. You let him break your concentration, and you will have trouble. Never mind buying Paradise Valley."

"He thinks he's right."

"He couldn't be more wrong—about most things. And I thought he'd done enough damage, proposing to Erin."

"We'll handle it." Putting an arm around her shoulders, Danny changed the subject. "That was a damn nice ride, wasn't it?"

"Better than the time I won first myself at Cheyenne."

He heard the pride, the loss, in her tone, and tightened his embrace. Would he be like Daisy next year? Buying his ticket to the grandstand, paying an exorbitant hotel bill, to watch someone else win the world in his event?

"You should give it another go, D.C."

"I can't. Sometimes I want to, but I'd never admit that to anyone else." She glanced at him. "I miss it so much. But I made my decision and retired in one piece." She paused, the smile returning full force. "Though if I had a horse like 'Sabe, I might reconsider."

"Let's go see him." Danny waved toward the nearby stabling area. He'd been heading in that direction when he nearly knocked Daisy over. Frankly, he worried about Kemosabe. When he and Tim had ridden in the Grand

Entry, the horse's walk seemed stiff and he had a welt on his flank that shouldn't be there. He didn't know Wes Turner well, but he meant to remedy that right now.

"I have to admit," Daisy said, "I was on my way to see him when I ran into you."

"Thanks a lot. Overshadowed by my own horse."

"I came to see you too."

"I know," he said, hugging her. Explaining his concern, he added, "Let's go worry about that old plug together."

Kemosabe's stall stood near the rear, past dozens of other cubicles with tired horses standing hip slung, their heads down, or horses who hadn't yet performed looking almost humanly expectant. From twenty yards away, Danny could see Kemosabe's dramatically colored hide. Then, closer, he saw the stocky, red-haired man with him and heard his angry voice.

"You miserable son of a bitch—Call yourself a ropin' horse? On foot I'd make better time." He picked up a water bucket. "Sinclair oughta pay me to keep you in hay, you bag of bones!"

The plastic bucket hit a post. Its metal handle clanged like a fire bell.

Tied in the open stall, Kemosabe shied but not far. His ears lay flat.

Before Danny reached the stall, Turner slung the bucket aside, bringing the flat of his hand down hard on Kemosabe's nose. Pulling against the rope that held him, the gelding whickered in pain.

"What's the matter, Wes?"

Danny's quiet tone soothed the horse, but Wes Turner spun around, shocked.

"You checkin' up on me?"

"Checking my property. Looks like a good thing I did."

"My lease says this horse is mine through finals."

"He's a good horse," Danny said. "I didn't lend him to you, for money or free, so you could tie him up and beat him."

"I wasn't beating him. Did you see the roping? He held back on me. I've made better time on a greenbroke colt."

"Maybe it's not the horse's fault," Daisy said, her voice hard. "Maybe you just can't ride."

"Easy, D.C."

Leaving her outside the stall, Danny slipped inside, running a gentle hand over Kemosabe's withers then his back, letting the horse nuzzle his belly, his pockets.

Kemosabe didn't find any carrots.

"Empty," Danny told him. He could sense Wes Turner standing beside Daisy. Anger emanated from him like the smell of horse manure all around, even though the area was super-clean and well-tended. "You know how it is when I'm working. I owe you one." He hunkered down, sliding a hand over 'Sabe's rear legs, then both front ones. On the left side, he felt heat.

For a moment, Danny hung his head.

Then he rose, his hands fisted, to glare at Turner.

"I had a bad feeling about you. If I hadn't needed the money I would have realized it sooner."

"What's wrong, Danny?" Daisy asked.

He spoke to the red-haired, red-faced man at the stall entry. "I left this horse home all last spring and summer. My boy and my wife took good care of him. When I leased him, he was sound." He took a step toward Wes, who shrank back. "He's got trouble again with that tendon. It's hot as a branding iron. I'd wager you knew that when you rode him tonight."

"I didn't—"

"Don't lie to me. You're the son of a bitch!"

"Danny, he's not worth it." Daisy grabbed his arm before he could throw a punch. "Let him go."

He shrugged her off, addressing Wes Turner in a low, deadly tone. "You're not using my horse again—"

"But tomorrow—"

"I'm on my way now to get the PRCA vet. If you have a

problem with that lease, take it to your lawyer and we'll see who wins. I'd suggest you forget Vegas, go home and tear it up—before I rip you into pieces."

"I got more rounds, money—"

"Come near this horse again during this competition, it'll be your last ride!"

With a disgusted sound, Turner wheeled around and stalked from the stabling area. Over his shoulder he called, "You want him, you got him. You pay his feed and stable bill! Or he can stand there and starve to death."

His hands on his hips, Danny stood looking at the ground between him and Daisy. He studied the toes of her obviously new tan boots, then the tips of his darker ones. At last, he pushed his hat back on his head and looked at her.

"What in hell have I done? Bringing this horse back on the circuit, all the way to the finals, just to help me pay off Ken, who's turning into another SOB? I must be out of my mind."

Nickering, Kemosabe turned his head, poking it over the stall as if to say he didn't think so. He'd never hurt anyone in his life. For all his size and strength, he depended on human beings to keep him safe, and well.

"It's okay, boy." Danny's throat felt tight. "I'll take care of you. You're gonna be all right."

"I'll stay with him," Daisy said. "You get the vet."

If I have to put this horse down . . .

He forgot his own victory that night. He forgot the check he hadn't yet picked up. He even forgot Ken.

All at once, the coveted nationals seemed less than magic to a man who'd craved that gold buckle all his life.

For the tenth round Danny drew a two-thousand-pound black bull by the name of Devil's Due. He'd ridden him before. A big twister, a muscled corkscrew. Definitely not a dink. But the bull had a mean streak, could be brutally unpredictable, and Danny's delight was short-lived.

He'd overcome his first anger at Wes Turner, gratified when the vet pronounced Kemosabe's tendon merely sore and inflamed, not torn. With rest and proper care he'd be okay, as Danny had promised. Guilt kept him supplying the horse the rest of the week with five-pound bags of carrots, enthusiastically delivered by Tim who also groomed the gelding's hide until Erin said she expected him to go bald.

"He'll ship easy," Danny told her with a laugh, "going home." They meant to fly Kemosabe to Montana. He sobered. "He'll weigh in at a hundred pounds less than usual anyway, thanks to Turner."

Behind the chutes now, Danny waited his turn.

Mentally, he ran through his moves.

He resined his bull rope, then added more, working it into a high-friction, sticky mess.

He swigged a Coke, as much to wet his dry mouth as to provide quick energy, wiping his lips on his blue chambray shirt sleeve. He couldn't deny it. With every round, he'd become increasingly tired. He took another first in the eighth round, but from the second day his bruised muscles had felt swollen, achy, and his favorite activity with Erin changed from lovemaking to having her rub him down late each night with liniment and lots of Icy Hot, a local anesthetic.

Last night, even that hadn't led to making love.

When the man ahead of him climbed lithely on board a wide-shouldered tan bull, Danny could have groaned. The kid must be no more than twenty-two or twenty-three, and he swung on like a monkey on a jungle gym. Youth, education—all those kids coming out of college, like this one, with degrees. Heading for the finals so quick. The sport was changing.

And here comes Danny Sinclair, on Devil's Due. Danny's from Sweetwater, Montana, folks—the world's oldest bull rider. Why, he's so old, he …

The gate slammed open. The tan bull leaped high, twisting its way into the ring as if it were spring-loaded.

The kid's hat flew off, and Danny's stomach clenched. From his perch on the chute boards near his own bull, he watched the few seconds' action.

The boy, who held second place ahead of Danny in the standings, had good form. Yesterday he'd taken the round. He kept his chin tucked, his hand high and moving, his knees tight, his spurs pumping. Then it happened.

At four seconds—it couldn't have been more, by Danny's automatic count—the bull spun, then whipped back again.

"Stay with him!" someone shouted.

"Keep tryin'! You know you can!"

The bull leaped high once more, swiping his head around and catching the boy in the face with a horn.

Danny leaped down off the chute.

"Sinclair, get back here. You're up!"

Adrenaline charging, he was already over the gate by the time the kid landed in the dirt, unconscious.

He reached him a split second before Luke did after waving the angry bull into the chute. Danny glanced around to make sure the gate was closed on an empty ring except for Luke's barrel man peering down at the body in the dust.

"He's out cold," Danny said.

Luke went down on one knee on the boy's other side, looking at Danny who searched for a neck pulse. He studied the kid's chest for the rise and fall action that would indicate he was breathing on his own.

"Any beat?"

Danny said, "I'm not sure."

He heard a moan, but wasn't certain it hadn't come from him. He studied the boy's eyes, hoping to see them flutter open, telling himself he saw a muscle twitch.

"Lie still. Stay down now, help's on the way."

A stretcher arrived, and paramedics carried the fallen rider from the ring to the cheers and shouts of encouragement from the fans.

Shaken, Danny got to his feet.

He didn't have much time to mount his own bull.

The announcer called Danny's name, his bull's, and by the time he said, "Sweetwater, Montana," Danny had his seat. No time to wonder or to think, to feel cold sweat trickle down his spine. No time to lose the rest of his nerve, like Daisy.

Accidents happened.

They were routine.

He'd been gored himself.

But he'd seen Lane Frost die at Cheyenne a few years ago. Twenty-five years old, and one of the finest bull riders the sport ever knew. Talented, young, good-looking. Married. Gone. He'd seen Trevor too.

He wouldn't let it matter. Not now.

Cowboys didn't grieve. They didn't feel pain. In the arena for those eight seconds, he preserved his own life. He didn't let himself think but used that bull's power for himself, pushed his own strength into the ride, and made them one moving mass of muscle, held on.

Still on board at eight seconds, he felt everything drain from him with the dismount as if he'd opened a vein and bled himself dry. When he dropped from the bull's back to the ground, he barely caught himself from crumpling to his knees.

He had himself a championship round, or damn close.

The crowd burst into applause and the announcer yelled his score. It didn't matter. Retrieving his black hat, Danny slapped it against his custom-made chaps. Yellow dust rose off the cognac-colored leather covering his thighs, and his heart pounded like a pile driver.

"*Danny?*"

He reached over his shoulder, pulling the cardboard square with his contestant's number from the back of his shirt. He walked from the ring, behind the chutes, straight into Erin's quivering arms.

"Oh my god, Danny. How did you do that? After that other rider—is he dead?"

"I don't know." He meant both questions.

"No one said. They just carried him off to an ambulance—"

"Someone'll know later."

She squeezed him tight, a python's embrace. She laid her cheek against his thudding chest, and he held her even tighter.

"I was so scared," she said. "Timmy started crying. Meg has him, she and Ken. Daisy's there too." She babbled the words. "I'm sorry to be a coward, but I had to see you, touch you . . ."

"I'm all right, Erin."

Eighty-four points. In the end, he'd won second place, not first; second place, which he couldn't help feeling he'd stolen from the boy whose life force he couldn't find with his fingertips.

"I'm all right," he said again.

"It's still good money, Danny."

The mantra stayed with him, all that night during the post-competition celebrations, but he couldn't seem to get his thoughts off that boy.

Luke finally brought him the news.

"University Hospital says he'll be okay. Some stitches in his face—some antibiotic to prevent infection from that nasty horn, wherever the hell it's been before—torn ligaments in his back. He was lucky at that."

"Lucky," Danny agreed.

Luke shoved another beer in his hand, and he drank it down, but he never felt the buzz it should have caused. He didn't notice his mother dancing cheek to cheek with Luke later, or acknowledge Erin's, "I'm worried about you," half a dozen times. He failed to notice Ken quarreling with Daisy in a corner, or wonder why Ken never asked him for the money. He didn't smile when he hit the payoff in a slot machine. When he and Erin went to bed near dawn, he didn't remember making love to her. Afterward, she held him, and he relished that but couldn't seem to talk much.

"You've seen people get hurt before, hundreds of times," she said, smoothing his bare back.

"I know."

"You've been hurt that many times yourself."

"I know that too."

"You didn't take anything away from him. If he'd made his eight seconds, he might not have scored high enough. You still might have won."

"Yeah," he agreed.

Erin feathered his hair, her eyes serious on his.

"I wish you could have gotten your gold buckle."

She didn't know what really bothered him.

He stared at the ceiling. Kemosabe. That kid flying off the tan bull, who might have been Jason Barker, if he'd stuck it out, or in a few years, Tim. Or Trevor. And Erin, who hated to watch him ride, but had come to Las Vegas and swallowed her fears to be there for him. His own selfishness all these years.

She raised on one elbow in the dark, her gaze searching his face. "I don't know how to ease your pain, Danny. I never do."

"You know how."

She didn't smile, and neither did he. And she didn't reach for him again, but Danny let her snuggle close, not taking the intimacy any farther himself.

"Let's go home," he finally said.

$\overline{\underset{}{20}}$

They reached Paradise Valley in a blizzard, driving down through the winding pass with the windshield wipers slashing, the road ahead a white-out in the dark December night. Home, Erin thought with a grateful sigh. The wind howled until dawn, when she heard Danny get up.

Propping herself up on an elbow, she yawned, wondering how he could leave the warm sheets—and her—so soon after the difficult trip from the airport last night. She watched him pull on long underwear, clean jeans, a green plaid wool shirt. When he added a heavy sweater, still without looking at her, she couldn't keep silent.

"Going somewhere?"

Perhaps he'd forgotten how treacherous even reaching the main road could be after such a storm. Outside the snow still fell in dizzying sweeps, and Erin heard the wind cutting across the back yard, slamming into the barn. Its double doors would be ice-crusted now, stuck shut.

"Butte." He tugged on winter boots. "I have to meet Kemosabe's plane."

In her gladness to be home, she had forgotten.

"Have you called the airport?"

"Still flying." He shrugged into a split cowhide jacket lined in sheepskin, then settled a worn brown Stetson on his head. "The flight's late but due in by ten."

It would take him easily that long to reach Butte. Towing a horse trailer behind her Jeep in such weather would take even longer. She'd worry all day.

Danny leaned down to kiss her. "Go to sleep. See you later."

He came back late that night. Erin had been sitting in the living room for hours on the chintz sofa near Meg's piano watching the driveway, straining her eyes against the blackness beyond the house, hoping to see headlights. When Danny stomped into the kitchen, she was waiting with fresh, hot coffee and a warm embrace. For Luke too. He'd accompanied Kemosabe from Las Vegas.

Luke's gaze swept the room.

"Meg went to bed early," Erin said with a smile. "She's exhausted from yesterday. Timmy too." To his obvious surprise, she added, "Welcome, Luke."

" 'Sabe survived his first flight," Danny said, though the airport had shut down, delaying the flight even longer. "I doubt he'll load in the trailer so well next time, but he's not going anywhere until spring. Maybe he'll forget by then." He slumped down at the kitchen table, sipping his coffee. "I hope you're glad to have me here too. Doesn't look like any of us will be leaving till at least April."

His words, only a slight exaggeration, alternately soothed Erin and set her thoughts spinning. She wanted Danny home, wanted their family together, more than she'd ever acknowledged to herself, but she didn't want him there without a willing heart.

She found herself listening for clues that he meant to leave. In the days before Christmas, he worked hard around the ranch, but Erin wondered if there was really that much to be done for winter, especially one night when she found him staring at a video of famous bull wrecks. Did his lost championship still bother him? If it troubled him too much . . .

She knew Ken's phone calls did, pressuring Danny for money he didn't have. The down payment, and his second place winnings from the finals, didn't satisfy Ken for long. Erin thought he just liked to needle his kid brother.

"I'm looking for a job," she heard Danny tell Ken.

But jobs were in short supply near Sweetwater, especially during the lean winter months when the town's trickle of tourists dried up and some businesses closed, their owners heading south until warmer weather.

Christmas proved lean though festive.

Erin had to fight her own guilt as she watched Danny and Timmy rip into their simple but useful presents, then later battle Luke and Meg with the water pistols her mother-in-law had given them. This year's silly gift was a family tradition passed down from Danny's boyhood, and still made Erin smile too. The cost of the presents didn't matter either; it was the joy they brought that counted. She fought that too, as if peering through a window at some long-coveted gift she didn't really deserve.

For the first time, she saw how much of his life Danny had relinquished to give her what she wanted.

The day after Christmas she realized part of the price she would have to pay.

Having left Timmy in the living room sitting cross-legged by the decoration laden tree and the electric train he'd gotten from Santa, Erin washed pots and pans in the kitchen.

She heard Danny's voice, then Timmy's laughter. Timmy was writing an essay on the true meaning of Christmas.

"That doesn't sound like subject-verb-object to me," she called. "You have half an hour to finish your paper before we review that math for your quiz with Ken tomorrow."

"The Grinch Who Stole Christmas." Danny appeared in the doorway, only half smiling.

"He has schoolwork."

"Every kid in Sweetwater's off until New Year's."

"Timmy missed a week while we were in Vegas." She had taken assignments with them, but somehow the time never materialized for home teaching, and she finally gave up. "It's too easy to let things slide. He needs a disciplined schedule."

"How about a disciplined hour helping me and Luke in the barn?"

"Yes. When he's finished here."

Danny threw her a look. "He can help us now. 'Sabe's stall needs mucking. Then Luke and I need him to hold nails and fetch tools while we knock those other stalls together."

"You won't need them until spring."

"We'll get the work done now, before we both find jobs for the rest of the winter."

Erin started to say something, like *what jobs?* but stopped herself. She'd seen him more than once, perusing the want ads in the Butte, Bozeman, and Dillon papers, and she'd heard him and Luke on the phone. If they found nothing, would they be forced south again? Last winter they had both worked in Texas for a stock contractor. Several winters Luke and Danny, like many cowboys, hired on as wranglers for Hollywood westerns. And they sometimes fell back, she knew, on odd-job construction work.

"Timmy can meet you in the barn after his essay is done. His math—"

"The math can wait too," Danny said. "And you can tell Ken I'll be teaching Tim his numbers from now on. I'll be damned if I'll have Ken hanging around the house, pushing me for money I don't have and giving my kid the impression I can't add two and two."

Erin planted both hands on her hips.

She knew Danny had given Ken every cent he could spare, and so far Ken hadn't sent any Realtors around, but he showed up often enough, and his very presence threatened Erin's peace of mind too, and Meg's. Ken had managed to remain civil during Christmas dinner but had left soon after they ate without even kissing his mother good-bye.

She sighed. "I know you don't approve of home teaching, but right now it's the best course. No pun intended." She waved a hand at the snowy landscape outside the kitchen door. "Unless you're willing to fight your way out this drive every morning for the next four months and all the way to Dillon to public school."

"I just might, or we'll all have cabin fever." He turned and opened the door. "I can add," he said. "One seven-year-old boy. A woman with a mind of her own. A man—that makes three—who intends to be part of this family. I know you're not used to it, but that's how it's going to be."

Erin stared at the closed door after Danny left. Then she whirled toward the kitchen window and watched him stalk to the barn, as if the path he'd cleared before lunch hadn't already filled with snow again.

She'd been on her own a long time. She was used to making—pondering—all decisions for herself and Timmy, or at least most of them. She'd had a difficult time when Danny commuted to finish his season. It had taken a while for her to rely on Meg's help at the store. Now, it seemed, she had another adjustment to make.

Having her own husband in the house. Full-time.

By New Year's Eve morning Danny had cleaned and repaired every square inch of the barn. He and Luke rode fence in Erin's Jeep, which had four-wheel drive, stopping and stalling in the snow to shore up a post here, to stretch cold wire there. Neither of them was accustomed to idleness, or to being in one place for long. He knew Luke was starting to chafe at their mostly indoor existence, brought on by a colder-than-normal winter in Paradise Valley and an already record snowfall. So was Danny.

Erin's balkiness didn't help.

Despite his near-miss in Las Vegas, the bull wreck he'd witnessed, and his acceptance of the finals as his last, he sometimes missed the circuit so much he could taste it. At other times . . . He rolled over in bed now, nuzzling Erin's shoulder, which tasted sweet and tangy.

"It's snowing again," she whispered, lying on her side with him behind her, spoon fashion.

Danny's Christmas present to Erin had been a new mattress. It felt like a warm cloud cushioning his body.

"All the more reason to stay in bed."

"Some of us have to get to work."

Danny's mouth stilled on her skin. "Is that a dig?"

"No, a fact. I'll close early for the holiday. Do you need the Jeep?"

"Yes," he said, making up his mind. It seemed he made every decision lately to counter Erin's, he thought with a frown as he got up from the bed. "I'll drop you at the store." His mother would stay home with Tim, to teach him piano and art. Danny doubted he'd ever have much need of either, but both were part of the curriculum—in which he had no say. "I need to talk to Ken."

On the way into town neither of them spoke. Even the Jeep slipped and sloughed through the slush along Denton Street.

"I'll pick you up at four."

Erin didn't wave good-bye. By the time he reached Dillon and his brother's construction site office, Danny had worked himself into a temper. The white trailer, with its cramped confines, gray metal desk and filing cabinets didn't help.

"Danny boy." Ken saluted him with a mug of coffee. "Didn't think you'd be up this early."

"It's hard to sleep, when I'm wondering if the first thing I hear some morning will be someone pounding a For Sale sign in the yard outside my bedroom window."

Ken's gaze shifted away. He gestured at the coffee urn, and Danny helped himself to a cup. The heater in Erin's Jeep needed work. His hands felt stiff from the drive, and the tip of his nose had gone cold.

"I've paid what I can," he said. "I figure the real estate market's dead until the weather breaks. Nobody's going to be able to dig or pour concrete foundations for those condos before spring."

Ken nodded once, as if reluctant to agree.

"I need a job," Danny said, looking into his coffee. "I don't care what, but I need a fair wage. I've answered every ad in the papers—which have been damn few—but I'm not cut out for assembly line work, or staying down in a mine tunnel all day. I'd go nuts, Ken." He looked at his brother.

"You're asking me for work?"

Danny swallowed. His pride too, he thought. "Yeah."

He needed to keep busy. Needed to be somewhere he could see the sky, the snow falling, feel the wind on his face. Otherwise, he would lose his mind. He'd start thinking about leaving before he bought his first bull or bronc, and ensured a future with Erin.

Ken watched him for a long moment. His gaze ran down Danny's frame from shoulders to boots.

"All I have this time of year is finish work. Inside. Some sheetrocking, cabinetry, painting."

"I can do that." He glanced around the skinny, crowded trailer, already feeling shut-in. He'd worked construction before and was good with his hands. He'd never worked for a brother who hated his guts, though.

"We start at eight A.M. We quit at five." Ken walked through the office to the neat stacks of paper on his desk. He selected a clipboard, shoving it toward Danny. "Fill out this application." When he caught Danny's look, he said,

"It's not for me—I know your history—it's for payroll. You have any medical insurance?"

"Through the PRCA," he said.

"You can start day after tomorrow."

Resettling his hat, Danny decided to push his luck. "I need a job for Luke too."

"Luke—" Ken threw up a hand. "Hell, why not? Same work, same pay." He named a figure.

"I'll take half of what I earn in my check each week, to help Erin and Tim." He paused. "You keep the other half, on account toward the ranch."

"Oh, that's just great, Danny boy. I pay myself for my own land."

"Dammit, I'll give you a full day's work. Where I put my pay is my business." Danny turned his back. "See you at eight. Day after tomorrow."

He spent the afternoon building a snowman with Tim and Luke, using two big black buttons from his mother's sewing basket for eyes. A huge carrot, which Tim hoped Kemosabe didn't see, made a nose, and gravel from the driveway lined up into a smiling mouth. Danny lifted Tim high to pull a red-striped knit cap over the snowman's head. Then he drove back into town to pick up Erin. Outside the emporium, he met Jason Barker with his girl-friend, home from college where they'd both made the dean's list their first semester.

That night Danny, Erin, Meg, and Luke stayed up to watch the entertainment shows before the ball fell in Times Square, on television. By eleven Tim fell asleep on the dark red print–cushioned sofa between Danny and Erin, his head lolling back against its wooden frame, as he had on the Ferris wheel that summer. Danny carried him to bed.

When the midnight countdown was about to begin, he set his beer aside, then Erin's.

For long seconds, with the New York noise in the back-ground, he held her face in his hands and looked deeply into her eyes. He'd spent too many New Year's Eves alone, and so had Erin.

"We should have thrown a party."

"No one would have come in the snow," she said.

"We should have plowed our way to Dillon. Out to dinner. Dancing. Something romantic."

"I didn't think you'd want to." She held his gaze. "I must not seem that romantic lately."

"It takes two," he said, and then, "I got a job today."

Her eyes lit up.

"Working for Ken," he told her. Shock filled her gaze. "He'll hold off about the ranch until spring."

"I've been thinking, Danny." She touched his cheek. In the distance his mother laughed softly, then Luke. The television audience chanted the seconds until midnight.

Seven . . . six . . . five . . .

"I could probably get a mortgage on my share of Paradise Valley," Erin said. "So could Meg." She laid a finger across his lips. "We talked about it, and that's what we want to do. You said we were a family. We should act like one."

Four . . . three . . .

"You have a point." His thumbs caressed her cheekbones, and his gaze held hers. A family, a marriage at long last. They had their share of compromises to make. He'd consider Erin's offer, but later. "Know what I'm thinking right now? What my New Year's resolution is?"

Her eyes darkened, and she shook her head. As if expecting him to take off for the winter circuit. Bending his head, he murmured in her ear, "I feel like a stud horse tonight."

"Danny." She buried her face in his shoulder.

"So let's go upstairs—and make ourselves a baby."

Two . . . one . . .

The strains of "Auld Lang Syne" struck up, growing louder as Luke pushed the remote control volume higher. He and Meg began singing. Erin raised her head, still blushing.

"Happy New Year," he whispered.

"Happy New Year."

He took Erin's mouth, parting her lips for the intrusion of his tongue, tasting her sweetness. He felt the rush of desire, her eager response. When at last he eased his mouth from hers, he couldn't seem to focus, and Erin's gaze looked blurry.

With a small sound, she wrapped her arms around him, kissing him again.

Across the living room, the singing stopped though the old song went on. Danny glanced over. Luke had dimmed the lamp and without touching her in any other way, was kissing his mother. It didn't look platonic. But that didn't bother Danny. He looked into Erin's eyes and smiled as she blinked.

"This song," she murmured, "always makes me cry."

"For what might have been." Holding out a hand, he pulled her gently to her feet, then moved across the room toward the hallway and the stairs. "Who was it who said, 'the best is yet to be?'"

After the holidays, on another snowy morning, Erin organized the emporium's annual January sale. This season she slashed prices on everything from percale sheets to canned cashews. She and Meg were making room for spring merchandise—and the new consignment area showcasing local crafts, Meg's pet project.

Erin supported the idea. Her hanging plants, Laura Ashley curtains, the store's old-fashioned, feminine look, to which Danny had objected, might bring business, appealing especially to the new residents who seemed to be trickling in around Sweetwater. Better profits would appeal to the bank when she and Meg applied for a mortgage on the ranch. If nothing more, Erin thought, Meg's enthusiasm was contagious.

"I spoke with the reverend's wife this morning," she told Erin, bustling about the store. "She's a wizard with that crochet hook. She's excited about a new afghan design and can give us half a dozen by March." Meg grinned. "Mrs. Eady was in yesterday to reserve one for herself, to cover her poor legs when she watches TV."

Erin, putting sale tags on merchandise, only smiled.

"The mayor's oldest daughter has promised us a nice supply of monogrammed hand towels. She does lovely work." Meg laughed. "I asked if she had anything in black on black."

Erin looked up.

"For Luke," her mother-in-law said, flushing. "Every time I clean the bathroom in the bunkhouse, those towels are a sight. Why is it men never wash the grime off, just wipe it on the nearest handy thing?" She paused, then added, "Hank did the same," as if to neutralize her mention of Luke.

"Danny too," Erin agreed. "He's a fine role model for Timmy." She glanced toward the office where Timmy was sitting at her desk working on his lessons. "And why are you cleaning Luke Hastings's bathroom?"

"A man's idea of clean is different from mine."

"He's a grown man, though. He's lived on his own."

"With bare regard for a tidy house."

Erin knew progress when she heard it. She'd seen Luke kiss Meg on New Year's Eve, and they'd seemed inseparable ever since. Danny thought they were sleeping together, but Erin knew they weren't. Meg's glow didn't seem of sufficiently high wattage. But Erin had hope for that, and more.

Meg swiped a rag across an empty shelf in the front corner of the store where she'd decided to display the consignment goods. Erin had also given her one-half the front window space hoping the crafts, in addition to the decorative wreaths and sensible women's wear already there, would draw customers. If it ever stopped snowing.

Montana had an undeserved reputation for frigid winters.

The air stayed dry for one thing, and normally the Chinook winds provided a respite from cold spells, but like the rest of the nation, Sweetwater was battling a brutal season. Erin had had enough cabin fever to tease her mother-in-law as a diversion.

"I think you clean house for Luke for the same reason you cook so much."

"I cook for the family. We have to eat."

"Fudge brownies? Whipped cream torte? Gingersnap cookies?" Erin grinned. "Lattice-top cherry pie?"

"I pitted those cherries myself. Last summer. They shouldn't go to waste in the freezer."

"So you had to crank some vanilla ice cream to go with them? I think Luke's getting a spare tire. And I woke up this morning to Danny doing sit-ups at the end of the bed."

"If you're implying that you've finally domesticated my son, that's the best news I've had." Meg smiled, swiping the rag across another shelf. "If you think Luke Hastings will join him, you couldn't be more wrong."

"I don't see him packing."

Luke and Danny had been working for Ken since New Year's, and they both came home so tired each night that Erin doubted either one of them could lift a gear bag—or a bull rope. Which was fine with her.

"It's not April yet," Meg said. "At the first honeyed breeze across the pasture, Luke will be in that camper. Even Kemosabe's ears will prick toward the nearest rodeo."

And what about Danny? Erin wondered. Aloud, she said, "Rodeo has been a part of Danny's life for more years than I have, really. Or Timmy. I wonder if we'll be able to hold him come spring." Or if she should try to. Hadn't she learned that lesson the hard way, long ago?

"Oh my, I shouldn't have spoken." Dropping the dust cloth, Meg crossed the store to the counter where Erin had been cutting prices on flannel nighties. "Once Danny buys a few head of horses, a nice bull or two, he'll settle in." She touched Erin's hand. "It can't be easy for him, working for Ken. Trust Danny, can't you?"

"Trust Luke," Erin said. "Maybe he's had enough time on the road himself. Maybe he'd even like to stay somewhere like Paradise Valley."

Meg's tone perked up. "And go into stock contracting with Danny?"

"He could still be a rodeo clown part-time," Erin said. "For Danny's outfit rather than some stranger's. He could spend winters here . . . with you."

Before Meg finished work and went home to start supper and teach several piano students, she and Erin had planned a perfect future, and Erin, if not for Meg then for herself, was trying to believe in it.

By mid-February Luke seemed a permanent fixture at the ranch. But Erin still didn't feel that certain about Danny. Late in January, without warning, he had competed in the Montana Prorodeo Circuit finals at Great Falls where he won, thereby softening the blow of his second place at Las Vegas. He also scared Erin to death by getting hung up in his bull rope as he dismounted—a potentially lethal complication she heard about afterward—but suffered only a chin cut, a common injury. Erin had caught him more than once since, watching videos of other near-perfect rides.

She began praying for the hard winter to continue into spring.

At the thought, which provoked fresh guilt on the morning of Valentine's Day, the poignant lyrics of "My Funny Valentine" began to play in Erin's mind. Then the emporium's bell jangled, the door swung open, and Daisy Chatworth rushed in.

Erin took a moment to greet her. She and Daisy were undergoing a still-awkward period following their quarrel months ago.

"God, it's cold out there," Daisy said, bundled into a hooded, red down parka, and beaming at Erin then Meg. "Is there anyone here who loves February in Montana? I hope not." She hurried toward the wood stove Erin kept stoked in the center of the store, its cheery heat radiating throughout the room. Holding her reddened hands toward the blaze, she added, "The furnace at the library quit. I figure that's a sign I should too."

"Don't thumb your nose at a day off with pay."

"Without pay." Flipping her hood back, Daisy grinned. "I played hooky when I went to Vegas for the finals. It was worth every penny of those tickets, the motel room too, just to see Ken's face each time Danny won a round."

Meg smiled and looked up from her arranging of a delicate pyramid of crystal snowflakes, a local artist's contribution to the new consignment area. "Daisy, you leave my oldest boy alone. He inherited his father's nature—his strengths too."

"Have you seen Ken lately?" Daisy asked Erin.

"Not much."

By *lately* Daisy probably meant since Ken's proposal. In Las Vegas, she and Erin had made up, but their friendship still seemed fragile, even with Danny home.

Daisy rubbed her hands together. "I haven't seen Ken Sinclair smile since . . . well, never mind."

"When?" Erin pressed, becoming irritated.

"Since Danny first came back in June."

The words of "My Funny Valentine" ran through Erin's mind again, and she blinked as she always did. He had come back—but how long would he stay?

"Ken's a lonely man," Meg murmured with a speculative look.

"No wonder," Daisy said.

In late March Ken strode through the house nearest his in the new subdivision at Wooded Creek. He'd sold it days before, just ahead of the spring real estate rush, and the finish work needed to be done by the time the buyers closed on the property.

"Danny? Luke?" he called out, a sheaf of blueprints under one arm, his yellow hard hat clamped on his head. Climbing the open stairs, he found them in a bedroom sheetrocking the walls. "I'll pay overtime—double time—if you can stay tonight. Maybe the rest of the week."

"Sounds good to me." Danny dragged an arm across his sweaty forehead. "You get half, I get half."

Ken's frown deepened. "I know the deal."

Danny turned away, lining up another panel. He worked hard but said little to Ken. The room was beginning to look like a room, Ken's favorite part of the construction process, but a small part of him always felt amazed when a house he'd built turned out looking like a house.

Which wouldn't surprise Daisy Chatworth, he supposed. If she ever learned about his self-doubt, which she wouldn't.

He thought he'd forgotten their stormy encounter in the rain last October, and its rehash the last night in Las Vegas. Then he had seen her again in Sweetwater, scurrying across the icy street in a bright red jacket, short skirt, and knee-high boots. He looked the other way, but he felt sure she'd seen him.

Ken lingered outside the bedroom on the landing.

Daisy wasn't his type. Long, lanky, all legs. That no-color hair, those big blue eyes. One time she looked mousy to him, the next ablaze with life. Like at the finals in Las Vegas. Maybe she only lit up around a rodeo. Or was she carrying some torch for Danny?

He went back into the room. "Can I talk to you?"

"About what?" Danny asked.

"It's private."

Danny glanced at Luke, who gazed back at him.

"Sounds interesting," Luke said. He took every opportunity to push Ken's buttons, especially about his mother.

"Give us a minute, Luke," Danny said.

Luke stuck a fresh wad of gum in his mouth and stepped into the hall. "Bubble break." Ken waited until he heard work boots scrambling down the steps, then the front door slamming.

"Why do I see him in clown face, even when he's not wearing any?" Ken said half to himself.

Danny leaned against the new wall. "What's this about? Am I fired?"

"You're doing okay." Ken paced the room, trampling paint-spattered tarpaulins. He jingled the change in his pants pocket then cleared his throat. "What do you know about Daisy Chatworth?"

Danny grinned, and Ken frowned. He hadn't seen that cheeky grin in a while.

"I'm just asking," Ken said.

"She's a good person. Honest. Kind-hearted. Like Erin," Danny couldn't resist adding. "She keeps to herself too much. I think that has something to do with her accident. She wants to put it behind her, to like what she does now instead of riding. Being a librarian, though," he said, shaking his head, "doesn't suit her somehow. She always seems to me like a fish out of water—a sleek salmon who flopped out on the bank going upstream and can't find her way back in."

"That's a hell of a way to put it."

Danny shrugged.

"She sure lit up about Kemosabe," Ken admitted. "Came by the ranch one time last fall, the day I moved out." And he had doused her fire with a few words, got some kick out of seeing her smile fade, as if he'd thrown ashes on it.

"Did she make calf eyes at you?" Danny asked.

Ken stopped pacing, his fists clenched.

"What do you mean by that?"

"She's been sweet on you for years. Don't tell me you never noticed. Every time you walk in that library . . . " He paused. "But then, I imagine Daisy never realized it herself. If she did, she'd probably run like hell."

"Don't bullshit me."

His reply was an innocent look, one Ken knew well.

He took a step. "What interest would she have in me? A man who hasn't been near a horse or a rodeo in years, except Vegas. A man she knows full well has no regard at all for her barrel racing . . . past, present, or future. I'm not her type any more than she's mine."

"Know what I think?" Grinning, Danny feinted a jab at him, a maneuver they'd used often on each other as kids. "I think you're stuck on her." He punched the air again. "Come on, admit it."

"You're so wound up with Erin—"

The second jab landed lightly on Ken's jaw. "Are you still wound up with her too?" Danny asked.

"No." He took his stance, bouncing on the balls of his feet. "I'm not." With the words, he knew the truth of them. The move to Dillon had cured him of his second-place role in her life. He had solitude, time to think, to heal the wounds he'd obviously caused himself. Daisy's interest— her supposed interest—pleased him a little too much. "Now what's this about Chatworth?"

"Find out for yourself."

Ken felt the years whizz backward. He and Danny, as teenagers, had taunted each other mercilessly about girls. And everything else.

"I think she's crazy for *you*," he said.

"*Me?*" Danny looked genuinely surprised. "Daisy and I have always been friends, nothing else, or maybe more like brother and sister."

Ken might have thought he was lying, but then Danny often seemed oblivious to other women's interest in him. Danny talked easily with females, always had, but never seemed to take the light flirting seriously—except with Erin. Ken sneaked a right in under his guard, hitting him in the stomach. Danny grunted, and Ken grinned.

"What's the matter? Not as tough as you used to be?" Ken asked.

He took the next left hook.

"I'll beat you any day."

The flurry of blows, none of them serious, soon had them doing a boxers' dance around the room, laughing.

"You can try, Danny boy."

Within minutes, they collapsed, laughing harder, the sound carrying, echoing through the empty house. Arms around each other's necks, they held on, foreheads pressed together, both breathing hard. Like brothers again.

"I can try," Danny said.

$\overline{2}\overline{1}$

Leaving his brother to finish sheetrocking, Ken drove straight from the construction site to the Sweetwater Public Library. One minute he imagined Danny might have a point about Daisy, the next he called himself names for believing something so ridiculous.

He should know better than to listen to his younger brother. It was Danny who had the easy charm, who'd grown up straighter, taller, better looking. Danny, who led a more exciting, if dangerous, life. He made Ken feel dull, like a flattened mound of mashed potatoes—no butter.

Ken parked his station wagon, then strolled inside the old brick building on Denton Street. He could prove Danny wrong about that long-legged librarian in twenty seconds sharp. Put his own mind back on track.

The library appeared empty.

Then, catching a glimpse of blondish-brown hair, he peered over the high mahogany counter littered with books and cartons to discover Daisy kneeling behind her desk, rooting through a bottom drawer.

"Why did you drive by my house?" he asked abruptly.

Startled, she sat back on her heels. "Curiosity," she said after a minute. "I had to see for myself what kind of monument a man might erect to his own crazy hopes."

Ken saw no light in Daisy's eyes, no liking for him. So Danny didn't have everything going for him. Intuition wasn't his strong suit after all.

She dumped a stack of papers into a carton.

"What are you doing?" he asked.

"Moving. Out. As in 'all gone, I quit.'"

"Did the library board finally come to its right mind and fire you?"

"Ken"—she shook her head—"don't take your rejections out on me. I don't know what other answer Erin could have given you except no."

He shifted his weight from one leg to the other, like an impatient horse. "Women don't always say no to me."

"Please." She gazed at him. "Leave the macho stuff to Danny. He can bring it off without a woman wanting to smack him."

"I didn't come to talk about Danny."

Getting up, Daisy heaved the carton onto the counter. "That does it." She lifted a pile of books and stalked across the room toward the shelves, her navy-blue heels tapping on the tile floor. "Now I know I made the right decision. I'll feel more at home among my own kind again—those rodeo people you so admire. *Not*," she added.

"Where are you going?"

He stared at her soft rose-colored sweater with the sleeves pushed up, her trim, faded jeans. She looked surprisingly good to him for a change.

"Back where I definitely belong. On the circuit." She shoved a book in place, her long hair swaying, then inched along the stacks, pushing a heavy volume between two others. "You know why?" She whirled around, blue eyes blazing. "Last week I saw you drive by, just like the night you offered me a ride home—only this time you pretended not to see me—and I said to myself, 'Chatworth, you are wasting your life.' So it's barrel racing again for me."

Something clutched at him, like fear. "I thought you had enough broken bones."

Holding a book in midair, she paused. "Apparently not."

"You don't even own a horse."

"I have a horse. Nugget's out of shape right now—definitely. She's pregnant and about to make me a grandmother, I guess. But I've saved my money. What is there to spend it on in Sweetwater?" She pushed the book into place, straightening its neighbors, lining up their spines along the front shelf edge. The way Ken sorted out his change each night. "I could use a few bright lights, the smells of dust and manure, the cheers from a crowd." She looked at him. "I'll lease a horse my first season."

"If you're so happy with that decision, what are you mad at me for?"

"I'm not mad at you. I wouldn't waste my time."

"Waste your time, waste your life," he repeated. What in hell was she talking about? He edged closer, remembering what Danny had said, but Daisy walked away. She rounded a corner and Ken followed. "My brother took off years ago, because of—"

She faced him. Her cheeks looked flushed, and up close he could see tiny pinpoints of red. "You and Hank."

Ken ignored that. "He's never let any grass grow underfoot since. Is that what you're doing, Chatworth? Running away?"

"What would I run from?" She glared at him. "A two-bedroom frame house within walking distance of this job? A couple of flower beds I never get around to weeding?" Her gaze slipped. "Spinsterhood?"

"Me," Ken nearly whispered.

"You," she repeated, as if he'd lost his senses.

"Danny says you . . . He . . . " Trailing off, he crowded

her against the shelves. "In his opinion, when you look in my direction, you like what you see."

"That traitor." She tilted her head, so close he could see the pulse beating in her throat. "And what do you think?"

When she tried to squirm away, under Ken's arm, he pushed her gently back against the shelves, gripping them at either side of her head. He stared into her eyes, hearing the rest of her books fall to the floor. One landed on Ken's foot but he didn't move.

"Is he right?"

"Ken Sinclair, you are the densest person. Do you have to hear the most obvious thing? Can't you let a woman keep her idiotic pride?"

He wondered whether she could see his pulse too.

"Then . . . it's true?" He kicked the book away.

"Do I have to hammer it home for you like a nail? Maybe I do," she said to herself. "Maybe that's what a thick-headed construction type understands. Yes"—she waved a hand, hitting Ken in the solar plexus—"when I look at you, I like what I see. Though I can't say it's because of your smiling face."

"Danny got all the family charm."

Her eyes softened and she smiled up at him, her lips curving just so, almost flirty. "You have your good points."

"Name one."

She shook her head. "Too obvious. And I don't like it that, when I look your way, you're always looking in Erin's direction. No wonder you never noticed me."

He'd noticed. He wasn't completely inept with women either. He'd dated his share, even had a brief fling or two. "Maybe my vision is improving."

Daisy wound her arms around his neck. "I have to tell you, I like my men with blinders on." She didn't give him time for a response. "No sharing." She pressed close to him.

"What?"

"Kiss me, then we'll see."

"See what?"

"Just do it."

The sultry command drew him in. Why not? Lowering his head, he dipped his mouth to hers. And learned why. At the first touch of her lips, he went hot all over. Then Daisy deepened the kiss, and he knew Danny had been right.

Slowly drawing away, he watched Daisy's eyes flutter open, looking soft and glazed. For a long moment neither of them spoke.

Then Ken said, not certain he could form words, "There's a new Western movie playing in Dillon next week-end."

He waited, but Daisy made him work.

"Maybe you'd like to go with me?" She still said nothing so he added, "You can pay your own way if you like. Pay for your own food afterward too."

She touched her lips. "I'm still going to buy a horse and go barrel racing for a living."

He passed the test with surprising ease.

"I've been around rodeo types all my life." Years ago he'd even ridden a few broncs himself, before Trevor died.

"I'm old-fashioned at heart," Daisy admitted. "You pay for the movie. The food too. Pick me up and bring me home."

Ken looked forward to it. Maybe, he thought, Danny didn't get everything.

Two weeks later, in the first days of April, Erin sailed into the house late from work. The emporium had been surprisingly busy that afternoon, and she'd stayed open an extra hour after Meg left. Driving home, for the first time in months she'd left a window cracked, letting the hint of early spring blow through the car.

As she shut the back door, her spirits plummeted. She

had news for Danny, but the house seemed too quiet. Usually she walked into chaos each night, with Timmy usually racing around, Meg's late afternoon piano lessons, and Danny working on some project. But no one was home this time.

She found two notes on the kitchen table. One informed her that Danny had taken Tim to McDonald's for dinner before the early show in Dillon. The Western movie they'd seen twice was being held over. The second note, from Timmy, asked her to fix his monkey again. The scrawled message was pinned to the yellow front of the well-loved toy between red suspenders, and she smiled at the underlined *please, please, please*. The monkey needed work; its head, nearly separated from its body, lay at a strange angle, as if its neck were broken.

Erin knew Meg had gone to town for dinner with Luke. Her stomach growled, but the refrigerator revealed no tempting leftovers for once, so she settled for a bowl of Frosted Flakes with plenty of milk.

She needed to eat more protein but didn't feel like defrosting something or driving back into town for groceries. She'd come to rely too much on Meg's cooking, on Meg herself. Erin was considering dividing the emporium in half, keeping part as the general store it always had been—which she hoped might draw the new, ex-urban residents beginning to build homes near Sweetwater—and giving Meg the other half for a boutique.

Pressing a hand to her lower spine, which ached, she slipped off her shoes then padded in her stockinged feet into the TV room and across the beige carpet, carrying Timmy's monkey and Meg's sewing basket.

Flopping down on the dark red print sofa, she aimed the remote control at the television on the shelves across the room, then dropped her arm before she had pressed the On button. Beside her lay a tabloid-style newspaper, facedown. Erin's heart sank. She didn't have to see its masthead. She didn't even have to turn it over. She'd grown up with that paper. Danny had subscribed before she was ten years old, and it was the first thing Timmy had tried to read on his own.

Pro Rodeo Sports News.

Erin laid a hand over the pages as if to block out what she already knew. She couldn't look. Wouldn't—especially tonight—find out that her dreams had gone up after all in a puff of arena dust.

It was almost spring. They had spent four months together. But she needed him home, tonight, needed his support in the next months more than ever. His love. Flipping the paper over, she proved her worst fears.

In red ballpoint pen on the closely-printed columns under Long Listings, Danny had circled half a dozen upcoming rodeos: Guthrie, Oklahoma; Columbus, Ohio; Beaumont, Texas; Ramona, California.

She had heard Danny recently talking in low tones with Luke, huddled together as if making plans.

Erin hugged Timmy's monkey close, as if it might comfort her, love her without disappointment.

Only last night Danny had made tender love to her, and she had almost believed in their adjustments being complete. On New Year's Eve, on so many nights and mornings since . . .

I feel like a stud horse.

What of his promises? To Timmy too? As soon as the snow melted, Danny would take him fishing for "porkchops," the weighty trout for which the Beaverhead River was famed. He and Timmy would spend a day at one of the commercial mines, sifting for sapphires with the tourists, Montana producing more gem-quality stones than any other state. He would take Timmy to Miles City, buy him his own horse. In the summer they would see hay piled as high as a house in the Big Hole, known as "the valley of 10,000 haystacks."

Erin didn't know how long she sat there without turning on the television or the lights. Cradling the stuffed monkey on her lap, she plunged the curved needle again and again through the gaps, sewing head back onto shoulders in the dark. When she heard the camper in the drive, she didn't move.

The back door slammed. Timmy dashed through the kitchen, along the hall, exploding into the TV room.

"Mom! You in here? Guess what? Me and Dad saw this movie about these guys on a cattle drive?" Everything seemed to be a question. In Erin's mind too. He jumped onto the sofa, crushing the newspaper. He smelled of crisp air, of popcorn. "Wow, you should have seen 'em! This one guy's horse . . . "

Erin resumed her sewing.

Standing in front of her, Danny thumbed his Broncos cap back. "Tim, better not give the plot away. It's late. Go on upstairs and get undressed for bed."

Timmy looked at her, then Danny. "Why don't you have any lights on?"

"Go on," Danny urged. "It's grownup time."

"You guys gonna kiss now?" His tone sounded hopeful, a small boy's preference to the quarrel he might expect.

"We'll see."

Flipping his hat aside, Danny dropped onto the sofa beside her as soon as Timmy darted from the room. She heard him fly up the stairs, his small boots seeming to hit every second step. "Thanks for fixing Monkey!" Then silence.

Erin broke it. "Guthrie starts the twenty-second. I suppose you'll leave a few days before."

Danny shrugged off his sheepskin jacket and picked up the paper. "You've been reading, have you?"

"Enough."

"And you decided I was heading back on the road?"

"That's what it looks like." When he scooted closer, a

smile twitching the corners of his mouth, the mattress needle pricked Erin's finger. "Danny, please. You've never
been a good liar. You didn't bother to hide the evidence."

"I'm not a sneak either."

She didn't hear a smile now. At least he wouldn't try to
charm his way past her going out the door.

Trust him, Meg had said.

Trust him to leave again. She'd seen him studying those
videos of himself too many times.

"Then go," she said. "Why don't you pack now, save us
both the trouble of good-bye in another three weeks? You
think I couldn't hear you and Luke the other night—that
conspiratorial tone, the laughter in your voices?" She set
the monkey aside, half-sewn. "You can both hardly wait to
take off again. Like spring birds migrating."

Danny gripped her shoulders. "Let me explain."

"Explain what? That you need blue sky over your head
and a rank bull under your seat to feel alive? I should have
known—"

His fingers tightened. "Why don't you stop making up
your mind about me before you hear the truth?" He held
her gaze. "I've been home all winter, I never said once
that I meant to ride bulls this spring. Why would you
think—"

Erin shrugged off his touch. "Because I see your face
sometimes! Because I've heard it all before! Because of
this—" She waved at the paper. As she did her hand
brushed Timmy's monkey, and Erin snatched it up. Its
head flopped to one side. "This is what our marriage is like!
A broken toy, like something you won at a carnival—I've
tried, Danny, half a dozen times it seems, but I can't fix it
anymore!"

He took the monkey and folded it against his chest as if it
were Timmy. "We are fixing it, dammit!"

"How? With another horn in your side?" Erin shot to her
feet. She flung up a hand when he would have spoken. "No,

I understand. Rodeo's a hard habit to break, isn't it? Don't tell me you don't miss that adrenaline high, the power. I can see it in your eyes," she said, "when you stare at those video tapes, like a yearning for some other woman."

"I do miss it."

She took a breath. "You didn't even make it through the winter, Danny. You rode at Great Falls in January."

His mouth tightened. "Because I qualified for the Montana circuit finals! I needed that money, Erin. Every dime went to Ken." He stood up, letting the monkey drop to the sofa. "Would you have me throw away last season here, all my entry fees and bruises?"

"What about Miles City?" she asked.

"Miles City?" He frowned. "You mean the Bucking Horse Sale coming up in May? I promised to take Tim and I will." Three days of bucking horses, parades, races . . .

"There's a rodeo there too."

He hung his head. "*Jesus Christ.*"

"What are you trying to prove? That you can climb on mad bulls until you're sixty? Drive me into a grave with worry? That you can win enough money, even win the world someday, and prove you're invincible? That nothing in this world can *kill you*—"

His gaze jerked back to hers. "I'm not trying to prove any such thing! Dammit, if I were, you couldn't keep me from it! You can't keep Tim away either!" On the verge of shaking her, he dropped his hands. "Daisy's going back into competition. She wants to lease Kemosabe. She's been away long enough not to know which are the good rodeos now in her event, so I said I'd pick the first few for her. I circled them for Daisy."

She wanted to believe him. But she'd wakened too many mornings in her life to cool sheets, to the sound of his pickup driving away. She'd watched too many rodeos. She had left him because of it. Rodeo was the love of his life, not her. Why couldn't she accept that?

"You really think I'd go back on my promise, when we've been trying to make a baby again?"

"I don't know." Her voice quivered. "Maybe I should have married someone with a safer job, like a policeman in some inner city."

"Maybe you should."

She opened her mouth, but he cut her off.

"Listen to me, Erin. I busted my ass this winter keeping things together, trying to earn enough to settle up with Ken, trying to be a good father to Tim and a decent husband to you—" He stepped toward her. "Why would I throw that away?"

She shook her head.

"You believe me or not?" he asked.

She tried to speak, but her throat had closed. The word *yes* stuck there like a chicken bone. She needed to believe, needed to tell him . . .

"You know what I think, Erin? You're hiding something from yourself. Maybe you're right about me. All my life I've been climbing on bulls, hanging on . . . but what are you holding onto right here in Paradise Valley?" His hazel eyes drilled into her. "I think you're waiting for your father to have time for you at last, to love you. And I'm just taking his place."

He snatched up his hat and strode to the door.

"Danny—"

He spun around. "Not to disappoint you, I am going." He jammed the Broncos cap on tight. "First thing tomorrow."

"Danny!"

His long strides easily left her behind. She didn't reach the doorway before the back door slammed shut. In her stockinged feet Erin didn't follow him across the still-snowy yard to the barn but sank down again on the TV room sofa, rocking Timmy's monkey in her arms.

She didn't tell Danny she was pregnant.

Meg and Luke were sitting close together—too close, she thought—on the green gingham-checked sofa in the bunkhouse, watching a television sitcom, or appearing to, when Danny banged through the door without knocking. Luke's hand dropped away from its slow caress of her shoulder, the nape of her neck. He took the bowl of potato chips off her lap, setting it on the tack trunk that served as a coffee table.

"What's wrong?" Meg immediately asked at the look on Danny's face.

"Nothing's wrong. Everything's fine." He glared at Luke. "Can you be ready to leave at dawn?"

"Sure, I guess so . . . "

"Good."

Without another word, and with only a brief glance at Luke then Meg, he slammed back out into the chilly night. He hadn't been wearing a jacket, only his plaid wool shirt and jeans with sneakers.

"What's eating him?" Luke wondered aloud.

"Something with Erin, I suspect."

To Meg life had seemed nearly tranquil in the last weeks of winter. Her extended family included Luke now, and she kept forgetting that couldn't last. Danny's abrupt visit was a reminder.

"I take it there's a trip planned," she said.

On the television screen two people traded comic insults, and the laugh track screamed.

"Me and Danny have been meaning to head over to Bozeman as soon as the weather broke." He gazed out the front window as if he could see spring there. "Guess he decided it has."

"We'll have another snow or two," Meg said.

Luke switched off the television.

"Are you upset that I didn't mention going? Danny

wants to check out a bull and a couple of broncs for sale at a ranch over that way." He paused. "Not professionally bred stock. It's said they've gone sour, and he thinks he can pick them up cheap."

She should have been soothed. Danny meant to start up his stock contracting business then; he didn't plan to rodeo this season, as Erin had feared all winter. Why, then, had they quarreled?

"That's all?" she asked.

He shrugged. "We both know Erin doesn't like stock contracting much more than she did bull riding. Maybe she took a strip off Danny just for practice."

She heard the resurgent disapproval in his tone and shook her head. "More than one marriage has ended in the dirt of a rodeo arena. But I thought . . . "

"Hell, what's marriage anyway, except a bunch of nasty words between people who'd be better off shaking hands in the morning and getting on the road again?" Luke's mouth turned down. "Maybe Danny got tired of feeling like a broken-down horse put out to pasture for the kids to ride."

Meg looked at him. "Is that how you feel?"

"Me?"

"Sitting around watching TV with Timmy's grandmother." She could understand Erin's doubts. She had some herself. With no effort she recalled that young rodeo official's pretty face. "As you said yourself, it's hardly your usual style, Luke."

She shoved the bowl of potato chips another few inches, laid her paper napkin on the trunk, and stood up. "I'd better be getting back to the house."

Luke gazed up at her from the sofa. "Why don't you give Erin time to think without adding your advice?"

His tone stopped her before she took a step.

"You think I'm meddling."

"I didn't say that. But you make things easy for Erin, for Danny too when you can . . . " He trailed off.

"Go on."

He rolled his shoulders again. "Danny barges in here, no apology, stomps back out again—and you're already on your feet, halfway to smoothing things over. Let 'em be."

"I had no idea that's what you thought of me."

Meg started for the door, narrowly avoiding a rattan basket of magazines by a chair. Luke came after her. He caught her elbow and swung her around.

"Sit down," he said. "I imagine Danny intends to spend the night here. But he'll stay away a while. Let's finish watching that silly show and keep letting the anticipation build. Pretty soon I'll switch out the lights, and we can pretend it's New Year's Eve again." He smiled a little. "Doesn't that sound better?"

It sounded lovely. Perfect. Absurd, considering what he'd just said regarding relationships.

"About that kiss, Luke . . . "

"And the others since?"

They spent most evenings together, here in the bunkhouse if not out somewhere, and most of them had ended with kisses, increasingly disturbing kisses.

"I wish you wouldn't remind me."

"I enjoyed 'em. Didn't you?"

She couldn't deny that. "Luke, I wish I'd known you years ago, while Hank was still alive. We could have left things at friendship then."

"Where are they now?"

"Friendship and"—she lifted her shoulders—"I don't know what else. Something confusing, something I have no business feeling." She looked away. "I'll be fifty-seven next summer."

"I'll be forty-nine next fall. So what?" He tipped her chin with a callused finger. "We're still alive, Meg. Hank's not. How long are you gonna try to bury yourself with that man? He may have been a good husband—though I have my doubts about him as a father, especially to Danny—but he isn't here."

"Life goes on?" she said.

"Sometimes better than before." He raised a brow. "I should know. My only previous attempt at anything but a one-night stand didn't set well. I admit, my marriage—the divorce—left me gun-shy. I apologize for what I said about men and women." He tried a smile. "Don't you think I'm showing signs of turning myself around?"

She couldn't resist the warmth in his brown eyes, the honest warmth, Meg thought. She liked a plain-spoken man. He led her back to the sofa, not bothering with the television program. Then he lowered the lights.

When he muttered something about music and turned his back to select an album, Meg went cold, and then heat swept through her. A lingering hot flash, she supposed. Luke needed a younger woman. She'd always known that.

"Where you going now?" His voice stopped her in the middle of the room. She'd meant to say goodnight from the door.

"Home to bed," she said.

"Meg, dammit."

"I'm too old for you, Luke! You need someone to give you children, someone like that girl at Cheyenne."

He groaned. "I knew we'd get around to that someday. She's nothing to me. Never was, never will be. We see each other from time to time at rodeos, that's all. Hi and good-bye, that's the sum total of our relationship."

"I doubt that."

Glaring, Luke took out a square of gum and popped it in his mouth.

"All right, so we fell into bed a night or two. Years ago. Nothing special. For either of us. What more do you want me to say?"

What she wanted frightened her.

"I don't recall asking either of you to marry me," Luke said, bringing her to her senses. "You think I want children at my age, as you might say?"

"You needn't worry," she told him. "I was married once—to a man I loved. I won't settle for less."

His mouth thinned. "Then I'm glad Danny and I are leaving in the morning. I could use some fresh air and breathing space—away from all you contrary females." Meg shut the door on his last words, but could hear him muttering, the gum snapping. "Just like a bunch of mares."

Later, Erin rapped softly at the bunkhouse door. It was after two in the morning, and Danny hadn't come back to their room. She couldn't sleep for hearing their quarrel in her mind.

She knocked twice before a rumple-haired Luke answered in low-slung jeans, scratching his bare chest and yawning. When he saw her, he stepped back as if she'd struck him.

"Erin. What are you doing out here?"

"Looking for Danny."

Clutching her gray tweed coat, she peered around him, but Danny wasn't on the gingham-upholstered sofa bed. It hadn't been pulled out, and alarm rippled through her.

"Have you seen him?"

"Nope. I expect he's sleeping in the barn."

"It must be freezing there." She turned to go, but Luke stopped her with a hand on her shoulder, none too gentle.

"He'll stay warm. Believe me, nothing keeps Danny up. He could sleep in the middle of a wild horse race."

She looked down at the sage-green carpet. "I suppose you'd know that."

Luke guided her into the bunkhouse living room.

"Come on in, let's settle this." Looking like a man with an axe to grind, he motioned her to a seat on the sofa. He slumped down in a rocker, throwing one leg over its broad wooden arm, his bare foot dangling. "If Danny's gonna begin contracting, and he and I are partners, you and I better find some way to get along all the time, not just when things are hunky-dory."

"Luke, I shouldn't resent your years with Danny. I know it's partly my fault he stayed away from Paradise Valley." Keeping her coat on to cover her flowered flannel night-gown, she studied her hands. "But I just can't accept his bull riding—"

"Bull riding?"

Erin explained about the rodeo newspaper, the circled dates. "He said they were for Daisy, but I'm not sure."

"They're for Daisy, I know."

Glancing up, Erin met his disgusted gaze.

"He told you the truth. If nothing else, Danny's an honest man. In the past months he's looked happier than I've seen him in years. He wouldn't take off now."

"Then where—?"

Rocking in the creaking old chair, Luke told her about the broncs and bull near Butte.

"We'll be gone a day or two, no more. There'll be other trips this spring and summer, I won't deny that. But we won't get any stock contracts with the season nearly under way, and we'll build slow this year. Quality bucking stock." Luke gazed at her steadily. "You got any more questions?"

"No," Erin said. She found it easier to believe Luke, a man she didn't know half as well as she did Danny. The realization shamed her. "Thank you, Luke. I guess I didn't give him a chance to explain."

She rose to leave.

"I envy you," he said abruptly, rising. The chair kept creaking. "Maybe that's been part of our inability to like each other much. But I do envy what you feel for him, what he feels for you."

He sounded as if he'd lost someone himself.

Luke followed her to the door. She opened it to the moonless night, with no stars overhead. A cold wind had picked up, blowing loose snow around the yard, drifting it in fine white sweeps against the barn door. In late January there had been a brief thaw, another in mid-March, both followed by vicious storms. But tonight the April air still smelled of new growth, and the coming spring.

"I wouldn't go after him tonight if I were you."

Erin looked at him with an unspoken question on her lips.

"Sometimes a man needs room for his thoughts. I'd be willing to wager Danny said a few things he shouldn't have either. Am I right?"

Erin nearly smiled. "Yes."

"Most of us do. He can be a prideful man."

"He's married to a stubborn woman." She hesitated in the doorway, letting her gaze wander to the darkened bedroom window opposite where she and Danny should be lying, sound asleep, together. Erin wrapped her tweed coat closer. "I needed to tell him something tonight."

"It'll keep till we get back."

But Erin couldn't hold the news inside her. "Luke, I'm . . . pregnant."

His gaze shot to her belly, which was covered by her coat and still apparently flat. He raised his hand to stroke her cheek. His eyes softened.

"He'll be real glad about that. I know he will." He started to smile, then let it become a full-blown grin. "Damn, he'll bust his britches—just the way he did when he learned you were expecting Tim."

"He did?" Erin hadn't been there.

Luke leaned close to kiss the tip of her nose. "I guess that makes me about halfway to being a godfather again."

He squeezed her shoulder, then walked with her into the yard and toward the house in the darkness. To see that she got there, or to keep her from going to Danny? She decided on the former. At the back door, Luke said goodnight.

"You tell your mother-in-law to take care, all right?" She nodded, and he shuffled back down the porch steps, dancing a little on his way across the yard to keep his feet from freezing. "We'll see you soon. Erin?"

Waiting, she watched him hop from one foot to the other.

"Don't worry about those broncs or that bull," he said. "I'll take care of Danny for you."

22

Early the next morning Danny let Luke rouse
him from a restless sleep for the drive to Bozeman. He'd
spent an uncomfortable night in Kemosabe's stall, both of
them sprawled at times on the clean hay with his arm
around the horse's neck. It was the only apology Danny
could give him for sending him away from Tim again later
that day. He didn't know how to make that up to Tim, but
he knew Daisy would treat the horse right. 'Sabe wasn't
ready for retirement yet. Maybe Danny wasn't either.

Erin never had understood his needs. Sure, he missed
riding bulls. He'd rodeoed most of his adult life. He
propped one boot against the dashboard as the Jeep, towing a stock trailer, pulled out of the drive onto the icy road,
leaving the still-darkened ranch house behind, and yanked
his cowboy hat down over his eyes.

"Erin's worried about you."

Luke's quiet tone broke through his thoughts, but
Danny didn't move his hat or open his eyes. He wrapped
himself in darkness, silence.

"I told her we were just running over to Bozeman," Luke said.

"I'm sure that eased her mind."

More silence.

Luke cleared his throat. "What would you say if I asked your mother to marry me?"

His attention captured at last, Danny shot upright. His hat fell off into the well behind the passenger seat, and he stared at Luke's profile. Luke didn't look his way but his face colored.

Danny thought his mother cared for Luke. He'd watched them all winter, and didn't think he imagined his mother's happiness. But the question still shocked him.

"Are you asking my permission?"

"Hell, I don't know. What do you think she'd say?"

"Ask her," Danny said.

"I think she'll say no." Luke fidgeted with the steering wheel. "She's determined to stay married to your father," he said, aiming the Jeep around a slow-moving semi on an upgrade, then swinging back into the right lane too soon. Inches behind the stock trailer, it seemed, the truck's air horn blasted.

Danny swallowed hard. He'd let Luke drive because he couldn't trust himself this morning. He didn't want to die on some frozen highway, though, with everything between him and Erin unresolved. As usual.

"Take it easy. Give us some space here."

"I had plenty of room." Accelerating, Luke pushed up the hill. He shook his head. "Hell, what would I want with a permanent arrangement anyway? I swore I'd never get hitched again."

"I know," Danny said. He'd heard that often enough.

"You sure as hell don't get much," he went on, gathering steam. "Women. Can't live with 'em."

"Can't live without 'em," Danny murmured.

The Jeep whizzed along on the drier pavement of the

highway, the odometer edging past seventy-five. "You want my opinion, we'd both be better off back on the circuit, chasing buckles, and bunnies. What man in his right mind needs to spend four months—or four minutes—trapped on a rundown ranch miles from a good road like this one?"

"I do," Danny said then retrieved his hat, pulling it low over his eyes. "I also need some quiet, so could you shut up for a while?"

Luke laughed. "That's it, give me some morning grump. It's sweet music in my ears. Makes me feel on top of the world again. What do you say we take a brief look at that bull, then keep going? And forget those two women?" He sighed. "What else do we need but the open road and another day behind the chutes somewhere?"

"You're full of it."

Danny leaned his head back against the seat and smiled in spite of his own bad mood. Luke had it worse than he thought. He felt as miserable as Danny did.

Outside of Bozeman, Luke missed a turn, and they circled around for an extra half hour before finding their destination, then listened to a lecture from the disgruntled rancher about being late.

"I got other things to see to," said the man in worn jeans and denim winter jacket, who was selling off his place and obviously feeling the loss.

"We won't hold you up." Carrying his bull rope, Danny matched the man's stride across the snowy ground to the corral. The fencing had seen better days, a few splintered boards lay on the ice-encrusted grass, and the barn—the only one in current use—looked ready to tumble down. "I'll just try out that bull and those horses, then we'll be on our way."

"You won't ride that bull," the man said.

His words bit into Danny's already wounded ego. The hell he wouldn't. "I can ride anything on four legs."

The rancher studied him, as if he were crazy. "You rodeo boys, something's wrong with all of you. My youngest son has it too. He'd rather try to break his own neck than do anything else. And when he almost does, he never admits to any pain. Just gets back on again. Why, last year he broke his arm . . ."

Danny stopped listening. In the far corner of the corral he spied the Black Angus bull, which had already seen him. They eyed each other across a hundred feet of uneven dirt specked with good-sized rocks. His blood began to sing. Four months, he thought.

He had his hand on the corral gate when Luke covered it with his. "You're not going in there. I am."

Danny gaped at him.

"I promised Erin," Luke explained, looking away. "It's not like I don't have experience. I spent enough years rodeoing myself before I started clowning."

"Riding saddle broncs," Danny said, his tone dismissive. It was a far cry from bull riding. "Get your hand off."

"I tried a few bulls before I met you." Luke's grip tightened. Danny wondered if he was lying, and why. "Didn't I ever tell you? I placed third one year on the Prairie Circuit, missed first another time by one bad ride." He grinned. "Why do you think I'm so fond of bulls that I keep dancing in front of 'em now?" He glanced at the Angus. "I'll buck him out for you. We're partners, aren't we? It's like earning a first dollar in the business."

"Yeah, we'll tack him up on the wall over the cash register." Prying Luke's hand away, he opened the gate on its sagging hinges, and the bull snorted, pawing the ground. Danny grinned. "Look at him. He thinks he's going to give me what-for this morning." As Erin had last night.

The rancher looked back and forth, between him and Luke. "You sure you boys know what you're doing?" He gazed speculatively at the bull rope in Danny's other hand. "You ever been near a rodeo? Or is that thing brand-new?"

"Every season, the last eighteen years. Take a look." At the end of the flat, braided rope, the bell, squashed like a penny on a rail from its many poundings in the arena, pronounced him a seasoned veteran. He was proud of that bell. Danny settled his hat deeper on his head. "Finished second in the world last December."

The man's eyes widened.

Luke stepped around him, between Danny and the Black Angus. Closing the gate, Danny glanced over Luke's shoulder.

"You better not turn your back on that bull. Now I'm losing patience, just like he is. Get out of my way, Luke."

"Erin had something to tell you."

"She can tell me tonight. I have a few things to tell her too. What's that got to do with bull riding?"

"You too-proud bastard! You've taken enough chances with your life." Luke held his gaze. "Trying to prove what? That Hank and Ken were wrong about you—or that you won't end up like Trevor did?" The flat of his hand slammed into Danny's chest before he took a step. "You're not ridin' today. By God, when I drive that Jeep through the ranch gates, you're gonna be sitting in that seat without a scratch . . . alive and kicking-mad. That's all right with me. It'll be all right with her too."

Danny shoved him.

"Goddammit, Sinclair, she's carryin' your baby!"

The breath went out of Danny, as if the Black Angus had charged and knocked him flat. He watched it paw the ground, sizing him up with a malevolent eye. He already loved that bull.

"Erin's pregnant?"

"She told me last night. I stopped her from tracking you down. I thought you needed cooling-off time but maybe I was wrong." He stared at the ground, both of them ignoring the rancher looking on. "It wasn't my place to tell you. I'm sorry."

Erin, *pregnant*. He tried out the notion, remembering New Year's Eve and all the nights since then. Mornings too. A few afternoons . . . He had new responsibilities to consider.

"Get on that ornery black cuss then and let's see how he jumps."

Even relinquishing his ride, it sounded easier than it proved. There was only a makeshift bucking chute for one thing. And Luke hadn't been on board a bull in years. With the rancher's lame assistance Danny helped him herd the animal behind the catty-corner gate with half its boards missing, managed to throw the bull rope around him, to get Luke seated. Then at Luke's nod he pulled the gate back, ran for safety and let him rip.

"He's a right-hand spinner!" Danny shouted, clapping his hat on his head. "Whoo-eee!"

In his mind he rode with Luke, whirling in the ring. The rancher hooted. Luke's face split in a sickly grin. The bull spun back—then took to the air. All four feet left the ground at once, daylight showing underneath, in a stiff-legged buck.

Danny's heart thumped. He had himself a damn fine rodeo bull, but the Angus was too much bull for Luke. He shouldn't have let him ride, even for Erin's sake. In the blink of an eye, the thoughts ran through his mind. Then the bull landed hard. At four seconds, its head went down and Luke flew over it, somersaulting onto the frozen dirt.

Danny heard the air rush from Luke's lungs as he ran toward him.

"Get 'im back in the chute!" he yelled to the rancher, who remained near the ramshackle gate in the corner of the ring. Danny's hat flew off. "Help me get him out of here!"

For precious seconds he ignored the fallen Luke. Shouting, he and the rancher stalked the animal, Danny playing bullfighter and taking the charges, barely evading the horns. Then, as if he heard an eight-second gun, the snorting Angus suddenly stopped before trotting like a docile calf into the next pen. The rancher slammed the gate shut, and Danny took off after Luke.

"Call the paramedics!"

Skidding to a halt in the center of the corral, he sank to his knees. He searched Luke for broken bones, for a pulse.

"Luke, wake up. Open your eyes!"

He slapped his cheeks, then slapped harder.

"Is he dead?" The rancher hovered over them.

God above, he prayed. If Luke died here, in this crazy-ass arena, because of him . . .

"I said call Emergency!"

The man jogged off across the yard to the house. Danny saw Luke's lips move without a sound. Then he heard a wheeze, his lungs refilling, and a feeble groan.

"Jesus, I'm dyin'." Luke cracked one eye, filled with pain. "I think . . . he . . . crushed . . . my chest."

Danny breathed again himself. "No, but you might have cracked a rib or two." He prayed that was all, but his whole body went weak with relief that Luke was conscious. If there were no internal injuries . . .

"Maybe my . . . rib's gone straight . . . through my lung . . . or even my heart. Remember Cheyenne."

"You're not coughing blood. You can breathe."

"Now and then." Luke clutched his arm. "Danny. Damn . . . I never rode . . . one of those . . . things before. Damn bull. If I don't . . . get home with you . . . tell Meg . . . "

"Don't talk. You can tell me later."

"No, now . . . Tell her . . . " He gasped, his eyes fixed on Danny. "I regret not havin' time with her . . . I wasted my life . . . doing what I felt like, staying by myself . . . Plain foolishness . . . Like you, Danny . . . Some dream."

Trembling, Danny gazed down at him. In Las Vegas he had called himself selfish, but for the first time, now, he really knew how Erin must feel, watching him ride. How she had felt last night. Her fears had never counted. He'd wanted to rodeo, so he did. When she left him, he never considered quitting, going back to Paradise Valley with less than that gold buckle to show Ken and his father. But would a buckle gain forgiveness? It certainly couldn't bring Trevor back. Crazy choices that had kept him apart from Erin. Maybe she and Luke were right about him. What was he trying to prove? That he, at least, was immortal?

He stared at Luke in the dirt. *Too-proud bastard.*

"Dreams can change," he murmured. "You tell my mother that when we get home."

He'd tell Erin too. No matter how he might miss the power, the surge, he had ridden his last bull. Thanks to Luke, risking his life in this piss-poor ring.

"Luke?"

He had passed out, escaping the pain.

With the dirt cold and hard under his knees, Danny leaned over his friend, as years ago he had bent over his youngest brother, but he didn't move Luke. "Oh, God." With no one else around, he slid lower, folding Luke close, lying with him on the frozen ground, feeling his heart beat against his own chest, pressing his cheek to Luke's temple. He envisioned Luke's strength returning as he tried to will life back into him, and tried not to remember the limpness of a much smaller body. So many years. He held him in his arms, and wept. For Luke, for Trevor, and himself.

At Paradise Valley that afternoon Erin stood outside the corral watching Timmy canter Kemosabe around the ring. Last summer he had become an adequate rider, though she would have preferred his staying on the ground a few more years. The fact that she'd started riding at five didn't sway Erin.

And since Daisy's phone call earlier she'd been dreading this last ride.

"I am so good enough to ride 'Sabe," Timmy insisted.

"Daisy's just leasing him from Daddy for the season until she can find a horse as smart and able as Kemosabe. Then he'll come home again."

"I won't let him go!"

Timmy had somehow dragged the heavy saddle up onto the horse's back himself, then gotten the bridle on. Erin checked the tack before he mounted, but he hadn't said a word to her since then until now.

Hearing a car on the drive, she didn't turn around. She knew who was coming. But to her surprise, Daisy wasn't alone. A familiar Taurus station wagon pulled the horse trailer, and two people got out.

"Afternoon, Erin," Ken called, striding across the mushy yard with the sun beating on his dark hair. His smile shocked her. So did his friendliness, and she waved back. Daisy had said they were seeing each other, but their clasped hands stunned her even more.

Ken leaned down to kiss Erin's cheek, and she smiled.

Timmy pulled Kemosabe into a trot, sitting the horse well and deeply even in the too-big western saddle as they swept by the gate. His expression looked mulish.

"Me and Kemosabe are pals. He doesn't want to leave."

Erin looked at Daisy.

"Seems I have my work cut out for me," Daisy said. "What did Timmy say when Danny told him I was leasing?"

"Danny didn't tell him."

"Oh, Lord." She rolled her eyes. "Where is he?"

Erin explained. "He left the bad news for me to convey—left a note on the kitchen table—and I can't blame Timmy for wanting to kill the messenger." She paused. "Are you really going on the circuit?"

"Sure am." Daisy looked worried.

"Come on in the house. Meg baked brownies this morning—at six A.M.—then disappeared after breakfast into her sewing room. I can't say there are any cheerful faces here today. Let's talk. I'll fix coffee."

"And put off the inevitable?"

They left Ken coaching Timmy from the fence rail. At the kitchen table Daisy dropped onto a chair, and leaned her chin against her palm.

"I'd come back another day, after Danny gets home and explains to Timmy in a way he can accept—but I made arrangements in Dillon with a trainer. He's expecting us today. He and I will work with the horse for the next couple of weeks until my first show. I need all the practice I can get."

Erin poured water into the coffeemaker. "It's not your fault Danny left me to take the heat."

"Maybe he'll get back soon."

"Maybe he won't come back." She sat across from Daisy while they waited for the coffee. "We had a terrible argument last night." She massaged her temples. "I accused him of lying about quitting rodeo." She gave Danny's side too.

Daisy looked as sympathetic as possible, Erin supposed, considering her longtime friendship with Danny and their own rift last fall.

"I've spent some time with Ken. I never thought he was an easy man to deal with, but he has his moments. He also has that Sinclair pride. I'm having to use a light rein."

Erin poured their coffee. "I've always thought Danny was footloose. This winter I've come to understand that I like having my freedom too. It hasn't been an easy four months, and I'm mad as a wet hen right now . . . but, Daisy, I need him."

"What aren't you telling me, Erin?"

She glided a hand over her stomach. "We're going to have another baby next fall. I need him with me, this time."

"Congratulations," Daisy said softly. "I'll bet Danny's crowing right now, stopping in every town on the way home to buy baby things."

"He doesn't know. I was so angry last night. Scared." She waved a hand. "I didn't want to keep him that way."

"If he comes back, if he stays, it has to be because that's what he wants. Not what you want, or even what you need." She smiled. "Danny's no fool. He'll be back."

She got up, dumped her coffee in the sink, and went outside. For long moments Erin stayed at the table, staring into her cup. She could hear Meg's sewing machine upstairs, whirring hard enough to punch holes in the ceiling. She could hear Timmy calling out to Ken and Daisy, "Watch me! I'm a saddle bronc rider."

She'd tried to give him everything she'd lacked as a child. Acceptance, a mother's unconditional love, security. This home she cherished so.

Her steps dragged from the house to the yard again to watch Timmy say good-bye to Kemosabe.

Timmy would survive, she told herself.

Instead of begging Daisy for another day, she went to the corral, knowing a few more hours wouldn't matter. Timmy would have to deal with it. She tried to harden her heart to the sight of him standing motionless on Kemosabe near the gate. His eyes trained upon the nearby horse trailer, his knuckles white on the reins.

Erin reached him and laid a hand over his.

"Daisy's a wonderful rider, a very kind person. She won't treat him badly like Wes Turner. And I'll take you to see the first rodeo she's in close enough to home."

"I won't go." Timmy bowed his head. "Why did Daddy lease him? You could tell Daisy he can't leave if you wanted to—but you don't like seeing me on a horse!" He chewed at his lip. "You're afraid I'll break my arm or something. You don't know how much I love him!"

Before Erin could speak, he spun and kicked Kemosabe into a gallop. Erin's heart leaped into her throat.

"Timmy!"

"If I was old like Daddy, I'd run away. I'd be a bull rider too!"

Erin clutched her coat tight around her neck. But she

didn't call out, didn't shout the warnings she might have months ago. She didn't even think of Trevor.

She remembered Danny as a boy, the daredeviltry in him on horseback, his natural balance and rhythm, his fine legs and hands. She remembered him in the rodeo arena at Cheyenne last summer, and the way her heart swelled with pride in Las Vegas as she stood with Timmy and Meg, shouting and clapping. Timmy was his father's son.

Quickly, he gathered his reins and brought the black-and-white gelding under absolute control. Seven years old, she thought, and born to the saddle.

Daisy started toward her, but that quickly, Timmy calmly worked the horse through its paces, as if gathering himself too.

"He's fine," Erin said.

At last Timmy walked Kemosabe on a loose rein over to them, then dismounted. Appearing to come to some agreement with himself, he glanced toward the trailer, then at Daisy. Holding Kemosabe's reins, he slipped both arms around the horse's neck.

"You be good for Daisy, hear?" He buried his face against the horse's furry winter hide. "Win lots of money. Look like a king."

The tears streamed down Erin's face.

Her seven-year-old son coped better than she did.

She swiped at her cheeks, her wet skin stiffening in the cold wind. Overhead the clouds rolled, thick and white, blocking the weak sun, and she knew it would snow again soon, that true spring wouldn't arrive until weeks from now. She could smell the moisture, as well as the steam rising from Kemosabe's hide. Like heartache.

Timmy planted a kiss on Kemosabe's nose, and Erin turned away.

"You want to help load him?" Daisy asked her son. "You can ride with Ken and me to the trainer's. Then I'll show you Nugget's new baby."

"She has a foal?" Timmy's voice brightened.

"Born last night. A beautiful little colt."

"Can I see him?" he asked Erin.

"Of course you can." She looked up. "Thanks, Daisy."

With a glance at the darkening clouds, Daisy half smiled. "A boy has his dreams too. And from what I just saw, he's halfway there." She slipped an arm through Ken's. "Good luck with Danny, Erin. I'll handle this guy."

By late the next morning eight inches of snow blanketed Paradise Valley, and snow was still falling from a pearl-gray sky. The wind shoved it into mounds and hollows, drifted it against the barn and the back porch steps.

From the kitchen window Erin watched the drive. Danny had called after Daisy and Ken left the day before to tell her and Meg that Luke had been hurt. His injuries weren't serious, but "he had his brain rattled," and the doctors in Bozeman wanted to keep him in the hospital overnight for observation. Erin nearly smiled now. So far that morning Meg had baked three cherry pies, two batches of the gingersnaps Luke loved, and was pummeling a meat loaf into shape at the kitchen table.

But Erin didn't smile. Luke might have been killed riding in Danny's place—for her.

Unable to keep still, after rummaging in her bedroom drawer for something she'd nearly lost, she shrugged into her hunter green parka, clapped a yellow knit cap on her head, and left Meg inside. She stepped out into what she hoped would be the last blizzard before spring.

Erin hunched against the wind, the sting of blowing snow. Luke was a better friend than she was a wife. As Daisy had said, she found ways to send Danny from her— had done exactly that again before he and Luke went to Bozeman. So afraid of losing him, she had wanted him in Paradise Valley, nowhere else. Yet this winter, hadn't he stayed? Given her what she wanted? What did she offer in return?

She rubbed her mittened thumb over the ring on her gloved left hand. She'd never really taken it off, in her heart. She'd never really left Danny either.

Making her way through the snowy yard, she gazed at the surrounding mountains that ringed Paradise Valley. Her home. But without Danny, it was only fifteen hundred acres, a small ranch, and a house. She hadn't divorced him, for one good reason: He was the man she loved, the only man she ever would love, ever could love. And she had stayed in Paradise Valley for thirteen years, not for Garrett Brodey, who had died long before Timmy was born, but for Danny. Waiting.

How many times had she imagined his return?

But come ye back when summer's in the meadow . . .

And when he had come last June, for Timmy, she'd ruined that too. The next time, she wouldn't. Somehow, she would bend for him.

A sound broke the thick stillness, and Erin swung around toward the driveway, the road. She heard a car's horn—or more accurately, the Jeep's. Towing a stock trailer. When it came near enough, down through the mountain pass into Paradise Valley on soundless tires in the snow, she could hear the angry bellow of a bull and the softer whickers of horses sensing a warm barn and hay.

Erin's heart, like her mittened fingers, twisted.

She'd always imagined his camper instead speeding the last hill—but never like this.

. . . when the valley's hushed and white with snow.

Suddenly, she was running, running.

In the center of the snowy track, she waved her arms. Danny was driving, plowing a path with the Jeep's front-mounted blade. Fifty yards from the house, he slid to a stop and jumped out, leaving the door open, the engine purring.

Erin stumbled toward him through the snow, keeping

her eyes on him every step—his dark felt Stetson, sheep-skin-lined jacket, tight jeans and black boots—blundering into his arms.

Her cap flew off. "Danny. Oh, Danny!"

"I'm home," he said, nestling his cheek against her hair. "I'm really home, Erin." He drew back to look at her, his beautiful hazel eyes serious. "Luke got hurt and I thought about Trev, and I knew—Erin, I just knew—it would be all right now. I knew I could come home."

"I waited for you. I would have waited forever."

"I know," he said, raising her face to his. His mouth covered hers, his warm and tasting of coffee, hers cold and tasting of fresh air. "I always knew."

The back door flew open. Meg skimmed down the steps without her boots. She wore no coat either, only a blue angora sweater and jeans that defined her slim figure.

Her brown gaze searched Danny's face. "Where's Luke?"

"In the Jeep." Danny grinned, his arms around Erin, rocking her. "All in one piece. And hungry as a bear after winter hibernation."

While Meg tended to Luke, Danny and Erin occupied themselves with kisses until Timmy apparently sensed his father's arrival, and, coatless too, ran from the house, barreling into Danny's knees. His breath frosted in the crisp air.

"Daddy, you should have seen me! I rode Kemosabe at a run then helped Daisy and Uncle Ken take him to Dillon. Then they showed me Nugget's new colt. You ought to see him, Daddy!"

"Hold on there." Danny scooped him up between him and Erin. "Don't I get a hug first?" He glanced at Erin and repeated, "Rode him at a run?" Erin shrugged, grinning. Timmy strangled him then slid to the ground and was off racing, shouting for his grandmother and Luke.

Erin and Danny were kissing again when he flew back toward them. His jaws worked furiously, and a big wad bulged his cheek.

"What is that in your mouth?" Erin asked.

"Uncle Luke's present." He showed her a tin box that looked suspiciously like chewing tobacco. "It's bubble gum, Mom. Just like Luke chews, only for kids."

"Lots of boys around rodeo like it," Danny explained, trying not to laugh.

"Well, aren't you just turning into a real cowboy?" Erin ruffled his hair. "If you're going to stay outdoors, put your coat on. And chew that one piece at a time."

Danny curled an arm around her shoulders. "That bubble gum's a good gift, Tim." He couldn't stop the grin any longer. "But you might take a look in the trailer. I picked up something for you in Bozeman too."

Timmy's head whipped around toward the Jeep. "A horse?"

Thumbing his hat back, Danny scratched his head. "Well, it's got four legs, a tail and a mane. A couple of eyes, a forelock . . ."

With a banshee cry, Timmy lit out down the drive again.

"Don't open that trailer till I get there," Danny called after him. He walked with Erin. "The guy who sold us the bull and broncs had this sweet little gelding. Chestnut with white socks and a blaze, a real kind eye." He hugged her close. "The rancher's daughter left for college last fall, and the horse has been pining for company. I told him I knew just the boy to spoil him."

"Oh, Danny." Erin leaned her cheek against his chest.

"The horse is perfectly safe. And not too large but big enough he'll be able to ride him for a long while." Reaching Timmy at the trailer's gate, he said, "I figure Kemosabe will need a companion during the winters." He kissed the tip of Erin's nose. "Now," he said, "you're cold and—as I hear tell—pregnant. Which is a matter we need to take up. Let's get this trailer unhitched, these animals bedded down, and you inside where it's warm."

"Be prepared to gain ten pounds. Meg's been baking all morning."

"She'd better start baking a wedding cake. Luke's a pretty determined man once he sets his mind to it."

Erin saw Meg hunched over Luke in the front seat of the Jeep, their mouths pressed together, but Danny's words drew her back. "Married?" she said.

He dipped his head to hers again. "Married."

That night in bed, Danny pulled the flowered coverlet and blankets over their heads, enclosing him and Erin in a warm cocoon. He was home again, and for the first time in years, he felt he belonged, that he could stay.

Despite a power failure just before dark, his mother had produced a perfect meal for her hungry men. Danny had meat loaf—not his favorite but one of Luke's—whipped potatoes, glazed carrots, corn bread, and raspberry creme cake in his belly. Plus two glasses of the champagne Luke had brought from Bozeman along with his headache and three bruised ribs.

Danny also had Meg's motherly lecture riding just below his heart.

"I know you think Hank didn't love you," she'd said after shooing everyone else from the kitchen after dinner. "But he did, Daniel." She handed him a blue-and-white dish towel, then a pot to dry. "He loved all his boys. Do you remember that first pro rodeo buckle you won, somewhere in Texas?"

"Tyler," he said.

She pulled a tissue-wrapped rectangle from her pocket. "You sent it to him and he kept it the rest of his life. In the top sock drawer of his bureau where he saw it every morning. He always said those socks kept it polished. He never saw you ride after you left home, but he treasured this buckle—even if he could never have said so. Like Garrett Brodey with Erin." She held it out to him, and Danny set the dried pot aside. "Your father would want you to have it back—for Timmy one day."

Danny swallowed, hard. He laid the towel on the counter.

"He didn't leave you a share of the ranch," his mother went on, her eyes warm with love, "but he left one to Erin, and I think I know why." She had watched him spread the tissue, find the buckle inside. "He knew you'd come back to her one day. That your love for her and this place would bring you home."

His father, Danny thought, a little muzzy now from the champagne. His remaining brother. Ken had agreed to a lower price for his share of Paradise Valley, so Erin and their mother wouldn't need that mortgage on the ranch— Daisy's doing, in part, he supposed. It looked as if his brother might have found a woman of his own, and since then, he and Danny were doing okay too.

"We were all affected by Trevor's death," his mother had said. "I believe we each handled that in our own way. Hank couldn't accept it. He tried to blame you. I made peace with it as I could." She ticked them off on her fingers, the people she loved, while Danny fingered the belt buckle. "Ken— careful Ken—tried to make certain nothing terrible ever happened again." She smiled. "Erin retreated into Paradise Valley as a refuge." She looked at Danny for a long moment before taking the dish towel to dry the last glassware herself. "And you, favorite boy, made a mission of riding anything on four legs to flaunt Fate itself."

With her back to him, her voice husky, she quoted to Danny from the Bible, a passage from Genesis that he'd heard many times on the circuit on Sundays.

"And God blessed them, and said unto them . . . have dominion . . . over every living thing that moveth upon the earth."

Shattering the moment, Tim burst into the kitchen, having obviously heard his grandmother's words.

"I thought I was your favorite boy, Gram."

"You are," she said, kissing him and then Danny. "You both are."

"You can't have two favorites."

"Yes," she said, "I can. More than that. With your Uncle Ken, I have three." But she gave Danny her special look. Luke appeared in the doorway, holding an ice bag to his middle, a round bulge in his cheek. "Then there's this man . . . "

And she dragged Luke upstairs. Danny watched them go. At the top of the stairs, his mother looked down. "Do you have a problem, Daniel?"

"I don't guess I have any problems just now."

He'd given her a thumbs-up sign, then Luke, who had his arm around Meg, his smile a little goofy from the wine and pain pills.

Danny grinned now in the dark. Luke, his stepfather? He could imagine worse things. He'd already promised to help Luke build an addition on to the bunkhouse so that he and Erin could have the ranch house. He thought Ken would supply plans, materials and labor if he asked. And he would ask anything, do anything, like Erin, to stay on this land.

He had no alternative. His yearning for bull riding would fade in time; it would seem paltry if instead he lost Erin. He might always miss the arena, the crowd's roar and the power of a bull beneath him, but the love she and Tim offered, the new baby's promise, his mother and Luke could fill the gap. Stock contracting would be enough, and with Luke's help, he would succeed at that too.

If he would never become world champion now, maybe one day Tim—in a safer, timed event like calf roping—just might. That second-hand hint of immortality tasted almost as sweet.

Under the covers Erin moved against him, and he held her close. "I love you, Mrs. Sinclair," he whispered.

"I love you too."

"About that baby . . . "

Her voice faltered. "Are you glad?"

"You know I am." He kissed her then Erin wiggled lower beneath the coverlet. "Mom's eager to work at the store," Danny said, holding his breath as Erin inched down his body, "so you should be able to juggle things. Unless that new business boom turns you into a tycoon or something."

"Or stock contracting does you." Erin kissed his collarbone. "I'm not that eager for so much change in Sweetwater."

"Like most Montanans." Her lips trailed across his chest and he sucked in a breath. "I'm not crazy about it either."

"But it's necessary to save the town and the emporium."

"That's progress." He held himself still as she kissed her way along his ribs. "Like people, if the town doesn't change to suit the times, it won't survive."

He meant himself too. Erin's mouth brushed over his belly to his scar from being gored by that bull in Cody years ago, the scar that had made her leave him, for fear of his life. She pressed her lips to the puckered flesh, sending a rush of need through him, of love.

"You're not doing bad already with that store. At first," he said, distracting himself, "coming into Sweetwater, I wondered. But you're gonna be all right there. It's good for Mom too to have something else—something satisfying." He paused. "Running your own business can be hard. I know, because all these years I've been my own business, even my own product . . . " He trailed off. "I guess I'm trying to say I'm proud of you, Erin."

"I'm proud of you too."

"Come on up here," he said, drawing her to him, his fingers around her hand—the hand that wore his wedding ring again. "I don't want to explode too quick." He kissed her, long and sweet, then raised his head to look into her eyes.

"I think Mom was right when she said I rode bulls"—the past tense didn't even stop him—"trying to prove I'd never end up like Trev. I mean, I loved riding, but Ken said the same thing, so did Luke, and it's true." He hesitated, gathering his words, the truth. "The ride's only half of it," he said. "As you know, the other half's a clean dismount, getting away safe."

He stroked the warm, enduring circle of gold on her finger, and Erin waited, as if sensing his next words. They didn't come easily, but when he said them, they seemed as much a comfort as the woman in his arms for the rest of his life. If he had Erin, that elusive gold buckle was only a cold piece of metal.

He cleared his throat. "Erin, that day in the corral . . . I've seen the same thing a few times on the circuit. My little brother didn't come off right." He swallowed, his voice low, shaking as he finished, but full of conviction. "Trev . . . he just landed wrong, that's all."

For long moments Erin said nothing. She heard the tone of his voice, but she also heard something more, like a current flowing beneath a stream. And just as Timmy, showing a wisdom beyond his years, had let Kemosabe go the day before, she knew what she had to say.

"Danny, I've tried to have my way, and only my way, long enough. I want you to know . . . you're the best bull rider I've ever seen." She paused. "Daisy was right. She said if you quit now, it has to be because you want to, not because that's what I need. Your mother implied the same thing."

He waited, watching her.

"If you buck out bulls and horses the rest of your life, whether in rodeo or stock contracting, I'll always be afraid, but that's who you are and what you have to do to be happy." He had said that once to her, when she couldn't really listen. "I can't change that, just as you can't change me. If we could change completely," she said, "we'd lose what we love in each other."

Through the lonely years, she had learned she could live without him; and Danny could live without her. But dear God, she didn't want that, for either of them. Just when she hoped their adjustments were complete, he surprised her all over again. She supposed she surprised him too—which promised an exciting life together. A real marriage at last. And so she said the rest.

She knew rodeo could be, and often was, on some level, a lifetime activity. Once, she'd dreaded that. "Your pro career may be over, but there's always weekend rodeo."

"You wouldn't mind?"

Erin couldn't help smiling at his swift response. She knew his heart, just as he knew hers.

"I'll try not to."

He rubbed her wedding ring, the back of her hand. "I'd wait until the new baby gets here."

"We'll all come," she said, "to cheer you on."

"You will?"

When she nodded, he studied her expression, then as if satisfied with what he saw, lowered his mouth to hers. As they kissed, he feathered a finger across one breast, and Erin moaned.

"That suits me fine," he said into her mouth.

"*You* suit me fine," she whispered against his.

Snow sifted past the windows. Through the dotted swiss curtains Erin glimpsed a streak of stars in the black sky. She savored Danny beside her, his warmth, his abiding love. The love she'd always had but didn't always accept. Perhaps she was Garrett Brodey's daughter after all. With the thought, Erin smiled and her last fears seemed to drift with the snow, the last storm before spring came.

"Danny?"

"What?"

She glanced toward the pine dresser where his first buckle gleamed in the low light.

"If you want more," she said, "if you wanted to try the circuit another season . . . I think you'd win that gold buckle."

He grinned. "Could be. I've gotten out of my own way, about Trev. I could keep my mind on business."

Erin stroked his hair. The notion didn't trouble her. If he competed again at the top level, she would travel with him as much as she could, teaching Timmy on the road and caring for the new baby, watching Danny ride. Despite her fears, Erin knew why. If anything ever happened to him in the arena again, victory or disaster, she would be there for him, with him. He wouldn't be alone. And neither would she.

"I'm here," she said, "for you. I always have been."

Rolling over, he gently pinned her beneath his weight, his overwhelming love for her showing in his eyes. Erin, cradled in his embrace, the place she loved above all else, even Paradise Valley, felt her vision blur. Meg's favorite song was hers too. The words were Erin's pledge.

She would be here . . . in sunshine or in shadow.

Oh, Danny boy, oh, Danny boy. I love you so.

"I'm not going anywhere," he whispered, "right now."

He covered her softening belly in the pillow-deep comfort of their bed.

"What would I be proving?" Danny said, bending to her mouth again. "I already won the world."

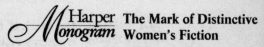

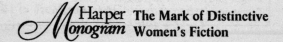

GLORY IN THE SPLENDOR OF SUMMER WITH

HarperMonogram's

101 Days of Romance

BUY 3 BOOKS, GET 1 FREE!

Take a book to the beach, relax by the pool, or read in the most quiet and romantic spot in your home. You can live through love all summer long when you redeem this exciting offer from HarperMonogram. Buy any three HarperMonogram romances in June, July, or August, and get a fourth book sent to you for FREE. See next page for the list of top-selling novels and romances by your favorite authors that you can choose from for your premium!

101 DAYS OF ROMANCE

BUY 3 BOOKS, GET 1 FREE!

CHOOSE A FREE BOOK FROM THIS OUTSTANDING
LIST OF AUTHORS AND TITLES:

HarperMonogram

____LORD OF THE NIGHT Susan Wiggs 0-06-108052-7
____ORCHIDS IN MOONLIGHT Patricia Hagan 0-06-108038-1
____TEARS OF JADE Leigh Riker 0-06-108047-0
____DIAMOND IN THE ROUGH Millie Criswell 0-06-108093-4
____HIGHLAND LOVE SONG Constance O'Banyon 0-06-108121-3
____CHEYENNE AMBER Catherine Anderson 0-06-108061-6
____OUTRAGEOUS Christina Dodd 0-06-108151-5
____THE COURT OF THREE SISTERS Marianne Willman 0-06-108053-5
____DIAMOND Sharon Sala 0-06-108196-5
____MOMENTS Georgia Bockoven 0-06-108164-7

HarperPaperbacks

____THE SECRET SISTERS Ann Maxwell 0-06-104236-6
____EVERYWHERE THAT MARY WENT Lisa Scottoline 0-06-104293-5
____NOTHING PERSONAL Eileen Dreyer 0-06-104275-7
____OTHER LOVERS Erin Pizzey 0-06-109032-8
____MAGIC HOUR Susan Isaacs 0-06-109948-1
____A WOMAN BETRAYED Barbara Delinsky 0-06-104034-7
____OUTER BANKS Anne Rivers Siddons 0-06-109973-2
____KEEPER OF THE LIGHT Diane Chamberlain 0-06-109040-9
____ALMONDS AND RAISINS Maisie Mosco 0-06-100142-2
____HERE I STAY Barbara Michaels 0-06-100726-9

To receive your free book, simply send in this coupon **and** your store receipt with the purchase prices circled. You may take part in this exclusive offer as many times as you wish, but all qualifying purchases must be made by September 4, 1995, and all requests must be postmarked by October 4, 1995. Please allow 6-8 weeks for delivery.

MAIL TO: HarperPaperbacks, Dept. FC-101
        10 East 53rd Street, New York, N.Y. 10022-5299

Name_____

Address_____

City_____State_____Zip_____

Offer is subject to availability. HarperPaperbacks may make substitutions for requested titles.

H09511